HEARTSONG

A Dark Fantasy Adventure

THE SPLINTERED LAND
BOOK V

RICHARD PARRY

Heartsong

The dead have no words for the living. **Except for Evanne.**

Evanne, a half-Vhemin bard with **a tune for trouble and a heart for heroism**, never expected to inherit a relic from before the world fell. Gifted an **ancient suit of armor** by a spectral warrior, she believes it holds the key to **restoring justice in a land teetering on the edge of chaos.**

But the armor is more than a relic. **It's a challenge from the past**, a summons that calls her across the **blasted plaguelands** to a place of myth—the **lost fairy sky city.** Her mission: **restore the armor, and tip the balance in their favor.** The catch? **She'll have to slay a vampire** older than history, a creature that has **outlasted empires** and for whom time has no meaning.

Evanne's journey is haunted—not just by ghosts, but by the fear of what she might become. **The necromancer's path** is paved with the souls of the unrestful dead, and even her closest ally, **the warrior fairy Tarragon**, fears for her soul.

No safe harbors. No grand armies. Just a **guitar that sings to both the living and the dead.**

If Evanne can't strike the right chord, the land will sink into silence. Forever.

You're Awesome

You could have picked any book, but you chose this one. That means a lot.

Your support keeps independent authors like me forging ahead, writing the stories we love (and hopefully, the ones you love too). Whether you're here for the characters, the worldbuilding, or just a little escapism, thank you for being part of this journey.

You. Kick. Ass.

Roll for Narrative

WHERE WORLDBUILDING AND OVERTHINKING COLLIDE

Love stories that linger in your brain long after The End? Ever wonder why some books hit like a natural 20 and others critically fail their way into the 1-star abyss?

Join *Roll for Narrative*, my hub for sci-fi and fantasy lovers. I explore storytelling like a rogue casing a dungeon, review movies, books, and games, and dish out writing tips like a chaotic-good bard with a grudge against bad prose. No spam, just good stuff.

Join the quest:
https://rollfornarrative.parrydox.com

For my Rae, always.

The Rising Sun

I t wasn't the bee that investigated his ear, or the gentle whisper of wind against his nose. Despite the deep reach the People had into the world, it wasn't the grass beneath him, nor the rock beneath the rich, loamy soil. The burbling of the brook didn't wake him, nor the rain squall that came and went in the night, or perhaps the night before. Or the one before that.

It wasn't hunger, or fear. Anger didn't make his heart beat hard, urgent, reminding him of tasks left undone. Much to his eternal chagrin, it wasn't love either. He'd known it, felt it trickle through his fingers no matter how he held on. Lost it, to time, or to the blade, or to the world that tried to mill all like him into a more pliable meal.

It was the call of the sky. It was the rising sun that woke him.

He knew he'd slept for days. *How many? Does it matter?* He flicked an ear, waved the bee away, and stretched. His tail *swish, swished*, disturbing the grass beneath him. The bee became agitated, and he focused on it. *It is very fuzzy.* Brown and black stripes, cautious in its bumbling way. He held his hand up, and it landed on his palm. He wanted to say, *See? We are not so different. Both are furred. You are lighter and darker than me, and it makes no difference. The dawn came for both of us, like she always does.*

But he couldn't, because the People were voiceless. A hive of industrious servants made for a time before this one, when humans were more monstrous.

Or, perhaps humans are as they've always been. He scratched his ear, worrying a burr from his fur, then rose. The bee alighted from his hand, trundling off to do whatever busyness the morning demanded. A quick pat down told him he had no weapons, not even the sliver of metal he'd made to keep him safe when a sharp wit or fast legs could do no more.

I'm at the bottom of a ravine. There was a trickle of water that wound beside his feet, too modest to be called a stream. The grass here was rugged, as much of this world had to be. Soft enough bedding compared to the stone it struggled through, but he'd have kinks aplenty. *I am far too old for this.* He scanned the side of the ravine, marking the telltale scuffs where stone and shale gave way on his descent. *I came down here the fast way, not the easy way.*

He scampered up the ravine wall because he had to find something. Or someone. *It's a someone. Definitely a someone.* Atop the ravine, he could see just how far down it was. It's a wonder he hadn't broken his neck. Who put him there? A small stain of dried blood marked the edge, and he bent, touched it, and sniffed his fingers. *Vhemin. Ancient enemy, but ... not this one. This one was a friend. Odd, that a friend would throw me to my death.*

The sun touched his face, reminding him he had business to be about.

The shale near the ravine's edge gave way to earth, then to trees that agreed to be a sparse forest. He followed the tracks laid by the one who'd thrown him. Weird, because there were no footprints, just scuffed dirt and rock, like something had been dragged. *Something like me! They dragged me.* No, that wasn't it, or at least not all of it. He felt his tail lash and grabbed it. It trembled in his grip, but he held it until it stilled. *There. No need for that.*

What if we were both dragged? It made a certain kind of sense, being the only answer that fit the facts. A dragger taking a draggee on a journey would take a lot of strength and a level of orneriness the People didn't possess. So, definitely Vhemin.

I know one of their kind. A brother, a friend, a strong stone wall at my back. But he wasn't here. He ... fell? That didn't seem quite right, but it would do for now. This one who'd dragged him had history with his brother. They'd known each other before the Knight with the hair like platinum metal had stolen his brother's heart.

No, he stole hers. That is the way it happened, I'm sure of it.

When he found the camp, he was surprised only at how ruined it was. Bedding, torn. Their metal cookware was bent, the wooden spoons broken. Even the small hut that stood for hundreds of years was smashed down, the bees who'd nested inside scattered on the wind.

The sun urged him on. He thought it said, *You've no time for that. You've got to find what you've forgotten.*

So, he picked through the camp. A bent knife lay beside a huge footprint. He puzzled over it, then looked up, following other prints through the smashed trees. *A machine did this.* His eyes rested on a small bedroll tucked out of the way. Unused, forgotten.

He hurried to it, lifting the bedroll. He smelled it and remembered.

Rust locks. A crooked smile, sharp teeth, but kind words behind them. A heart that wasn't strong enough, and that's why he'd given her a guitar—so she could make music instead of war.

Evanne. I remember you.

With her name and face came a rush of other memories, rattled free from the fog of his stubborn skull. How she'd tricked him—him! —by leaving him on watch and skiving off. How he'd heard the Artifices coming for them, and how Barret had said, *Well, I guess you'll have to get her after the rest of us are dead*, and knocked him out.

He had no memories after that because the matriarch had thrown him into a ravine. He couldn't imagine how she'd made the decision to die, just as she'd made the decision to save him. He, furred, not scaled. He, who'd lost a child, and couldn't be relied on to save another.

Sight of Day looked at the sun, then brought his hands between them. He pressed them together in supplication. {*Don't ask this of me. I'm not made well enough.*}

The sun watched him. He felt it, a burning glare that made a mockery of his Handspeak. And one more memory came, the key to the lock inside him. The sun gave him back his name.

Roars Like the Singing Sun.

Ah. Well, if you're going to be like that, I'd better get to work.

Chapter One

The lands breathed a story of loss and betrayal. A city, vanished. A people, murdered. War between those who had, and those who wanted.

"I'm not buying any of it," Evanne said. "You're telling me there's a mystical fairy fortress that someone buried under a pile of rock and water?"

"All know the tale." Heser the Cheg didn't face her, casting his glance out over a long, narrow valley. Below sat a small township that struggled with airs of grandeur: a crenelated keep stood amid the squalor of ramshackle wooden buildings in a lean workman's district. The workman's district would smell; that heady aroma abetted only marginally by the river that flowed freely into the Burroughs, and somewhat more sluggishly out, laden with all manner of vileness that promised a bad time for anyone foolish enough to try bathing in it. Drinking it was out of the question. "It is famous in Ravenswall. M'lady's father tried to make amends and found naught but misery and hardship."

"It's true." Morgan sat cross-legged, apart, her back to Heser the Cheg, but still *quite* close. Her spine was straight as a mast, chin high, the slightest hint of grey about her raven locks. *That's new*, Evanne thought. *I wonder if being used as a bonfire to heat the fires of a demon gate takes it out of you?* "My father heard the drums of war and looked to broker peace. By the time he made it here, there was little left but ashes."

"Was it ashes or hardship?" Tarragon fluttered to land on Evanne's shoulder. Evanne lent her a warm smile, leaning her cheek against the fairy, who leaned right back, if but for a moment. "Or ashy hardship? Hard ashes?" She glimmered. "Can ashes be hard?"

Heser the Cheg sighed as if the world were suddenly a hundred times as heavy, and he was the one doing all the lifting. "The tale involves love and loss." Did he look at Morgan for a moment? "The fairies held themselves aloft—"

"That's because we have wings," Tarragon purred.

"A flying city," Morgan murmured. "It was no standard keep. A relic of a bygone age, kept high by their magics. The city soared in the clouds but didn't move. It stayed up there," she pointed to the north and west, "never descending to where people suffered. It was said riches stayed with them, a magnificence of wonder. Ovens that made cakes without the need for chefs, or even flour. The weather... it was always spring, even when sleet coated the ground below. I heard tell that dragons once roosted there, but there were none by the time I was a little girl." She chewed a lock of raven-black hair, as if forgetting she was the queen of Or'sen.

"Let me guess." Evanne joined Heser the Cheg on his small hillock outlook, visoring her eyes to stare into the valley. "They didn't share their toys, and so a mighty force embarked upon a quest to take back the forgotten riches of a bygone age. Share, and share alike! There would be plenty for all, if only the fairies didn't control it."

"Are you telling this story, or am I?" Heser the Cheg gave her a little side eye. Evanne admitted it looked good on him, because his eyes didn't so much crinkle as crease at the edges.

"Morgan said—"

"My lady can say as she pleases," the big man rumbled.

Evanne snorted. "If you say so."

The side-eye turned to a glare, but Morgan tinkled a laugh. "She's right, Heser the Cheg. I rule no kingdom. Not anymore." She stood, the length of her gown teased by the breeze to flutter eastward. "Where's that useless cat?"

"*Here.*" Pakhet sat behind Evanne, tail curled about her forepaws as if she'd been there for hours. A small buck, neck at an unwholesome angle, lay before her. The grey-striped tiger looked pleased with herself, and if cats could smile, this one grinned ear to ear. "*I brought breakfast. What have you done to earn your keep, hmm?*" She leaned down, her sheer size the kind of thing that would stop the heart.

Morgan bunched fists onto hips and glared at the cat. "You call that breakfast? The way you eat, it's barely a snack."

"How does she do that?" Tarragon whispered into Evanne's ear. "You know. When she's done something wrong, she makes it someone else's fault?"

"Leadership," Evanne hazarded. "I'm more interested in how a cat the size of a Clydesdale snuck up on us without anyone noticing."

"*It is because you're blind, stupid, and possibly incompetent,*" Pakhet rumbled, her grin not dimming a mote.

"At least I've got fingers." Evanne turned from the cat to stare into the valley again. "So, down there are a mess of people who felled a flying city? And we want, what, directions?"

"We want to know what really happened." Heser the Cheg held up a hand. "Aye, quit your sniping. I know I said all know that tale. But it doesn't mean that's what happened, just what's remembered. The town below holds a secret or two. Near as we know, the city fell with the old world. Perhaps the people's names in the story changed so it could keep pace with time. Mist descended on the facts and there's no knowing the truth of things. If Queen Morgan's father found no trace of the city, it likely fell..." He trailed off, looking at Tarragon. The fairy's wings wilted further with each word. "It is but a story. I mean to say, I'm sure there are fairies left."

"The story *was* true, to a point. There was a city. I've been there! It was around here *somewhere*. You can't just lose a city! If nothing else, the town below may also hold a map." Tarragon turned away from Heser the Cheg, and clambered up Evanne's hair, perching atop her head. "I want to know where they think the entrance to my home is."

"Because you don't remember," Evanne said.

"I remember, sort of," Tarragon countered. "The thing is, I remember the city flying. If it's no longer flying, things will be quite different. The kinds of inbreds who'd crash someone's home into the ground probably have a map."

"They might know why there's a lake there now too." Evanne pulled out her knife. "I guess it's breakfast then a bit of old-fashioned spying, no?"

EVANNE PULLED UP HER HOOD. IT WAS A NICE HOOD, ATTACHED TO A cloak she'd liberated before leaving the strange temple that was supposed to heal people, but hurt them instead. The deep grey material was soft, as if it was made of pressed angel's wings, and warm as anything she'd owned, but a third the weight. It didn't get dirty, and water beaded right off it.

For all that, it didn't seem to draw the eye. She'd been concerned people might want to take it from her, but when she wore it, eyes slid right past her. The seam about the collar had runes stitched into it she didn't recognise, but Tarragon didn't either. The fairy had huffed something about *exams* and fluttered off in a disconsolate way only those of very small stature could manage.

The runes didn't glow, itch, or call to her soul. They did *something*, and that was good enough for a Vhemin going into human lands. Her face wasn't scaled like her father's, but her teeth and eyes set her apart enough for the obvious mistake to be made.

It's not a mistake. I am Vhemin!

Except, of course, she wasn't. She was half one thing, half another, and those two parts didn't quite make a whole. *At least my heart works right now.* Evanne rubbed the ribbon of scar above it, remembering how Requiem had slid through her ribcage. Remembering the hand that held the magic blade, and the eyes above that gave nothing but hate.

So: a cloak of shadows, a light step, and no fucking about.

A merchant on the road had called this place Wandermere. He'd argued with Heser the Cheg about who ruled, and both left dissatisfied, although the merchant had a bloody nose to boot. The Raven, as Evanne liked to think of her, hadn't even blinked when the merchant said Queen Morgan's reign had ended, but her Queensguard pursued the conversation to its natural conclusion.

A light drizzle started, affecting Evanne and her cloak not at all. Tarragon hid beneath it too, her warmth by Evanne's cheek, peering out while bunching the fabric about her head to stay dry. "I think the weather is worse."

Evanne snorted. "How can it be worse than the plaguelands? That was a killing desert only the foolish enter and only the strong leave. The sun hit like ten hammers, the heat stealing any lick of moisture from your body, and—"

"Not that, silly." Tarragon huddled into her hair. "Across the whole, um, world."

"I don't follow." Evanne found a line leading through Wandermere's gates. Ahead, a bored trio of guards played dice in the lee of a small hut, while a pair of their fellows inspected wagons and collected 'tithes'. "I don't like the look of those guards."

Tarragon stood a little taller. "Is it the sloping chins? Oh, I see: that man doesn't have all his teeth."

Evanne gave her cloak a companionable enough tug, jostling the fairy. "Back to the weather, sprite."

"Oh. Um." Tarragon sighed. "Since I came back. Like, eight hundred years ago the weather was fine almost all the time. The Three nudged the clouds over crops as much as was needed. Now it seems so … accidental."

"It's just rain."

"It's *wet.*"

"That it is." Evanne touched the handle of her scattergun, Fusillade. The weapon she'd looted from the temple didn't come with a name, so she'd given it one. It hung from a sling at her shoulder to just below her hip. Easy enough to grab if the situation called for action or bluster. A knife as long as her forearm lay in a sheath on the other side. She'd found it among the dead in the temple. The blade wasn't bright like her mother's Smithsteel armour. It was dull, the colour of the skies that delivered drizzle on her now, but even after eight hundred years it held an edge that only glass could beat.

Her guitar lay across her back, oiled canvas covering it, although like the cloak, Uncle Day's present didn't seem to mind the weather. It was banged up plenty by her adventures, but still sang a sweet enough tune.

By any account, she'd left the temple with riches. A scattergun that fired more than two shots without reloading, a cloak of shadows, and an eversharp blade. Hitch's armour, though? That was broken. She'd left the suit back at their camp above the town, because every time Evanne even looked at it, Tarragon got huffy again, said *exams*, and fled. *But I didn't leave with Cleo.*

"That's enough of that." Tarragon pulled her hair.

"Ow. Enough of what?"

"You're thinking about something bad," Tarragon said. "You're thinking about the things you didn't do, or someone you didn't do it for."

"True enough. You seem to know me better than most." Evanne tried for a little bravado, but it didn't land right. "I'm ... I'm happy you're here."

"Me too. I mean, I'm happy *you're* here. Um." The fairy glimmered for a moment. "How are we getting into the town?"

"Simple." Evanne let a breezy grin touch her lips. "We're going to walk right in."

THE ROAD THAT LED THROUGH WANDERMERE'S WESTERN GATE RAN atop a bridge, making it difficult to sidle off this close. A guard shack, and by association the resident guards, was stationed at the end of the bridge. The shack was the usual affair. It sported a roof in dire need of repair, shutters against frames with no glass, a rickety balcony to keep near zero sun or rain off, and a bell. From the bell hung a weathered rope still firmly attached to the knocker. Such a device promised reinforcements if Evanne cocked this up. Beneath the bridge ran the sludgy remains of the river that looped outside then through the township. From up here it didn't smell too bad, although the breeze holding hands with the rain did a little heavy lifting on that front. The river gave Evanne something to go on in case Plan A didn't work out, but it was far enough below she knew going down the fast way would hurt.

She approached a guard who wore a bored expression like most people wore pants. He was a little bent in the spine, and was draped in too-large chain armour, sporting a too-small sword. She fished about for just the right Trick. *I need a slight smile, but no teeth, at least not yet. Don't appear lazy, yet let my hair fall forward—yes, like that. Shoulders are too straight, slouch a little, everyone here does. Now I look just like anyone else, and since I'm wearing this boss cloak from ancient times, they won't even notice me.*

Trick in mind, she made to walk right past the guard, who was having exactly none of it. Despite his mismatched armour and ancient hand-me-down weapon, he swivelled to Evanne, then blinked. He adjusted his helmet, ensuring the visor wasn't in his eyes, shook himself, then placed a hand on her shoulder, firmer than would be considered companionable, and said, "Oi."

Evanne stopped and gave him a little side-eye. "Do I look like your daughter?"

"You what now?" The guard squinted, his brow furrowed as if he couldn't quite see her right. His brain tried valiantly for the right excuse, and despite the drizzle, came up with, "Damn sun in my eyes."

Evanne glanced heavenward, the steady drizzle still present, the expanse of clouds not breaking even a hands breadth horizon to horizon, then looked at the guard again. "Your daughter. Do I look like her?"

"Not especially."

"Then take your fucking hand off me," she hissed. "Right now."

"Here now," he dropped his hand, "just doing my job. Say. Don't I know you?"

"I've never heard that pickup line before." She gave him the up-and-down. "Besides, you're too old, and entirely too grody."

"It's not a..." He trailed off, rubbed his eyes, squinted harder, blinked, then grimaced. "Wait here." He ambled to his companion, a woman in her mid-forties. She looked bored, not just with her job, but with life. She was in the middle of shaking down a merchant for a few barons, but he dragged her away from that lucrative pursuit, back to Evanne. "Look at her."

The female guard looked past Evanne, then back to her companion. "Look at who?"

"Her!" The guard stabbed a finger at Evanne. "Right there. Plain as day, except—"

"Except it's raining," Evanne said. "Day's not clear at all, is it?" She glanced at the merchant, who was high-tailing it through the gate as fast as a man could with a donkey-drawn wagon.

"There's no one there." The guardswoman turned to the three lounging by the shack, bawling, "Captain! Yuro's been in your stash again."

"Have not," Yuro said. "Not today, leastwise."

One of the three playing dice made a great show of standing up, arched his back, adjusted his sword belt, then his pants, scratched an armpit, and trudged over, still carrying a battered tin cup. Attired like the rest in shit armour, with a shit weapon, he wore a cloak of rank as if it was a mighty benediction from the Three. His eyes slid over Evanne, back, then away. "What is it? Can't you see I'm busy?"

The guardswoman said, "Yuro's losing his grip."

"I'm not. It's just, this woman here—"

"What woman?" asked the captain. "I don't see..." He trailed off, glancing into his cup, and muttered, "Might be a bit strong this time."

Yuro rallied. "Here, this young woman tried to get past me—"

"I walked," Evanne said. "If I'd been *trying* to get past you, you'd never have seen me."

"She's different," he said. "Can't quite see her. But can't not look at her now neither."

"I can see why you're stationed here," Evanne said. "This post is the most miserable in the city, no? Wandermere's refuse toils its way downriver, sliding beneath your perch. You've nought but lice-ridden merchants to shake down for a spot of coin. Hard times, no mistake." She sidled next to Yuro companionably close. Evanne hummed a small tune, just a few bars, but the temperature dropped just as she knew it would. "You did something wrong," here she switched to song, her breath frosting the air, "and now you're stuck here." As she sang, her voice captured the attention of the captain and the guardswoman, even if their eyes struggled to see her.

FOLLOW THE WHISPERS, HEED THE CALL,
  Under this enchanting sky, stand tall.
  Trust the guidance, let your heart unfold,
  In the dance of destiny, do as you're told.

THE ANCIENT WOODS, THEY BECKON AND SWAY,
  In the melody of wonder, let yourself obey.
  With open eyes and a heart that's bold,
  In the tapestry of dreams, do as you're told.

"STUCK HERE," YURO REPEATED.

Evanne kept the song in her voice. "All you need do is repent."

"Repent," agreed the guardswoman.

"And let me pass," she crooned as she stepped behind the captain.

"Let you ... fuck that!" The captain rounded on her, grabbed Evanne by the collar, and hauled her close. His breath smelled of sweet wine, which wasn't too bad, but it caused her hood to fall away. His eyes cleared as if the sun had come out. "Yuro, I think we've got ourselves a thief."

"Bard," Evanne corrected.

"A what now?"

"Singer of songs. Teller of tales. A master of—" She cut off as he gave her a shake. "I don't steal things. People give them to me instead."

"What's wrong with your eyes?" He peered at her. "You sick?"

"There's nothing wrong with my eyes," she gritted. "What's wrong with your face?"

He loosened his grip a fraction, touching his face. "There's nothing ... oh, I see. You tried for a clever rejoinder."

"It was pretty good under the circumstances," Evanne said.

"Should I do something?" Tarragon fluttered free. The captain gave a small scream, pushed Evanne away, drew his sword, got tangled in his cloak, stumbled, and fell.

As he dropped, the guardswoman drew steel, as did Yuro. The two guards remaining by at the shack sprang into action, one hefting a pike, the other a stout club banded in iron. The one with the pike rang a bell against the shack, *clang clang clang*, while glaring at Evanne, who in turn glared at Tarragon. "Yes. Stop helping!"

"He fell down by himself," Tarragon said. "I didn't do a thing. It's like he's never seen a fairy before." She settled into a hover, crossed her arms, and gave a tiny *humph*.

"Sorcery!" the captain shrilled. "A sinner."

Evanne closed her eyes and rubbed her brow. She started with, "If I was a sorcerer," then stopped as Yuro tackled her from the side. She went down in a clatter of scattergun, guitar, and knife, the air going out of her in a *ugh*.

"Should I help now?" Tarragon fluttered, perhaps a shade anxiously.

"*Maybe* I *should help*," said Pakhet. The cat lounged against the guard shack, which creaked in protest due to the grey-striped's huge size.

Three things happened.

First, Wandermere's reinforcements arrived through the gate. These were a seedy-looking group of malcontents but held weapons that would let the sticky red out well enough. They approached at speed, with enthusiasm, a giant Vhemin at their head.

Second, the crowd waiting for entrance panicked, some running back down the road, but most running toward the malcontents masquerading as guards. There was a lot of screaming, yelling, braying of donkeys, and whinnying of panicked horses, all of which Evanne suspected had never seen a tiger larger than them. The one ray of sunshine in the confusion of livestock was a barking dog that looked like it was having the time of its life. The crowd pumped through the gate, a tide that brooked no argument, sweeping the malcontents and their Vhemin leader back inside Wandermere.

Third, the captain, Yuro, the guardswoman, and their two helpers made as one and vaulted the bridge's railing and into the murk below.

It might have been the captain who screamed as he fell; Evanne was never sure on that detail.

She stood, brushed herself off, and looked at Pakhet. "Really?"

"You looked like you could use a hand."

"You don't have hands."

"That's right, play on my deepest insecurities. Way to go, hero." The cat's tail lashed, and she stood, rubbing against the shack, which collapsed. *"Should we go into the city?"*

Evanne grunted, waited for Tarragon to land, pulled her hood up, and faced the gates. "I guess so."

"I *was* helping," the fairy muttered.

"I know, love." Evanne adjusted her guitar, then followed the final trickle of screamers through Wandermere's gates. "See? Just like I said. We'll walk right in."

INSIDE THE TOWN LIVED UP TO THE PROMISE OF THE SLUGGISH RIVER outside. It smelled bad, a mixture of rotted cabbage and old sweat. The houses were in various states of repair, but none shone with new paint, and Evanne couldn't see any signs of repair or renovation. Everything was slumping into miserable disrepair. No dogs wagged their tails. Cats arched and hissed, but in Evanne's experience that could just be cats. Not many creatures liked the Vhemin in her.

"This isn't what I expected a human town to be like." Tarragon huddled into Evanne's cowl as the misting drizzle threatened to turn back into rain. "I thought there would be more Bigs. I mean ... humans."

True enough, there were not many humans out and about. Evanne didn't find the raw number interesting, but rather their demeanour. "They all look so downbeat."

Hitch drifted through a house to slouch along beside them. He shoved not-hands into pockets. "What did I miss?"

"Nothing." Evanne gave her shoulder a shrug to keep Tarragon from interrupting. "Straight in. No problems at all. Scouting report?"

"Report? Hah." The spectre seemed distracted. "This town isn't a good place to be. Word on the street is there's a moderately bad man in charge of everything."

"Isn't there always? Explains the downtrodden air." A woman holding a broom with hardly any bristles left did a double-take as Evanne strode by, then bustled back inside a house and slammed the door shut. "And the unwelcoming visage."

Tarragon glimmered, shedding a little warmth into Evanne's collar. "I know I'm out of touch. I was in prison for eight hundred years. But don't towns these days have, I guess, shops? Malls? Arcades?"

"There's a market." Hitch pointed to the east. "It's closed."

"What's an arcade?" Evanne frowned. "You know what? Never mind. It'll be something I won't understand, leaving me more confused, or something I will, and then I'll want it even though I can't have it."

"And so it goes," Hitch agreed. "The moderately bad man in charge of everything is called Grind."

"Hold up a minute." Tarragon peered around Evanne's cowl at the ghost. "Why 'moderately bad'?"

"Doesn't eat babies. Kept the biggest tavern open. Overthrew the last dictator. Usual stuff." Hitch glanced skyward. "I don't miss rain at all."

"But he's still bad?"

"Of course. He made himself a dictator. Well, a robber baron, perhaps. He raids the countryside, ever since they put fire and sword to the neighbouring town up north. Place called Hollyhead. Used to trade with Wandermere, before they burned Hollyhead to the waterline."

Evanne glanced around. "Where is this biggest tavern?"

"Follow me." Hitch picked a slightly less dingy alley than most, guiding them south and east. "Hollyhead was a fishing village. It held—"

"Fishing?" Tarragon stepped free of Evanne's cowl, hanging on with one hand while she leaned out to peer at Hitch. "First we hear my city was crashed into a lake. There's no lake there! The fairy kingdom drifted above a plain, without water for klicks. Now it's a big enough lake to sport a fishing village?"

Hitch raised not-hands in mock defence. "People hereabouts talk of a fishing village. Eight hundred years is a long time. Could have rained a lot."

"Don't be a dick," the fairy advised. "While it suits you, it's not nice."

"So there's a ... *big* lake now. The fairy kingdom no longer flies the skies. Why not, and where it's gone, are what we're trying to find. Perhaps this Grind will know more?" Evanne crossed her arms under the cloak, shivering a little. "Grind sounds like a Vhemin name. I don't know much about how cities in Or'sen work but I thought humans ruled humans, and Vhemin ruled Vhemin here, just like everywhere else. Wandermere is a human settlement."

"Might be why everyone hereabouts is puckered at both ends." Hitch beckoned. "It's just around this corner."

True enough, rounding the corner let them out onto a wide road. It had cobbles, but they looked in a less-than-average state of repair. The road held very little in the way of traffic. People hunched, hurrying about their business. A lone donkey stood in the drizzle, looking less happy than Tarragon. No horses. No excitement.

Just the tavern.

It was big, the size of two ordinary taverns put together. A wide, welcoming gate immediately to the right of the inn proper led to a stables but Evanne couldn't see an ostler. Nor were horses in attendance: the stables held naught but a few clumps of rotting straw. The inn itself could use a lick of paint but was otherwise in decent condition by Wandermere's standards. Shutters were closed against the cool of the north, but a glimmer of warm orange light played around the sills. The main double doors of the inn were closed, perhaps to ward against the chill, but had a well-worn pair of handles that beckoned Evanne's touch. She sighed. "It's been a long time since I had a cup of chilled rice wine."

"Two things." Hitch stood before her. "First, you're working. Keep your head clear. Second, it's going to continue to be a long time, because they serve nothing but ale here."

"Hmm." What Hitch said wasn't useful, so she ignored everything about it. "Have you seen this Grind? Is he a tough guy?"

"No clue." Hitch shrugged. "People talk as if he's there in the room, but..." He trailed off. "I can't hear him."

"Wards." Evanne spat. "Maybe he's a shaman."

"Or he's got one on retainer." Tarragon left the safety of Evanne's hood, breathing deep. "This place stinks."

"It's a human town. They all stink." Hitch looked at his feet. "Okay, here's the thing. If they think you've got a spectre with you, they might start some shit. I'd like to try something new."

Evanne gave him a sideways glance. "You don't normally ask my permission when you're about to do something stupid. Why start now?"

"Because I need your help."

"Oh, great!" Tarragon giggled. "You're enabling Evanne to lose IQ points. I can't wait to hear about this."

Hitch looked like he glared at her, but it was hard to tell, what with his face not really being there anymore. He gritted, "It's a good idea."

"Cool," Evanne said. "Let's hear it."

"And it *should* work."

"I said let's... wait a minute. What do you mean, should?" Evanne amped up her eyebrow game.

Hitch leaned closer and told her. As he spoke, she nodded, then smiled, then grinned. "I love this idea."

"This is a terrible idea," Tarragon said. "It's the worst idea he's had, and he's had some super bad ones."

"We're doing it." Evanne squared her shoulders, then marched to the inn. She let her fingers rest on the cool metal doorhandles, then pushed the doors wide and strode inside.

SMOKE. PORK FAT. FRIED POTATOES. ALE. SWEAT. THE SOFT ROAR OF many voices. The clatter of cutlery, and the pop of logs on a fire. The tavern interior was one big common room, with a set of stairs leading up to the north, and a door to the east leading to the yard. Tables were arrayed in a rough semblance of order within, and enough people sat there to make it look busy.

A serving girl a shade older than Evanne carried mugs on a tray. A kitchen glowed cheerily from behind her. A bartender, thick with muscle sagging to fat with age, gave her a jaundiced stare. By the enormous hearth sat a Vhemin of giant proportions. He had the look of a man who'd seen his fair share of combat, but a prosperous waistline suggested he'd spent time on the bench since then. His chair was more throne than functional furniture, with what might have been a baby dragon's skull mounted to the wall above it. At least, it looked like a dragon's skull; Evanne hadn't met a dragon before, so it could have been a horror creature native to Or'sen.

I don't remember seeing a fat Vhemin before. Evanne took it all in. *So many people. I haven't seen this many all at once since...* The smile fell from her face. *Since Imshir died.*

"Keep moving," Tarragon hissed. "Everyone is looking at us."

"That drunk guy over there isn't." Hitch pointed. "It's possible he's drowning in his wine."

Evanne gave herself a mental kick and reached for a Trick. *Make it look like you meant it.* "Which one of you assholes is Grind?"

The hubbub faded away. Someone out back in the kitchen dropped crockery, which crashed over loud in the relative silence. A cat *rowl'd*. More silence, then a deep, rumbling voice came from the fat Vhemin. "Who's asking?"

She reached for another Trick, putting on a lazy smile as fat as his paunch. "Evanne. You may have heard of me."

"Seriously?" Hitch glanced between them. "You're playing that game?"

"What game?" Tarragon's voice was smaller than usual. She huddled in Evanne's cowl.

"And what would Grind, ruler of Wandermere, conqueror of Hollyhead, and slayer of dragons know of a sixteen-year-old named Evanne?" The Vhemin stood.

Evanne faced him head on. There was some distance between them. She had time. "Ah. So you *have* heard of me."

He paused. "Come again?"

"Well, you know my age. Stands to reason." She crossed her arms, tapping her chin. "One thing doesn't stack up, though." She pointed to the skull. "You killed that?"

She could see him trying to resist the pull of looking, but the rest of the tavern followed her finger, and with the force of the retreating tide it pulled his gaze around. Grind's shoulders hunched, and he turned back to her. "I did."

He knows he's being played. Excellent. "That skull is barely larger than a horse's. Are you in the habit of slaying infants?" Evanne waited a handful of seconds, just until he looked ready to retort, then laughed. "I'm kidding! Even a baby dragon is harder to kill than, well, a baby chicken." She buffed her fingers, then examined them. "But that's not why I'm here."

Wait him out. The monster waddled a few steps closer. "And why are you here?"

Got you. "Because it's my birthday. And you're going to give me a present."

"It's your birthday?" Tarragon glowed. "You should have said."

"Didn't you have a birthday last year?" Hitch seemed surprised.

"Just like every year," Evanne murmured out the side of her mouth. To Grind, she beamed. "And what you're going to give me is a story. And, because I'm fair, I will give you a story in return." Grind was close enough for her to make out subtle details. His snake's eyes were ordinary yellow, but his shark's teeth were crooked on the left side of his jaw, speaking of a terrible injury he was tough enough to walk away from. He was well, if not cleanly, dressed, sporting a stained waistcoat above a pearl-buttoned shirt. While his waist was big enough for two regular Vhemin, so were his shoulders. He might have given Armitage a run for his money.

Don't think of Papa. Not now.

The monster had a sword belted to his hip. The hilt was exquisite, suggesting a marvel of Feybrind-forged steel within. He rested a meaty paw on it. "And if I'm not in a giving mood?"

She eyed him up and down. "What if I give you my story first, and you tell me one if it's worthy of the tale?"

"Are you a bard?"

"I knew you'd heard of me." She whirled, heading toward the hearth, leaving his wide-eyed gape in her wake. The hearth was warmer than she'd like, her half-Vhemin blood not as sluggish in the wintry north as his pure cold-blooded red. She righted an overturned stool, pushed her cloak out behind her, and sat. The guitar found her hands as if by magic, and she strummed the strings.

If the inn had been quiet before, it mimicked the grave now.

"I see him." Hitch pointed. "There. In the nook by the stairs."

Evanne let her eyes wander the room, eventually landing on a cloaked shape huddled in the step's lee. A man much shorter than most, with a cloak far dirtier and worn than her own, face hidden within a cowl. She raised her voice. "Come, sir. Don't hide from good song and fine wine. Join us in the fire's warmth."

Grind blinked. "Here. You don't give orders in my house."

Evanne's fingers plucked the strings, and she turned her violet eyes on him. Those eyes that were so Vhemin, yet so different than anything he'd seen before. The notes from her guitar entwined in her fingers. "But Grind, my lovely. It's my birthday. And you want to please me on my birthday."

"I do," he admitted, sounding surprised.

"It is settled." She stilled the strings. "Come out and enjoy the hospitality of the house."

The hunched figure came from the shadows, a shuffle-step at a time. He was shorter than she'd first thought, standing no taller than a child, but gnarled like an old tree, and broad enough. As the light touched his face, she saw he'd been burned as if marked by the Three's lightning yet lived to tell the tale.

"Merciful Three," Tarragon whispered. "What's that?"

"An accident of birth." Hitch's voice carried the certainty of experience, and Evanne remembered the vision of his past he'd shared with her. "A thing most can't tolerate."

The man *was* Vhemin. Broad, yes, but stunted and twisted. Evanne couldn't imagine the tribe that had birthed him letting him live. It wasn't the Vhemin way, not if Papa's tales were to be believed. The monsters were strong, and anyone in the clan that wasn't mighty was food wasted. And maybe he'd been cast out or put on a pyre. The burns Evanne could see were a horror.

Wait a minute. Vhemin ... heal. Just what is he?

A moment later: *He's like me. Different.*

She didn't let her fingers leave the strings, or the smile walk off her face. "A drink, then?"

The gnarled monster spoke with a voice that was half-gravel, half-lisp. "I want nothing from you or the leech that feasts on your soul. Aye, spectre, I mean you." He raised a hand, pointing a crooked finger at Hitch. "You would take until there is nothing left."

Hitch looked at his own chest, then behind him, then back to the little Vhemin. "You're talking to me?"

"Aye."

"And you can see me? Well, *obviously* you can see me. How remarkable." Hitch clasped invisible hands. "Are you a shaman?"

"I am your ending," the little goblin promised.

"You are too short to even be a start," Tarragon glittered. "And it's Evanne's birthday. There should be no fighting on a birthday."

"Come, now," the Vhemin husked. "There should be no lies between us. You've come here to fight, and fight hard."

"I don't know about that." Evanne hunched over her guitar. "For a hard fight, there'd need to be hard men. All I see is the ruinous cast-offs of a tribe that forgot its way. See? A warlord who's let himself go to seed, and a man too short to reach the top shelf."

Tarragon winced. Hitch sucked in not-air. Evanne touched the strings again, feeling the temperature drop. And despite that, the warlord Grind stuttered into motion, rallying against the hold her music put on him. He opened his mouth, closed it, frowned, belched, then said, "What?"

Evanne stood, kicking her chair back. Tarragon fluttered into the hearth behind her, wreathing herself in the flames, while Hitch stepped *into* Evanne. She drew her hood close, plucking a bass string. "Hear me, Grind. Hear me, failure of your tribe. Hear me, and fear me, for I will remind you of what a chieftain *is*."

. . .

In the hush of twilight's breath, I weave my song,
To chill the air, to make it cold and strong.
With words and melody, the frost I'll bind,
A spellsong cast, an icy chill combined.

Zephyrs still, the world holds its breath,
Whispers on the wind, a touch of death.
With every note, I call upon the freeze,
To make the air an icy, biting breeze.

With the chill of the north, the frost's embrace,
I command the air, a frozen space.
From tundra's heart to mountain's crest,
I bring the cold, a wintry test.

As the notes fade, the spell is done,
The air grows cold, the battle's won.
With Frostwind's touch, I have my way,
A world in ice, until the break of day.

THE FIRE AT HER BACK ROARED, BLASTING FLAMES TINGED THE colour of verdigris into the chimney, then guttering out with a snap. Evanne's breath frosted from her lips, curling free like cigarillo smoke. The bass crept through the tables, her fingers teasing the string, coaxing it, making all who heard remember all they had left undone. The fields, fallow. The hunt, deer still on the hoof. Thatched roofs that let in the weather, and hearts that let in traitorous thoughts. Through it, Hitch's power, *her* power, and the ever-present cold that grew from her, the floor glittering with hoarfrost.

Grind's eyes widened, and he reached for the Feybrind-forged weapon. It flew from its scabbard, and a pretty thing it was too, the blade glittering like it captured all the stars above in the edge of its smile. In a human's hand it might have been called a greatsword, but in Grind's huge paw it was merely adequate. He took a step toward her, foot crunching on ice crystals, then another.

Then he stopped, the colour draining from his face. Unlike Evanne, he was all the way Vhemin. Stronger, and faster. Maybe meaner, too, although she wouldn't admit that even over liquor. But he was also cold-blooded, his snake-eyes holding onto all that came before him and slithered. And without the fire, the great hearth's heat now held within Tarragon's tiny body, the room was cold.

The first of the inn's people came at Evanne from the side, and Hitch held her hand through all the moves. She stepped from a blow she didn't see, the ghost's eyes where hers weren't, and he made her body crouch, spin, and curl a leg behind her attackers. Her attacker gave a surprised yell, cut short as she stood half-way through his tumble, shoulder in his gut, and upended him face-first into the stool behind her. Teeth clattered to the wooden floor. Evanne's fingers coaxed the strings, the music's tempo moving higher, the pitch evening, but still urgent, still judging those here for the things they hadn't done.

WHISPERS IN THE DARKNESS, VOICES FROM THE PAST,
　　Unfinished dreams and promises that couldn't last.
　　With words and melody, I'll demand all,
　　The echoes of your past, your failures all.

REGRETS LIKE SHADOWS, LURKING IN THE NIGHT,
　　Mistakes and missteps, casting their blight.
　　A mirror to your soul, reflecting all you've missed,
　　The chances left behind, the opportunities dismissed.

ECHOES, ECHOES, HAUNTING STILL,
　　All you've left undone, your will to fulfil.
　　Echoes, echoes, a solemn tide,

A reminder of the moments when you let life slide.

SHE BARED NOT-QUITE-SHARK-TEETH. "YOU LEFT HOLLYHEAD TO die, people of Wandermere. They were your friends, your allies, and now they moulder beneath a frigid lake."

Then she stepped to the left as a chair sailed toward her. It clattered to splinters as it hit the wall behind her, showing evidence of manufacture that was most definitely not Feybrind. She stormed from the hearth, a muse leaving her stage, bringing music to the people who needed it the most. Evanne kicked a man in the groin when he made the mistake of swinging at her with a tankard, then kicked his woman in the groin for good measure as she tried to get involved.

Hitch touched her heart, her soul, and she shivered with the power of it. Her breath left her, ice crystals shimmering like Tarragon's glitter. She marched toward Grind, ducked a swung club, and raised an elbow into the jaw of her attacker without slowing her roll. Four meters. Her cloak cracked with ice, tiny shards dropping in her wake, because the grave was the coldest thing there was. A woman charged her, chair held high, and Evanne stepped back, foot out, tripping her and sending her into a gaggle of labourers. Three meters, and Grind's snake-eyes held desperation. Evanne held the guitar in fingers so cold they were blue. She couldn't feel the instrument anymore, but her heart knew it, *loved* it, and the strings hadn't moved. They were where she needed them to be.

The inn was *alive* around her. Her music touched the guilty, and the innocent fought for her. Some could see her, but the cloak hid her from others. All could hear her.

Two meters and she swung the guitar free of her shoulders. Another step. She grinned like firelight, ready to knock this clown back to the plaguelands.

"Enough." Gravel and lisp, followed by a flash of purple iridescence. Evanne blinked away stars, then stumbled as Hitch was knocked from her, the spectre shrieking as he flew from the inn, cast aside. She screamed, dropping to one knee, which was lucky because Grind had worked up the motivation to swing that fancy blade at her neck. The blow was slow and crude with the cold, cutting nothing but air, but it was best not to take pride in that since she was currently on her knees before him.

"Hitch?" Her teeth chattered in a spasm so hard Evanne thought they might break.

Tarragon flittered close, warmth falling from the fairy like summer rain. "He's gone. You've got to *move*."

Fuck that. Evanne rose, fended off Grind's backswing with a shove, and stepped clear. The little goblin fucker stood in a ring of purple light, a stick of charred wood rescued from the hearth in one hand, runes he'd scribed with coal into the floor glimmering with a light that reminded her of the demon gate. *A shaman for sure.* She gritted her teeth to stop them chattering, feeling the cold in her bones now, and snarled. "You trouble powers that are not to be disturbed."

The grotty little man sneered. "Spoken like one who is blind in the land of the sighted."

Buy time. Where is Hitch? "Hang about. Aren't you the sighted in this metaphor? Because a shaman's got *gifts*, man. But there aren't many of you. I think it should be a sighted person in the land of the blind, right?"

The little Vhemin frowned, the muscles of his face pulling his scarred visage. "What?"

"I think you might be wanting something like, 'spoken like someone who is awesome in the land of the less awesome'." She tried for a glittering smile, feeling the rime on her face crack.

"Listen, fuckwitch," the little man snarled. "*I'm* the one with the power here. Me! You're just a, a," he spluttered, "*musician*."

"Oh, my poor summer child." Evanne took another step back from Grind, who still had the look of a man spoiling for a fight despite being blue edge to edge. She hefted her guitar. "With this, I can change the world."

The shaman peered at her, as if seeing an unusual insect for the first time. "And with this," he stamped the floor with a boot, and by inference the circle he stood within, "I can summon those who will end it."

Ah, one of those. Evanne took another step back. "My Uncle Day said something once when I asked him why there were no sorcerers among the People. Vhemin have shaman, the consorts of demons. Humans have all the powers under the stars. They command fire and lightning and can draw hope from a dead man's chest. Thaumaturgists cause the world to tip on the head of a pin, and ritualists can bend what should be into what is. Feybrind have none of those things. Do you know what he said?"

The little horror pursed his lips. "I'll bite. What?"

"He said," and she used Handspeak, her motions clear enough if not as beautiful as Uncle Day's, {We like the world as it is. Who are we to put our will upon it?}

The grode chortled. "Spoken like hunted, not hunter."

Evanne felt the anger pull at her. "You know what? I think it's time we end this." She roared, grabbing the guitar by the neck, and swinging it like a bat at Grind, who'd taken that moment to lumber forward in a frigid approximation of a charge. The instrument *clanged* against his face, making him lose his grip on that beautiful sword. The Feybrind weapon clattered to the frozen floor. In the little space left by his wide-eyed stagger, she drew Fusillade, cloak billowing wide. The weapon sang as her hand found the grip, and she pointed it at the shaman. He shrieked, hands moving through the air, and wind curled around Evanne's feet. Evanne pulled Fusillade's trigger, ignoring the worry of its diminishing ammunition count, because if this heretic summoned demons here, they were *proper* fucked.

The weapon roared. Purple flared about the circle the little Vhemin stood in, the scattergun's round flaring into boiling metal. As if on cue, a hole into darkness gaped beside the summoning circle. And that's when Grind punched Evanne in the side of the head.

It was her turn to stagger, weapon falling from her nerveless fingers. It hit the ground, bounced, landed on its grip, and roared again. The scattergun's shot hit the dragon skull above the throne, which splintered into about a million pieces, revealing it was made of cheap plaster. One of the million pieces pinged into the ceiling, ricocheted off, and came down right onto the shaman's head, showing he'd made a protective wall rather than a sphere. This threw off his concentration for a moment, but the really exciting part was how it made him teeter like a child's top losing spin.

The shaman took a step, then another, hand to his forehead, blood trickling free. He screamed, "I will kill you," and then a horrible, clawed arm reached from the demon gate and grabbed him, because he'd stepped outside his summoning circle.

He didn't have time to scream.

The purple runes snapped out, the gate shut with a slam, and Evanne spun, decking Grind with a fist of fives so epic his ancestors would have felt it from the place beyond. The massive Vhemin slammed to the floor, causing tankards to jostle.

She panted into the silence. "Anyone else want some?"

Tarragon hustled across the bar top, leaving a trail of glitterdust in her wake. To and fro, back and forth, her frown growing with each stretch of the two metre stretch of polished oak. Evanne waited her out from her perch on a stool, the comatose Grind splayed on a chair next to her, a thin line of drool trailing from his open mouth to the bar. *A Trick I learned long ago is silence can do the best talking.* Evanne swirled the ale she'd ... appropriated, which wasn't half bad, and nibbled what tasted like three-day-old bread, which was pretty bad. The kitchen was out of anything that wasn't spoiled, apart from the ale, bread, and oats. *And I don't want to cook oats.*

Tarragon made her way back down the bar, step-step-step, wings aflutter, then when she reached Evanne's position at the midway point, rounded on her. The fairy shook a furious fist at Evanne. "That wasn't the plan!"

Evanne took another sip. "It kinda was."

"Wasn't!"

"The plan, if you'll remember, was to use Hitch to—"

"And look how well that turned out." Tarragon crossed her arms and glared.

Evanne raised an eyebrow. "It worked pretty well until it didn't. Then we improvised."

"You hit a man with your guitar."

"Like I said, it worked pretty well."

"Then you shot someone else. Accidentally."

"Also worked pretty well." Evanne swirled ale. "What's the problem, Tarragon? No, don't stamp a tiny foot at me and get angrier. We planned to come in here. Release the spell we thought Grind," she elbowed the brute, "was under. Free the town and be recognised as heroes. And, yay, here we are. Heroes all, the town freed, and the villain dead." She pursed her lips. "I hope he's dead. Where he went, I can't see living being much fun."

Tarragon looked about to stamp her foot anyway, then fluttered her wings, glowing a hot orange. "You've killed half the bar—"

"Truth, but they mostly killed themselves."

"And you don't even know if this imbecile" she threw an arm out toward Grind's head, showering him with sparkle, "knows anything. He could be the villain. And don't get me started on Hitch. The spectre was borderline useless. He lasted all of thirty seconds before he was cast aside, and—"

"I admit, that was odd." Evanne chewed the inside of her cheek. "I don't know how it happened."

"Spectral dissonance generation of the subatomic layer of reality." Tarragon sighed. "It's a subset of quantum entanglement and leads to the banishment of entities incorrectly bound to this plane. Don't you know anything?"

Evanne thought that through, trying to find any words she understood. "Huh?"

"And to think I'm the one who failed her exams." The fairy blew a stray strand of hair from her face, which was entirely too fetching. Evanne felt herself blush and looked away. "We had a thing for it. A wossit."

"You don't remember?"

"I don't remember." The fairy looked like she wanted to shriek but was running low on fucks. "I don't think I ever knew. I know it's possible. I can almost feel how it's done, but..." She trailed off.

Evanne leaned back, rolling a shoulder. Something had snared it in the ruckus, and it would take a while to sort itself. *Think, Half-Made. She isn't angry. Tarragon's scared, and that's worse.* "You're mad because you thought I was going to die."

"You were going to die!"

"And you said we shouldn't do this."

"I totally advised against it." Tarragon crossed her arms, slumping. "No one listens to me."

"I listened." Evanne gusted a sigh. "I listened all the way. I just thought this," she gestured behind her to the destroyed inn, "would be cooler."

"And you'd get to be a hero."

"That, too." Evanne fetched her guitar from its rest against the bar. She turned a peg, plucked a string, then winced at the off-key note it made. "Ballads don't write themselves."

"That guitar's not going to be much good if you keep hitting people with it."

"Now you're a musician?" Evanne turned the instrument over. "Come to think of it, there's no instrument I've ever touched that would bear the strain I've put on this. The belly is sound. Fretboard without mark or bend." She sighted down it anyway. "It's just the strings."

"The strings were made by your people, not mine." Tarragon turned away.

"What's that supposed to mean?" Evanne bridled. "Is this a Vhemin thing?"

The fairy cringed, turning about, hands out. "No, love. Not that. I meant ... I meant where, or *when* I came from, we made things to last. Sometimes we were successful. Like with the guitar. Sometimes less so, like with the Skyforges. These days, all those wonders and the knack to making them are lost. It's all just ... *stuff*, now."

Evanne relaxed a shade. "I get you. We suck."

Tarragon gazed up at her. "As an aggregate? Everyone sucks. But *you* don't. Not really." She looked away. "I was so worried, Evanne. I was worried until I felt sick. That snotty little man tried to open a demon gate. There is nothing good on the other side, and lots of bad things. You can't..." She kicked the bar top.

"I can't defeat a demon lord?"

"No one can."

"I think someone can." Evanne thought of Mama's stories of the Tresward, and a red-haired Champion who left them to fight the demons on their own plane. Of her Holomancer lover, and the dragon they both called friend. Then she thought of Vertiline's story of how the other people left in Imshir all died in a final fight that left the city sundered. Stories told with the certainty of a lived experience, no fables to be found. *I do not think Geneve is alive. It is impossible to think it might be true, and yet we recovered her still-glowing sword.* She hedged. "Maybe."

"We tried and tried and failed. The world died. We lost a war we didn't know we were fighting." Tarragon slammed a tiny fist into her palm. "I was taught to hate people like you." She gave a nervous laugh. "Now we just need him," she nodded to Grind, "to wake, and then we can work out what's going on."

"We also need to find Hitch."

"Do we?" Tarragon fluttered her lashes. "Really?"

"Really, fairy." Evanne stood, slugged back the rest of her ale, and faced the ruined inn. "Man, we really destroyed this place. Not bad for a birthday party."

"Is it actually your birthday?"

"Actually is." Evanne hitched her belt. "I'm sixteen. Or was last week."

"Sixteen and one week is a very pivotal age." Tarragon landed on Evanne's shoulder, voice grave. "So many things happen between this week and next, you will think it a lifetime."

Evanne laughed. "Let's see if we can find the ghost."

"You could try calling him." Tarragon clambered into the folds of Evanne's hood that nestled about her neck. "You are a necromancer."

"Bard."

"Potato, potato."

Evanne sighed. *Worth a crack.* She closed her eyes, trying to feel where Hitch was. *I know you, Lance Corporal Eric Hitcherson. I know your real face, and the colour of your eyes. I know where the rest of you remains, while a shadow of you is here. Come to me.*

"What on earth are you doing?" At Hitch's voice, Evanne's eyes snapped open. There the spectre was, arms crossed, leaning forward as if to inspect Evanne as a circus curio.

"I was, uh." Evanne gave up. "Never mind. We need to get this asshole," she jerked a thumb at Grind, "talking."

"Excellent," Hitch said. "I love talking."

EVANNE STOOD, HANDS ON HIPS, SURVEYING HER HANDIWORK. Grind was tethered to a chair, and that was the iffiest part of the whole opera. The man was a monster, huge in every way, and like as not to wake in a monstrous mood. She imagined rage, straining muscles, splintered wood, and a punch to the face.

I like my face well enough. He hits like a runaway cart. Let's avoid that.

So, she triple-checked his bonds. Stout rope from the stable, designed to hold a heavy load pulled by proud equines. The chair was from a guest room upstairs. It had the look of Feybrind manufacture, the wood smooth, oiled, and harder than iron. She could make out no nails in its construction, which was a mark of the People. *Good enough.*

They'd cleared out space around the man. By 'they', Evanne did all the work, being of both appropriate size *and* tangible, qualities that Tarragon and Hitch lacked, respectively. Tarragon supervised, claiming knowledge of knots—*'I'm a spy. Tying people up's what spies do'*—and Hitch muttered to himself while pacing. Evanne kept Grind's chair separate from anything he could shuffle toward as leverage or weapon. *Also good enough.*

The bucket was an inspired choice. Evanne found it in the stables, and it took a lot of swearing to get it in here, what with the icy sluice she'd filled it with. The cold here was bitter, the drizzle outside turned hard like diamond sleet, but it meant the bucket was filled with a fun surprise.

Her guitar leaned against a chair. The axe sang sweet enough now after she'd spent some time teasing the strings. She brushed back rust locks. "I think we're good."

"We're not good," Tarragon said. "But we're possibly not terrible."

"I think we're terrible." Hitch sighed, the air chilling a degree or two. "But we need to know what happened."

"Light the fire." Evanne waited as Tarragon sped into the laid hearth. The marvel of her glimmer made Evanne blush, because the fairy was so damn beautiful it hurt to look at sometimes. The little sprite ducked into the wood, hunching with fists clenched. She dimmed for a moment, then flared. The fire burst alight with a *woosh*, which Grind would appreciate after his surprise. Evanne threw back her cloak, bent her knees—*Uncle Day said to treat my back like glass, because it won't last forever*—and hefted the bucket. It felt cold even through the banded wood, but that was the point. She tipped it over Grind in one swift motion, stepping back to avoid the runoff.

The monster awoke with a scream, snake eyes wide and panicked. "Murder!"

Evanne leaned close, eyeballed him, then strode to her chair. She sat, picking up her guitar. "Good morning, sleepyhead. Did you have a nice rest?"

"Everything hurts," the monster growled. He tried to stand, noticed his bonds, and bared shark teeth. "This your doing?"

"Seems likely," Evanne admitted. "I would like to sing a song. It's my birthday, after all."

"No," Grind said. "No more music. Please. The last was..." He looked away.

"Stirring?" Tarragon hovered before the Vhemin.

The creature flexed in a valiant struggle against the rope, then sagged as much as his ropes would allow. "I've no skill with words. But what I felt wasn't good. I ... I *did* things. Do you see what I mean?"

The fairy fluttered back, her voice uncertain. "We'll ask the questions here."

"It's okay." Evanne stroked the strings, the guitar taking a moment to weep into the silence. "The question is good enough. Grind, you stand ... well, sit, really ... accused of treachery."

"War is not treachery." The monster lifted his chin.

"You waged no war," Hitch spat.

Evanne glanced at the spectre. "He can't hear you." She faced Grind. "My companion claims you brought ruin on those who sought only peace and trade."

"I said nothing of the sort," Hitch said.

"Your companion?" Grind blinked.

Evanne leaned forward. "I am Evanne the Half-Made. I stand between two worlds. My father was Vhemin, my mother human."

"Impossible," the monster growled.

"And yet." Evanne tickled the strings again. "My companions are the queen of a broken land, a guardsman in love with one he cannot touch, a soldier who fell while the world was yet whole, and," she glanced at Tarragon, "a fairy who's heart is purer than gold. I came here—"

"Don't forget the tiger," Pakhet said from her massive puddle of cat by the fire. *"The tiger is the best part."*

Grind screamed, flexed, broke the chair, spun, and ran, eyes never leaving Pakhet. He made it seven rushed steps before he went face-first into the wall, the impact making a noise like a drum. The wall shook, the ceiling shed dust, and the Vhemin slammed back onto the floor, out cold.

Evanne sighed, putting down the guitar. "We need to work on your entrances."

"I've been here the whole time."

"It's hard to misplace a giant cat," Hitch said.

"She was *not* there the whole time," Tarragon said. "I was just in the fire. I didn't see her."

"That's because she is invisible sometimes." Evanne stood, faced Pakhet, and put her hands on hips. "Right?"

Pakhet raised her nose from where it nestled against a grey-striped tail. *"Close enough."*

Evanne ran a hand through her hair, straightened her cloak, and flexed her back. "Come on, cat. You're helping me fill this damn bucket."

EVANNE DECIDED IT WAS BEST TO ROLL SOLO. PAKHET WOULD terrify Grind. Hitch would provide unwelcome commentary. Tarragon would flutter, which was fetching and equally distracting. So, Evanne husbanded them all away. The tiger was outside, ensuring no interruptions from thirsty townsfolk. The fairy and the spectre argued upstairs. It left Evanne and a comatose Grind, and a newly filled bucket of ice water, in the inn's common room. *Let's try again.*

Evanne tossed water on Grind, the monster jerking awake again. He blinked, wiped his eyes, then looked at his unbound hands, then to Evanne, and then convulsed as he tried to look everywhere at once for a giant tiger.

"Hush, now," Evanne said. "The bad kitty isn't here anymore."

"That thing is *real?*"

"*She* is real. She eats a lot, too." Evanne examined her nails, then looked back to Grind. "You're probably wondering why you're still alive."

"I am?"

"You are. And by association, you're wondering why you remain unbound, hands ready to choke the life from me." She leaned forward, arching her neck. "Go on. I dare you. I *double* dare you."

Grind glanced behind her, then to his hands, which had curled reflexively. With visible effort, he relaxed. "I don't think so."

She patted him on the cheek. "Good man. Now, about my birthday present."

"Your what now?"

"Birthday. Present." Evanne grabbed a chair, spun the back toward Grind, and straddled it. "See, I've saved you and yours from a painful life of deceit. You'll get an opportunity to make amends. You can save your souls. And all you've got to do is tell me what happened to Hollyhead."

The monster sighed. "I could wait, you know."

"Sure you could. Make sure the cat isn't here, then murder me from behind."

He seemed surprised. "You've thought this through. I admire that." He gave her a speculative up-and-down as if seeing her for the first time. "You and I could—"

"Ew," Evanne said. "Gross."

"I didn't—"

"Sure you did. You're old enough to be my grandfather, and you're too..." She trailed off.

"Awesome?"

"Male." Evanne favoured him with a smile anyway. "Don't look so downcast. It's a numbers game, Grind, and today you didn't roll the right number. Keep at it." She let the smile fall. "Let's stay focused, shall we? Hollyhead."

"We killed everyone," he growled. "That's what you want to hear, isn't it?"

"No. I knew that part." She pointed to the wall, and by inference the direction where the Raven and Heser the Cheg should be. "My crew—"

"The same crew that has a queen and a runty guard?"

"You remembered!" She beamed. "I thought we'd hit you too hard."

"Hit meself," he admitted. "Ran into the wall. I've never seen a cat like that."

"No one has, not for eight hundred years." She snapped her fingers in front of his face. "Hollyhead."

"Seemed a good idea at the time. Head over. Break some skulls, the Vhemin way. And we did. Murder. Pillage." He tugged an ear. "Got most of 'em, I think. A few stragglers we left to rebuild. Mistake, though."

"Don't tell me your flexible moral compass pointed you to a new true north." Evanne could see she'd lost him. "What happened next?"

"What do you mean, what happened?" He glared. "We killed—"

"The part where you realised it was wrong." Evanne kept her voice low, calm, a little husk in it. A Trick she knew would calm him, keep his anger low, banked for another day. "Where you realised you'd been tricked."

"How'd you know about that?" He glanced away, as if ashamed. "Grit said—"

"Grit was the goblin?"

Grind nodded. "Grit said there'd be riches."

"Grit lied." Evanne crossed her arms over the chair back. "Grit wanted souls for his magic. And you were the sucker to deliver. Oh, aye, I know the story. Vhemin don't get what's deserved." She slapped her chest. "I'm half Vhemin, and I see it well enough."

He gave her a baleful glare. "What's the other half? Camel?"

Evanne put her chin on her arms. "Human. It's the part, I think, that lets me talk to the dead, to sing songs that wake the world, and holds me back from killing people like you."

"But you killed Grit."

"What's it to you?" She sighed. "I didn't kill him. Tried to, and that's the truth, but his own summoning took him away." Evanne stood, parking the stool to the side. "Well, good day to you."

"Uh." He stood, but nice and slow. "That's it?"

"That's it." She nodded. "You told me what I needed to know. Hollyhead died because a bitter man wanted souls to make himself big."

"Wasn't his fault." Grind grabbed the hem of his stylish-yet-stained waistcoat, twisting it. "He was born different."

"So was I," Evanne said. "Taken me a long, winding road to get to the point where I realised it was a strength. A *power*, Grind. When people see my eyes or my teeth or get a look at my skin—don't get any ideas—all they see is something that's not enough of one thing to stop being another. They don't hear the songs I sing, right up until I make them. I started on this road after revenge. Now I'm here to fix the world." She brushed her cloak down. "Now you get to choose."

"Choose?"

"Choose," she nodded. "Grit held you in thrall. A magic that twisted your soul. Oh, aye, I know you were twisted enough to start with. Had to be something there to work with. But you didn't do it all yourself. And I broke that hold. Gave you back yourself. Now you get to choose what to do with the rest of your life."

He frowned, brows furrowing in more thought than he'd ever tried before. "What should I do?"

Evanne shrugged. "Up to you, innit? You get to walk out that door, greet the citizens of Wandermere as an equal, help 'em rebuild, and teach them not to fear. Or you get to stay here," she pointed above his faux throne, "with your make-believe kingdom, the hate gnawing at your gut, the bitterness twisting you. You learned might is the Vhemin way, but you can learn a new truth too." She turned to go.

"Wait." He touched her shoulder, and when she whirled, hand going to Fusillade, he held his hands up in surrender. "Maybe I could travel with you."

She eyed him up and down, then shook her head, but sadly. "Not this time. Your path is different to mine."

"Yeah? Why's that?"

Evanne strode to the inn door, barging it open, then looked over her shoulder. "Because your path lets you live. Mine ends in blood and terror." And that's how she left him, astonishment on his face, hands empty, relaxed by his side. No anger in his heart, just hope.

It's all anyone needs.

Chapter Two

Tarragon perched atop Pakhet's head while Evanne told all. Evanne had summoned the fairy and tiger back into the common room to explain just how her conversation with Grind had gone. Hitch absented himself, drifting through a wall and into the cold. And of the titanic Vhemin Grind there was no sign. Apparently his new leaf blew outside and he went to follow it. *Just as well*. Tarragon didn't like being shut out, because the gorgeous maybe-Vhemin trended toward action that would command hazard pay for a military fairy. Without Tarragon there, something bad could have happened. And the story she told didn't make Tarragon feel better! Just one new demon summoner had killed Hollyhead and put Wandermere into fear and panic, its citizens hiding from those that should have protected them.

When the maybe-Vhemin was done, Tarragon huffed. "I admit, it was okay for you to talk to the bad Vhemin alone."

"Admit?" Evanne blinked, those wondrous lavender eyes sparkling like precious stones. "I fucken *nailed* it. When we tried to do it together, he got spooked. Saw *you*," she glared at Pakhet, "and near as shat himself."

"I am majestic as fuck."

"You are troublesome." Evanne scowled. "Why'd you follow me anyway?"

"Because terrible men attacked Morgan and Heser the Cheg, so I ran away."

"Wait, what?" Tarragon flitted away from her perch on Pakhet's head and turned on the tiger. "You're ... *huge.* You're a tiger the size of a horse that—"

"Bigger." Pakhet licked a paw. *"Horses are quite small. Usually they can only be ridden by two humans, or pull a cart."*

"And you can ... pull a bigger cart?" Evanne looked to Tarragon, a plea in her eyes.

"No. I don't pull carts. Do you remember the majestic part?"

The maybe-Vhemin rallied. "I remember how you ran away from humans who attacked—"

"Who said they were human?" Pakhet turned golden eyes on Evanne. *"They haven't been human for some time. They were dead men."*

"Hang about." Evanne paced. "You're telling me while I found out Grind was a stooge for a horrible gnome, undead horrors whisked away our allies and you ran away?"

"I guess so. I was not aware you discovered Grind was a stooge, but it tracks. Vhemin are terrible judges of character."

"I will knock you the fuck out." Evanne shook a fist at the cat.

Tarragon flitted between them. "Easy, now. Let's discuss the part where undead horrors crept up on you."

Pakhet turned those golden eyes on Tarragon. She felt very small. *This creature could eat me in one bite. I hope she doesn't like the taste of fairy.* *"The undead horrors shambled up in waterlogged clothing. They shambled, like their minds were gone. I estimate,"* the cat yawned, showing a cavern of razor fangs, *"they were your typical mindless husks controlled from afar."*

"Back to the running away part?" Tarragon smiled, perhaps too sweetly, but she wanted to rage and this was the best alternative.

"Ah. You assume I did nothing, but I did everything! I, Pakhet, she who scratches, tried to scratch the humans at camp. First, I tried to nudge Heser the Cheg awake. The man slept as if drugged. Then I pawed the Raven, who at least made a noise, but not a happy one. At this point I was out of humans, and my support crew had long abandoned me, and thus I was forced to flee."

Evanne growled. "And just how many were there?"

"*Two. I think.*"

Evanne made a small noise that sounded like she was drowning her own words in the bath, so Tarragon put on a little more glimmer. "That makes sense. One undead for each human. To carry them somewhere, see? But where, and why did they not turn up with three undead porters?"

Evanne sounded weary. "Because they knew we were here, so I didn't need carrying. And they knew we were up to something. And they want *leverage*." She smacked her fist into palm. "It's a terrible idea."

"I know," Tarragon murmured. "Hostages are never a good negotiating tactic. You have to feed them, and stop them running away, and—"

"No, it's a terrible idea because I don't even like the Raven," Evanne said. "I don't care if she's eaten alive by—"

"*I think the Raven Queen is lovely,*" Pakhet said. "*She uses her clever fingers to scratch behind my ears.*"

"Unbelievable," Evanne said. "My own cat, a traitor."

"Your *cat?*" Pakhet narrowed her golden eyes.

Evanne started pacing again. "And the thing is, we've got to go after them, because otherwise people will think *I* ran away." She gazed at the heavens. "Why me? What did I do to get lumbered with this?"

"Good timing." Hitch drifted through the wall, then leaned against it. "See, while you've been ranting and raving, I've been doing recon. Hollyhead yet lives, but in a shadow state. It has but one serviceable inn, fisherfolk, and not a single flying fairy fortress anywhere." He sighed with the chill of the grave. "There is one curious point of note. There are no sorcerers, hedge witches, cunning men, illusionists, necromancers, or evokers in the entire hamlet."

Evanne scowled. "So?"

"So, the problem we face is bigger." He pointed toward the faux throne. "The horrible gnome snared Grind to wage war upon Hollyhead. The why of it is murky, until you wonder what might be near Hollyhead."

"A fairy fortress?" Evanne hazarded.

"A fairy fortress." Hitch nodded. "Except, as we know, it's not anywhere you can see. It doesn't fly the skies like in days of old. It is not a crashed wreck in a hillside."

"It's underwater," Tarragon guessed. *Oh no. This is bad.* "The whole thing crashed and made a huge lake, and it's at the bottom."

"That's where I was going," Hitch agreed. "If you're about to dredge up untold prizes from a forgotten age, you don't want witnesses. You generate a war between two friendly towns, using one to wipe out the other. Then you let humanity's natural stupidity do the rest. With a little luck they'll run away or murder each other in the night." He shrugged, pushing not hands into invisible pockets. "I say that as a recovering human."

Tarragon swirled around Pakhet, who'd gone back to ignoring them, choosing to worry at a burr, then flitted to face the spectre. "There's another sorcerer calling the shots?"

"Grit had a partner. One summoner to get demons to ride the souls of the people here. Then a necromancer at the other side to engage a legion of helpers to dredge up lost artefacts. Unholy monsters that can go where anyone who needs to breathe cannot."

"Well, fuck," Evanne said. "We've got ourselves a basic rescue mission. Get in, get our let's-not-call-them-friends-just-yet, give the necromancer a fist of fives, save any surviving fairies, and if we can, raise the flying fortress from the muck below a lake to ride the friendly skies."

Tarragon pursed her lips. "When you say it like that, it doesn't sound like a basic rescue mission."

"Hmm." Evanne went back to pacing. "I've got a scattergun with limited ammo, a guitar, sharp knife, wonky invisibility cloak, and—"

"It's not an invisibility cloak," Tarragon said. "It's a cloak of shadows."

Evanne blinked. "That's what I said."

Tarragon resisted the urge to explain as if to a child. "No, it's not. The classic invisibility cloak, also called a cloak of many colours, is a fabulous device. It is hard to make, requiring the toil of many Builders, an evoker, and a thaumaturge to boot. A cloak of shadows needs a journeyman evoker at best, and a little time with a loom."

Evanne picked at the hem of her cloak. "You're saying I've got the copper baron version of a platinum solar cloak?"

Tarragon winced. "I wouldn't put it that way, but—"

"*The mite speaks true. A cloak of shadows is a novelty gift given at children's parties.*"

"Fuck sake," Evanne breathed. "We're all going to die."

"*Yes,*" Pakhet rumbled. "*But you'll look fabulous doing it.*"

THEY'D DETOURED BACK TO THE CAMP WHERE THEY'D LEFT QUEEN Morgan and Heser the Cheg. Tarragon thought it should be hard to misplace a monarch, but of the Raven Queen there was no sign. The camp wasn't a shambles, Morgan and Heser having been carted off without a fuss. The creatures hadn't even taken Hitch's armour. It lay, still broken, by the fire. The whole business smelled of magic, and not the good kind. In Tarragon's experience, enchanters were a shady lot, right up there with necromancers, although she was starting to warm to one particular necromancer.

So, naturally, Tarragon worried about Evanne. The maybe-Vhemin's shoulders were back, head high, as they rummaged through the camp, but the fairy sensed a subtlety about her posture that didn't scan. *She's afraid, but not for herself.* Sure, there was a lot to be fearful of. The world was full of nonsense that tried to eat you, enslave you, or generally ruin your day. Eight hundred years ago, someone put Tarragon in a cage and she'd missed a lot of that. Like the fall of her home. Tarragon hadn't even had a chance to fight for it, and here she was, a stranger to this time, and she didn't even have a sword. "This sucks."

"Hmm?" Evanne turned. "It's quite nice out here."

"This world," Tarragon clarified. "It's broken."

"Only one we've got. Besides, it's not the world. It's the people in it." Evanne toed the armour. "We need to fix this. If we had it, we'd..." She glanced at Tarragon. "Oh. Your exams. I didn't mean—"

"It's fine," Tarragon said. "If we had a sword, or even better timing, things would be okay. Ish." She hovered by Evanne's shoulder. "Let's get on, love."

"Let's." Evanne didn't sound convinced. "Where's the damn cat?"

"*Here*." Pakhet was perched on a large rock overlooking the town, and Tarragon was *sure* she hadn't been there a second ago.

"Right, you're carrying the armour," Evanne said. "Come here."

"*I'm not a horse.*"

"I heard that part." Evanne beamed. "I also heard you're *better* than a horse. So large! So strong."

"*Shit*," Pakhet offered, after a moment.

THE ROAD TO HOLLYHEAD WAS PEACEFUL, WITH SMALL HILLS AND flat grasslands, the odd tree breaking up the monotony. The lack of trade between Wandermere and Hollyhead meant the road wasn't a ruinous mess after the rain. The village wasn't as large as Wandermere and nestled between a moor on one side and a lake on the other. Their party, being just an invisible cat, a ghost, and a maybe-Vhemin seemed small to overcome an enchanter.

Don't forget the fairy. Tarragon bit her lip as they looked toward the township. It wasn't much to look at, being in about as good repair as Wandermere. She felt afraid, and didn't know if it was because Evanne was being weird and distant and all *I'm-a-leader-so-I-shall-bear-this-load-alone*, or because Tarragon didn't have a sword, or...

"It's because you're small." Evanne was there, right *there*, the Big having crept up on Tarragon to stand beside her.

Tarragon let out a tiny shriek. "Don't creep up on people like that!"

Evanne glanced to the side, at the suspiciously empty moor, then the other side, toward the lake. "There is literally nothing here to hide behind. I am not creeping. I'm standing. Right here." She leaned forward, and Tarragon backwinged, all aflutter. "You've been quiet, sprite."

"Aye?" *I sound defensive. Why do I sound defensive?* "What of it?"

"It's because you're worried about me." Evanne jerked a thumb to her chest.

"You almost died!"

"I *did* die," Evanne corrected. "It was bad, I'll admit."

"You're not helping my nerves. *Hic*."

"Thing is," Evanne turned to Hollyhead, then crouched in the sodden grass, "If someone's got to die, it shouldn't be you. You're wonderful. Special, I mean. Uh." The maybe-Vhemin glanced away. "And Hitch is already dead, so."

"No one has to die."

"Someone probably does." But Evanne's tone had dropped its joking tone. "I'm not saying it has to be one of us, but... did you see Wandermere? People died there because of a small-minded grode." She stabbed a hand toward Hollyhead. "Tell me what you see."

"Um. *Hic*." Tarragon flitted higher, squinting. "It's a small fishing village, I guess. I don't know much about fishing but there are docks, and a boat on the lake. Which I admit doesn't mean much of a fishing industry. *Hic*. Not many people about, but a lot of houses."

Evanne sounded grim, her lips pressed in a line, violet eyes hard like deep ice. "Hollyhead died because someone killed an ancient fairy city a long time ago, and now grave robbers want to paw over the corpse." She stood. "So, someone's going to pay."

"Why does it have to be you that makes people pay?"

"Because the same kinds of people that killed Hollyhead killed *my* home. Imshir, gone. And they got into the head of, of..." Evanne bit her lip. Tarragon admitted it looked fetching. "Cleo followed them to her end. And many more, I think. I feel their line behind us. Dead beyond counting, all because we can't stop killing. Trust me, people die fast enough without help."

"We could just ... leave." Tarragon wrung her hands. "You and me. Or, *hic*, you, or, um. *Hic*."

Evanne didn't seem to notice her tongue-tied nervousness. The maybe-Vhemin was on a roll, all shining eyes and youthful enthusiasm. "See, what we need to do is get in there, smash the bad people down, and show the remnant of the village a little freedom."

"Or we could leave," Tarragon suggested again, but in a smaller voice.

"Okay, let's do that." Evanne squared her shoulders. "Into the village. Nothing to keep us here."

She set off down the small incline, leaving Tarragon fluttering in the gentle breeze. When the maybe-Vhemin had gone twenty metres, safely out of earshot, the fairy sighed. "I don't want another person that I love to die."

Chapter Three

Evanne glared at the fortress. It was shitty top to bottom. Old stone, complete with crumbling masonry. A couple towers on the walls that needed re-thatching. Lichen roamed, and vines scaled. It looked like the ramparts had taken a beating in some faux war an age past, and no one had got about the task of repairing them.

The guards were *also* shitty, because they were alert. The pair by the busted main gate were hands-on-pikes types, hard stares and a no-fucks-given view on the drizzle. On the wall above, archers patrolled with the lofty superiority of people who could put an arrow in you and knew there was nothing you could do about it.

She turned to Hitch. "You're *sure* this is the place? Why couldn't you take me to a place with lax security?"

"Don't hate the player. Hate the game." The spectre seemed distracted. "There's something not right here. I can't quite—"

"Of course it's not right," Tarragon hissed from the safety of Evanne's cowl. "There are people there," she jabbed a tiny arm, "who will kill," she tugged Evanne's hair, "her!"

"Ow."

"Sorry. Making a point."

"Make it with your own hair." Evanne felt the smile in her voice, no sting in it at all. *Odd. Where's my biting wit when it's most needed?* "What's up, ghost?"

Hitch sighed. "It's probably nothing."

"Means it's something," Evanne countered. "C'mon. You're usually the one who wants to go in swinging."

"That's because it's not his fists doing the swinging," Tarragon muttered.

"I think there's a bad person here," Hitch said. "I think there's a *really* bad person here."

"Well, *duh*." Evanne straightened her cloak. "There's only one thing for it. We're playing a confidence trick."

"No," Tarragon said. "We will die, because I'm a terrible liar."

"It's fine, fairy." Evanne beamed. "This is what I *do*."

EVANNE STROLLED UP TO THE GATES. THEY WERE, UNLIKE THE REST of the keep, in relatively good repair. The road leading to them was rutted, muddy, and unsuited to horses. She kept her eye out for undead horrors, but nothing looked like a shambling wreck from beyond the grave. Just the standard poor maintenance common across all the Kingdom of Or'sen she'd had the dubious pleasure of seeing.

The guards watched her wander closer, not doing much other than giving her a curious look every so often, as if she were a two-headed duck. As she drew near, she could see the stone wasn't just crumbling, but rough-hewn. *No one spared a bent copper baron when putting* this *one together*. The tower roofs in need of re-thatching were actually bad repairs thrown atop chipped and sun-faded blue tiles. They reminded Evanne of her mother's eyes. Vertiline had the colour of the sky in her eye.

When she made it within hailing distance, a guard hollered, "Halt!"

Evanne stopped, gazing up at the archers, who appeared to be taking a professional interest in her. She waited, hoping they wouldn't nail her feet to the muddy road. Her boots were standing up well, the ancients' material keeping them snug, but an arrow through the top would spoil waterproofing for all time.

After a handful of moments that stretched to the point of discomfort, the guard said something that sounded like *come closer*. Evanne tossed a squint in his direction. "What?"

"I said, come closer!"

"Will your friends shoot me full of arrows?"

The guard thought about it, glanced to his friend, then up to the archers. One archer looked down, shrugging, so the guard faced Evanne. "Probably not?"

"You don't sound certain."

"Uncertain times, friend." The guard shifted his pike from left to right hand. "Let's have a look at you."

Evanne put a little lazy roll into her stride as she drew closer. *Be cool.* She stopped about ten metres back. "Look all you like."

The guard gave her an up and down, then another go-over. Tarragon leaned into Evanne's ear. "I don't like him."

She ignored the sprite, giving the guard a sly grin. "You get what you need?"

He stopped doing the up-and-down thing, looking her in the eye. "You look ... different."

"It's the cloak." Evanne tugged it open. "Got it from an Imshir merchant who said it was one of a kind."

"And you believed him?"

She snorted. "I liked the colour."

He laughed, a good-natured sound. "It suits you."

"My thanks." She gave a mock bow. "I am here to play for the lord of the manse. I have a talent with the strings, and—"

"Now's not a great time." The guard looked at his friend who was as if cut from stone, eyes front, but Evanne noted a slight twitch in her eye. "See, Lord Gyles is ... indisposed."

"He's not here?"

"He's not available." The guard sighed, a micron of his poise slipping as he leaned on his pike. "He's here. But not for you."

Evanne widened her smile. "That's okay, sailor. I'm not here for him."

EVANNE AND HITCH TRUDGED IN THE GUARD'S WAKE, THE SPECTRE'S not-eyes downcast, his mind on something else. Tarragon remained in Evanne's hood, glimmer hidden, but still warm. The keep's design was unconventional. The immediate courtyard past the gates was wide and thin, no ostlery in sight. A few stray piles of rotted straw to the east suggested livestock were more welcome in that direction. To the west lay a cobbleway so worn the stone sagged in the middle.

Evanne frowned. "Maintenance not a big priority?"

The guard gave her a backward glance. "Not for a long time. Lord Gyles doesn't notice things like that. C'mon."

He led her further, the passage to the west jinking north into a wide, circular walled enclosure. Here the age of the stone was more apparent. To the east lay a shitty, rotted double door that was open, one half laying on the old stone floor. A barred gate to the west called to her because the door was the only thing she'd seen that looked new, but she resisted the pull. To the north a passage barred by a ruined portcullis and slump of broken masonry spoke volumes. Evanne pointed. "The boss not give a shit if you die when the roof caves in?"

The guard glanced to the north, startled as if seeing it for the first time. "You know, I think ... there's something about that..." He trailed off, sounding befuddled.

Tarragon leaned into Evanne's ear, whispering, "Careful now."

"It's all good." Evanne spoke expansively, arms wide. "You said we were going to meet your captain?"

"Ed," the guard nodded. "That's right. This way." Predictably he led Evanne to the east, not the highly attractive west.

Evanne gave a last, longing glance westward. "What's that way?"

"Eh?" The guard frowned. "Don't rightly know. Only the lord himself goes that way. Not even Ed gets a look in."

Evanne sighed. "If only we knew someone who could walk through walls."

The guard laughed. "If only."

"Oh!" Hitch's blue brightened. "You mean me." At Evanne's nod, he drifted west while she followed her escort. Another north-south corridor promised an ache to the brain if she tried to get out of here in a hurry. *This place is a warren.*

Her chaperone headed north. She glanced south, flicking a *shooing* motion in that direction. *I don't know if Pakhet is here, but if so, she can go for a look-see.* Evanne jogged to catch up to the guard. "I never got your name, and 'sailor' seems so presumptuous."

"I was a sailor, that's the thing." He scratched under his helmet, then straightened it. "Pay is shit and there's a high chance of getting wet."

She laughed. *I don't want to kill this one. He's ... likeable!* "They call me Evanne the Half-Made."

"They call me Quinton, on account of it being my name." Quinton gave her a shy smile. "What's half-made about you? Everything seems to be in working order."

"Here's the thing, Quinton." Evanne waited for him to open the door at the end of the corridor, which he did with the help of a large ring of keys and a lot of grunting. "You and I? We can flirt a little. Hell, it's fun. I'm enjoying it."

"But."

"But, and here's the thing, you're just built of all the wrong pieces." She batted her eyelashes at him.

"Shame." Quinton shrugged it off. "Don't begrudge a man for trying."

"The Three love a trier." Evanne glanced up. "At least, that's what Mama said. Papa had a different view."

"Here we are." Quinton pushed the door wide.

Behind lay a large room, complete with dogs, men, women, tables, smoke, the smell of burnt meat, ale, and sweat. Evanne loved everything about it. First, the dogs. There were four, big mongrels that looked made of spite and the souls of the damned. All were black, slavering hounds. The men and women were what you'd expect at first glance, but scratching deeper left a more irritating itch. Sure, they had armour and weapons, but only a few had the muscled look of those used to hitting other people for money. A few didn't look used to outside work, or inside work for that matter.

The burnt meat smell came from a massive fireplace with a spit. The remains of an animal that could have been a pig charred merrily away. Ale was easy to place, the large open casks about the room suggesting a group used to the crutch of liquor to tide them through the watch.

Evanne glanced at Quinton. "You're not really a guard, are you?"

"Careful," Tarragon warned again. "Things aren't what they seem."

"I..." Quinton frowned.

"Used to the sea," Evanne urged. "More like, a lake. Hollyhead's waters. Hmm?"

Quinton's frown deepened, the furrows on his brow looking like mountain ranges. "I—"

"Quinton!" A woman stood from a huge chair in the middle of the room. She was striking, once black hair falling like a silver-grey waterfall over her shoulder. "Was I in any way unclear?"

Quinton had the look of a man finding himself in a pickle not entirely of his making. Before he could speak, Evanne dredged up a platinum solar smile, and stepped in front of the guardsman. "My lady." She dropped the words like she dropped her bow: elegantly, with poise, and assurance that went dragon high.

"I'm no lady, you imbecile," the woman barked. "I'm the captain of the guard. And the whimpering quim behind you is—"

"Quinton, your master of ceremonies," Evanne purred. "He knows how hard it is here on the edge of the world. Naught but sheep for company, assuming you can handle the smell." Was that a twitch of a smile? "Truth, there aren't enough sheep to go around." That brought a chortle from a brave hero near the fire—Evanne couldn't mark the man, but she wanted to thank him. "I am but a lonely traveller on the road, seeking shelter, company, and but a sip of broth."

"We're no charity."

"Nay, you are..." Evanne frowned, then turned to Quinton, jerking her thumb at the angry woman. "Who the fuck is this?"

"Ed," the guardsman said.

"Ed's a boy's name," Evanne, as if to someone very young, and inexperienced in the ways of the world.

"Short for Eden," he said.

"Ah." Evanne turned back to Ed, smile just as wide as ever. "Ed, you run a fine house. And such a fine house deserves song for all under its roof. I promise I will play you music the likes of which you've never heard." She unslung her guitar, ignoring the shift of hands to weapons and straightening of spines that promised a readiness for bloodshed. *Tough crowd.* "I swear before the night is out—"

"You will play and only take our food if we like it?" Ed snorted, clearly liking the bargain. "You must be very stupid or very good."

"Why not both?" Evanne stroked the strings, fingers gentle, coaxing, comforting the guitar. The chord drifted from the instrument, sifted along the old stone floor, and stilled all within the room.

"You're really very good at that," Tarragon said. "Where did you learn to play?"

"Imshir," Evanne said out the side of her mouth. "There was nothing to do but get drunk or play."

Ed relaxed a whisker, raising her chin with interest. "And with one note, you have my attention."

"Three."

"What?"

"Three notes," Evanne said. "It's a chord, and... you don't care, do you?"

"Do I look like I care?" But Ed was smiling with it, something less harsh in her voice. Something almost wistful. "I think..." She listed for a moment. "I think I need more wine!" She held her goblet aloft.

A general chorus of agreement sounded from the men and women scattered about. Evanne took that as a good sign and navigated toward the fire. While her heart was better than new, and her human blood warmer than the Vhemin other half, it was still too cool in Or'sen by far. She settled in an empty chair by the open hearth, feeling it creak beneath her. She allowed herself to relax. *I'm in.*

Chapter Four

Tarragon did not like being in this place. Underneath the smell of Bigs was an odour she couldn't put her finger on. It felt like something she should know from the Manifest, but of course she didn't *have* one of those. But Evanne was here, and so there was nowhere else she'd rather be. It didn't stop her wishing Evanne, and thus Tarragon herself, were somewhere else though.

Evanne's fingers had drifted to the strings, the maybe-Vhemin getting that far off look she had when she made music. Tarragon didn't think of it as *playing*, because she'd heard people play before. They held instruments or used their voice, and sounds came out, no problem. That part was similar.

But until she'd met Evanne, she'd never found someone who held music inside them. The notes in her chest, right next to her heart, and urged into life because Evanne wanted everyone around her to experience the same thing she did.

The bard didn't sing. She made you *feel*.

Tarragon wiped a tear from her eye, which was a special kind of bullshit because Evanne wasn't even playing the soppy stuff yet. *This won't do*. As the song wound down and a man brought Evanne a flagon of ale, Tarragon leaned close the maybe-Vhemin's ear. "Do you mind if I take a look around?"

Evanne shook her head. "No." A hesitation. "Are you okay?"

"I'm fine," Tarragon lied. "I want to see what's keeping Hitch."

"Good idea," Evanne said. "I'll stay here until, well, they feed me." Tarragon could hear the smile in Evanne's voice, one of those ones Tarragon knew was real, not made up for show or pageantry. It was small, and uneven, but just for the fairy. "Be careful."

"I'm always careful," Tarragon lied again. "I'm tiny. What could go wrong?"

"Hmm." Evanne turned away, attention drifting to her music and her crowd. Tarragon reached a hand to stroke those rust locks, then took wing.

She's not ignoring me. She's just ... focused on other things.

Tarragon fluttered through the crumbling shitpile that tried to stand up to the memory of being a castle, ignoring just about everything. The darkness didn't bother her, because she glowed. Cobwebs she didn't fear. Spider's silk couldn't withstand glimmer, no matter the size of the spider. She zipped past mouldering tapestries. A *proper* Builder might know how they were made. *Weave? Or is it weft?* She scrubbed her hair, wanting to get fingers into her brain, to comb through the Manifest's gaps to get to the truths other Builders had.

All except those in her clutch, barring Helio, who had it all. Tarragon had nothing. *Not even a sword.*

It was with that unfortunate thought Tarragon realised she was lost. She'd flown through a passage that smelled of rotted wood and chalk, then darted into an old dumb waiter, up, out into a disused bedroom, down another passage, and then about forty other turns she didn't remember.

Which left her in a dark corridor with no paintings, the slumbering remains of an ancient tapestry decaying quietly to itself against a wall, and no clue where to go next. *The obvious path is to find Hitch, because he might know where the Raven Queen and Heser the Cheg are. Once we have them, we can get out, and stop consorting with people who don't know how to decorate.*

As plans went, it was a good one. Find their maybe-friends, take wing, and get gone. They'd even talked it through, just the ghost, Evanne, and Tarragon. Tarragon didn't remember them talking about how the fairy would get lost and spoil everything.

I've screwed everything up.

She bit her lower lip, glimmer subsiding in shame. *Think, fairy. I'm good at thinking. They made me to be good at making stuff they couldn't. Surely I can make my own way out of here?*

Tarragon glanced left, then right, then gave a tiny *hic*.

Laughter.

She spun, eyes trying to pierce gloom her glimmer couldn't reach. The laughter wasn't close. It was sepulchral, male, and made her feel uncomfortable in her stomach, but it was at least someone who sounded like they knew where they were and how to get to where they wanted to be.

Good start.

The fairy fluttered along, weaving a little in indecision. After a turn of the passage, she spotted a door cracked ajar ahead. A slender lick of orange light lay against the old stone floor. The light showed dust, highlighting the lack of broom use. There were no convenient places to hide, but that was okay because she'd heard *laughter* not *mad panicked screaming*.

Tarragon poked her head around the doorway. The room beyond had a cheery fire laid in a wide hearth. A table sat before it, and by the table, two chairs. One chair held a man who looked regal in the way gaunt people seemed to do by default. The other chair was empty. The table held a lantern that emitted an eerie, ghostly blue.

Along the wall were all manner of weird things. Tarragon spotted a shield next to a weathered coil of rope. A tricorn hat sat atop the handle of a spade that leaned nonchalantly against a saddle. The junk went on and on, a menagerie of items that defied explanation. *I mean, why does a man keep a spice box, a dustpan, and a single book on the same shelf? It makes no sense.*

"Hello, little one."

Tarragon gave a tiny scream, then clamped her hand over her mouth. The gaunt man looked at her with an expression that could be described as *hungry*, or perhaps *thirsty*.

Wait. Why do I think he's thirsty? Get a grip. I'm a front line-fighter in a war that spanned the world. I can do better than an outcry and a lot of hand waving. Tarragon lowered her hand, glimmering a little, but it faded when the man's gaze didn't leave her. Most people's eyes moved around, taking in things like your eyes, mouth, nose, or even a little lower, if they wanted to leer. This guy? He was locked on, a house cat's pre-pounce stare at a mouse.

"Um," Tarragon started, then, "*hic*. Um. Do you know how to get down to the main hall?"

"Mmm." The gaunt man rose from his chair, eyes never leaving Tarragon. "Why would you want to go there?"

"Because." Tarragon fought a stammer. "It's where I came from, and I got lost."

"Here is so much nicer." The man fielded the lantern, raising it not as one might to illuminate the room, but to gaze on it like it was a prize possession. He didn't hiss or flinch, suggesting it gave off no heat, or he was staunch. "Here is where *you* are."

"*Hic*," Tarragon offered. "That's a strange thing to say."

The man started to navigate around the chair toward Tarragon. "A stranger thing to say is, 'I have your friend'. Which I do." He stopped walking, turned the lantern over in his hands, then fiddled with the wick crank.

"Run." Hitch's voice came from the lantern. "Run away fast. Get Evanne and go." His voice was strange, stretched, thinner, much like the old man. Like he was feeling all his eight hundred years but didn't have Tarragon's good genes to carry him through.

A few thoughts entered Tarragon's head. First, *This asshole has caught the spectre in a lantern.* Second, and she couldn't help herself, *Maybe he'll stop following Evanne around.* The fairy crushed that one, her brain struggling to keep up, and it offered one final pearl of wisdom. *I've been so stuck in the past, I forgot to think about what the world is like now. There are no machines of war, reactors, or ships that sail the stars. There are just people, and even people who aren't people anymore.* She let out a breath. "You're ... a bad man?"

"I'm the worst." The gaunt man gave a chortle, lips peeled back, teeth showing, and this was how Tarragon noted his canines were more pronounced than in most humans. "Like you, I've been sitting on this rotting carcass of a world for hundreds of years. Unlike you, I think I like it. People have mostly forgotten about my kind, which lets me hunt, and feed, and," he widened his arms expansively, lantern at one end, empty-and-somehow-now-clawed hand at the other, "have my own slice of paradise. Do you know what I used to do? Before I got," he made scare quotes with his crooked, gnarled fingers, "sick?"

"*Hic. Hic.*" Tarragon backed up, exiting through the door. "I don't need to know. Bye!" She turned, dropped the virtual hammer, and fled, glitterdust glimmering like star fire in her wake.

"Come back," the gaunt man called. "We can talk about how I repaired machines too lowly for Builders before I got the bite. And then we can talk, perhaps over dinner, about how I never had to fix another machine again."

Tarragon headed toward the end of the corridor where it crooked to the left. She didn't drop speed, just kind of bounced off the wall in a shower of sparkle and boosted into the dark. A part of her brain screamed, *I am panicking! Slow down and think!* But another part of her brain, wiser perhaps, and quieter, whispered, *I'm right to panic, because his voice isn't getting quieter with distance. He doesn't sound like he's breathing hard and he's gaining on me.*

She spied a rickety door ahead, a single board out of true. Tarragon aimed for it, ducked her head, and ploughed right on through in a shower of dried, rotted wood. The wood ignited, dust burning along with her glimmer, but she ignored it. *I can't burn to death, but I can be sucked dry!* Just a mouthful, that's all she was. And after the monster took his mouthful, she wouldn't see Evanne again.

She darted about, seeking an exit. The room had cots lining the walls. The screaming part of her mind said, *It's just a dormitory, now get going!* But the quiet voice said, *Morgue.* And the quiet voice was right, because all the beds were full of dead people. Some looked *super* dead, wizened and twisted with age, reduced to desiccated husks. Tarragon buzzed down the room, and as she got further, she saw the bodies were fresher. Still dead, sure, but more recently so. She glanced back just in time to see the gaunt asshole smash through the door, lantern in hand.

He looked delighted, those hunter's eyes finding her spark no problem. "You've found my larder. Look at them all. I've saved each one. Kept them here so I can remind myself of all the people who wanted me to fix their toasters." He cruised to the bed nearest the door while Tarragon backwinged, her breath coming in short gasps as she sought an exit, a hole, *anything*. "This woman tried to command me. Do you know what it's like when your food talks back at you?" He patted the aged remnants almost affectionately, as a parent might to a wayward yet charming child.

"I'm not very *hic* tasty." Tarragon realised she was babbling. "I'm too small. I'm barely a bite."

"Ah." The gaunt man didn't look at her, still stroking the head of the woman who died before the war burned out. "You are just a bite, but my, the *flavour*." He looked at her, free hand moving to his lips as he made the classic chef's kiss. "Exquisite."

"Why are you doing this?" Tarragon wailed.

"I'm doing this because I can." The gaunt man marched forward. "But I'm also doing this because I need your ritualist after my last one, ah, gave up her position. And for that I need all the ... pieces under my control. Leverage, to make people work the way they must. You? I don't *need* you. But I do *want* a snack."

Fuck. Tarragon glanced to the walls to the left and right. She'd been turned around on her way here, but she was sure the one on her right led *outside*. It was stone, no doubt half a metre thick, but if it had open air beyond she might have a chance. A chance to get to Evanne and follow Hitch's advice: *run*.

If she was wrong, she'd just pop into another room, where she would die, because this creature was a vampire, and she didn't have any way of fighting him. Not a lord of the dead, champion of the evernight.

Right wall it is! She flitted to the left wall, bunching knees beneath her like a champion swimmer streamlining, and then fired to the opposite wall. The vampire was almost on her, hand outstretched, but she was burning now, a tiny piece of a star, her skin alive with heat, the fires of her creation liming her flesh, her wings incandescent.

Tarragon burned right through the asshole's hand and hit the right wall. The old stone gave way with a wet *plop* as she boiled the stone to magma in a moment, and then she was through, falling.

It was a long way down, pieces of molten stone glowing, her now ordinary-looking skin dull, her fires spent. But the air here didn't smell of rot. It smelled of wood and rain. *Thank the Three. I made it outside.*

Tarragon landed in the courtyard where Quinton had led Evanne to the hall with Ed. Same impenetrable door with the Raven Queen— *probably*—behind it. Same broken door to the north, and an open one to the west. Evanne was that way, if only Tarragon could muster the strength to stand.

Oh no. Above her she saw the vampire peer down, his hungry eyes eager. The master of his demesne, king with a crooked crown, enjoying the game more than the end. And beyond him, doom: the sky no longer tinged with light.

Night had fallen, and vampires only feared the sun.

Chapter Five

The ship nudged the broken dock of Ravenswall's piers, the captain red-faced as he shouted orders for someone, *anyone* to make fast. Vertiline eyed the man from where she stood on the forecastle. The ship eased with the swells, the cries of gulls above. Aside from his bluster, and the ruined city beyond, it was a lovely day. She tugged a rogue strand of hair from her face, hand on the hilt of her sword, but without any desire to use it.

"This is fucked," Armitage said.

"Aye, monster." She pointed to Ravenswall's streets where charred buildings showed their blackened skeletal ribs to all. "Much has happened since our last visit."

"Not that." He nudged her arm around, pointing it to the broken dock. "*That*."

"I am not blind."

He showed shark teeth. "Your eyes are too high. Lower them from the horizon to see the sands beneath your feet."

Vertiline showed her own teeth. "There is water beneath my feet."

"There's wood, if we're being honest." He widened his smile. "Don't get pissy at me if you can't see it."

"I am not 'pissy', monster." She glared at her husband. "We must *find* her."

"Aye, aye, I'm not arguing that point. We'll find her, and bring her back to hearth, safe as houses. Not those ones, I mean," he eyed the ruins in Ravenswall, "or the ones back home, come to think—"

"What is this important thing I must see?" She felt her words were showing some strain and tried to soften them. "I miss her."

"That's the thing, though. You *can't* miss her." He jabbed his large fingers toward the broken dock. "Someone sailed a ship right into this wharf. Then they sailed the fuck off," he waved at the ocean, "without leaving a wreck. There are some odd things that happen between sea and sky, but I've not seen a vessel hit ground that hard and not leave a carcass."

"Seen many vessels hit docks?"

"A few." Armitage's tone was a shade evasive. "Point is, our girl was here."

"It could have been any—"

"The *gods*, Tilly." He stamped about a few paces. "You said they must not set foot on land. They shouldn't get involved. What would happen if that black bitch Cophine took a ship and rammed it here?"

"The spring goddess is less a sailor than Khiton."

"Khiton, Ikmae, I don't give a shit. They're your gods, not mine." He saw the look on her face and picked up speed. "Point is, someone got all the wicked way across the sea to here in less time than it took us. This damage is long done. See the breaks in the wood? Weathered, salt-stained. But it was done well and done hard. Like a god took their fist and smashed it here, keeping to the letter of their bargain. No foot on soil, yet Evanne delivered safe and sound."

She chewed that over as the deck shifted beneath her, the ship scraping against the broken timber of the dock. Vertiline heard the captain's voice go up an octave as his ship felt the claws of land. *It's a good reminder. This vessel is no harbour skiff, and it can't tousle with the shore. Someone who wielded power came here. A sinner, perhaps, but...* She sniffed the air. *My husband is right. This is a god's work.* "What does it tell us?"

"It tells us we need to hurry." He looked down. "She might carry their favour."

"They promised no harm," Vertiline gritted. "They will not have our girl."

"No, they won't," he agreed, implacable as the sky. He ran a hand across the seam of the scar that ran from his shoulder and across his rib cage. "The last who carried their favour is lost."

"We will get Geneve back."

Armitage eyed her. "Aye." The monster tightened the straps of his pack, then vaulted the railing, landing on the remains of the dock, then sauntered toward the city's ruins. The short blades belted at his waist suggested anyone getting in his way was in for a rough day.

She watched him a moment. That strong stride. Confident manner, a jaw that caught her eye, but the beautiful soul within that caught her heart. *I have been blessed.* Vertiline eyed the clouds scudding in on a westerly breeze. *Is there a price to pay for happiness? It has always seemed so.*

She shook herself, put her metal hand on the railing, and leaped over to land on the dock. She ignored the captain's howling. The few school's Novices they'd found lurking Imshir's streets would be along. They weren't the type to need mollycoddling, and she had no patience for the task anyway.

First order of business was finding someone who knew something. Vertiline glared at Ravenswall's keep, nestled in the heart of the Queen's district. *Now how does a keep remain intact while the city burns?* Time to find out.

I miss Geneve. Vertiline trudged up the small hill toward the keep, eying the detritus of a lost city en route. There, a smithy, coals dark. Beside it, a horse trader's yard, empty of mounts. On and on it went, taverns quiet, dry, vacant, clothiers without customers or cloth, bakers without bread.

But everywhere, the dead. The smell of them ripening in the street. Bloated bodies, some hacked to pieces, some dropped from starvation.

"It's cozy, innit," the monster grumbled. "I think there's just the right amount of bullshit swept into each corner."

"This city has seen horrors before, but this..." Vertiline frowned. "It will remember this for all time."

"I would've thought the dragon landing by the castle was the thing people would mark for their grandkids, but maybe everyone dying tops it off." Her husband drew one of his blades, poking at a body. "See here."

She stopped, leaning against him for a moment, borrowing a little strength against what would come. "You're right. I'm not sure how I could have missed he was dead."

He chuckled. Vhemin grew up with death as their constant companion. The monster wouldn't be phased by any of this. "He wasn't cut down. Here and here," he pointed with his blade. "Holes."

"Arrows," she guessed.

"Makes sense, but what's better is this guy over here." He stomped a few paces to the left, where a man lay sprawled against a rotting grain sack. His face was grisly, eyes gone, mouth open. "An arrow to each eye."

She bit her lip. "The People did this?"

"Some of it, sure." Armitage slid his sword home. "I'm used to their handiwork. No, don't go caterwauling at me. I don't bear any particular grudge. All I'm saying is, the Feybrind came here, and kicked the *shit* out of these people. Probably had a lot of help, but..." He trailed off.

"But why are the Feybrind waging war on humans?" She glanced at the keep. "Let's find out."

"We'll have to get the gates open."

"Leave that to me, monster."

VERTILINE EYED THE GATE GUARDS, WHO EYED HER RIGHT BACK, not an ounce of respect shared between them. True, she wore no Smithsteel, because she'd given her armour to Evanne. But she still walked like Tresward. The Storm answered her call. *Have these churls forgotten the footprints we left on this land?*

Seven guards stood watch before the main keep's closed gates. One wore captain's stripes, him a little leaner and meaner than the rank required. He had an eyepatch, a nasty scar running from brow to cheek beneath it. Last time she was here, there was just a ceremonial pair set to remind casual visitors they needed an appointment. This group was more mob than army, the usual shine of Morgan's Queensguard's armour lacking, and a few belly bulges indicating the rank and file had forgotten the importance of exercise.

"Sirrah," she addressed the captain. "You will take us to the Raven Queen."

He chortled, all false camaraderie with his mates. "Look lads, she and the horror want a special session with her majesty." It didn't matter they weren't all 'lads'; Vertiline marked two women. Seven against one was no particular challenge, and her husband would do more than his share. *I've a pattern for this.* She eyed the battlements. *No archers.* She furrowed her brows. *I would have expected one or two, but Feybrind are masters of remaining unseen.*

Armitage made a great show of looking behind him, then narrowed his eyes. "Are you calling *me* a horror?"

"You, and all like you," the captain said. Chin jutting. One-eye narrowed right back.

Vertiline sighed. *This isn't going to end well.* "Perhaps we can—"

"That so," Armitage rumbled right over her. His voice lowered, almost becoming conspiratorial. "Do you know why they call us horrors?"

"The teeth," said a woman to the captain's left.

"The smell," chortled a man beside her.

Armitage lunged, grabbing the captain by the neck in one huge hand. He hefted the struggling man one-armed, and while his companions struggled to draw steel in the late morning light, he spun, arm moving like a windmill, and slammed the captain to the cobbles.

The man was stunned, moving only weakly, but the monster wasn't done. He stepped forward, stamping a heavy boot into the man's skull. It popped with a hollow sound, bloody gore spraying out like water from a puddle. Armitage drew his short blades, spinning back to the gate guards. He roared, "It's the fucking mess!"

Vertiline closed her eyes, hand falling to the hilt of her sword. She breathed out as she stepped forward into *Certain Winter*, blade flowing from its scabbard with a faint hiss. She carried the movement out and across, and she *knew* the edge passed through the neck of the man closest to her. The sound of falling water as blood spattered on the cobbles. She opened her eyes, bringing her blade up as the pattern demanded.

It was plain steel, not glass like she loved, nor Smithsteel she was used to in a pinch. She'd salvaged the weapon from Imshir, and it was sturdy enough. The sword's length glowed with golden light, the Storm infusing it with divine purpose.

Thunder roiled at her back as a man screamed, "'Ware! Tresward!" Vertiline was only three steps into *Certain Winter*, the pattern commanding her purpose. She didn't look up as the arrows fell from hidden archers, her sword slicing shafts from the air before going through a woman's shoulder, across the ribcage, and out near her hip. The body smoked as her blade burned.

Armitage took a man's lunge against crossed blades, then shifted forward, swords skating along his opponent's steel before he pierced the man's stomach. Bloody points ruptured from his enemy's back. He heaved the man up and aside and took a blade to his shoulder for the trouble. He grunted, but before he could lash at the man who stabbed him Vertiline ran him through.

The rest turned to run, but the closed gate at their backs was still closed. The remaining woman hammered on old timber. "Let us in!"

Another arrow, and Vertiline followed *Certain Winter's* demands, feet stepping just so, blade up, cutting arrows into burning chaff. She finished the pattern, a half-smile on her lips, then closed her eyes again.

The lightning hit, so bright she could see it through shut lids. The noise was enormous, shattering wood and stone, tossing humans and their works aside like toy blocks. The ground heaved, but she kept her footing, because the Storm was with her, *inside* her, demanding justice.

The quiet after the Storm was broken by the pattering of stone and wood returning to earth. Vertiline opened her eyes and looked to Armitage. He was flat on his back from where the blast had tossed him, but with a fierce smile of vicious delight on his face. The gates were a smoking ruin, and the battlements above glowed, the stone red and sagging with heat. *No more archers.* No more guards either. All they'd been was rendered to ash, lost on the bitter wind.

"Fuck me," her husband said. "I had it, you know."

She sheathed her blade, then turned, hand out. He gripped it and she hauled him upright. "I know. But you were taking too long."

He rubbed the gash in his shoulder. "So, now what?"

"The Raven Queen does not own this city. We will find out who thinks they do and disabuse them of the notion."

Armitage frowned. "Tilly—"

"I will know who has our baby," Vertiline hissed. "I will tear down the kingdoms of men and beast alike to get to her."

He nodded. "Aye. Just..." He trailed off, frowning at the wreckage before them. "Dead men tell no tales."

"You, counselling *me* for patience?"

He growled, frowning. "It's not that. It's... They don't remember us here."

"Then we will remind them."

"Hold a moment." He sighed. "On the sands, we had a saying. None of us are irreplaceable." He held up his index finger. "This is you." He pointed it down, making a stirring motion. "This is you, in a pool of water."

"The day is wasting—"

"I know what time it is." He held up his finger again. "Imagine you are removed from the pool. Does the pool remember the finger? Does the pool even look like it noticed you leaving? No. It just closes up as if you never were."

"The Tresward were more than a finger."

"The Tresward aren't here anymore." He eyed the wreckage. "All I'm saying is, maybe we put the finger back in, rather than throw out the bucket of water."

She swept platinum hair back from her face. "I hear you."

"Great." He grinned shark's teeth. "Now let's go make some noise."

Chapter Six

Amir watched the Justiciar vault the railing of the ship, and wondered, *Why me?*

It was a thing he asked himself a lot. He asked it the first time he'd called her *Justiciar*, after which she said *I am no Justiciar, sirrah* and beat him so bad it felt like she'd handed him his ass as a hat. Her eyes were haunted as she'd said it, but he'd still wondered, *Why me?* as he landed on his backside with what felt like a broken jaw.

She had a mean left hook, and he'd felt all the knuckles of that metal hand of hers when it hit his jaw. Surprising to all was he hadn't lost a single tooth, and perhaps that was part of the Light. How to hit a man just enough to make him aware of the precipice between life and death, and then make him feel a right dick for sauntering up to it so casually.

He glanced at Faust. "It lands to us, then."

The giant didn't look perturbed. He never did. Amir imagined what Faust would be like in armour. Probably like an impassive anvil. The only time Amir could remember Faust changing his expression was when the kitchen ran out of peaches. The man loved a good peach. "It always lands to us. And by 'us', I mean you."

"Why me?" Amir couldn't help it. It was like the words just wanted to come out by themselves.

"You're the pretty one." Faust pressed his lips into a line. "She likes you the best."

"She's never decked you!"

"That's because she can't reach that high." Faust adjusted his belt, glancing around. The deck was a confusion of fuckwittery, men and women falling over themselves, and the school's best students, which was also the students left alive, trying to hop to it after the Justiciar.

Slim hope and no hope, that one. Amir caught a glimpse of platinum hair and then Justiciar Vertiline was gone from view, swallowed by Ravenswall. He knew the city would choke on her, because she didn't go down easy. Not that one. *Good teacher. Be better if she didn't hit me so often, though.* "Where's Larochette?"

"About," Faust said.

"That's cryptic. That because you don't know?"

"Maybe," Faust allowed. "You're in charge, brother. You should know where we lay."

True enough. Amir was proxy head of their trinity. They'd joined Vertiline's school in Imshir about the same time. Had the same onboarding speech. All failed to take Vertiline with steel when she used naught but a wooden practice blade against them. Swore, on bent knee, learned the Light and struggled with the Sway. None held glass yet, because the Light wouldn't bend to their will as it should. There had been better students, but the burning lava of Heaven's Gate took them.

It was enough to live and be able to call Faust and Larochette his friends. "I think she's getting supplies."

"You mean she's looting the liquor."

"I mean exactly that, friend Faust." Amir clapped the giant on the shoulder, by now used to how high he had to reach. It wasn't clear why Faust was so large. He was easily the tallest man Amir had ever seen, taller even than the Justiciar's husband, although perhaps not as wide. Armitage had laughed when Faust looked down on him one time, and then sat the giant on his ass, just as Vertiline had with Amir. It turned out you didn't need to hold the Light on a chain to beat a giant. You just needed to be more ornery. "Let us help her. It's the honourable thing to do."

That earned him a sideways glance. "You want free booze."

"I want free booze," Amir said breezily. "Let's be about it."

LAROCHETTE WASN'T, AFTER ALL, LOOTING LIQUOR. SHE'D LOOTED blades, which lay at her feet.

They found her after doing a circuit belowdecks. She waited for them above, hair tugged in the breeze, as if she'd been there for hours and honestly, what kept them? How she'd slipped past them was a mystery, but not one Amir wanted to dredge too deeply. He knew her knack for being unseen, which was uncanny because of how she drew the eye.

Larochette was lighter skinned than Amir, although not as pale as Faust. The giant looked carved of ice, but Larochette's skin held the tone of milky coffee. Buxom, so much so he worried for her back. Her hair was straight jet to Amir's ringlet brown, both the envy of Faust's bald pate. Her face could stop the sun in its tracks, a beauty sufficient to cause carters to pause while unloading their wares.

She didn't encourage the looks or the oft-followed gropes, and was a fighter who knew her way about any kind of blade you were careless enough to leave within her reach. He remembered the time three newcomers to the school left nursing splints about broken wrists after they were free with their hands. Vengeful, but just: they still had their hands, after all.

"Ho, Larochette," Amir called.

"What kept you?" She tossed him a scabbarded broadsword.

He snatched the blade from the air, pulling steel in a smooth motion, feeling the weight. It was his sword, but the Justiciar taught them to feel the weight of even the best-known weapon. *They change,* she'd said. *A weapon loses fragments in each clash. Over time, the weight changes. If you want the Light to make a home in the edge of your steel, you will show it the respect of perfect balance.* So Amir spent a lot of time feeling the weight of this sword. He hadn't named it yet but wanted no other. "We were looking for you."

"You weren't doing a very good job." She didn't grunt as she hefted Faust's greatsword, offering the giant the hilt, but she looked like she wanted to.

Faust accepted the sword almost absently, gazing toward the dock, where a clot of robed imbeciles tried to calm panicked horses. "What are they?"

"Assassins, most likely." Larochette didn't follow his glance. "They've been waiting for us to disembark."

Amir gave his blade another twirl. *Is the steel thirsty today?* "They don't look like assassins."

"No assassin does." The scorn in her words made him wince.

"Perhaps." Amir thought that was an over simplistic view of the world. There was plenty of scope for an enterprising assassin to strike fear through a bit of mummery, but it wouldn't do to belabour the point. "Shall we go spring the trap?"

"You first," Faust said.

"Why me?"

THE IMBECILES DRESSED WELL. AMIR SIZED THEM UP BEFORE reaching them, targeting an almost painfully slim man of unnatural height as their likely leader. The slim man wasn't as tall as Faust, but then many trees didn't get that high either. Despite being near bridling horses, which could do a soul injury, he seemed very interested in people coming from the docks.

He also appeared to have missed Vertiline and Armitage, which made this all the easier. Amir sauntered right on up, putting a little mosey into it, tied on his best sunrise grin, and said, "Ho there, man. What news?"

The slim man smoothed his robes. "We are here to greet High Justiciar Vertiline and her—"

"Oooh," Amir winced. "Don't call her a Justiciar. Doesn't like it."

"Ah." The slender man looked temporarily adrift. "What should I call her?"

"Vertiline works well enough. She's worn the name longer than anyone else alive." Amir glanced at the sun, which was making its slow wander to the horizon. "She's right there." He pointed at Larochette.

The slim man looked at Larochette, who looked right back with just the right level of frost. Amir imagined the slim man had been sent to collect Vertiline, who as a matter of public record was tall, athletic, and sported hair the colour of a platinum solar. Larochette was buxom but could pass as athletic if your eyes moved past the obvious anchor points. Her hair was completely the wrong colour, though. "This is, uh, I mean."

"Are you here to take me to our quarters?" Larochette fingered the blade at her hip. "Or are you here to stare like a dolt?"

That seemed to do it. The slender man jerked his mental train of horses into a swift canter, gesturing to the mounts beside him. "We are. These steeds will carry you to—"

"No." Larochette glanced about, the horses already forgotten. "We'll walk."

The slender man paled with anger, lips pressing into a line so thin you couldn't get a playing card between them. "I was given instructions."

Amir stopped examining his nails. "Did your instructions say to die in a pile of your own entrails on the street? You've called Vertiline a Justiciar, said she must ride when she clearly means to walk, and *you are standing in her way*." He sighed. "It's our fault, really."

"It is?" The slender man looked between Amir and Larochette. "I mean, it is."

"Because of the school."

"The school," he repeated, clearly not getting it.

Amir slapped the man on the shoulder, leaning in conspiratorially. "We have the school in Imshir, see? But there's not been even a Tresward's hair this side of the ocean in, what, fifteen summers?"

"Sixteen," Faust murmured.

Amir snapped his fingers. "Of course. I was counting time by the years of the school's mascot, but there was time in the oven too."

"She would use you like a sock puppet if she heard you call her a mascot," Faust warned.

"That's the best thing about it," Amir breezed. "She's not here."

"Who?" The slender man looked completely lost.

"Doesn't matter," Amir assured him. "Now, where's that carriage?"

"Carriage?"

"For pity's sake, man." Amir clapped his hands together smartly. "The Justiciar means to ride in a carriage. Be about it."

"You said not to call her—"

"Aye."

"And she said she'd walk—"

"Aye." Amir nodded, encouraging.

"I'll get a carriage." The slim man sagged in defeat.

Chapter Seven

Evanne thought there might be a problem when she heard a *whine-crunch*. She'd heard something like it once before, back when they'd made landfall at Ravenswall. She'd known less of Tarragon, yet the fairy had put her all into a fight against Feybrind, burning a hole through one before falling, spent.

The sound as the little fairy charred through Feybrind sounded a lot like the *whine* part of what Evanne heard.

Because she was surrounded by a group of people who were, while not openly hostile, slowing the giving of their mead, Evanne stood as her fingers dropped from the strings, beamed like a thousand suns, and said, "I need to piss. Where's the jakes?"

Quinton, ever helpful, stood with her. "I'll show you."

She gave him another up-and-down, allowing her smile to dim perhaps two millimetres. "Not wanting to be a dick about it, but I don't need your kind of help. Is there a woman who knows the route?"

A slight complication stood up: Ed. The woman brushed down her leather armour, slopped a little too much ale from her cup while listing, and slurred, "I'll take you."

Evanne was near certain most people in this room weren't guards. Not originally. She'd played for only a half hour or so, but during that time she hadn't seen the usual posture of people used to doing hard work for harder pay. Aye, she understood the Trick of seeming a thing you weren't, but after enough ale these people showed insufficient care to be working blades. The one outlier in all this was Eden, a misnamed woman if ever there was one. Her eyes were a shade too close together, her nose broken one too many times, and she had the shoulders of a Vhemin, not human.

Still, she was drunk, and Evanne needed an escort, so here they were. Evanne nodded her thanks, slung her guitar behind her, and held her hand out. "After you, m'lady."

Ed snorted. "I'm no lady. I'm, a, a, wossit."

"Captain?" Evanne hazarded.

"One of those." The woman listed again, turned it into a stagger, and headed for the southern exit. This was the passage Evanne entered from, which was perplexing because Evanne remembered no doors leading to washrooms at any point. *Fine. She wants to take me on a mystery tour? No problem, because that's where the noise came from anyway.*

She followed Eden down the passage, minding her distance. "You're captain of the house guard? For how many summers?"

"Aye." Eden sounded confused about it though. "Years."

They made it into the open courtyard with the strange locked door. Evanne noted two alarming things as they cleared the doorway. To the south lay a small pile of glowing stone and crumpled fairy. Beside this sad pile stood a gaunt man who held a blue-tinged lantern. Evanne felt a tug in her chest, one emotional, the other physical. Emotional: *that's Tarragon!* Physical: the gaunt man was no man, and he carried Hitch in the palm of his hand. He was a vampire; she knew it in her core, the same way she could see ghosts or reach the hearts and souls of those lost to death. And that meant he was bad news and would probably kill them all without breaking a sweat.

Unless. She thought fast, landing at a simple Trick. She stopped, glared, and said, "Mother*fucker.*"

The gaunt man paused, half-bent toward Tarragon. "Excuse me?"

"No, you're not excused," Evanne said. "You're a wanker. You're about to lay hands on my friend, and you've got another friend in a glass jar. And I won't stand for it."

The man turned to Eden, gaze heavy like winter snow, and said, "Deal with her."

Evanne pulled Fusillade from under her cloak and smashed Eden upside the head with it. The guard captain stretched her burly length on the old cobbles, face bouncing on stone. Evanne swept the weapon's muzzle toward the gaunt man. "'Deal with her'? Did you see a copper baron stage show and steal lines from it? No, don't tell me." She put a weary hand on her forehead. "It was a group of lesser thespians. Idiots putting on a show without the right training. This, I promise you, is why no bard gets the credit they deserve any more. *Amateurs*."

The man blinked, the snow going right out of his gaze. "What?"

"And you," Evanne stabbed the weapon toward him, "are supposed to be scary? Is that it?"

The man looked like he'd found firmer ground. "I *am* scary."

"You're a two-bit clown," she corrected. "What's the play here?"

"I'm going to use you as a fountain, drinking eternally from your flesh," the monster beamed. "You smell so sweet. Half human, yes, but half Vhemin too. Someone who won't die so easily. Someone who can stay bound here forever, at my mercy, your companions doing my bidding for fear of your death while I live on the delicate juices in your veins."

"Gross," Evanne said. "Wait. You..." She laughed, slapping her knee, then began pacing. She knew she looked nonchalant, but her pacing had a purpose. She angled around to the southern exit. "You think the Raven is a friend of mine? You want her to do something for you?"

"Ah." The vampire's enthusiasm cooled for a moment, then he brightened. "I still have your spectre in the lantern. The very heart of your power. And your fairy, well. I know you'll do anything for her."

Evanne stalked further toward the exit. "So?"

"So, you'll bewitch the ritualist to do as I say, then—"

"Wait. You want me to bewitch Morgan to do what you want, for fear of my death?" Evanne scratched her head. "This feels overly complicated."

The vampire scowled. "I can work out the kinks. I have the time, and the patience."

"Huh." Evanne blew a stray rust lock from her face. "You're a crea-

ture from beyond, something like that?" She lifted her chin in professional curiosity. "Vampire? Yeah, I thought so." She tapped Fusillade's
muzzle against her chin. "Got the whole place in thrall, amirite?"

The vampire beamed. "Look behind you."

She gave a quick glance, taking in the twenty 'guards' who'd come
out to gaze with unwavering eyes at her. "Huh. Well, got to go." She
gave a quick grin, levelled Fusillade, and fired.

The scattergun roared once, blowing the vampire's hand off at the
wrist. The lantern holding Hitch fell to the ground. *Good enough*.

The man screamed, so Evanne bolted.

The horde behind her howled in pursuit. But none were as fast as
the vampire.

Chapter Eight

Tarragon huddled, arms over her head, as a legion of Bigs stampeded past her. The little crumbing of rock and molten stone created a natural lee that their river flowed around, but she didn't stop trembling until they were all gone. *I can't fly. I can't even stand. I am small, and this world wants to kill me.*

After they were gone, she struggled upright. Laying on its side was the lantern. It was rocking slightly as if someone inside were trying to get out. She pulled herself to it, placing a hand on the opaque glass. As she suspected, it wasn't hot at all. It was so cold she shivered and pulled her hand back. "Hitch?"

"I'm here," the lantern said. "I don't know *where* here is, though. I can't see much. Shapes, mostly."

"How'd you get in there?" Tarragon limped a circle around the lantern. "Never mind that. We need to get you out. Evanne's in trouble."

A soft laugh came from the lantern. "When is she not?"

Tarragon bit her lower lip. "This is serious. I can't fly. She doesn't have you. The Raven Queen and all her magic are absent." She thought of Heser and how he smelled strong, like an anvil. "I don't know where Heser the Cheg is."

"That's easy. Heser is where the Raven Queen is."

Tarragon looked to the sealed door. "Is she in there?"

"I can't see." Hitch sighed. "If it's a big door that looks new, then yes. I went in, and that's when he got me. This lantern is some kind of trap."

Tarragon tapped the glass. "I don't think it was meant for you. I mean, not specifically. We used them, back before, when we wanted sight beyond sight."

"You assholes trapped ghosts?"

"I guess. Not me personally, but sure." Tarragon looked about for a way to open the door that held the Raven Queen captive. It was huge, designed by Bigs for Bigs, and even if she wasn't tapped out, she'd never get it open. "How do we open that?"

"Easy," Hitch breezed. "You ask someone for help."

"Everyone here is bewitched!"

"A minor problem at best." Hitch was silent a moment. "Is there an unconscious woman near you?"

Tarragon glanced at the fallen form of Eden. "Yes, but I don't know if she'll help us."

"Do you have any other ideas?" Hitch sounded like he was buffing his nails against his shirt. Smug, aloof, and very punchable.

She gritted her teeth, curled tiny hands into fists, and stamped over to Eden. The woman's face was a mess, blood from a broken nose pooling beneath her. Tarragon kicked the woman's chin. "Hey!" No response. She glared harder, but it didn't do much.

"Is there a handy pool of cooling magma about, perchance?" By the Three, Hitch sounded like he would be better in a wood chipper than a lantern, but was thinking clearer than she was. The stone she'd boiled through was just *sitting* there. Waiting. Wanting to be used.

Tarragon stormed to it, grabbing a hunk of rock resting near the magma. It was hot as a brand despite the colour cooling to a sullen red, but Tarragon was from a race of reactor technicians. Mere *heat* wouldn't hurt her. She humped it back to Eden, eyed the woman's face, then took pity and headed for her hand, then hesitated. "What if she's angry?"

"That's the point, isn't it?"

"Right." Tarragon pushed the glowing stone against Eden's exposed wrist.

There was a sizzle and the smell of searing meat, then Eden screamed, slapped Tarragon and her stone away, then bolted upright. The fairy tumbled end over end, coming to rest a couple meters back. The guard captain held her wrist to mouth. "What the hell was that?"

"A super hot rock." Tarragon got up, winced, and scrubbed at her hair. "I need your help."

"So you burned me?"

"Yes. There wasn't time to do it another way." Tarragon looked at her feet. "Look, here's how it is. You were bewitched, and I'm hoping you're not any more. Because of the pain, you see? Usually busts right through that kind of thing. If you want to kill me that's understandable, but I'd prefer if you could open that door first." She pointed.

Eden turned. "Huh." She sucked her wrist, then faced Tarragon. "Why should I?"

"Because there is a vampire here who is hundreds of years old. Maybe as old as me. And he wants to kill people forever." She gave her wings a tentative flutter, but they were sluggish. "And, *hic*, he wants to kill Evanne."

The guard captain listed. "I'm drunk?"

"Yes, I think so. You smell drunk."

"I don't remember getting drunk." Eden looked at her hands, then arms, and down at her body. "I don't remember getting dressed." She looked around. "I don't even remember this place. You think I'd remember, right?" She frowned. "But ... I remember music. Notes falling like the tears of the Three. Soft, but strong." Her voice faded off in wonder. "Was that Evanne?"

"Yes." Tarragon nodded. "She makes music."

"She plays like the angels. I *felt* it." Eden rubbed her chest above her heart. "Right here."

"Well, she's going to die." Tarragon frowned. "I don't want to hurry you, but she's going to die *soon*."

"Right." Eden ignored the lantern, headed to the door, and examined the stone beside it. "Where's that catch..? Ah, here." She pressed on the stone, and with a *click*, there came a rumbling sound. The door slid sideways.

Heser the Cheg roared out, hands in fists, eyes wild. He made Eden in two steps, smashing the guard captain in the side of the head. She went out like a light, laying her length on the cobbles for the second time in five minutes. "Who else wants some?"

Tarragon looked at Eden, then Heser the Cheg. "Smooth moves."

Morgan walked from the shadows beyond the door, cool hand resting for the briefest of moments on Heser the Cheg's shoulder. Then she strode to Tarragon and crouched. "Fairy. What is our status?"

"Evanne's in trouble."

"Of course."

"I said the same thing," the lantern said. "Tarragon didn't think it was funny then."

The Raven Queen looked at Tarragon a little closer, a little longer, then nodded. "Nor now, by the looks."

"Evanne is trying to save us all," Tarragon said. "And she's all alone."

"What about the cat?" Heser the Cheg looked like a man who wanted to beat a few more people down.

"Pakhet? I haven't seen her." Tarragon pointed to the tunnel Evanne ran down. "Evanne went that way. But I don't think you should go there."

"Why, prithee?" Morgan stood, glancing to the passage.

"Vampires," Tarragon explained. "There is a room above full of fetishes. I believe the vampire holds people in thrall. He wants you to do that to more people."

Morgan nodded slowly. "So, he would spare me, but kill Evanne?"

Tarragon frowned. "Yes?"

Morgan smiled. "I knew I was the likeable one." She glanced to Heser the Cheg. "Captain, I need you to buy me time."

Heser the Cheg looked to Morgan, the passage, then back to Morgan. "You want me to fight a vampire?"

"If that's what it takes." Morgan's smile widened. "The fairy and I have other business. Attend, Queensguard. I need as much time as you can buy."

"You will have until the end of all things." Heser the Cheg lingered but a moment, then straightened, duty stiffening his spine. He ran after Evanne.

Morgan bent and picked up Tarragon. Her hands were warm, but not as gentle as Evanne's. "Where must we go?"

Tarragon pointed to the hole in the wall above. "There."

The Raven Queen sighed. "Always, stairs."

"A little help," Hitch said. "If you could, you know. Get me out?"

"My," Morgan said. "Is that Hitch?"

"You can hear him?" Tarragon blinked. "It must be because of the lantern."

"A ghost is of no use at all," the Raven Queen said. "But I really like the idea of a talking lantern."

Chapter Nine

Evanne ran, and made good time. *I am motivated.* Her reforged heart hammered in her chest, breath sawing through her throat, but despite the hounds on her heels she felt invigorated.

It's a long-ish shot but I think it'll work.

She pounded down the corridor toward the gate, bounced off the bend to the left, dropped her head, and ran harder. *I can't fight. Not without Hitch. But I still know how to play.* Evanne kept her guitar in a death grip, left hand around the neck like she was saving a drowning man. Her right hand held Fusillade just as tight.

I've got to lead them away.

Fusillade was running low on ammunition. Worse, it wasn't a holy weapon. The last hand that held it was Tresward, but the long dead Knight Champion left no blessed ammunition that could purge the living dead from the world. Without a Tresward's Storm, it was just a gun, and Evanne figured she'd need a cannon to take out a vampire.

I hope Morgan does her part. I hope I haven't trusted like a fool.

Evanne heard the pounding of feet behind her. She careened off another junction and slammed into a door. Her momentum took her right through the sagging wood, hinges and splinters following her.

Her right foot found nothing but air, and she pinwheeled, too panicked to scream, and descended into darkness.

Her shoulder hit stone as she fell. Evanne's chin slammed into a stone edge. The pain was a bright spark in the gloom. She lost her grip on the guitar, and heard it clatter into the darkness. Fusillade tumbled away as she hit her elbow. Evanne rolled, still falling, feeling the edge of stone bite her shoulder, wood slap her upside the head, and then she came to rest at the bottom.

Howling from above.

She scrambled, fingers scrabbling at stone, reaching. Evanne almost cried with relief when her fingers found the wood and metal of a fretboard. She grabbed the instrument, surged upright, spun, and ... paused. Her Vhemin eyes pierced the gloom well enough. She was in a basement that moonlighted as a storeroom. She spat a tooth, glaring at the stairs she'd fallen down, then kicked a stray board from beside her feet.

By the Three, it clattered against Fusillade. The weapon's barrel watched her from the dark, a gimlet eye before a length of gleaming promise. Evanne panted her way to it, hefted the weapon, and looked around.

Barrels. Shelves. No weapons she could see.

There. A hunch of stone lurked, a dark blue iris to a black portal. She hustled, reached the archway, and cursed the maker of this place who saw fit to put a portcullis here. Evanne slid Fusillade into its holster, propped the guitar against the arch, grabbed the base of the portcullis, and heaved.

Nothing. Not even a flake of rust.

I'm fucked, I'm fucked, I'm fucked. The refrain ran through her mind, because she couldn't stop here. *Here* would leave Hitch in a lantern forever. And *here* was a place where no one could help her.

She heard feet on the stairs, and what sounded like sniffing.

Evanne's shoulders bunched. She strained, heart hammering, teeth clenched so tight she thought they might break. *Curse you, weak human flesh. My father could do this. Why can't I?*

Someone chuckled from the darkness. Evanne knew the hundred different weights of laughter, and this was laden with malice, cunning, and hunger. She screamed, heaved, felt her left shoulder *twinge*, screamed louder, and then the portcullis shrieked right back at her as it crashed upward. She wanted to weep, but grabbed the guitar by the neck, tight enough to choke, and stumbled into the gloom beyond.

Evanne's feet splashed through muck. She kept going, hand out, collecting cobwebs as she ran. The guitar banged against the tunnel wall. The passage was narrower than she expected, a tightness she felt in her chest, and she thought this might be where she died. Buried in a culvert beneath the earth, locked in the deathless embrace of the evernight.

Fuck that.

It was almost a relief when she rounded a bend, the dark greys and blues of her blood heat vision giving way to the startled red-yellow of living flesh. A woman, sword in hand. Evanne was surprised, because *how had they gotten ahead of her?* and *what do I do now?*

The sword came for her, a hungering slip of edged malice. Evanne stumbled back, Hitch's hand no longer on her shoulder, the spectre not with her. The cut was sloppy, because of course this was a human, and the human could see just two things in the dark around them: jack, and shit. Driven by the vampire, sent here to stumble into the enemy.

That's no way to treat your vassals.

Evanne steadied herself, stepped back, and grinned in the lamp-black dark. *Be gentle. Be strong. Be a darker night, but hope in the dawn.* She layered Tricks in her tone, a finger on her fret board, touching a string for comfort. "It doesn't have to be this way." The sword swung again, the woman panicked, and Evanne felt a pang for her. This person was a slave like a Commanded Feybrind.

So, when she stepped in on the woman's overswing, she only clubbed her as hard as necessary with the guitar.

The woman dropped like a sack of millet. Evanne ignored the fallen sword, because she couldn't use one, and hurried on through the dark. Above, a ladder she ignored—perhaps how the woman had come down—and then an intersection. Voices to the right. *So, left it is.*

Left. A right. Daylight.

She hurried, human eyes shouldering their level of the burden.

Evanne found a door with a grill set at eye height. Beyond, the crimson gold of sunset.

Oh. Oh, no.

If there was one thing everyone knew, it was that vampires feared the Three's Light. And the meagre glimmer remaining was draining from the sky, minute by minute.

Evanne glanced over her shoulder, then put a hand on the door. Old wood, but not rotted. It was barred from this side, and a metal bolt set into the frame for good measure. She hefted the plank, dropped it with a splash, then slide the bolt free.

Evanne stepped into the dusk beyond, glanced at the onyx sky, and fled.

Chapter Ten

The problem with Evanne is she's Evanne. Morgan, Raven Queen of Or'sen, thought of the half-Vhemin girl who kept stumbling into danger, stumbling out with the queen in tow, and leaving Morgan owing her one.

And I hate debt. She gave Heser the Cheg a sideways glance. "We should leave."

The guardsman had returned after pursuit of the enemy. His report suggested he'd waylaid five of the enemy but lost the rest when they went to ground. He looked unhappy about it, but Morgan wasn't sure if it was because he'd left Evanne alone, or because he'd only had his vengeance on five. Heser listened to her, pursed his lips and nodded, but in the way he did when he wasn't agreeing. It aggravated Morgan no end, because the man wouldn't have the decency to start an argument with her. It was always, *Yes, my queen,* or, *As the Raven wills,* but never a good, *Get bent.* She thought of Lord Meriwether du Reeves, a man who reeked of insurrection, and then looked away.

My lord Meriwether would have made a good match, but he wouldn't have been as good a man as Heser. Not that it matters, because Heser is a guardsman, and I am the Raven Queen. I could as easily touch the Three moons as his face.

Not that there were any of the Three still in the sky. Morgan glanced up, noting the light bleeding away, leaving the dark, as it always did, and smiled. "If we leave, we will have the cover of darkness. I saw no hounds for tracking. The Lord Gyles who keeps this manse is a sloppy warden. We will be free." *Of everything*, she wanted to add.

"You can't leave." Predictable as ever, the fairy struggled upright. Morgan looked down on the pitiful creature. She was usually a sparkling wonder, but her wings drooped, face similarly so, and there was no glimmer about her. "Evanne risked all to set you free."

"And without Evanne, we would not have been captured in the first place. I believe this makes us even." Morgan raised an eyebrow. "Would you disagree?"

Tarragon glanced at Morgan, the lantern she held, and then at Heser the Cheg. "No."

"Good."

"I would call you an imbecile," Tarragon continued, as if Morgan had said nothing. "I would say you are unfit to rule a just kingdom. And I might—"

"Mind your tone," Morgan bridled.

"Mind your face," Tarragon snapped. Morgan felt the sting, but long years atop the Raven Throne kept her expression a mask. *I hope it's a mask, anyway.* "The maybe-Vhemin is risking all for your kingdom. Your people. Bringing justice to a rudderless land."

"Hmm," Heser the Cheg said, in the manner of a man with something on his mind.

Morgan ignored him. "I do not need the whelp's help to regain a kingdom I've not lost. A quick tally." She counted on her fingers. "I've lost a ship, and some good men. My capital is aflame, but it isn't the first time. My lickspittle brother thinks to govern, but the man is incapable of tying his shoelaces unaided, so I've little to fear there. With a few good people I will put this to rights."

"Hmm," Heser the Cheg offered, but louder this time.

"I think I would like to get out of this lantern," Hitch said.

"I think I would like to not be surrounded by cowards," Tarragon said. "You're afraid, queen of nothing, ruler of invisible subjects. You're afraid because you have tasted death, and Evanne rules that realm better than you hold this one. Your power is that of rituals, held in the muddy hands of Vhemin, and all might wonder how one of your lordly line got it." She looked down her nose at Morgan, an impressive feat because the sprite didn't come half-way up the Raven Queen's shin. "I don't think your ancestors lay with the enemy. I just think you're made of the same dirty material."

Morgan lunged for the creature, and there was Heser the Cheg, the impossible man the size of an ox, face as impassive one too. His hand was up at her chest height but didn't touch her. "My queen."

"She dares!"

"Hmm," he said.

Morgan hissed. "You agree with the creature?"

He gave that some thought, looking as if he were chewing some internal cud. "Not on all matters."

"Sirrah," she snapped. "You forget yourself."

"I have forgotten many things. I've lost my name once or twice. I lost my way more than that. Found myself in your house, rose through service, then lost that too. But never have I forgotten myself." He lowered his hand. "I remember the Raven. A black bird, but so clever. I remember when you reached out to the lost, brought them close, tried to build something with the sorcerers who'd been hunted by the Tresward. Worked with the Knights, those who could see, and did something great." He stood aside, showing Tarragon behind him. Giving her permission, perhaps. "I have never seen nor remembered you to be weak. Perhaps I was wrong."

Weak. Morgan wanted to scream. Curl her fingers into a fist, slug Heser upside the head, and storm out. She felt her jaw clench, feared her teeth might break. Heard the snarl more than felt it, and knew the mask wasn't holding. "You think I am *weak?*"

He didn't meet her eyes. "I said I remembered no time when you were."

"You mean to say something else. Just get it out."

The slightest hint of a wrinkle touched the corner of his mouth. *By the Three, is he smiling?* "Tarragon is small. No, sprite, I mean no disrespect. It is merely a fact. I am large." He breathed deep, chest expanding, then let it out. "Only the weak hit the small. That is all."

The Raven Queen felt her gut clench. *She deserves it.* Morgan wanted to storm past Heser, lay about with righteous fury, make the fairy take it back—

Righteous fury? There would be nothing right about it. Morgan stilled herself, straightened, and breathed for a moment. "And what do the strong do?"

"Hmm." Heser the Cheg sagged a little. "For truth, I don't know. My queen, I have strayed. I am not the man you need. I'm too old to hold the blade steady." She raised an eyebrow at this, looking at the breadth of his shoulders, the biceps that were like coconuts, and the chest that would make a Vhemin jealous. "I believe I owe Evanne. I have shared a road with her. We tried to drag her to us. And," he waved a hand at her look, "Knight Champion Vertiline. We needed aid against your brother. Help against those who turned on us. We brought our best to Imshir and failed. Barret ... fell." He looked at Tarragon. "There have been precious few who stood by us. Fewer still who did so with nothing to gain. The fairy. The bard. And the spectre."

She waited for him to continue, but the silence stretched between them. "And you think we should help them?"

"I think they are helping us. The least we can do is meet them halfway."

Morgan sighed. "Fuck."

"Good talk," said the lantern. "Can someone get me out of here?"

"About that." Tarragon was cautious, as if she felt she and Morgan still needed a set-to. "I have an idea."

"Oh?" Morgan lifted the lantern. *I still like the idea of a talking lantern. What a shame.* "Let me hear it."

"Um." Tarragon toed the ground. "Well, before when I said you were dirty—"

"Yes, yes, lay with sows, all of that." Morgan rolled her eyes. "What of it?"

"We need you to be dirtier."

HESER THE CHEG LED THEM. HE STALKED LIKE A VERY QUIET ANVIL. Tarragon sat on his shoulder, clutching his ear, the man's bald head giving her no purchase. Her guardsman didn't seem to mind.

Morgan followed with the lantern. The task seemed impossible. Tarragon spoke of a room of relics, explaining they were probably tokens used by the vampire to bind his thralls. He needed a ritualist to make more. *Odds are*, the fairy hazarded, *a good ritualist could unmake the ones he has.* Then she'd bit her lip, which was perhaps the cutest thing Morgan had seen in her life, and added, *It's not that I don't think you're a good ritualist.* Hic.

The keep was a sprawl. Ravenswall's castle had fewer twists, Morgan would swear her life on it. Tarragon insisted they go up, so Heser the Cheg tried to find stairs. They rounded a promising bend and came face to face with a startled man. He had the look of a wood-cutter. A bit simple but made of stern stuff. He wore armour and a surprised expression, a broadsword belted to his hip.

Heser the Cheg said, "Ah," leaned back, and punched the man. Not in the face, but right in the chest, into that armoured breastplate.

The man flew back as if kicked by a horse to clatter in a stunned pile. A low, long groan came from him. Tarragon fluttered her wings uncertainly. "Why didn't you just knock him out?"

"An unconscious man is unlikely to tell us about the stairs." Heser the Cheg stamped forward, grabbed the front of the woodcutter's cuirass, and hefted the man to a sitting position. "Stairs?"

Morgan noticed the cuirass was dented where Heser's fist hit. The woodcutter looked at Heser, then at his fist, somehow magically cocked for another hit. "That way." His chin jerked from the direction he'd come.

"Thank you." Heser stood, let the man's breastplate go, then helped him up.

"No, thank you," said the man, then fell over unconscious as Heser's fist clocked him in the jaw.

Morgan wasn't sure if she should gasp or smile. Tarragon glittered, then put a tiny kiss against the large man's ear. "I know why Evanne likes your style."

WHEN THIS IS DONE, I WILL OWE HER NOTHING. MORGAN STAMPED UP stairs, the refrain beating in her head. *Owing people leads to repayment plans you can never meet. It leads to overreach of the royal treasury. Before you know it, you've lost a kingdom.*

That was it, wasn't it? She'd lost Or'sen. For a moment her feet slowed on the old stone steps, sickness in her gut, hand against the worn stone wall. Tarragon glanced back, saw her distress, and flitted to land on the railing beside her hand. The fairy was worn thin, faded like ancient parchment, but by the Three, still in the fight. "Are you okay?"

"Your concern for my welfare is touching," Morgan said.

"I'm not concerned for your welfare. I'm concerned whether you'll be able to do your job, so we can get out of here without dying, or worse, becoming undying. That would be bad." The fairy didn't glimmer, just stood there, looking like she weighed about thirty kilograms for all her tiny size.

"Fairies can become the living dead?"

"Evanne could," Tarragon said. "Fairies can only be fairies. We're really good at it." She glanced away. "I don't hate you, you know."

"You don't?" The Raven Queen felt a smile on her lips. Delicate, only half there, but miraculous.

"I hate what they made you." The fairy cocked her head. "If I look at you like this," she framed Morgan in her hands, as if the queen were a painting, "I can see the girl you were, then the young woman you had to be. And I can't believe what you are now is what you wanted, when you were a girl."

Morgan saw Heser the Cheg pause, the man fidgeting, wanting to press on, but also tethered to her. His fate, hers. *I am responsible for what happens to this man.* The thought was another kind of debt, but it didn't feel bad. Important, perhaps. "You see all that from thirty centimetres of height?"

"Not really." Tarragon dropped her hands. "Evanne told me."

"The Vhemin?" Morgan frowned. "She's sixteen."

"She's Evanne." Tarragon glimmered, suddenly bashful, one foot behind the other. "Can you do your job?"

"This is a difficult conversation to follow. You flit from topic to topic."

Tarragon clapped her hands, surprisingly loud for such a tiny creature. "Keep up! Bigs are slow. I get it. But you're not stupid. You made all the good things in the world, once. You can do it again." She took wing, struggling up to Heser the Cheg, alighting on the big man's shoulder.

Heser the Cheg didn't seem to mind.

We made all the good things. We can do it again.

Morgan looked at her hands. Long, delicate, soft. Used to ruling, not doing. *We made all the bad things too though, didn't we? We made everything stop, when it was so good.* She glanced up. "I don't know if we should be in charge."

"First smart thing you've said all day," Tarragon said. "Now hurry up."

"Please," said the lantern. "It's cramped in here."

THE ROOM OF TALISMANS AND RELICS SMELLED OF AGE. WHEN Morgan was young, her father had shown her the castle library. He'd explained, hand out, *Everything you need is here.* Then he'd smiled, touched her head, then her chest. *And here, and here.*

She hadn't understood, until she'd found a book where a princess lived in a castle. Kept prisoner by a dragon, a thing that breathed fire and ate knights. Not Tresward, just the ordinary kind of knights, because a dragon needed to be mindful around even a lowly Adept.

Morgan loved how the library smelled. It wasn't until much later she understood the dragon was an allegory, a creature that stood in place of something the reader needed to see. From one side, it was the dangers untold, the thing we must face to get the prize.

I am not a prize, she realised when she was eight. *I am the knight. The princess, too. And the dragon is doubt. It is fear. It is the uncertainty in the hearts of men.*

And then she'd realised, *I am no man.*

The library smelled of knowledge and wisdom, timeless and ancient. She'd loved that smell.

This room smelled nothing like it. It was the crooked part of time, where mould grew, and all the lessons were bad. Where doubt festered, and the hearts of men failed.

"We are here, my queen," Heser the Cheg murmured. He perhaps felt it important to remind her, because she'd been standing in the doorway for thirty seconds.

"She knows," Tarragon hissed. "Give her a minute. It's a lot to take in."

The fairy wasn't wrong. There was a hearth that promised warmth with a little rekindling, but the wood was gone. The walls were lined with knick-knacks and bric-a-brac. A helmet. A spinning wheel. A hoe beside a fishing rod. A wheel from a ship. Canvas. The shuttle of a loom. A sword, but bent and old. A halter too large for a horse. It went on and on, and made the room feel large, as if Morgan was eight, in Ravenswall's library again.

"The doubts of men," she said.

Tarragon glittered in the gloom. "The who?"

Morgan bared her teeth. "Have you ever met a dragon?"

"Umm." Tarragon glanced at Heser the Cheg, who remained impassive as basalt. "Yes? Not really. I've seen a dragon, but never been introduced. I'm sure they're very nice."

"I've met one." Morgan strode into the room. "She was huge. The world shook when she walked. Ormeon breathed fire and could destroy the Artifices that ruined a legion of my best soldiers."

"My queen," Heser the Cheg said. "Ormeon has been lost these many years."

"I wonder." Morgan rubbed her arms. "I don't think you meet a dragon and don't take a piece of her with you." She turned a slow circle, examining the relics. "I don't think dragons are supposed to make you afraid."

"You what now?" Tarragon looked lost at sea.

"I think we're supposed to be the knight, the princess, *and* the dragon." Morgan sighed.

Tarragon glittered for a moment. "You've no idea what to do."

"Not a clue," the Raven Queen admitted. "I had a coterie. They would know."

"Probably not," the fairy argued. "Ritualism is ... different." She crossed her arms while she fluttered. "Why not give it a shot?"

"A ... shot?" Morgan blinked. "We need a plan! Some kind of system, a way to control—"

"There's no controlling it," Tarragon said. "This is magic, witch queen, and it controls you."

Morgan strode about the room, stopping before the ship's wheel. She threw an arm toward it. "You're telling me I'm supposed to stand here and take it?"

"I don't know," Tarragon said. "I'm a Builder. But the last time I saw you go all googly-eyed—"

"I do not have googly eyes! I am the Raven Queen of Or'sen!"

Tarragon pursed her tiny, perfect lips. "You're right. They're a bit squinty, not googly."

"*Squinty?*"

"Not important." Tarragon flew a small loop. "Last time, you were in a demon summoning circle. You had no control. And the time before that was at the docks." She sighed. "That seemed a long time ago. I thought Evanne was the enemy. I thought I could find my commanding officer and help win the war."

Morgan let her hand drop, felt her heart slow. Looked at the fairy for a moment, really *looked* at her. Saw the angel face, the wondrous glow and glitter, and the impossible sadness hidden in the green gaze that held the cold of the ocean depths. "And now?"

"Different war. That's all." Tarragon looked away. "Why don't you try touching one? See what happens."

Morgan scoffed. "One does not simply touch a thing and expect magic to happen. To think that your best plan is for me to place my palm against this wheel and hope? Hope is not a strategy!" For emphasis, she slapped her hand on the ship's wheel.

Felt ocean spray.

And fell overboard.

QUINTON HELD THE WHEEL IN A GRIP MADE IRON BY FEAR. THE SKY WAS *shot through with spears of lightning. The Three warred above, he was sure. Threw their might against the clouds, tried to shatter the storm with a greater fury.*

They weren't helping.

The skiff surged through. They called her Dancer, *because she skipped over the water like the graceful performers who'd come to Hollyhead's fair ten seasons past. He and his wife had laughed, ate toffee apple, talked of their future, and bought a boat.*

The boat would bring luck.

He gazed to the west, squinting through the squall. The rain befouled his vision, and made shadow monsters of simple waves. He'd come out here looking for Wolrif, or some news of his boat. The lad had gone out after Yvette or some such nonsense and wouldn't hear about how unlikely it was she wasn't anywhere on the water. Not in this storm. Not even a fool would come out here.

A fool, or someone who had a dancer to keep them safe.

Quinton grinned, feeling the fear still with him, but mindful of another emotion. Hope would be too trite, but he could admit to excitement.

No, to the west there was something. It had the look of a man with great wings. Lightning gave him the gift of sight, throwing the night back with a casual flash. The man was like any other, excepting the wings, and how he flew over the whitecaps.

Hand on the wheel, Quinton wondered if this was how he'd die. Will I know my killer? Will he make it quick? Is this how Wolrif died?

The man landed on Dancer's *deck with a wet thump. The wings became the billowy flutter of a great cape, so long it dragged like a train. A gaunt man, but strong against the storm. Wet, he but didn't look mad about it. Like he'd been wet before and knew it would pass. Quinton kept his hand on the wheel, rubbed more water from his eyes, and said, "Help you?"*

The man smiled. The expression might've been meant as a kindness, but it wasn't a smile like you'd get from Jenna as she glanced your way while tending the flower cart, or even the type little Jack would throw your way while scampering off with a few coins he'd 'found'. It was the smile of a corpse, fixed, held a little longer than the living ever would. "What an interesting question."

"Only, you've come at a bad time," explained Quinton. "We're out here looking for Wolrif. Storm's bad, and if it's all the same, perhaps you could come back later." He wondered why he'd said that.

"You're trying to be polite, because this is an unusual situation." The man looked at his hand, turning it over as the rain lashed about them. "Men used to offer a handshake to let each other know they had no weapon. Courtesy is the same. A platitude to let someone else know you're trying not to offend them. It won't help."

"It won't?" Quinton looked at the wheel, his hand on it, that iron grip holding the rudder true. "Why not?"

"I'm not here for your courtesy. I am not interested in coming back later. I am Lord Gyles of Drastow Stronghold, and I need your soul."

Quinton eyed the man, the deck, and the distance to the railing. He flashed a quick, nervous smile, doffed an imaginary cap, and turned for the rail. He sprinted as if his life depended on it, and in four short strides he was on the railing, then over it, heading for the chop below. An icy embrace, true, but he would have a chance in the water. Because he knew whatever Lord Gyles was, he wasn't here to give Quinton any kind of chance.

It was only a short distance from the railing to the waves. Quinton fell.

He never hit the water.

MORGAN SCREAMED. THE WHEEL WAS IN HER HANDS, THE WOOD smoking, charring where her fingers gripped it. Water drenched her, the clean saltless ice sluce of an inland lake. She felt her body shake with the cold, the fear, the knowing she was about to die.

The wheel shook as she gripped it. Heser the Cheg was there, of course. He shouted at her, but his words meant nothing. Past him Tarragon fluttered, glitterdust shedding to the floor. The fairy wrung her hands, anxious, but Morgan wasn't seeing her either.

Past both was a shadow. A gaunt man with a cape, but it wasn't a cape at all. Wings, leathery and long, a grotesque distortion of a bat. He had an inhuman smile, not like the Vhemin at all. The monsters weren't human, but they knew passion. Lord Gyles had nothing in his smile but a yearning, desperate hunger.

I am the princess and the knight. I am the dragon.

She screamed again, lightning forking from the wheel, arcing to the stone walls. Morgan felt her hair rise, wanted to drop the wheel.

Couldn't.

It flashed blue, then smoked more, licks of flame curling through her fingers. She fought it, tried to pull away, and the wheel came apart in her hands. Wood splintering, it clattered to the old stone floor, each piece a burning ember.

Heser the Cheg staggered back. Tarragon flew forward, hand out. Lightning caught the sprite, a great coiling loop of white power.

Silence.

Morgan blinked, momentarily night blind. "Heser? Tarragon?"

"I am here, my queen." Strong hands on her arms. A lesser man would have run. She could smell the maleness of him, wanted him to hold her, just fucking *hold* her for a minute.

Not yet. She put a cool hand on his. "Tarragon?" Morgan blinked, the room coming back in dim flashes as her sight returned. *There.* Twin motes of azure blue instead of the expected emerald green.

The fairy floated before her, eyes glowing with icefire. "I think you found it. I think you found how to break the ritual."

Morgan stepped past Heser, walking around the fairy. "You're unharmed?"

"It's just lightning."

"It's *exactly* lightning. It destroys rock, houses, and people. It chars the earth and blasts ancient oaks to pieces." Morgan felt heat coming off the sprite like a coal forge.

Tarragon shrugged. "It can't hurt me. Not really. About now I could jump start a reactor."

Morgan felt more adrift than when she'd been Quinton. "Reactor?"

"Doesn't matter. Do another one." The fairy pointed to the wall of relics. "That was one. Only about a hundred to go."

"Are you insane? I'm not touching another one of those." Morgan crossed arms still soaked from the lake.

"Ah." Tarragon nodded, sad, but not arguing. "Then Evanne will die. I'm going to find her. Because she shouldn't die alone."

"Wait." But the fairy didn't wait, because the maddening creature didn't care she was the Raven Queen of Or'sen. The fairy cared about Evanne, and Evanne was going to die.

"My queen." Heser the Cheg spoke cautiously, as if words were feet placed about the rim of a pit of spikes. "Tell me how it is done, and I will do it."

Honest. Forthright. Carrying all my cares. Has it ever been so, and I didn't see it? She looked at Heser, stepped to him, and took his face in her hands. "Dear man. You can't do this for me."

He took her wrists. Lowered her hands. She wanted him to step in and kiss her, to taste the lake on her lips. But instead he said, "Someone must. The sprite is right. Evanne will likely die this night."

Morgan wanted to wail *there are so many!* Because the wall behind her held relics enough to capture the souls for an army.

But wailing had never fixed her life. She looked at the door. *Perhaps it is time to run, then.*

Chapter Eleven

The throne room's décor was much as Vertiline remembered. The high, vaulted ceiling brooded above. The windows were high set within solid stone, allowing enough sun through that a young queen could glower with just the right lighting effects from where she sat on the ornate throne. The throne hulked atop the steps at the far end, made by men to impress other men. It had always been too large for Morgan, but the Raven Queen's presence was bigger than a single chair. She owned the room and the kingdom beyond.

The young queen is not here, though. Neither is she young any more. But who is? Vertiline stood at the door with her husband, his presence by her right side a rock. In the room were a collection of assholes, vagrants, and inbreds, all wearing the Queen's black. The assholes lounged on the steps, or in ornate chairs about the room. Morgan had never held with sycophants, so the assholes were a new addition.

The drapes were new, too. They looked like just the kind of thing a person could hide behind, which meant either hidden archers, or bad planning because assassins could be there just as easily.

On the throne sat a young enough man as Vertiline counted such things. Perhaps thirty summers, and all of them easy. He'd perfected sneering down his nose to an art form she admired despite the situation. He held a slender dagger, to which she took professional interest: it had the look of the People's craftsmanship, not the gaudy toys aristocracy tended to favour. *Not as if I am an expert in the wants of the blue bloods. It has been many years since I lent my blade to the service of a lord or lady.*

"Bunch of assholes, vagrants, and inbreds," Armitage rumbled.

Vertiline's lips quirked, but her hand remand as stone on the hilt of her blade. "I was just thinking the same thing."

"Great minds," he muttered.

"And small minds never differ." The dandy atop the throne collected his sumptuous robes as he stood. He was slender, that sneering nose just a shade long for him to be attractive, but his face was otherwise comely enough. "I see you've brought blood and death with you."

Vertiline made a great show of looking beside and behind her. "There is no death here." *There is plenty in my wake, but let's not let facts stand in the way of a good entrance.*

"My lord," he said.

"I am no lord," Vertiline purred. "Nor lady, but that would be closer."

"You will address me as 'my lord'," he sneered. "I didn't mean *you* were a lord."

"Raven crests all, yet no Raven Queen." Vertiline took three steps forward, watching as the assholes came to attention. "Morgan deserved respect, and yet I wouldn't bend the knee to her either. Tresward kneel only to the Three."

The dandy blinked, then guffawed, a great show of manufactured mirth. His lackeys shared his good humour, one even wiping a faux tear away. "The Tresward are a fairy tale. A myth to scare naughty children with."

"Only evil children, sirrah." Vertiline took another step closer. "The good and righteous never need fear our blades."

"Well, there was that one time," Armitage said.

"Hush," she muttered.

"And that one time lasted a *long* time," the Vhemin said. "My people bled plenty, and—"

"Ah, yes, a monster." The dandy smiled. "Your kind have walked from the wastes to my doorstep, taking much and giving little. My dear dead sister accorded you too much favour."

Vertiline frowned. "You mean to tell me that Morgan, Queen of Or'sen, has a surprising younger brother kept hidden all these long years?" She beamed. "A marvel, I admit, and I congratulate you on your good fortune for finding yourself, perhaps miraculously so, in such esteemed lineage." She let her smile fall. "There are but two problems."

The maybe-not-Morgan's-brother took two steps down, hand clutching the dagger's hilt so tight his fingers went white. "You tread dangerous ground, Knight."

"Ah, so you admit I am Tresward. It is good such peskersome details are behind us." She held up her metal hand, two digits extended, watching as his eyes widened. "Yes, this hand is metal. That is not the issue. First, for Morgan's younger brother to be on the throne, it would mean the Raven Queen is dead." She folded a finger away. "Second, it would suggest the only child of the rightful ruler of Or'sen was terribly forgetful, never once mentioning to those closest to her that she had a long lost relative." She let her hand fall.

"I've had enough," said the dandy. "Archers, kill them!"

Vertiline's blade left its sheath like one of Meriwether's magic tricks. One moment it was hidden, waiting for purpose, the next the steel was in her hand, a slender tooth waiting violence. She waited for the first arrow, but nothing happened.

"I said, kill them!" The assholes at the dandy's feet looked uncertainly at each other, then drew blades reluctantly, perhaps because to Vertiline's eye they knew very little about which end to hold. Before they could step closer, one of the drapes at the side of the room billowed, a body sliding out to slump on the stone floor. A bow clattered to rest beside the body. A moment later a Feybrind with marvellous golden eyes stepped out, polishing a dagger with a fragment of cloth.

Sight of Day seemed like all Feybrind: lean and ready. His tail swished once. Vertiline swallowed the lump in her throat. *If he is here, where is our baby girl?* The Feybrind appeared weary, a look that suited him not at all. The cat sheathed his dagger. *{It's good you got here in time. I wasn't sure how I was going to get through all of them alone.}*

Armitage opened his mouth, closed it, then tried again. "Cat? What are you doing here?"

The dandy, who'd spent the last handful of seconds looking at the Feybrind and the dead archer at his feet, rallied. "This is preposterous! I demand—"

"Hold up," Armitage rumbled. "Ain't done talking. If you're here, where is Evanne?"

Those golden eyes softened. *{There is much to speak of, and much is owed besides.}*

"Stop waving your hands," the dandy demanded, every inch the high-pitched imperialist. "Soldiers, I demand you—"

"If you're going to demand they arrest us or kill us," Vertiline levelled her sword at him, doing a quick tally, "you should consider whether you think twelve men and women are good enough to beat a Tresward Knight."

"Oh, my Queensguard are good enough to beat a fairytale, and many other things—"

"Queensguard guard a queen. Right there in the name." Armitage squinted. "You don't look much like a queen to me."

"Needless to say—"

"Maybe it's the uniform." Vertiline pitched her voice, keeping it level, thoughtful almost. "The Raven Queen always looked good in black. Why throw out a good wardrobe with the rightful ruler?"

The dandy's face flushed. "*I* am the rightful ruler of Or'sen, and I demand—"

"Assumes the queen is dead, and that she had a brother." Armitage nodded, as if considering the argument. "How do we know she's dead?"

"Ah hah!" The dandy's hand surged up, index finger pointing. "Her ship was wrecked off these very shores—"

"Wasn't," the Vhemin said.

"I beg your pardon?" The face flush turned a dangerous shade of red that, in Vertiline's experience, was a precursor to a heart attack.

"Her ship wrecked off the shores of Imshir," Armitage explained, as if to a child. "Stands to reason it couldn't also wreck here."

The dandy spluttered, blinked, turned to his men, clutched his robes, let them fall, then shrieked, "*Kill them all!*"

"There are only three of us," Vertiline said. "'Them all' sounds as if we are an army." She sighed. *Best get on with it.* She stalked past her husband as the clatter of hurrying boots sounded from the corridor behind them.

"I've got the rearguard," he said.

"I know," she murmured, then put on a burst of speed as the faux king's vagrant army surged forward, all flailing weapons and brigand-like screams. *There are but twelve. Is the legend of my fallen brothers and sisters so easy to forget?*

No matter. The lesson begins.

The first man came at her with a mace, a weapon no self-respecting Queensguard would hold. She stepped beneath the swing, the pattern of *Seasons' Rhythm* holding her steady. There were four seasons, but it would do for the first four combatants well enough. She pulled her blade from low guard to high as she passed, the glimmering steel passing through the man's hip, ribcage, and out his shoulder. His mace went up, hand loosening as it rose.

Vertiline caught the lunge of a pike against her steel, and the Storm rumbled. The pike head glowed with heat, the shaft shattering, and she continued the movement, separating head from shoulders, then faced a flaxen-haired woman who came at her with a greatsword too large for a person twice her size. Vertiline slipped to the side of the clumsy thrust, her steel cutting her enemy's sword in half, then she cut the woman in half, tip to tail, the two parts slithering to a messy heap.

A man screamed his rage, and her thrown sword took him in the face, lodging in his skull. It was a move Geneve would be proud of. *She kept throwing her weapons away.* Vertiline pivoted, took a step back, and reached her sword hand behind her. The mace she'd sent toward the Three earlier came back down, the haft hitting the palm of her hand, and she swung it against the shield of a toothless man who leered behind his guard. The force of her blow, backed by the Storm, smashed his shield into him, pulverised his body, and sent the remains splattering against the steps below the dandy.

One of the guards turned to the dandy, a slip of steel in his hand, and an arrow took him in the side of the head. Vertiline glanced to see Sight of Day with the fallen archer's bow, another arrow ready to take another life. She turned back to the fight, stepping into *Sunset's Next Sunrise*, a pattern meant for harder jobs than this.

A woman, clearly smarter than her peers, decided attacking Vertiline head-on was a fool's game and swung a morning star at the Knight's feet. Vertiline felt the Storm with her, the strength of the Three *within* her, and stepped down onto the morning star's head. Thunder roiled as the head shattered, brilliant coils of electric blue coiling up the chain. The woman stiffened, skin blackening as the lightning coursed through her, arcing into a man behind her, and then into a third nearer the throne. *And that's eight.*

Thunk, thunk as Sight of Day's arrows took two more. Vertiline tossed her borrowed mace aside, heading for the dandy, her face blank, but heart filled with murder. She fetched her sword in passing, the hilt warm to the touch, the blade smoking as it burned the blood clean.

The remaining two guards took a defensive position below the faux king on the steps. Vertiline could hear the song of Sight of Day's bow, the roar of Armitage's fury, and the screams of the dying reinforcements behind her. She put it aside, because this man knew something about her daughter, and she was going to find out what it was.

The guards before her had a more seasoned look. Perhaps they were Queensguard once, before their vows were traded for easy coin. Or maybe hired steel, ready to do things that others wouldn't. It didn't matter to Vertiline. They had the high ground, but she had the Three.

The left man lunged, and she parried, running her steel against his, shearing through the cross guard, and taking his hand off. He stared at his smoking wrist, and she jerked her blade right, through the raised shield of his colleague and through his skull. Then she ran the man on the left through, letting both bodies tumble down the stairs.

The dandy took a step right, then left, looking for an exit.

Vertiline borrowed some of Ormeon's grin as she climbed closer.

"Fairytales, was it?" She heard the trouble behind her cease, no one left but this one before her. "Have you forgotten all the Tresward were?"

"I remember now," he assured her, head bobbing like a woodpecker's.

"I don't think you have. Not really. But that's okay." She kept on, and he backed into the throne, sagging into the seat in a tumble of limbs. "I'll help you remember."

Chapter Twelve

As far as carriages went, it wasn't half bad. Plush seats with cushions, and not a hint of blood from the previous owners. Curtains, to keep the bad out. A hint of cedar, without being cloying. Lots of black and red, dark tones, nothing that would excite the blood and get the humours going. Amir liked it. *A good enough place to die, if that's how it'll be.*

"What kind of trap do you supposed this is?" Faust bent his head forward because this carriage was designed for humans of a different scale to him.

"Usual kind," Larochette said. "Get us to a place with food and wine. Slip a little poison in. Do us in right quick."

Amir nodded. "It's how I'd do it."

Faust nodded, then winced as he cracked his head against the carriage's roof. "Why'd you let them take our weapons, then?"

Amir spread his hands. "Because they wouldn't fit in here."

"But ... we'll need them."

"Maybe." Amir leaned back, trying to get more cedar and less Faust-meets-Larochette. They'd been aboard together for weeks, and none had the chance for a refreshing turn at the baths. "Vertiline is off doing hero stuff." He waved a hand toward the carriage's wall, and by inference, the greater city of Ravenswall. "She's taught us well. Time to put those skills to good use."

"We're not even Adepts." Larochette looked depressed. "Not a Trial among us."

"Chin up." Amir closed his eyes, enjoying the ride. "There's every chance of a field promotion in our future."

The taverna was underground, but not dingy. Lamps with good oil gave a warm, smokeless cheer to the place. The walls were hidden behind tapestries, hushing the echoes and smothering any damp that might linger. The place was constructed about a central box-like bar, a faux prisoner bartender in the middle, ever ready to refill your ale handle while you enjoyed fine conversation.

There weren't many souls inside. The slim man, his entourage of six thugs, and a nervous-looking barmaid. She was perhaps thirty summers, but she hid the terror behind a bright smile and brittle voice. Amir thought it gave her the taught, tensioned look of someone a little older, but he was used to such. He'd grown up around thugs.

Larochette led in her role as Vertiline. Amir admitted she had their teacher's imperious manner down like it was her own. She stalked to the east side of the bar, put her elbow on it, and said, "Where is everyone?"

"The city is regrettably at war." The slim man steepled his hands. "Refreshments?"

"Of course," she said.

Amir sauntered to the southern face of the box-like bar, tossing a quick look over the side. No assassin hid behind. So, just the seven in here against their three. *Should be just about fair.* Faust was doing a slow circuit, making every show of a man admiring the tapestries. "Ho, barkeep."

The barmaid curtsied, scurrying over. "What does my lord wish?"

"He wishes to not be called a lord, and to get a tankard of ale."

Amir smiled to soften his words. He wished he could say, *It'll be okay soon*, but that wasn't certain.

She nodded like a woodpecker, all quick jerky movements, and bustled behind the bar through a clever hinged part of the east section. She drew him an ale, putting it on the bar in front of him. Amir ignored it, wondering how to get the action started as quickly as possible.

Larochette put her hands on the bar, leaning forward. Amir heard her back pop as she stretched. The slim man gave her a cautious look, then sidled up to Amir. In a low voice he said, "What's she doing?"

"Limbering up, I'd imagine." He beamed. "Fierce tight quarters aboard a ship."

"Ah." The slim man brightened as a boy arrived from the back room carrying a platter. The platter was festooned with all manner of treats. Candied plums. Smoked meat and dried sausage. Bread, fresh-baked too by the look, and a good crock of butter. Grapes, dates, and cheeses.

Amir resented all of it. He craned his neck left then right and was rewarded with a *crack*. "Let's be about it, then."

"I'm sorry?" The slim man backed away a step.

"It's not lost on me that in a war-torn city without a regent, having horses and a dock escort is unlikely." Amir smiled, but apologetically this time. "Your task was to waylay us at the docks, then poison us."

"The city has a regent," the man spluttered.

"Curious you didn't jump on the poison angle first," Amir noted.

"Ah." The slim man took another step back. "Only because it was so preposterous."

"Then perhaps you'd like a plum?" Amir's smile turned wolfish. "Come now, don't be saying you just ate. You, sir, have the look of a man with a case of worms. You could eat all day and not gain a gram."

It wasn't lost on Amir that while he was talking with the slim man, his opponent's compatriots were fanning about the room. No doubt they thought to put two against one and take Tresward on the blade, which showed just how unused to seeing Smithsteel these people were. The best option was to amass your forces against a single opponent, hoping your war of attrition would win. Bring enough people and you can solve almost any problem.

The slim man did a quick tally, perhaps satisfied his gang were in position. Two brutes were behind Faust, who was still giving every appearance of a man studying an apprenticeship in tapestry manufacture. Larochette enjoyed the attention of another pair who had the look of ordinary sellswords, a lean hardness about them that would normally encourage you to offer your coin purse without being asked. The slim man was now backed by a man and woman who were so alike as to be cast from the same mould. Amir hazarded them as twins, but if they didn't share a birthday, siblings either way.

Many thought having someone you knew almost as well as yourself in a fight was an asset. In Amir's experience it could be, but only if you didn't care about them. Otherwise it was a hazard, the kind of thing to distract the mind and eye both. *While I have three against my one, two of them will be crippled by concern.* It wasn't a bad way to start an imbalanced fight.

"When will the regent arrive?" Amir fingered his belt, wishing he had a sword there.

"We are men of action," the slim man chided. "There should be no lies between us."

"Since it's come to this, I feel I need to come clean." Amir brightened. "We are not Tresward."

"You're ... not?" The slim man backed between the twins. "But ... you arrived on their ship."

"True enough, but you missed Vertiline by moments. We, sir, are common vagabonds who stowed away." Amir spread his arms. "What can you do?"

The ruse might have worked on a country rube, but Amir had spent too much time cementing these people's view of them as Vertiline and her retinue. At this, the play's third act, it held less water than a sieve. The twins lunged past the slim man, both with evil-looking curved knives that seemed to sprout from nowhere.

Amir's hands sought weapons behind him. His right found the back of a chair. His left came back with a spoon from the bar top. *Teacher said we should make anything a weapon, and each weapon our own.* Amir skidded the chair under the feet of the sister, who went down in a tangle of wood, limbs, and curses. He took a fighting stance, left hand brandishing the spoon in vertical guard.

The brother's eye twitched the barest fraction as his sister fell, which was perfect, but he didn't pause his assault, which wasn't. The man's curved knife came in a savage cut that went inside Amir's guard and up toward his neck. Amir swayed left in an approximation of the first step of *Deer's Passing*, kicking out with his leading foot into the man's shin. It was nobody's foot sweep, and he could hear the Justiciar saying *wrong pattern for the wrong attack*, seconds before she smacked him upside the head, but it staggered the brother well enough. Amir stepped forward and, using the man's arm as a convenient guide to run his strike along, rammed the haft of his spoon into his foe's neck.

The man choked, stumbled back, and dropped his knife, which Amir saved from a swift fall. The brother wasn't dead, but his collapsed throat promised that outcome, so Amir changed his focus to the sister. *Deer's Passing* was a poor choice for this, which was why he wasn't yet an Adept, so he discarded the form and went for *Spearing Hawk*. This pattern assumed a downed opponent which fit the rules of engagement.

Downed, but not out: the sister hissed and spat like a cat in a sack, kicking the chair at Amir. It hit his shins, which hurt more than a little, and overbalanced him also more than a little. Her knife came up at him, so he decided to join her on the floor. He slapped her wrist aside with his right hand as he fell, turning his back toward the floor as he went. He focused on landing on his right elbow, and unfortunately for the sister she was between it and the ground. The air went out of her in a rush as she spasmed.

Amir swung with his left arm as she curled up, embedding her brother's knife in her throat. He turned away as blood sprayed and attempted to get to his feet.

The slim man hit him with a chair, and Amir went down again. He turned the fall into a roll, getting just the right momentum from it, came up beside a table, grabbed the vase upon it, and spun. He sent the vase in a tumbling motion that was a better semblance of the first movement of *Sparrow's Flight*. For the barest moment he smelled cinnamon, but no Light touched the vase. It broke against the slim man's nose with a satisfying crack. Amir was already running, and as the slim man stumbled Amir tackled him, taking the man to the ground—*again with the ground!*—and punching him in his already broken nose.

The man looked to be putting up a fuss, so Amir gave him a judicious slug across the jaw. He sloshed the slim man's brain in his skull well enough, and his opponent went unconscious, his head banging the hard wooden floor.

Amir stood in a fighting stance, hands at the ready, but the action was already over. Faust had inserted a giant into the wall, showcasing the tapestries hid wood panelling that wasn't very strong. He'd put the other giant into the hearth, which smoked and guttered. Larochette had opened a sellsword from throat to navel with her opponent's blade, then nailed the other to the bar with it. The only thing she looked upset about was her spilled ale.

"Ho, friends," Amir said. "We emerge, victorious."

"We emerge without the Light," Larochette spat. "It will not come."

"Perhaps with time," Faust murmured.

"Easy for you to say," she said. "You don't need the Light to beat anyone."

"Last summer's day, I fought an impossible foe of immense size—"

"You fought an ox," Amir said. "You don't believe us, but you were so drunk you tried to wrestle livestock. That's why you lost."

Larochette looked about. "Where's that damn barkeep? I need a refill."

"I'm not sure our coin's welcome here." Faust dragged the man free from the hearth. "Burning hair smells bad, and flesh worse."

"Our coin spends well enough," Amir assured him. "Besides, we need time to question this asshole." He pointed to the unconscious slim man. "I figure they were sent to murder the rightful queen's retinue, and any Tresward with her. Anyone want to take that bet?"

"Not I." Larochette headed for the back. "I'll find us something to eat that's not poisoned."

THEY DIDN'T EAT AFTER ALL. THE BARMAID HAD LEGGED IT, GONE on the wind, and without her sage counsel none of them were willing to risk eating or drinking anything that might have hemlock's kiss. Larochette gave a half-hearted effort to find something in the kitchen anyway, and during that found a final foe hiding behind a shelf in the kitchen, by way of him trying to bury a blade in her neck.

After that problem was squared away, with Larochette alive and her assassin with a crick in his neck he would never recover from, she drew their attention to the man's hidey-hole. It wasn't so much an alcove as a passage and swept clean of the usual spiderwebs. It screamed *secret tunnel.* There were no lighting sconces within, and it travelled down old stone steps before vanishing into the dark.

Amir eyed the hole. "I think we have to go down there."

"Are you mad, man?" Larochette busied herself with propping up the assassin-slash-guard against a box of potatoes. "There. He looks like he's sleeping."

"Come now. You can clearly see his neck is broken." Faust rubbed his chin. "I think we need to go down there, too."

Larochette tossed curled locks. "You're mad, too. Was it something you ate on the ship? Some men go wild on the whipped seas. Telling tales of mermaids and such."

"There are no mermaids down there." Amir hitched his belt. "Here's my thinking. These men were sent to kill Vertiline. Stands to reason they had instructions from someone. With the queen gone, the regent is the most likely suspect. I would imagine this tunnel is one of those escape routes royalty use when their castle is besieged."

"Because it comes out into a less than vainglorious pub?" Larochette's words were hung on a scaffold of sarcasm.

"Exactly so. There will be other guards ahead in case the Tresward split their forces."

"Which we did," Faust said.

"Aye. Although that was more through luck than skill." Amir gave

Larochette a glance. "Do you think we should be the saviours of our Justiciar?"

"If she needs saving by the likes of you, we're proper fucked." Larochette sounded thoughtful, rather than argumentative. "We'll need a disguise. And it just so happens there are plenty of discarded clothes here on the bodies of the fallen. No uniforms but at a distance we could be the people they knew." She sized up Amir. "Yours were brother and sister, no? We could play the part."

"No one here carries my size." Faust sighed. "I trust we will use the tired ruse where I am your prisoner?"

"Of course," Amir breezed. "Let's be about it."

And this is how they hurried through the passages beneath the city of Ravenswall. A lantern liberated from the pub's storeroom cast light enough for the three of them. *And, if we've learned our patterns well enough, we can fight in the dark.* Amir wasn't sure if he was ready for that test. He was good with a blade, but the Light didn't come to heel.

The passage didn't run straight, nor was it well maintained, but it hadn't seen a cave in. Amir held the lead, Faust in the middle, and Larochette guarding the rear. Their 'siblings' clothes were good enough if you ignored the blood-soaked nature of the garments, so Amir donned a cloak to cover the worst of it.

The lantern burned steady, confirming the publican didn't use the cheap oil. They came, after much walking in the dark, to the base of another set of steps. They marched to the top, silent as a dream, pausing at a door. Amir put his ear to it, making out voices on the other side.

A gruff man said, "We should be up there already."

A man with enough weasel in his tone to steal a henhouse countered. "We've our orders."

This was good enough for Amir. He'd done his share of gambling, and if he had a copper baron on the outcome, it would be this being a rearguard force or some other mischief. He put hand to handle, flipped the latch, and strode into the room. "Ho, friends. What news?"

Faust was on his heels, hands manacled before him, playing the mummer's part of prisoner. Larochette closed the door behind her, hiding her face for the brief moment's advantage they had. Amir took in the room. It was a barracks of a sort, windowless and cheerless, with benches about the sides. On the benches were a strong assortment of killing folk, rough-looking readies who had blade or cudgel near at hand. Two men stood by the wide exit door, currently shut and barred from the inside, and Amir would put another copper baron beside the first that they were Gruff and Weasel.

Blank looks. No responses. But no immediate signs of murderous intent. Amir tightened his smile, making sure it wouldn't come off. "We've a prisoner. This one took down four of our best."

Gruff looked up at Faust. "I didn't know they grew that high in the foreign lands."

Weasel looked a little sly. "Did he have one of those pretty glass blades? I've always wanted a souvenir."

"This was naught but an Adept, unless I miss my guess." Amir swapped the smile for a puckered, sour face. "Plain steel, and lads, not very good with it. The tales we've heard about the fearsome might of the Tresward feel less real than a vial of unicorn's blood bought at a three-baron hawker."

Gruff was in the business of nodding along, but Weasel's sly face sobered. "And where are the rest of you?"

"Gone, and the abyss take them." Larochette stepped from behind Faust's bulk.

This turned out to be the wrong action. While she was hidden behind the man mountain of her 'prisoner', in plain view of the room her face showed. A man on a bench surged to his feet, pulling a metre of steel from his scabbard, and screaming, "'Ware! Traitors!"

No one seemed to move, so Amir gave a delicate cough. "I beg your pardon?"

"That is not the woman I slept with three days past." The man pointed his steel at Larochette. "But she's wearing her clothes."

Weasel sidled closer. "Come to think, none of you look familiar."

"I'm not surprised." Amir drew his sword and ran Weasel through.

"That's torn it," Faust murmured, before bedlam took whatever else he might have had to say.

Gruff approached Amir at an unexpected pace for a big man. Amir waited for him, preparing *Sparrow's Entrance*. Left foot forward, weight on the back foot just so, blood-slick blade swapped to off hand. The pattern said a big man moving fast would go for centre mass but had the flexibility to take the attack high or low. The trick, Vertiline explained, was to take high or low without favour, treating them as a gift. *No Tresward should be concerned if the blade comes at throat or balls*, she'd chided over a prostrate Amir, who'd taken it in the balls that time. *A Tresward should be concerned about the Knights at his back, the foes he's yet to meet, and how to make this one perish.*

No problem. Faust was behind him, so Gruff was about to perish. The enemy went less predictably for throat-not-balls, perhaps a kindred spirit in things you just didn't do to people, so Amir pivoted around his load-bearing right foot, swaying like a sparrow around a gust of wind. Quick, effortless, as a small bird could ride winds that tore a kite from the sky, and make it look fun. Amir was the sparrow, he was in the moment, and he was—

A fist hit the side of his head mid-pivot, turning it into a graceless tumble. Amir thought *motherfucker* as he went straight for the worn flagstones, landed, spat blood, and bounded to his feet in time to stick his knife into a woman who was going balls-not-throat. He wasn't kind about it, because she went for his balls, and left her fountaining blood, trying to find his sparrow's grace in the spray.

Faust and Larochette were doing a favourable imitation of *Shoaling*, a partner pattern where each Knight moved from an enemy, presenting nothing but emptiness, the other closing around the space to dispatch their shared foes. Amir heard a tiny chime, like a waiter's bell, and thought it was Larochette's near-perfect strike that called the hint of Light.

A woman made for the door, perhaps to unbar it, so Amir kicked her legs out and knifed her as she fell. A man strong-armed Larochette from the side, a blow that would have winded an ox, but she bounced off, taking the hit like a boxer in the first round. Amir threw his blade, steel tumbling end over end to embed in her foe's chest. A man swung at Amir, all overhead strength and nonsense, so Amir stepped into the grey space between strike and safety, inserted his elbow into the man's throat, and liberated his mace.

A swift strike on the back of the man's head, and he went down atop the dying woman.

This is bullish creativity but none of us are masters of steel, let alone glass. Amir felt the weight of his borrowed mace. The haft was old wood, cut from a single branch, but the head was a bad forging. The let's-call-it-left side of the head was a shade heavier than the right. Two men surged toward him, clearly trying to take the easier opponent while trying to avoid the thresher that was Faust.

Amir thought, *I will be a master of glass*, and met them on the charge with *Buck's Challenge*. The left-heavy mace felt like his own arm as he flicked his wrist, tossing the weapon into the head of the right opponent. It bounced as he expected, and he tickled the haft as it rebounded into the skull of the left man. Amir caught it, tossed it heavy side down into the ground, and was rewarded with a *crunch* as it bounced upward into the chin of Faust's opponent.

Over. It's over! Amir felt the breath rasp in and out of his chest, turned, and spat blood. "Ho, friends. All's well?"

"All's well," Faust agreed.

"Mostly well," Larochette groused, rotating her shoulder. "The man hit well, and I should've seen it."

"All fights are lessons," Amir said. "I've learned a thing or two myself this time."

"You got clocked good," Larochette agreed. "How's the jaw?"

"Fine." Amir considered. "I think I've a loose tooth. Let's see what the morrow brings."

Faust roamed the dead. "All are gone." He paused by his last fallen opponent. "Friend Amir, there is hope for you yet." He shifted the body before him, then pointed to the ground beneath the corpse where Amir had bounced the mace.

The pavers were cratered rather than merely cracked, sunken as if hit by a great force. Larochette whistled. "The Storm comes."

"It is no Storm," Amir argued. "I felt nothing, heard no bells, and saw no wonders. This is merely bad workmanship, maintenance, or both."

"Perhaps." Faust sounded like he one hundred percent disagreed.

The door rattled. Amir whirled, realised he had no weapon, and looted the floor where there were plenty. He came up with a short sword with a wide blade, a bloodletter's weapon for dark deeds. He stalked to the door. Faust took one side, Larochette the other, the pair handling the bar.

At Amir's nod, they flipped the bar away. Amir yanked the door wide, blade high, a war cry on his lips. It died there, the tip of a sword right under his chin.

Vertiline stood there, poise perfect, arch eyebrow raised. "Sloppy." She looked behind him at the ruins of a troupe of men and women. "But perhaps effective." She flourished her steel, then slipped it into her scabbard.

"Knight Champion," Amir said. "We were, uh."

Faust counted on his fingers. "Uncovering a plot to assassinate you. Dealing with poisoners and insurgents. Killed assassins and turncoat Queensguard." He sighed. "It's been a busy morning."

Vertiline looked up at the big man, then to Larochette, and finally back to Amir. She nodded, nice and slow. "Is this true, Adept?"

"I am no Adept," Amir said. "I cannot call the Storm."

"Time and practice." Vertiline sounded distracted as she scanned the dead behind them. "Just you three did all this?"

"Aye." Amir met her eye.

She gave the ghost of a smile. "Do you want a medal? Or a hug? Get yourselves together. We are Tresward." The Justiciar turned on her heel, and Faust and Larochette hurried to catch up.

Amir held a moment, considering. Vertiline had said *We are Tresward*. He heard the words, but beneath them, something deeper. A feeling, almost like hope.

Vertiline said it as if she were starting to believe it.

Chapter Thirteen

The countryside was dark, not a human hamlet with cheery hearth for klicks. Hollyhead was murdered by Wandermere, but this countryside had been licked clean by Lord Gyles. Evanne missed her desert home of Imshir, and the people she'd known. *I don't like being alone.* Evanne felt the chill of the dusk more than usual. Her half-Vhemin blood let the cold in more than if she were human, but this was deeper. Always she'd had someone with her. Tarragon lately, but before: Hitch. Always Hitch.

Now there was no one.

"*Hello,*" Pakhet said.

Evanne gave a small scream. The giant cat was perched on a rock, licking a paw. She rallied, clutched her guitar tighter—*I will need it before the night's done*—and glared at the tiger. "Where have you been?"

"*Hiding,*" she admitted. "*Did you know there's a vampire after you? He is quite old. Probably cunning, more than usual for one of his kind. I expect he wants to siphon you dry.*"

"Not super helpful," Evanne said. "I *know* he's a vampire and wants me dead."

"*Don't forget the siphoning part.*"

"Hard to ignore." Evanne glanced at the keep's wall behind her. Old stone, easy to climb, but she didn't want back in. She needed to be a long way away from a creature that could drain her as easily as a man downing a cup of cold water on a hot day. "How long have I got?"

"*The mob will exit the front of the keep in moments.*"

Evanne frowned. "Seems like it's taking them a long time."

"*I helped. I'm helpful. This is me helping.*" The cat offered Evanne a yawn full of teeth. "*There were horses.*"

"What do you mean 'were'?"

"*They are now panicked horses.*" The cat gazed over the darkening hills. Evanne wondered whether she saw with the blood-heat of Vhemin vision, or the false daylight of the Feybrind. "*Heser helped. His clever fingers were useful for opening the stalls.*"

"Ah." Evanne glanced away from the keep and to the west. The keep rested atop a gentle decline. Down the decline was a scraggly forest. *I might be able to lose them in there.*

"*If you're thinking about losing them in the forest, I give you excellent odds of deferred success.*"

"Deferred what?"

"*You're going to fail, because the vampire can smell the blood inside you.*"

"Ah," Evanne said again. "That might work, actually."

"*I'm confused.*"

"Stick around, cat. We're going vampire hunting."

"*We are so, so not.*" Pakhet vanished.

Evanne grinned despite herself. *I saw it! I saw the moment the cat went invisible.* It wasn't in a puff of smoke. One moment she was there, the next she wasn't. No pop, no sparkle, but a kind of *absence,* like losing your belt—you forgot where you left it, rather than throwing it out.

Maybe I can work with that, too.

EVANNE HURRIED THROUGH THE WOODS. THE TREES WEREN'T VERY big, which was a blessing from the Three, because otherwise she'd have been slowed. The dusk turned to early evening, and if she'd been on a porch, brazier cheery beside her, and with mulled wine at hand, it'd have been a pleasant evening.

All things considered, not a bad night to die.

"Hello?"

Evanne froze. The voice was uncertain, male, and sounded alone. *Frightened.* She oriented toward it, wondering why her Vhemin's eyes hadn't seen the hot blood inside the man. *Ah—there.* A piece of ancient masonry nestled between the tangled trunks of old oaks. It didn't take much imagination to guess how a hunk of the keep above had rolled here to be held in the tree's embrace. And a good lesson to be more careful, because a wise person could hide their heat behind a rock.

Hang about. That voice sounds familiar. Her hand went to her knife, but she didn't release her grip on the guitar. "Quinton?"

"Evanne?" The man stepped from behind his rock. He tugged at his guardsman's armour like a noble with a too-tight collar. "I thought I'd dreamed you. I thought—"

"You thought you'd died. Captured by a creature of the black beyond. Saw sights, aye, and heard sounds of strange things, as if in a dream." Evanne let go her knife, pulled her guitar close, and plucked the strings. "But then you heard this. Felt it beneath the ocean of sleep. And then—"

"And then I saw her." His voice held more awe than fear now. "The Raven Queen."

"What?" Evanne did a double-take. "Not the amazing bard and her song?"

"Sure, the bard." He waved it away. "But the Raven was everywhere. A presence in my dream, a black-feathered angel of hope. She held me close right as I leaped from the *Dancer* to my death. Carried me from the world of dreams to this one." He hugged himself. "I'd rather be asleep."

"Night's not too cold for you?"

"Night's too full of vampires." Quinton relaxed a shade, then drew his sword. It wasn't an elegant move. He almost overbalanced. "I am here to help."

"Great. Where's everyone else?"

"Who?"

Evanne blinked. "The rest of the keep's guard. The household. The rest of you."

"There is no one else. I came alone."

Evanne sighed, rubbing her forehead. "She had one job, Quinton. One fucking job!"

"Who?" The man looked between her and the rock. "Are we expecting someone else?"

Evanne heard the rustle of leathery wings above. She glanced up but couldn't see a swarm of bats. Still, it never hurt to be cautious. She lowered her voice. "Do you know where we might find shelter?"

"Against the rain, or against a vampire?"

"Vampire." Evanne showed her teeth in the night. "I'm tough. I don't mind the rain."

"No where is safe against Lord Gyles. He will come for us no matter where we hide."

"Thought so." Evanne nodded. "But you came anyway."

He offered her a shy smile. She could see the way his lips moved, the tilt of his head as he looked to the ground. "I came because of how you played. I came because I've never heard anything so beautiful."

Evanne felt her cheeks warm. "The good news is you'll hear more before the night's out. Come on."

QUINTON HUSTLED WELL ENOUGH FOR A MAN WEARING ARMOUR HE woke up in, and holding a sword he didn't know how to use. He kept up a steady stream of babble, all *I am a merchant fisherman* this and *Wait until you see me sail the seas* that. Evanne let it wash over her as they headed downhill.

The forest gave way to a ruined road, which she ignored, favouring the fields beyond. A lone farmstead beckoned from beyond rich clutches of corn gone to seed. No lights glimmered, very much in keeping with the abandoned vibe she got from the fields.

Evanne headed between the cornrows, shouldering through with a little Vhemin grit and human grace. Black, cold fingers of corn leaves tried to hold her in passing but she ignored their need. Quinton struggled to keep up. "Hold a moment, bard."

She turned. "We don't have time. The monster will find us soon." *So, why have I stopped?*

The sailor caught up to her. "You are powerful strong. I can barely keep pace and I'm a man grown."

"You're strong enough." Evanne eyed him up and down. "It's fair to say the curse of my birth has left me some ... advantages."

Quinton looked up at that. "Curse? Don't you mean blessing? You've come to save us. A guardian sent by the Three for sure."

"Huh." Evanne glanced at the sky again. Still no giant bat. "You say the nicest things. Doesn't change the truth though." *There is no Trick in his words. Why do I feel like there should be?* "I was born against the Three's rule. A human mother and a Vhemin father."

Quinton tossed her a glance. "What's your point?"

Evanne frowned. "Isn't it obvious?"

He laughed. "I've yet to meet someone young who thought their place in the world was right. It's a part of being human." He sighed. "Or, you know. Whatever you are."

She wanted to be angry with him, but she laughed instead. "You should never become a bard. You've no Trick with words."

"Never used words well. I'm better on the unsteady land of the ocean swell."

"And yet, poetic." She jostled further down the cornrows. "Come on. We've got to build a defensible position."

"Against a vampire lord?"

"Something like that." She didn't know if he could see the glint of her smile in the night. "There are other things that go bump in the night."

THE BARN WAS A WASH, BUT THE HOMESTEAD HAD POTENTIAL. THE roof was gone, but the dwelling was a lofty two storeys. It allowed her some protection from attacks from above.

The fireplace held flame well enough, giving the illusion of warmth and safety. She held her shiver back, because Quinton was having enough trouble with the night as it was. They'd made space before the fire by pushing rickety furniture into the stairwell. Quinton used the little patch of heat and light for pacing. "Okay, here we are. What's the plan?"

"The plan has two parts." Evanne held up her guitar. "This is the second part."

"A lute?"

"Guitar," she corrected. "It's an instrument the ancients played."

He seemed suspicious. "How is the music of the ancients going to help us when Lord Gyles descends, ready to avenge his lost pride?"

"Well, that's where the first part comes in." Evanne felt nervousness eat at her belly like sickness. "I hoped the Raven Queen would have released the totems on more of the vampire's followers."

There was a tiny knock at the door. They both stiffened, then Evanne moved to open it. Quinton grabbed her arm. "Don't open it!"

"The vampire lord will not knock." Evanne shook him free, unlatched the door, saw no one, looked down, and felt her heart lift. "Tarragon!"

The fairy glimmered a little brighter. "Found you."

Evanne couldn't help but notice the fairy was alone. "No one else, then?"

Tarragon flitted in. "The Raven Queen struggles with her own demons."

"Good." Evanne shut the door behind the sprite.

"What do you mean, 'good'? This is terrible." Tarragon gave Quinton a wide stare. "Hey. Isn't he—"

"The guardsman, yes." Evanne retrieved a stool from the stairwell's barricade, placed it in the middle of the room, and sat. "It's good because we each need a nudge. The gentlest of pushes to do the thing we're made to do or be. Do you see?"

"Not really. The queen pitched a shit fit and looked about to cry."

"Even better." Evanne plucked strings. The guitar wanted to give her a haunting melody, so she let it. The sound washed from her fingers to all corners of the room.

"Oh, my." Quinton drew closer. "What tune is that?"

"It doesn't have a name. Not yet." Evanne eyed the door. "Here he is."

"Who?" Tarragon turned to the door, just in time for it to be smashed aside, wood turned to fragments.

Evanne weathered the storm of splinters, fingers still drawing notes from the strings as Lord Gyles, vampire lord, stormed inside. She gave him a welcoming smile. "My lord. You made an impressive enough entrance, but it will avail you not in the slightest."

Quinton stood by her left shoulder. "Uh. He's a vampire lord. Ever-living lord to a host of the damned."

"And still." She widened her smile. "All things must die, in the end."

"He doesn't look dead yet." Tarragon landed on her right shoulder. She was warm and bright.

Gyles glared hatred. He was gaunt as ever and looked a little sickly now. "I have come to—"

"Seal my doom?" Evanne gave an encouraging nod. "Rip my life from me? Aye, I know the Trick of it. You hope to remove the ritualist's friends or use them as leverage. Isolate her, and if you can't, bind her. Corrupt her purpose, and make it slave to yours, nay?"

He blinked, his face slackening as he entered uncertain narrative terrain. "That is the plan. You should be terrified. Why aren't you?"

Evanne plucked another string, teasing a note free. "There's one thing you don't know about the Raven. A thing that all men ignore at their peril. It's the thing that's bound her to the purpose of Or'sen and made her travel across the seas to find my parents. Carry me with her, and still be at my side. Do you know what it is?"

He took a step closer. "Enlighten me."

Evanne smiled, a cat with a whole tureen of cream. *It's time to stop playing.*

Chapter Fourteen

T he room remained daunting. Full of other people's lives, the
things they'd done, the folk they'd known, the families they'd
made. Morgan knew people well enough. She'd ruled the
kingdom of Or'sen, seen to their cares, and balanced their needs as she
navigated war, destruction, and the return of the Three. This was more
personal, though. In this room people weren't a name on a ledger.
People you knew, really *knew*, had far more weight and substance.

"I'm afraid," Morgan admitted.

"You are nothing of the sort," Heser the Cheg countered. "You've
never been afraid of anything."

She snorted. "That's a lie."

Her Queensguard offered her a horse's bridle. "Try this one."

She pushed it away. "I don't think so."

He laughed. "I see it now."

Morgan brought herself up to her full height, looking down her
nose at the man. "See what?"

He lowered the bridle. "I wonder if Evanne knows it. If she's
planned this down to the moment. It seems impossible, yet..."

"Out with it, man," she snapped. "I've little patience for—"

"You don't like being told what to do." His voice was low, a smile playing in his eyes. "All of this isn't about fear or who to help. You are the Raven Queen of Or'sen, and no one tells you what to do. Leastways, not a child gone feral in the forgotten Tebrani lands, daughter to the Tresward Knight Champion Vertiline, who wouldn't bend the knee. And her daughter hasn't fallen far from the tree."

She glared, opened her mouth, closed it, tried again, failed, started with, "That's," closed her mouth with a snap, and glared harder.

"And the thing is," Heser the Cheg offered her the bridle once more, "Evanne hasn't told you to do anything. The vampire, though? He will make you do things until you're bled dry. Perhaps now is the moment to do something right, even if it chafes, so you can do the rest on your own terms."

And here you are, telling me what to do. She could have screamed or laughed at the irony of it. Instead, she snatched the bridle from him. "Give it here."

Ed struggled with the bridle. The horse reared, but she'd expected that. Always a bit iffy, this one. A champer and a tramper, her father would have said.

Just the way she liked it. A horse without spirit was like a body without a soul.

She placed a hand on the roan's neck. The beast was having none of that, all tossing mane and wild eyes. Eden smiled without teeth, loosening the bridle. "Maybe tomorrow, hey?"

Morgan sagged, the bridle turning toffee-like in her hands, then the leather parted like cobwebs. She leaned into Heser the Cheg before she realised where she was and didn't remember she was supposed to mind his arm about her. "Rest," he said.

She offered a weak smile, croaking, "Still trying to coddle me?"

"My queen," he started, then fell into silence.

"I'm no queen. Not anymore."

"Perhaps next week, then." She heard the warmth in his voice. "When we've put this vampire lord to rest, there will be time enough to rebuild."

"Give me the next one." The Raven Queen stood, back straight as a shaft of light. "Give me *all* of them."

Chapter Fifteen

When the horde arrived, Evanne wasn't surprised. Tarragon's face said *we're deeply fucked*, and Quinton paled like new parchment, but she held strong for both of them. The people who Lord Gyles bound about his fist like a halter surged against the farmstead's walls. The walls creaked, dust silting from the rafters.

Evanne shifted on her stool. She found the Trick of pitching her voice just right, to let it carry above the cacophony, to be heard by all. "This the best you've got?"

The cloak about Lord Gyles swirled like smoke. His eyes took on a reddish tinge, embers at their heart as he hungered. She felt his need for the blood inside her, ignored it, and settled the guitar across her knee. She plucked a string.

Gyles lunged for her, the creature surging forward as the note left her guitar. She raised her chin, unflinching, the everliving's hands reaching for her, all smoke, shadow, and hate. The note twisted about her, found its level, and with it, brought strength.

· · ·

WITH A SONG AND FIERY CHANT SO BOLD,
 Turn this sword from steel to molten gold.
 Cophine's fury, let it rise in fame,
 As I command, burst into blazing flame!

QUINTON'S BLADE CROSSED HER VISION, THE SAILOR BRINGING THE weapon to guard her. Its silver-bright edge was a Trick itself, the old sword borrowing starlight from above, and a little of Tarragon's glimmer to rim the edge. The vampire reared back, hissing as smoke billowed from his cape, shadow seeping about Evanne's feet.

Evanne plucked another string, the note finding the shutters, a way outside, and to the waiting people beyond. "So, that's a yes, then?"

"A what?" Gyles' eyes locked on the glimmering edge of Quinton's blade.

"Them. They're the best you've got." Evanne teased more notes from the guitar.

"This is but one man." The vampire drew himself upright, more of his form seeping into shadow. "I've killed many like him."

"Hmm." Evanne continued to strum. "Do you know the Trick of a man's heart? I do. You sat above us in your throne room surrounded by your trinkets and planned my murder. You wanted me gone and the Raven for your own. But you tried to take by force what could have been given freely."

"The strong, take. The weak, bargain." Gyles stalked around Quinton. The sailor turned to follow him, blade held cross guard, edge curling with rimfire as Evanne stroked new life from old steel with her music. "The victim, submits. You're young. It's understandable you don't know the way of the world."

"Aye, that's common enough wisdom many follow." Evanne lowered her voice, conspiratorial. "But a thing with the young? We can make our own path. We don't need hand-holding, and not from the likes of you. You're missing the big Trick here, my lord Gyles. You're missing a really big one."

He lunged forward, and Quinton swept the blade once, twice, and the vampire dodged back. "I miss nothing. I see a girl barely weaned from the teat, out of her depth, and without allies."

"You see, but you don't hear." Evanne dropped another handful of notes on the floor, cocking her head. "Listen."

"I hear nothing." His face creased with a frown, the leathery skin showing the marks of time beyond reason.

"Exactly. What of your horde? What of the people in thrall? They should be here clamouring for my blood."

The vampire screamed, lunging forward. Quinton fought like a dervish, but he was just a man, and a sailor rather than soldier. The blade in his hand was half moonbeams and lies, time-worn metal well cold from the forge that birthed it. The vampire's hands sparked against the steel. The metal screeched, then cracked.

Steel tinkled as it fell.

The creature seized Quinton, sinking fangs into the man's throat. Tarragon leaped from Evanne's shoulder, burning incandescent, smashing into the vampire's face. The creature roared as he staggered back, head aflame, then swatted the fairy from the air.

Evanne felt her guitar tremble. She wanted to toss the instrument aside, to run and help. She almost got up, but a glimmer from her right stopped her. Tarragon took wing again, screaming like a tiny banshee, flying with starlight-tinted fury at the monster. Her heart thudded in her chest when she saw the fairy fly aside, hitting the wall, her glimmer gone. *I must play. I can't stop. All will be lost.* She pressed fingers against strings, locking the tune to the fretboard, fingers coaxing life from the instrument.

Giving another life away as she sang.

GATHER 'ROUND, BRAVE HEARTS, STAND STRONG AND TALL,
Heed the call to help, lest evil's shadow fall.
In unity we'll conquer, our spirits ignite,
Join the fray, together we'll win this fight!

. . .

G YLES TOSSED Q UINTON TO THE FLOOR LIKE A USED WASHCLOTH. H E stalked toward Evanne, bloody drool dripping from his chin, eyes molten. "I will drain you right to the point of death, then leave you to heal. Then do it all over again. This will be your lot until the end of time, your screams unheard by any except—"

A *chunk* sound sliced through his diatribe. He fell over, a crossbow bolt stuck in his head, which looked to Evanne a very uncomfortable thing. The vampire surged upright, his cloak of smoke swirling. At the door stood the guardswoman Ed, crossbow already falling to the floor, sword in hand.

Behind her, four others. Through the door and beyond them, Evanne saw the crowd. The people she'd freed. *Nay, see it clearly: Morgan did the freeing. I just gave them a little strength.* It was difficult to kill a vampire lord. They were fast, strong, and cunning. But this one had come into a room with no exits. And Evanne brought her own cunning, and the strength of a hundred people who'd been locked in thrall, families lost, friends dead, time lost.

In the hearts of those with courage and might,
Enchant these weapons with a radiant Light.
Magic's glow, with each swing and thrust,
Turns these arms to weapons we can trust.

She carefully, *very* carefully, stood. Music continued to drip from the guitar. Evanne backed to the wall, watching as Ed's sword glimmered, the heavy-set man behind her lifting a hammer with a glowing head. The woman to his left holding naught but a pitchfork, but the tines gleamed ember.

The people howled forward.

E VANNE WAITED BY THE STAKE. S HE STILL HELD HER GUITAR AND hadn't stopped playing the entire time.

Quinton is dead.

The refrain kept rolling through her mind. *Quinton is dead.* She gazed at the stars, her guitar weeping enough for the both of them. *Quinton is dead.* Evanne brought her eyes back to the monster.

The stake was a big affair. It had the look of a fulcrum used for moving hay bales from storage to cart. The top was a fire-charred ruin, a victim of whatever had killed the farm, but the stake itself was still strong. Evanne had called it a stake because that's what you burned people at.

Tied to the stake: the vampire lord. Gyles hissed and snapped, his teeth long, but thankfully bloodless now. *Quinton is dead.* The crowd had beaten the monster, held him down, smashed him to the floor over and over. Others had died, because a vampire lord is a monster of power, but enough lived to drag the fiend out here.

Quinton is dead.

Evanne played the whole time Gyles was being subdued. The guitar was hurt, angry, and sad. But mostly angry, like her. The music was a timeless loop she played over and over, chords used to bind like rope, the guitar's strings like a tether. Lord Gyles, stuck fast, unable to move to his smoke form.

"Stop playing," the monster hissed. "I can't hear myself think."

"No." Evanne kept her fingers on the strings, ignoring how much they hurt. *Don't look. They'll be bloody, but Quinton is dead. Keep playing, because Quinton is dead.* "Do you know last night I played this song for your people? I played it for you, too. I made sure I bound you from the first. I'm not a good bard, so I needed time. And time you gave me." *Quinton is dead.* "Hubris. You thought yourself too strong, and us too weak. And here we are."

"You are weak," said Gyles. "You are an insect to me."

"I'm not the one tied to a stake." Evanne glanced to her right, her eye catching movement. Around the side of the old barn came a man and woman. It was too dark for her human eyes to make out detail, but her Vhemin eyes saw their blood's heat well enough. She didn't need light to know who they were. Their walk, aye, that was familiar. But how they walked *together* told her who they were. "Just in time."

The vampire craned to see. "The ritualist and her paper soldier."

Morgan and Heser the Cheg drew near the stake. The Raven put hands on hips and looked at the vampire lord. "So much fuss for such a small man."

"My queen, step away." Heser the Cheg almost put his hand on her elbow. Almost.

Quinton is dead. "I killed Quinton," Evanne blurted.

Morgan turned, giving her a long stare, then shook her head. "The sailor? I remember him." She looked down. "He had a ship that loved to race. The *Dancer.*"

"It's not too late to take my side," Lord Gyles said. "Cut me down, and we shall rule all."

Morgan's lips turned in the slightest hint of a smile. "You know me as a ritualist. All these years, I didn't. Perhaps I lived too close to people, or among too many. My power was hidden by another." The vampire looked doubtful but said nothing. "I don't need you to make me a lord. I was *queen.*" Her voice lowered to a mutter. Evanne thought she heard *Princess* and *Dragon.*

Lord Gyles stretched against his ropes. "Speak up, woman."

Morgan snapped, "I am the Raven Queen of Or'sen, little man, and you shouldn't forget it. You were brought low by—"

"Oh, aye, by moonbeams and magic," the vampire snorted.

"No. By a woman who believed in us more than we believed in ourselves." Morgan glanced at Evanne, her gaze falling to the bard's fingers. "And hurt herself for us too."

Evanne sighed. "It's almost time."

"Am I late?" Pakhet curled at Evanne's side. She had not been there moments before. Tarragon fluttered to perch atop the cat's head. The fairy was battered, one wing bent, but she had a little glimmer back. The bard felt her lips quirk in the ghost of a smile. *"I hate being late."*

"Did you find her? Did she bring them?"

"Of course. She is almost back."

As if on cue, Ed strode from the barn's lee. Behind her was a gaggle of people. Her guards, or whatever they were before Morgan freed them. Evanne raised her chin in acknowledgement, but kept playing, lifting her eyes to the sky. The horizon behind Gyles held a tint of purple.

"Late for what?" the monster asked, because he couldn't see what was coming.

Ed drew near. Her nose looked swollen and painful from earlier, but her eyes were bright and hard. She stopped before Evanne. "I hear we owe you thanks."

"Not yet." Evanne kept playing. "Soon, perhaps. Is this everyone?"

"It is." The guard captain looked uncomfortable. "All that lived."

That punched Evanne hard. *I killed Quinton.* The thing she'd done was monstrous, worse than the creature tied to the stake, and it needed to come out. "It's my fault. I killed Quinton."

She saw how Tarragon's face fell. The sprite buzzed to Evanne, her crooked wing fouling her flight. She landed against Evanne's shoulder rather than on it, scrabbled for purchase, found a rust lock, swung, and hauled herself up. "No, love. Not that. Not ever. There's only one here who killed the sailor boy."

"Come closer and I'll kill the rest of you." The vampire gnashed, too-thin face and too-bright eyes ever hungry.

Ed stormed toward him. "I will knock you the fuck down."

"I like her," Tarragon murmured.

"Aye, I do too." Evanne felt her fingers stumble a little, saw the creature strain, and held her song steady. "Come away, Ed. He can't be trusted."

The guard captain looked over her shoulder. "You hold him in thrall well enough."

"She struggles," Gyles confided. "She holds me in a lock of song so thin it may as well be prayer." He lifted his chin toward Pakhet. "That's the only creature here that could hurt me, but even I can see something's wrong with it."

"*I am curious about this.*" Pakhet took a step forward, thought better of it, and sat. "*I am curious from a distance.*"

"A construct of those you call ancient. People of my kind, and my time." He shrugged, but the movement didn't get far. "Think of what will be lost when you lock me away."

"Lock?" Eden laughed. "It's the gallows for you."

"*Construct?*"

"What does that make me?" Tarragon's glitter dimmed.

Gyles snorted, ignoring the cat and fairy. "I can't be killed with a rope. Ask the necromancer."

Ed followed the direction of his glance over her shoulder, landed on Evanne, did a double take, and laughed again. "She's no necromancer."

"I am." Evanne didn't want to play anymore, but the guitar held her hand for a few bars. "I have a spectre as my companion. I see the dead."

"You don't see the dead," Ed said. "You see souls. I met a necromancer once, and you're nothing like him." She turned back to Gyles. "If she were a necromancer, she would have you wrapped around her fist like a sock puppet." She glanced about. "This here is an everliving husk trying to remember what it was like to be a person. It is undead, and a necromancer would own it totally."

Evanne wanted to believe, but she felt the thing inside her that yearned for the songs of those long dead, that hung up on the ghosts following her about, and of Hitch, ever her companion, since the day she was born. "It is nice of you to say, but," and that's where her guitar gave up.

It might have been the abuse she'd given it. In hindsight, using the instrument like a weapon was a bad call. Dragging it through the muck and rain and Three knows what else was definitely a no-no. And she'd used it to draw the dead near, to bind their power, and hold a monster prisoner.

A string snapped. The song died.

Gyles was free fast as you please, the ropes about him snapping like twine. Before Evanne could process the fraying string under her fingers, he made it to Eden, put an arm around her neck, and held her close, teeth wide.

Tarragon flared, making to speed forward, so Evanne grabbed her on the wing, a mixture of Vhemin speed and human heart. *No, love, you'll die.* She was burning hot in Evanne's hand, which made the bard grit her teeth, but she held on anyway.

Pakhet vanished. People screamed. Morgan stood tall, perhaps thinking a ritual might save the day, but Evanne knew these things took time. She stood, kicked back her stool, felt for her bag of Tricks, and called, "Hold! By the Three, hold!" Gyles stopped, which probably surprised him more than Evanne. She put Tarragon back on her shoulder, ignoring her scalded palm, and leaned the guitar against her stool. "My lord Gyles, this is not the way."

"What are you doing?" Tarragon hissed.

"I am curious too." Gyles took his teeth away from Ed's neck. "Your instrument is broken, your power with it. I can do as I please."

"He makes a fair point, and puissantly so." Morgan strode to Evanne's side. "Count me among the curious."

Perfect. Evanne knew Gyles would see dissent among them, not that they stood united against him. *The Raven Queen knows politics.* A point to remember for another time. If there was another time. "Lord Gyles, you spoke of what would be lost if you were to be locked up."

"Kill him," Ed hissed. "Don't listen—"

Gyles shook her by the neck, tightening his grip. Her face turned red. "Aye. I know this world. I know it now, and I know it from before."

Don't look at the horizon. Evanne kept her tone light, her gaze on Gyles. "We have no immediate quarrel with you. We're here because you wanted me dead and the Raven in a cell, and—"

"The Raven?" Morgan gave her a little side eye.

"Roll with it." Evanne smoothed her burned hand against her leather tunic, feeling for a different Trick, the way the words needed to roll off her tongue. "We are people of pragmatism. We could offer you much, but as *partners.* Not as slaves."

"You're insane," choked Ed. It sounded like *grrl insurrrl,* what with Gyles' hand about her neck.

"Those who don't rule don't understand." Evanne offered a wide smile.

"I could take what I want, as I always have."

Evanne nodded, not really disagreeing. "Perhaps a convincer?" She turned her tone harsh. "Pakhet! Come!"

The huge tiger popped back into visibility, a slightly guilty expression on her face. "*What?*"

"Kill him." Evanne waved her hand at Gyles.

The vampire lord, having no real idea how to read a tiger's expression, or know the great cat was terrified of butterflies, held Eden between him and the tiger. "A moment."

"And so we stand." Evanne nodded, pacing in time to the Trick she needed. "Here it is, Gyles. We need passage through your land, three good horses—nothing lame or old, do you understand?—and a guide. We need to get to Hollyhead lake, and we need to do it quickly."

"Why Hollyhead?" Gyles narrowed his eyes. "Why not coin instead? And what do I get out of it?"

"You get to live, first." Evanne looked down her nose at him. "Or, close to it."

"You have a plan," Morgan said *sotto voce* as Evanne's steps took her in front of the Raven. "Please tell me you have a plan."

Evanne kept her pacing up. "The other thing you get is an ally in the Queen of Or'sen. And your mutually beneficial arrangement will bring a ready supply of food—and by that, I mean living people with blood inside them. We get your knowledge. How the ancients worked, where they kept their wonders, and how to demand service from this ragged husk of a world." For emphasis, she slapped fist in palm. *Too much? It felt like too much.*

Gyles' eyes widened though, the vampire lord growing thoughtful. "Aye. This approach pleases me."

Tarragon hissed, "If he knew the secrets of the ancients, he would have—"

"He had not the support nor the loyalty of his vassals to unlock the ancient's power," Evanne declared. "We bring him both."

Heser the Cheg cleared his throat. "Normally I provide a voice of counsel against my queen's more rash statements, but—"

"Please tell me of these statements." Morgan's voice was honeysuckle sweet.

Heser the Cheg blanched, but like any man of action, charged right into danger. "There was that one time you said—"

"I think she was being rhetorical," Evanne suggested.

"Right." The man cleared his throat and looked Evanne right in the eye. "You are talking as if you've had a head injury."

Evanne smiled wider. She smiled with radiance, warmth, and satisfaction. She smiled like the crescent sun, which chose that moment to nose above the horizon.

Gyles turned into an incandescent pyre. Eden screamed, which was good because it meant she wasn't on fire and also didn't have a hand around her throat anymore. Black, oily smoke belched from the creature, and he screamed counterpoint to her, but just once.

Then he exploded into flaming hunks of gore.

Evanne brushed a chunk from her lapel, picked up her guitar, and asked of no one in particular, "Where can I get more guitar strings?"

Chapter Sixteen

It's been a big day. Tarragon fluttered about the old broken-down farmstead. She couldn't get much height, so it was hard to tell what'd killed it back in the day. Fire? Plague? *The Bigs of this age are without basic medicine or tools. They struggle so.*

She roosted on a windowsill with broken fangs of glass still in place. *No, not 'this' age. It's just ... now. What I knew before is gone. It is more gone than Gyles.*

She gave a tiny smile, thinking about how the vampire lord turned into a greasy residue, then took flight again. Her wings buzzed, no longer true, and she knew she needed to stop throwing herself into harm's way. *They made me small. They also made me fierce, and the two don't mix. Not anymore. Not in this 'now'.*

The sounds of merriment reached her on the early morning air. The people of Gyles' keep were free. Morgan had seen to that, because Evanne had seen to *her* freedom. They looked the kind of folk who would make merry with ale, but it was breakfast time, so they were making do with open fires, eggs, bacon, and crusty bread. It smelled really good, and Tarragon knew she should eat something.

I don't want to. I don't want to be here.

There was something missing from the laughter, so she buzzed around the corner of the farmstead to see what was going on. She hovered in place, struggling with it a bit as the breeze caught her, but she gritted tiny teeth and held herself steady, bung wing and all. *Yep, people. Lots of Bigs.* She scanned the crowd, seeing smiles, worn though they might be, and a lot of people getting to know each other.

Under Gyles, they were slaves. They were made anew into what he needed, and now they were back to what they'd been. But because Bigs thought they owned the world, a lack of identity didn't bother them as much as it might a tiny fairy eight hundred years out of place. They were all just kind of mucking in and getting to know each other. At the heart of it was Ed, the 'guard captain', who was nothing of the sort. Her bill of materials was mightier than most Bigs, but it's because she loved horses and knew hard work well enough.

Ah. Tarragon smacked a tiny fist into palm. *That's what's wrong. The centre is Eden, not Evanne. Where is she?*

The fairy rose higher, cocking an ear for music, but got nothing. Over there, Morgan and the gentle man inside a warrior's shell. Beyond, a flattened patch of grass that looked like where an invisible giant tiger might be grooming. She flitted further. The faintest glimmer of blue caught her eye by an old oak at the edge of a field.

She hummed as she drew closer. Sure enough, Hitch's lantern rested in the nook of the old oak. But no Evanne. She was going to fly away, but the lantern said, "Hold a moment."

Tarragon frowned. *I shouldn't be churlish. I can't even remember anymore why I don't like him.* She settled to the ground by the lantern. The morning sun hadn't warmed the ground yet. Dew drops clung to grass. She clambered up the roots of the tree, feeling the age of the craggy bark. Settling herself, she glared at the lantern. *Just because I don't hate him anymore doesn't mean he has to know that.* "What?"

"Can you get me out?"

She snorted. "Morgan needs to do that."

"The Raven Queen thinks a talking lantern is 'neat'. I fear I will stay here forever."

Tarragon frowned. "Your voice sounds ... thinner. Everything okay in there?"

"Not really." She imagined his shrug, those not-hands shoved into pockets. "I'm a memory of what used to be a man. I'm not ... *alive*. Not in any way that matters."

"Do you need a hug, or...?" She let the question hang.

He laughed. "I do, sprite. But it won't happen until I see my love on the other side of time." This sounded a bit melancholy even for a ghost. Hitch seemed to realise it and tried harder. "Hah. Listen to me. It's like I'm afraid of dying or something."

"That *was* a bit weak."

"Just like me, hey?"

Tarragon laughed. "Neither of us are made for heavy lifting." She swung her legs against the tree bark. It was rough, but she didn't mind. *I can still feel. He can't.* "What is it you need, spectre? It's not someone to let you out. There's something else, isn't there?"

The lantern was silent so long she thought he'd decided not to answer. "I need a favour."

"I'm the person least likely in the whole world, and I mean the entire *planet*, to give you a favour."

"True as that is, I think you might do this one small thing for me." She imagined him pacing. "Thing is, I don't think I have much time. Evanne is growing. She gets bigger, and I get smaller. No, don't interrupt. I don't *mind*, Tarragon. I think it's why I'm here. But ... when I'm gone, see? There won't be anyone else. So, will you stay with her? Will you be her guide in this place, shepherding her against the ills of the old world?"

"Umm," Tarragon said.

"That's better than a no."

"I don't know why you'd ask *me*." Tarragon looked down. "I failed my exams, Hitch! I am the most worthless fairy that ever lived. I know how to use a blade, but no one makes fun-sized razors anymore. I don't *do* anything. I am the least important person in her life."

The lantern looked at her for a long time. She looked right back. The lantern gave in first. "I don't think you understand what's going on between you two."

"What's that supposed to mean?"

"It means not everyone needs to kill monsters to be useful. Sometimes, it's the people who kill the least that are most needed."

"You're a cryptic light source."

"I'm not supposed to be in a lantern!"

Tarragon looked up. The boughs above her were a gentle protector. Light leaked through the oak's leaves, dappling the ground. She put a hand against the bark. *I wonder what stories you'd tell if you could speak.* "I don't know if I can do what you want. But I'm not going anywhere."

"Cool." Hitch sounded relieved. "Really cool."

"You don't even like me."

"Tarragon, you annoy the shit out of me, but every time Evanne looks at you her face lights up like Cophine's moon. Lustrous, brilliant, and full of hope. She looks like that at no other. Three save me, but I think I love you. Worse, I think Evanne loves you too."

"Umm." Tarragon hopped down, walking to the lantern. "You're a weird person."

"Thanks."

"Do you know where she is?" Tarragon put a hand on the lantern's glass. Inside, impossible pressure. Heat, light, and pain. She could *feel* it, like the sun against the palm of her hand.

"Not from in here."

"You should've said." Tarragon walked around the lantern, found the latch, flipped it, and pulled the door open.

The lantern shuddered, then hopped like a kettle over-boiling. It skittled around a moment, then Hitch hissed out like steam. He formed beside her, looking down at his not hands, pale blue eyes wide. "You could *do* that? Why didn't you do it earlier?"

"A talking lantern is cool."

"I take it all back. I hate you."

"Good talk." Tarragon tapped her foot. "Where's Evanne?"

I can't believe he left me. The spectre had ghosted, leaving Tarragon beside a dead lantern in the middle of a field. He'd done it with a jaunty probably-a-wave-but-difficult-to-tell-because-he-didn't-have-hands, then vanished.

He went to find Evanne first.

Tarragon spent the next while buzzing about, then decided to annoy Pakhet. She found where the tiger was because it was an empty sunny spot beside the festivities of breakfast. It was the sort of place treats could go missing and was about the size of a giant Big-eating creature. The grass looked crushed, as if someone of significant weight were sleeping there. A slight drone hung on the air.

Tarragon settled on the tiger, which elicited a heavy sigh from the invisible creature. *"How'd you know I was here?"*

"Simple." Tarragon counted on her fingers. "Flattened grass, no people, and you snore."

"I do not snore. At best, I have a gentle buzz." Pakhet came into view, all grey-black majesty and huge fangs. Tarragon found she was sitting on the tiger's rump, giving her an excellent view of said fangs as the feline yawned.

"You don't need to do that all the time you know."

"Yawn? I like yawning."

"Yawning with intent." Tarragon sat, a little glimmer settling on the tiger's pelt. It shone like motes of sun against the night. "You do it a lot."

The cat looked down on her for a moment, then stared at the crowd, who more or less ignored her. *"Do you know why I ... yawn with intent, was it?"* At Tarragon's nod, the cat shook her great head. *"I don't fight, fairy. I don't like to fight. I hate it. Fighting leads to screaming, and people getting hurt, and there was that one time I got punched in the nose."*

"Evanne got you good."

The tiger settled giant head on equally giant paws. *"They made me to fight. Didn't ask me. Just did it. But they left something out of the mix. I know how, Tarragon Greyflight. I know which part of my claws go where to pull the tasty red from inside someone. But it scares me."*

"You're ... scared?" Tarragon blinked.

"I'm scared," Pakhet agreed. *"I am scared almost all the time. I came from a world that is eight hundred years dead. I was made to keep the wounded soldiers of the last, great war safe while they recovered. All,"* she chuffed a laugh, *"so they could go back and do it again. Then something happened. I went*

to sleep before they could finish the job and when I awoke, I had no courage. So, here I am."

Tarragon leaned her head on hand. "They made me wrong, too. No wonder they lost the war. I was a Builder. I make machines and reactors. Anything breaks, that's me, fixing it. Except I can't. I'm like a hammer without a head. The haft might fit well in the hand, but you can't do anything with it." She sighed.

"You do a good sigh."

"Thank you." They sat in silence while the Bigs finished breakfast and drifted off in ones and twos to start more trouble they'd need a fairy to get them out of. Soon, there was almost no one left, except for Eden, who sat alone at a table near the middle of the field enjoying the dregs of probably-coffee. "Do you think she wonders why she's here? She wasn't a guard captain but did guarding just fine without a Manifest. Are Bigs different to us?

"In every way. They believe themselves above. Better than. Made to rule, and when they ran out of people to lord over, they made things to collar and chain." The cat sneered, a hint of giant fangs behind it. *"I'm glad their empires fell. We are better for it, despite my fear. And I think they gave me that too."*

"Why do you say that?" Tarragon perked up.

"I think I'm supposed to be afraid of them. Some of them, anyway. The ones who hold the leash and lash. They were supposed to tell me, 'go there, do that', and I'd obey because of the fear they put in me. The Manifest would have said who I feared and who I loved, and I'd follow it until I died doing what they wanted. So, here I sit, in this very nice field, enjoying the sun, and the company of a fey of impossible beauty, wondering where the world will take us next."

Tarragon boggled. "Umm."

"Don't fret, little one." Pakhet turned gemstone eyes on her. *"I'm not afraid of you. I'm not saying that to make you scared. I'm saying that because I feel comfortable around you. One broken machine finding peace with another."*

"I see." Tarragon snapped her fingers. "You let Gyles get into your head."

"Gyles was just telling the truth. We were made, but those who set atom to atom, building us mote by mote, are gone. We can be at peace."

Tarragon thought about that for a long time, until Eden finished her coffee, gave a wave, and set off toward the keep. A butterfly made its flitting way across the field, carried by the warm morning air. She watched a bee buzz nearby. Then Tarragon stood, stretched, and smiled. "I know what I'm going to do next."

"*You're going to fly somewhere so I can nap in peace?*"

"I'm going to find Evanne, and we're going to save what's left of the world."

"*Huh. I—*"

"And you're going to come with us."

"*You what now?*" The tiger seemed confused, rearing to stare down her nose at Tarragon.

"We like having you around. We don't need you to fight anyone. Evanne hasn't asked anyone to do anything they don't want to do. She doesn't want what they were *made* for, but what they *yearn to be*. She sees that in us." Tarragon bent, touching the tiger's fur. It was coarse enough, but soft deeper in. "In you."

"*I'll think about it.*"

"You're wrong, you know. About courage, I mean." Tarragon took to the air, gritting her teeth at how her wing pulled her from her customary graceful swoop. "You came with us across a desert. Do you remember when you climbed into the Artifice for the first time? And then you walked into a vampire's castle. You've done a zillion amazing things that need courage. Just because you don't want to kill people doesn't make you afraid."

The tiger watched her hover. "*You don't know what it feels like.*"

Tarragon touched her stomach. "Water, here. Nothing but ice in your veins. Your hands, or paws I guess, shake. You can't think. Running seems good, but so does hiding."

"*Huh.*"

"I'll find Evanne and we can set off." Tarragon gave Pakhet a wave, then headed for the warmer air above. It was going to be a good day.

Chapter Seventeen

T he part of the field Evanne lurked in was empty. She'd chosen it for that reason. It was a long way beyond the barn, where old bales of hay were trying to decay in peace. She heard the sound of people being free, and it felt good, but the good wasn't as big as the bad of Quinton dying. So, Evanne brooded. She knew she did it well; it was a Trick like any other, but she meant it this time. *I don't know what to do next. There are people here who need help, but I'm on a mission to save the whole world, not just this part of it.* The thought chafed at her. So many people needed so much, and she'd barely crested sixteen summers. *I don't know how to do it all.* The thing inside her that was Vhemin hissed, *We do what we must.*

The hay bale she used as a stoop felt uncomfortable, so she stood. Her hand went to the scar on her chest above her heart, where Requiem had parted her flesh and left her bleeding out her last. She felt the steady *thump, thump* beneath her fingertips, and realised: *It wasn't the Vhemin in me that snarled. It was the human piece. The bit that gives a shit for those outside of the tribe.*

Was that wrong? Did Vhemin not care? Weren't humans just as angry?

She snarled, turned, and kicked the hay bale.

"Nice," Hitch offered from behind her.

Evanne startled, whirled, grinned, ran to him as if to snatch him in a hug, then faltered. She dropped her hands, toeing the grass. "Hey."

"Hey yourself." He blinked not-eyes. "Oh, I get it. You're sitting on hay."

"Took you a while."

"I've been stuck in a lantern." He gazed at the sky. "Tarragon let me out."

"Tarragon ... wait. The fairy let you out?" Evanne boggled. "Why didn't she let you out before?"

"Could be many reasons. Maybe she wanted to see if Morgan was on the team." Hitch shrugged. "I think mostly she liked me being stuck in a lantern."

Evanne felt warm, like that delicious feeling when you put your foot in a bath just the right temperature. "I'm glad you're okay."

"I'm sorry I left. The vampire caught me flat-footed. I haven't seen an artefact that captures ghosts before. Could be useful to have around." He looked away. "I'm glad you're okay, too."

"What do I do, Hitch?" She threw an arm out at the farmstead behind them. "There are people here who need me. But we need to save the world."

Hitch glanced at her. "Have you had breakfast?"

"I don't have time to think about food."

The ghost laughed. "That's a first. You eat six times your body-weight daily. Come on. We'll find something."

FOOD WAS GOOD. EVANNE ATE WITH PURPOSE, TRYING TO FIND WAYS to stick all the eggs, bacon, and sausage in her mouth at once. The bacon was overdone, but she liked a bit of crunch. The sausage was perfect, if a bit cold. She ravened in the farmstead's old kitchen. The south door led to the room where Quinton died. Someone had cleaned it up before people made the old farmstead's kitchen hum again. There was a lot of leftover food and only one person to eat it.

Mama didn't raise no quitter. Evanne took another bite of sausage as Hitch stepped through a wall, then spoke around a mouthful. "Where'd they all go?"

"They're having a meeting."

She gave him a little side-eye while she chewed. "About what? Specifics, ghost."

"They're talking about the usual things. How they fell thrall to a vampire lord. Where their families are. It's pretty standard stuff, really."

"Like you rescue castles full of people on a daily basis."

He paused, glancing just over her shoulder for a moment. "You know, I think I used to. I don't remember."

"Convenient."

"It's not. If I remembered I could tell a good story. Be the talk of the party."

Evanne pushed a piece of toast through runny yolk. "So, how do we help them?"

"I think that's a problem that'll solve itself. One moment." He tapped a not foot. "Any second now."

The exterior door opened, the sound of footsteps drawing closer. Eden walked in. The guardswoman had colour in her face. "Hello."

Evanne pointed with her toast to a stool across the kitchen bench from her, inviting the guard captain to sit. "Sup."

She got a raised eyebrow for that, but Ed sat. "How are you?"

"Great." Evanne gritted her teeth. *Take away the Trick. Be honest.* "I don't know what to do."

Ed pursed her lips. "What do you mean?"

"I came here for Hollyhead. There's a lake, I think." Evanne finished her toast. "I need to save the world, you see, but then I found you. Gyles needed stopping." Ed looked down for a moment. "Now Gyles is gone, I need to get back to Hollyhead. But I can't leave all of you."

Ed raised the same eyebrow. "Are you nuts?"

Evanne ran that through her head again. "I don't think so."

"You *saved* us. You don't need to do anything at all." Eden stood, all nervous energy, and paced the kitchen. "You defeated a vampire lord. You freed us. You liberated the land. What else is there?"

"I got Quinton killed. There's that." Evanne turned away from her plate. "I need to..." She trailed off.

"Oh, honey." Ed came to her. "No you don't. That's not on you."

"Quinton is dead." Evanne bit her lip to stop it trembling. "Quinton is *dead*."

Ed nodded, not disagreeing. "He is. And he's not coming back. But he chose his fate. Died, fighting a tyrant."

"Save the dragon, and the princess." Morgan leaned against the door frame. She'd arrived, doing a passable impression of Pakhet's turning-up routine.

That woman can move powerful quiet. "Oh. It's you."

"It's me." The Raven straightened, then held out a sheet of parchment. "A map."

Evanne took it, then glanced at the queen. "You worked that out by yourself?"

Her lip quirked, then the permafrost returned. "It shows where Hollyhead lies."

"What are we waiting for?" Eden straightened. "We must away."

"Hold up a second." Evanne examined the map. "There's a lake, but no fairy kingdom."

"I was waiting for you to notice." Morgan's face was deadpan.

"You're coming along nicely." Evanne rolled the map, then tapped her chin with the tube. "Can you do me a favour?"

"Perhaps." The queen examined her fingers, then met Evanne's eyes. "It seems I have some small skill with magic after all."

"Great," Evanne said. "I need you to stay the fuck here."

Chapter Eighteen

F inding a man crazy enough to lead them into the blasted
plaguelands was difficult, which is why the High Justiciar
asked Amir to do it.

They'd spent enough time kicking the cobbles of Ravenswall to last
him a lifetime. Misery was everywhere. It was a foe he found a hard
time meeting on the edge of his steel. Hollow-eyed waifs watched from
the doorways of burned-out tenements. Livestock lay in the streets,
bellies swollen in death. Few hawkers sold wares, and what they had
was priced piteously or outrageously, depending on your point of view.
A gold band for a loaf of bread, if it please. In the seller's position, Amir
would've kept the bread. There wasn't enough to go around.

And the *smell*. Ikmae's sometime balls, but Ravenswall smelled like
a tanner's yard, everywhere, all the time. To stay was madness, but
stories of reavers beyond the walls meant leaving was suicide. Unless,
of course, you had Storm and Sway at your beck and call. Smithsteel,
and plenty of it, between you and the world.

Which sent Amir toward the docks. Ravenswall was the capital of
Or'sen, but also a fair port city in its own right. Ships farther out now
steered clear from the pillars of smoke, but a few that hadn't managed
escape still huddled at anchor, waiting for skilled crew to assist.

Amir walked the docks for most of a day, watching, listening, and waiting. And as the sun sighed into the hills beyond Ravenswall, casting long shadows against the chop and surge of a salty sea, he approached a man short on luck and desperate on time. A merchant, used to wealth but uncomfortable with its luxuries. His clothes were fine enough but clung to a lean frame. He stood on the forecastle, surveying the empty main deck of his ship, looking like what he wanted more than anything was a lemon to suck. The ship was fine enough, aye, the sails wrapped against the wind, the paint on the main-mast still glossy with a fresh coat. The timber of the deck was sanded smooth by the passage of many feet, but well cared for, not a plank out of true.

Pasting on a brilliant smile, Amir wandered up the gangplank, pausing before the railing. "Ho, friend. Permission to come aboard?"

The merchant puckered. "You know the sea well enough, then, to ask for permission before standing on another man's deck?"

"Aye," Amir agreed. "Not well enough to sign on for paltry wages, though. Which is what you're about to offer."

The merchant bristled. "I don't think—"

"Your ship bobs at anchor. Her belly is light and in need of trade goods. You have no crew, no pilot, nor boatswain to do the necessary to the needful." Amir spread his hands almost apologetically. "You've a mission in mind, and no souls to help with the practicalities of what-ever venture you've in mind."

"Uh," said the merchant.

"The thing is," and Amir paused for dramatic effect, eye upon the rigging, "you're a man familiar with the sands. I can see no water weight on your frame. You've come to these shores hoping for Vhemin trade, but none will take position as guard while you walk into their blasted lands. Precious few would hold steel against a monster even in peacetime, and Ravenswall hasn't known true peace for many moons."

"Ah," the merchant said, though thoughtfully this time.

Amir's eyes found the deck before he glanced back at the merchant. "I represent an interested party. We've good swords, one and all, not unused to the dirty work of a bloody moon."

"You're a poet, sirrah," the merchant said.

"I try."

"I'm not," he said. "I'm a man used to trading a thing for something of hopefully higher value but letting the other feel they've the better of the bargain. And you've come to me, all offer, but no ask. While you've the silken tongue of a courtier you've asked for naught, and that makes me more than a little suspicious."

"That's the problem with these foreign lands." Amir shook his head ruefully. "No trust between strangers."

"Friend, we are at war."

"Fair point." Amir considered. "While we have swords, we lack a guide."

"You propose a trade of ... services?" The merchant bit his lip, considering. "Your steel for my map?"

"Aye."

"Preposterous," he said. "The map of my trade routes is invaluable. If you knew what I—"

"I'm going to stop you right there, *friend*." Amir raised his hand, palm out. "We both know the moves of this dance. I imagine you a fair fiend across the table as a haggler or card player."

"Gambling is a low vice."

"But a fun one." Amir smiled. "We hail from Imshir. Our business is steel and glass. We've no wont of your maps and baubles. We must find a girl and save the world."

"Aye, aye, a quest of ... wait. Did you say steel *and glass?*" His eyes bulged.

"Truth, only one of our number can use the glass. The rest of us are but squires, learning the Three's ways."

"Glass?" the man asked again, perhaps redundantly.

"We are from the High Justiciar's school across the seas. We come on a quest most urgent. One that takes us into the plaguelands, and beyond. We've need of your knowledge and will keep you safe while you are about your business."

"And you want *my* help?"

"If it's available." Amir shrugged. "If it is not, we will find another, or go brave the desert without it."

"You'd die."

"It's possible. Service to the Three guarantees no safety."

The merchant paced. "What is your quest?"

"We believe this war involves a new faction. One made from the fragments of fallen houses. They take brother and place him against brother. Our once allies now bare blades against us. The queen flees her city, and a degenerate tries for her throne. The Three are absent from our skies, and everywhere is death." Amir sighed. "Our quest is to fix the world."

"Oh, is that all?" At Amir's nod, the smile faded from the merchant's face. "You mentioned a girl?"

"Barely sixteen summers."

"How can one so young help?"

Amir glanced to the duskening sky. "She is a child born of two worlds. The enemy wants her, for what purpose I don't know. But I tell you, we want her because we love her. She is the daughter of the Three."

The merchant's face soured a shade. "I thought the Saviour of Ravenswall was the daughter of the Three. How many can there be?"

"Did I lay it on too thick?"

"A little."

Amir laughed. "She is a child of the universe as are we all. We love her still, regardless of her provenance."

A woman stepped through the doorway from the captain's cabin. She was elegant, all flowing silks, her hair flowing on the gentle sea breeze that tickled the rigging. The merchant sagged the merest fraction but Amir saw it all the same and resisted the urge to drop his smile. The woman flowed across the deck like a dancer schooled in ballet, anchoring herself to the crooked elbow of the merchant. "Brother, who is this?"

The merchant, perhaps sensing a trap, introduced Amir with a flourish. "A man of no import, sister mine. A stray and a waif, brought to our deck on the promise of work."

"That's a lie," she murmured. "He came with a great quest. He's offered to take us into the desert."

"Ah, you heard that?" The merchant's tone held fondness.

"You spoke at the volume of braying yaks. They heard you in the next town."

Amir cleared his throat. "It's not strictly a lie, or perhaps just a polished half-truth."

He got a raised eyebrow for his troubles. "Sirrah, I heard you well enough. My brother called you a man of no import, a vagabond after small coins for simple work."

"He was true on those accounts." Amir gave a modest bow. "Amir of Imshir. I am indeed a vagabond seeking work for my blade. The lie, if there is one, is that I offered to take you into the desert. The truth is the opposite. I need you to take me to where I can't step without death dogging my heels. And we will keep you safe."

"Safe." She leaned into her brother. "I like him. Can we keep him?"

The merchant laughed. "It seems my desires are of no import. Amir of Imshir, I am Amber. This is my sister, Jade. We are sand merchants by calling. Our haunt is the plaguelands and the secrets within."

"Then we have a partnership?"

"Partners share maps, friend Amir. We have an accord." Amber looked to the west. "We will find your child of fortune."

Amir felt his smile falter. "A strong statement."

"My brother does what he says," Jade said. "He has made wealth enough from finding things upon the sand even the Vhemin don't know about."

Interesting. Amir touched his brow in salute. "Good enough. When will you be ready to ride?"

"Tomorrow." Amber glanced to the captain's cabin. "No later than two hours after sunrise. Will that suit?"

"Perfectly. Until tomorrow." Amir swept a bow to the pair, then made his way down the gangway. Time to give the good news to the High Justiciar. For once, she would be pleased.

"I AM NOT PLEASED." VERTILINE LOOKED DOWN ON AMIR. THEY were in the throne room, currently missing its ruler, so the High Justiciar was seated on high. Someone had fetched a steward or two to clean up the mess left from her last conversation in here. "You had one job, Adept."

The Feybrind leaned against a wall, looking as if he had no stake in the conversation, but Sight of Day was always like that. It was one of the reasons Amir thought he was good people. *Listens. Watches. Waits. Acts when needful.* There was something he'd like to learn from the cat, but he didn't feel he could talk to him. Not because Sight of Day would turn him away. Amir, for all his charming experience of the world before coming to the school, couldn't Handspeak better than a child.

Time to get this moving. Amir glanced to Larochette on his left, and whispered out the side of his mouth loud enough Vertiline would be sure to hear. "What did I miss?"

The High Justiciar leaned forward, her eyes cool. "You missed nothing while you weren't here. But it seems you missed everything before, when you were. I need a guide to take me to Evanne. Evanne is west, but we know not where."

"No problem," Amir breezed. "The merchant will find her."

"I ... what?" The High Justiciar looked the barest hair's breadth off-balance, and it made Amir want to high-five someone, except that would've gotten him killed.

"The noble Amber and his sister Jade seek riches. Your daughter is well known to be attracted to the same." He raised an eyebrow. "Am I not wrong?"

Vertiline gave him a stare hard as granite. "My daughter didn't come here for coin."

"I didn't come here for beer, but I'll find it all the same." Faust's comforting rumble came from Amir's right.

The High Justiciar's look became stormy. "I don't like your tone, Adept."

"I don't like getting thrashed daily but here we are." Faust almost sounded apologetic.

Amir verbally stepped into the conversational breach. "He was well dressed. The ship was maintained above the usual standard. No frayed lines, no sail out of place."

"You're an expert on boats?"

"I'm an expert on most things," Amir said. "Point is, he makes money, this Amber. He is good at it. He gave his word, and my feeling is if we have a little faith, we—"

"We will not put my daughter's life on the scales of faith!"

Amir held his peace a moment, then he nodded. "Perhaps we should split up. Leave a force here in case there is word. Others go with Amber and Jade."

Vertiline surged from the throne, stalked the floor, then glanced at Armitage. Amir had to admit for a big man he made very little noise and, like Sight of Day, didn't draw the eye unless he needed to. "Husband?"

"She's going home," he rumbled.

"She's never set foot on this continent. Did the voyage addle your brain?" Vertiline sounded on the verge of murder: her voice was quiet and almost reasonable.

"The sand calls." The Vhemin shrugged. "She is mine and yours. We've kept her safe in a city, like a human needing coddling. But the monster in her—"

"Do I look like I need coddling?" Vertiline's voice had clicked up an octave. Amir winced.

"The monster in her," Armitage trundled on, "needs the sands. Blood calls to blood where the sun scorches the earth."

Vertiline turned to Sight of Day. "I suppose you support this hair-brained scheme?"

The Feybrind detached himself from the wall. {Your clever daughter ditched me.} He paused, examining his hands as if they'd turned traitor. {She left me to go into the wasteland. I failed her, and I will find her. I will go with the merchant while you stay here.} Golden eyes found Armitage. {If you need coddling, that is. While you coddle, I'll get to work.} He padded toward the hallway exit.

Vertiline rounded on Amir. "Did they set you up to this?"

"No, High Justiciar."

"Call me Justiciar one more time and you'll lose another tooth," she warned.

"Yes, High Justiciar," Amir said mildly. "Tomorrow, when we meet Amber and Jade, we should be ready for an attack."

"What do you know?" Larochette hissed. "You didn't say anything about an attack."

"Oh, we're just lucky that way." Amir looked to Faust. "Wouldn't you say, brother?"

"Aye. We are the luckiest alive."

Chapter Nineteen

Sight of Day worked his way toward the docks. He wasn't taking special pains to not be seen, but only thieves, assassins, and other Feybrind used the rooftops. Rarely would a human look up from the mud beneath their feet. It was a marvel they'd survived so long. Then again, they ruled the world, both before, and now. Being a human had its perks.

Humans take everything so seriously. Perhaps it's their mayfly lifespan.

The sun was well and truly set, only the faintest hint of blue-yellow light touching the sky above the western sea. Ravenswall had its own beauty. Gulls flew above on their way to roost. Night birds called to each other. Sight of Day marked an owl taking wing. *An early night hunter. Just like me.* The rooftops below his padding feet were mostly tile. They kept the sun's heat even after it had set. He was in the Artist's Borough, the area the Raven Queen set aside for those with more heart than body. The Borough led to the docks, or near enough. A slight detour was well enough.

Sight of Day liked human artists. They reminded him of Feybrind craftspeople. Dedicated to a perfection others couldn't see, let alone pursue. He used to be one before life took him elsewhere.

His path took him past music played on harp and mandolin. It led past bakeries where cakes were made into works of art. Sight of Day ghosted beside a window open to the night air, the faint *scritch-scritch* of quill on parchment reaching his sensitive ears. While he could hear the music and smell the cakes, he couldn't read the poem without going inside.

I wonder if it is as magnificent as the words Evanne teases from the heavens. Probably not, but all art had its place. It wasn't a competition.

The Feybrind's path took him down a level onto a low roof. He used a drainpipe to scamper down, landing silently on a long roof. Now just one level above the street, a passerby might have seen him if the sky weren't so dark. Two thugs clearly had the same sense of safety; they stood before him above the lintel of an open window. One was large, with a shaved head, and the other larger, with an impressive beard.

It is strange how humans put so much hair on their faces. Is it to make up for the lack on the rest of their person?

Sense suggested he slip on by. There was naught to be gained here. But the *tink, tink* of a hammer on steel drew his ear. It reminded him of his own smithcraft, the delicate shaping of metal that led to wonders like the blade at his hip. In the room below the lintel was another smith. Not a Tresward artisan forging Smithsteel for the will of the Three, just a man or woman intent on their craft even in these trying times. The presence of thugs suggested the smith was good at their job. Word was out, and covetous people wanted wonders that weren't theirs.

The *tink, tink* stopped with a grunt of disgust from within. "I'll never get this right!" A man's voice, young by how humans measured their brief span.

How curious. He makes marvels yet is not satisfied. The thugs were still, perhaps waiting an opportune moment. The bearded one put lips to the ear of the bald, his voice so low only Feybrind ears would hear it a metre out. "We must get the sword."

Ah. A weaponsmith. Sight of Day crept closer to the thugs. The bald one nodded but had a restraining hand on the bearded one's arm. "When he's gone. No witnesses."

"There are other ways to remove witnesses." Beard drew a thin slip of steel. The blade was dulled with lampblack, but Sight of Day didn't think the old metal had much gleam left to give. His Feybrind eyes saw the state of the pitted metal.

"Fair enough." Bald freed a kosh from his belt. In Sight of Day's opinion, a kosh was the kind of weapon you beat a man with until he couldn't move, and then kept going if you wanted him dead. It wasn't pretty, or merciful. The best thing you could say about a kosh was the price. It was cheap, for tawdry work. While there was surely a moral quandary in whether allowing the weaponsmith to live would deliver more death to the world, or save lives because people had steel against the claw and fang of the world, the man below the lintel was an artist. He was like the Feybrind, unsatisfied with his best, and wanting more from his art than his skills could provide.

That's cinched it, then.

Sight of Day sighed, pulled out his own blade, and ran Beard through. The man arched, clawing at the handspan of steel sprouting from his chest. While he choked on blood, Sight of Day freed his blade, sweeping it across the throat of Bald as the man turned in alarm. He slipped back a couple metres while blood fountained and two men died. They fell to the roof, which made a noise.

"Hello?" The smith within sounded nervous. Sight of Day hurried forward, grabbed collars, and pulled the men back from the edge. Lantern light's fingers parted the night as the man looked out below. Sight of Day waited, silent, and after a few moments the light withdrew, the shutters closing behind it. He fussed with the bodies, tossing them into an alley below, before slipping to the street. He had the People's curiosity, and wanted to see the art the weaponsmith was about.

The window was latched, a trivial matter. He used a twist of metal from his belt and liberated the window, then eased it open. Inside, a workshop gleamed. A forge gave a sullen glow from the northern wall. An anvil was before it. It wasn't large, more for the manufacture of horseshoes than ploughshares. Leaning against the anvil was a sword, or the makings of one. No hilt or crosspiece adorned the blade.

He helped himself over the windowsill and retrieved the blade. The metal was light, and flexed when he tested the metal. *Ah. It lacks tempered strength*. He made his way about the room, finding charcoal, a hammer, iron ingots, and other such used in the making of fine steel. A chalk board was on a workbench, angry scrawls marking a failed attempt at the perfect recipe. Sight of Day erased it, fetched a nub of chalk, and wrote:

Step one. Clear your mind.

Step two. Use no more than 7 parts charcoal to one thousand parts iron. Less than 6 is also a mistake.

Step three. Folding the steel takes time. Here is how it is done among the People.

HELPING MAYFLIES WAS AN ARGUMENT LONG TRADED BY THE People. On the one hand, the obvious: their short-lived species couldn't hope to equal the mastery of the Feybrind, and their petty natures could let them make weapons that would cut Feybrind just as easily as Vhemin. Sight of Day had a different take.

They are children, and all children deserve to learn and grow.

It was a matter unsettled between him and his son, before the latter had his name and then life taken by perverted monsters. Sight of Day didn't mind that his son had a different perspective. Viewing things from a different angle and sharing the findings made for better craft, no matter the vantage. That he'd helped a human put a lift in his step as he traversed the rooftops. The docks were close, salt tang on the air, and the buildings closer to the ocean carried a more weathered look be they wood or stone.

Some few ships bobbed at anchor. They were all sound enough vessels, but Sight of Day wanted the thing Amir had seen. A *worthy* ship. Something that drew the eye. *Ah. There it is.* It wasn't the neat rigging, or the ropes coiled just-so. Nor was it the clean and clear deck, not a bucket astray, nor a hawser unlashed. No, it was the goons who lurked on the decks, hulking purpose directed toward the captain's cabin. A cheery little light shone from the rear window, a sea lantern set to warm the heart while at harbour's rest.

That's enough of that. The Feybrind slipped down from a warehouse roof, padding along the wharf toward the ship. A lookout lurked by a stack of crates sheltered by a waxed tarpaulin. Sight of Day relieved him of consciousness with a well-placed rap to the base of his skull, then tossed his crossbow, sword, dagger, kosh, darts, and garrotte into the ocean. He kept the man's purse, because humans loved shiny things, and there were many things that glittered within. *Perhaps Tilly will want them. She doesn't smile, and for good reason, and I don't expect baubles to change that. But a friend keeping her in their heart will help, if only a little.*

He jumped the paltry seven-metre gap between dock and ship, grappling the rearward lintel of the open window. The lantern gave a gentle light, but he turned golden eyes away, because the night was not yet done. Breathing came within, soft under the gentle wayward creaking of the ship. Two people, not at all alarmed, perhaps reading books and sharing wine.

Sight of Day entered through the open window in a smooth movement, one hand on the sill, the other pushing the lantern aside. He landed on the carpeted floor, spreading his hands wide. *I am a friend.* The two people within were very surprised to see him. The man knocked a goblet over, so Sight of Day moved the three metres between window and table, caught it before it could clatter on the deck, and put it on the table.

The woman sucked in a lungful of air, no doubt to scream or shout for aid, so Sight of Day liberated the man's half-drawn blade, vaulted the table in the same motion, swished behind her, and clamped a fursoft hand across her mouth. He held the sword about her front, holding it by the tang, not hilt. An offering, not a threat.

Everyone took a moment, which was good. Sight of Day waited them out. Humans moved very, very slowly most of the time, but this deserved an abundance of care. The man looked between his empty scabbard and the blade now in Sight of Day's hand. The woman relaxed a fraction, then gently, so very carefully, took the sword.

Sight of Day stepped back from her reach, because while he was confident in his skills with a blade, he didn't know hers. {*Hello. I am*

Sight of Day. There are six men on your deck who wish you harm. Do you know why?}

The woman looked to be sucking in more air, so Sight of Day put a finger to his lips. Feybrind couldn't speak but the gesture was universal. *Be quiet.* She closed her mouth, pursing her lips as if she could swallow sound. The man sketched a short bow. *{I am—}*

{I know who you are.} Sight of Day's tail lash, lashed. *{What is in question is who is on your deck.}*

The woman lifted her skirt, crouched to keep her shadow off the windows, and made her way to the door. *Clever, that one.* She lifted the bar, dropping it with exquisite care into its stays. Sight of Day shifted golden eyes to the man. The Feybrind knew humans found their jewelled eyes beautiful, captivating perhaps, and the People were no strangers to leveraging every advantage. The man looked into Sight of Day's eyes, relaxing a micron. *{I don't know who they are. Our crew are—}*

{I know you have no crew.} There was nothing for it but to burn precious time with stupid explanations. *{This afternoon a son of the Three visited you. He holds no Storm but it is within him waiting for the right moment. He said this, yes?}* The man nodded. *{You are sand merchants, prowling the blasted plaguelands for trinkets to sell to humans. The curious part of this is how a human could do a thing the Vhemin, who call the wastelands their home, struggle with. It is a thing the People do not know how to do, and we know how to do almost everything.}* He gave an encouraging nod. *{So, why do six men with murder in their heart roam your deck? It doesn't bother me. I can leave through the same window I came in. It might worry you, if you cannot use steel like Tresward.}*

The door creaked as the handle turned slowly. The bar held it, and after a moment, someone set shoulder to it. *Whump.*

"A moment," the woman called, cementing herself as the brains of the pair. "I but need my coat."

The man's eyes flicked to the wall, the tiniest motion but not lost on one of the People. Sight of Day moved whippet-quick to the wall, eyes spotting the almost invisible panel more worn than others. He knocked it, and it opened, revealing a small device. The man rushed Sight of Day, so the Feybrind stepped behind him without taking his eyes off the device, then tapped the back of the man's knee. He stumbled, and Sight of Day helped him to a sitting position.

The device was similar to one the Feybrind had seen out on the plaguelands. They'd found several in a temple that birthed a lost friend, the dragon Ormeon. The devices were made of a curious mix of metal and glass. The one Sight of Day had seen could provide the true name of a Feybrind, the hidden one they trusted only to their closest friends. Knowing this name let Feybrind be Commanded, robbed them of will, could turn friend against friend, or worse, son against father.

I want to destroy this thing.

Still, there was something different about it. The panel of glass affixed to the device's front was larger, and it had a curious weightiness to it, like the inside was larger than the outside, with all the world's secrets packed within.

Perhaps this thing is not like the other things.

The door shook as a large fist hammered against the outside. Sight of Day rolled his eyes, popped the device into his pouch, winked at the woman, then drifted through the window to hang from the lintel. He gave the humans another encouraging nod, then lowered himself from view. Listening, and waiting.

He heard the door's bar lift, and the *slam* of it opening. The bar rattled against the deck, and an *oof* suggested the man had taken a stout blow to the stomach. The woman didn't scream, bless her, but Sight of Day heard the sword she held clatter to the deck beside her brother.

No matter.

Heavy footsteps spread out within the room. The desk was knocked aside. The door of the cubby where he'd found the device rattled, then muffled scraping as a hand probed within. A sea chest lid opened, a thud as contents hit the floor. Sight of Day waited until footsteps approached his window, then he reached in, helping the surprised man within to exit over the side.

He took the man's place in the room as his startled shout ended in a splash. Five men remained, one hulking in the door as lookout. *Well enough.* The man by the sea chest lunged for Sight of Day with a heavy cutlass swinging about like a kite in a storm. He may as well have offered the blade to the Feybrind as a gift. Sight of Day took it from him, considered the fine carpet beneath his feet, and decided not to run him through.

The dumbfounded man's eyes crossed when Sight of Day rapped him on the head. As the man began his slow slide into gravity's embrace, the Feybrind scampered over the table, because on the other side was a man with a small crossbow. The weapon fired, releasing a bolt to where Sight of Day had been what felt like ages past. Sight of Day borrowed the weapon, cudgelled the man against the wall with it, turned, and threw it at the man coming through the doorway. This served as a useful distraction, the man shouting as the stock broke his nose.

Armitage is better at this. But Armitage wouldn't have kept his head when he'd found the device, because his brother from another world took that kind of thing personally. The Feybrind felt his breathing hurry, his heart picking up the pace, and felt happy there was just one foe remaining in the room.

The enemy had the look of a fencer. Classic guard pose, blade tip higher than hilt, just so, stance a little weighted on the rear foot. She paced about the table, feet moving with care across the carpet. Sight of Day bent, grabbed an edge of the rug, yanked, and then moved forward as she fell backward. Her sword clattered to the feet of the merchant brother, which might be a problem in moments but wasn't presently.

The swordswoman flailed, knocking her wrist against the table with a wince-worthy *crunch*, screamed, and then passed into uncon-sciousness as Sight of Day punched her in the temple. This but left the man with the broken nose at the door.

The merchant sister was clambering to her feet, leaning on her brother's recaptured sword, which wouldn't do at all. If she got killed then the brother would be difficult, and Tilly had no time for difficulty. Sight of Day helped her up, took the sword from her, sidestepped her brother, took his sword as well, exited the cabin, and ran both blades through the chest of the man outside.

The fellow he'd tossed out the window arrived up the gangplank, so

Sight of Day waited for him, two blades in hand, blocked his clumsy lunge, and removed the man's head.

That job done, the Feybrind tossed his liberated weapons overboard, then returned to the cabin. He surveyed the unconscious forms. *{I didn't want to mess up your carpet.}*

The man looked at the fallen bodies, then at Sight of Day. "We are in your debt."

{Of course you are. Your whole species is in our debt. We make your tools of living and killing. You are infants who can't clothe yourselves.} He noticed the man eying his pouch. *Best get this done, and done well.* He fetched forth the device. *{I have seen one of these before.}*

The merchant's sister looked surprised. "You've seen a star atlas? This is the only one we've ever found."

Sight of Day looked closer at the device. *{A what?}*

"Star atlas." The man held out a tentative hand. "Let me show you."

They didn't smell like they were lying, but humans were duplicitous creatures. He felt a stab of guilt. *Tilly is not a liar. Geneve was no liar. Meriwether was a sometime liar but not about the things that mattered.* Perhaps he was judging because he'd seen much evil. Pocketing the device, he hefted unconscious people out the window. The waters below the ship would be crowded, but he didn't have a better place. *{Perhaps you can show me later. You should sleep elsewhere. This place isn't safe.}*

"We need that." The man's hand remained outstretched.

{You need a good night's sleep. This trinket is a want.} Still... *{What does a star atlas do?}*

"It shows the realms of the ancients. Where they were, and where their relics might be found." The sister looked more angry than afraid. "But it needs a special knowledge to use it. And you need to be human."

{Of course you do. You ever kept your slaves at knee.} Sight of Day winced at the words his fingers carved into the air. *{I'm sorry. You probably don't know that part.}* He took the device from his pouch, placing it on the table. *{May I tell you a story? I promise it is not a long one.}*

The woman sat, and after a moment so did the man. "They call me Amber."

Sight of Day raised an eyebrow, then turned to the woman. *{And you are Jade. I find it convenient you chose names that rest easy on the fingertips of the People.}*

"I find it convenient you know our names," Jade shot back.

The Feybrind turned the full force of his golden gaze on her. *{You met a friend of mine earlier. He, not being a simpleton, remembered your names and offered them to me. I have kept them safe.}*

She bridled a bit, but Amber nodded. "Amir."

{The very same.}

"Tell your story." Amber crossed his arms.

{Sixteen summers past, or winters if you're feeling depressed, a small group of,} his fingers hesitated, *{friends walked two continents to save the world. The wonders they saw were like gazing into the sun. One such wonder was a sky forge, a creation of the ancients that made dragons. And thus, a dragon became their friend too, and promised to save the world it had been born into.}* Sight of Day looked away. *{The sky forge was in a temple that held many wonders of the ancient world. One such was a device like your star map, but it was a map of the heart. It could take the hidden name of any of the People and speak it aloud. Our most sacred thing, presented as a bauble. We were bent, broken, and afraid. When Commanded, we stop being us, and become another. We can betray a friend, or cross blades with a father.}*

"This device," Amber pointed to the star map, "knows your name?"

Sight of Day shrugged. *{Perhaps. I don't know how they work. Their magic will not answer my call. Your people did not want their leashes in the hands of the cattle.}* Despite the age of the memories, he shivered. *{One friend on the journey took all devices and broke them. He never used my name, but he knew it. Another friend knew my name, and used it to save me. Yet, it wasn't according to my will. I was ... taken from myself.}*

"Like when you're drunk?" Jade seemed doubtful.

{Nothing at all the same.} Sight of Day shook his head. *{The People are just ... gone. What remains is a machine wearing our faces, doing the bidding of another. To see this star map makes me afraid, and I don't know if anyone should have one.}*

"What if," Amber started, then settled, thoughtful.

"What if it could find what's lost?" Jade's eyes were piercing. "Would that be a worthy price?"

{Merchants always think things have a copper baron price. I mean no offence.} The Feybrind leaned back. *{It is how you are made, like the sun is made hot, or water is wet.}* He breathed in, then out, slowly. *{One of my dearest friends in all the world has lost her child. The vile thing here,}* he shook the star map, *{could find the child, and set that world to rights. I do not know if the rest of the world would spin out of balance, and the People would fall off. Do you understand?}*

"I don't understand at all," Amber admitted. "I am a merchant, and I know whether things are worth barons or solars. I have never had myself taken by another. But I know things have value that is not measured in copper or platinum." His eyes flickered to his sister. "What if you held the device? What if you controlled it?"

{For how long?}

Amber shrugged. "I don't know the future. I know the device has never told us a Feybrind's name. But I don't know if it wouldn't or couldn't. So, how long? For now, at least. We know the reading of it. Together we might find wealth," again his eyes moved to his sister, "of a kind we desire."

Sight of Day felt around the edge of the star map. Cold, but not icy. Hard, but not brittle. Nothing about what it was made of told him what was within. It didn't look like a sword, but he'd yet to see a thing the ancients made that wasn't a weapon. Not even the People. He stood. *{I will hold it. We will travel a road. Both will learn from the other. Then we decide.}*

"But, uh, we need that." Jade half-stood, then stopped. "Without it, we are lost."

Sight of Day padded to the window. *{With it, all could be lost. Even you.}* He slipped over the sill, leaped for the wharf, and slipped into the night.

Chapter Twenty

The dockside was warm, if a little smokey. Amir eyed the sky, and the sun eyed him right back. It was hued with orange and ochre, burnished like bronze. This late in the morning it should have burned a clean yellow-white, but Amir figured even suns could have an off-day.

Larochette tugged at her jerkin. The air in Or'sen was cooler than Imshir but she seemed to run hotter than anyone else. Aside from that slight movement, she appeared composed, calm, ready for the day. Faust glowered as only a giant could, but Amir didn't think he meant any particular thing by it.

The three waited behind the High Justiciar, her husband, and the cat. The Feybrind seemed twitchier than usual, his tail *lash, lashing* every so often, a tension belied by the calmness in those golden eyes. The remains of their school were scattered about in twos, sometimes threes, a rag-tag army of the willing waiting to do the needful. *If that's the poet in me, I shouldn't quit the soldiering life. I suck at poetry.*

The wharf area was ripe for an ambush, the warehouses presenting ample roof acreage for seedy types to lurk with crossbow and ill intent. Amir rubbed his face, waiting for the inevitable.

Larochette nudged him. It wasn't pleasant; the woman had pointy elbows. "Quit fidgeting."

"I was born to fidget." Amir eyed the empty expanse of dock before them. "We're missing a merchant and his sister."

Vertiline turned, offering him a cool stare. "You had one job, Adept."

"I am no Adept." Amir pressed his lips into a line. "By the Three's grace, perhaps one day, but today dawns weary upon my laggardly soul. Without dedication, I will ever—"

"Three's mercy," she breathed. "You prattle like a child."

"Be as may." He sketched an insincere bow. "Perhaps it was the glint of your ire that scared them off. Sand merchants are brave, hardy souls, but even the stoutest heart can wither."

As if on cue, Amber and Jade rounded a bend not five buildings further up. The alarming thing was the retinue accompanying them. Amir saw horses and handlers for the horses, and Khiton's ass but was that a *camel?* This wasn't a problem because of logistics; Amir was confident the merchant had that avenue covered. It was a huge deal because last night there were no people on their ship. Not crew, nor hands, nothing. Now: a party.

Amber and Jade were late because they'd been recruiting.

Recruiting this number meant loose lips, which would sink the caravan, metaphorically. No way that many people could be offered coin for a dangerous trip into the plaguelands without casting a wide net, and the minnows that slipped through would trade information to darker sorts.

Right on cue, Larochette elbowed him again. "There. On the roof." She threw her arm out at the warehouse roof nearby, over the top of which a ragged assortment of dirty men and women scrabbled. They had both weapons and ill intent. "'Ware!"

The High Justiciar offered Amir a withering glance, drew glass, and swiped a crossbow bolt out of the air absently. Armitage set off at a hulking run toward the merchants, because the villains on the roof weren't targeting the heavily armed what-they-presumed-were-Knights. They were after the caravan, no doubt for whatever secrets a sand merchant kept for combing the plaguelands for riches.

A second crossbow bolt sought Vertiline. If Amir lived to be a hundred, he swore he would never see movements as perfect as that woman's. She slipped around the bolt, blade caressing its edge, holding it glitter-tight. Golden light glimmered as she spun, holding the bolt against her blade, giving it more speed, and the power of the Light. The bolt flew back as if tossed from an arbalest. It hit the cross-bowman in a flare of ruddy glory. His body exploded into flame and ruin, the blast picking up a handful of his comrades and tossing them into the street.

As appealing as it was to watch the High Justiciar work, Amir knew he needed to get closer to Armitage. He ran down the docks, and almost lost his footing in surprise as he passed Jade sprinting in the opposite direction. No time to think, head down as he was, but something nagged at him. It continued tugging at his mind as a woman wielding a mattock engaged him on his left. He used a rough parody of *Ice's Embrace* to step inside her guard, removing her weapon from her by severing her hands at the wrist, took off her head, and almost took a blade to the gut as her companion rushed him.

It was sloppy, even for Amir, and he knew it was that glimpse of Jade that did it. She wasn't running for safety. He gritted his teeth, *Ice's Embrace* about him now, the cold of it almost in his bones, as he placed left foot behind right, stepped, and cut his opponent from skull to groin.

She wasn't afraid. She was determined.

Amir paused, trusting his comrades Faust and Larochette, those two that made them three, and looked back. Larochette stood behind Faust. The giant resorted to brute strength, tossing a wiry man into the harbour. Larochette was already on the way to back Amir, eyes fixed on the enemy.

Amir spied Jade. She was heading to the spot Tilly, Armitage, and Sight of Day had been but moments earlier. The horses were troubled, but good Tresward beasts didn't fret at the spilling of a little blood. The merchant's sister was rifling through their saddlebags. Not one to be bothered by a bit of honest stealing, Amir didn't mind the intent so much as the brassiness of the move, what with her brother beset by murderers and their guard scattered about dealing with malcontents.

"Attend! Trouble." Amir pointed his blade toward the horses and stray merchant's sister.

Larochette arrived at his shoulder, squinted, and said, "Go."

Head down, running fast as wind and twice as hard, Amir vaulted a woman tangling with Sight of Day. She was struggling to pull the arrow from her throat while the cat lay her on the ground almost tenderly. He breezed past two large men with outstretched arms, ducked beneath the swing of a club, and then went down as a woman tackled him.

He rolled, found his feet, punched her in the head, and was off. He went around the mass of horses—where *was* the damnable sister—and lurked between a Clydesdale and a roan, calmed his pace, then sauntered past the rear of the Clydesdale as if he'd been there for hours, just in time to confront Jade. The woman had the common decency to look both surprised, alarmed, and ashamed. She had a device in her hands, which she quickly transferred behind her back. "I was, uh, trying to hide."

"Me too," Amir confided. "You know, it's probably best if you stay here."

"Uh," she offered. "I need to get back to my brother."

Amir swatted an arrow out of the air headed toward her head. It clattered to the cobbles, and Jade jerked at the noise. "If you think that's a good idea." He leaned close, putting a little husk in his voice. "I can escort you. It is quite dangerous."

She fumbled with a satchel, patted the lid closed, and glanced toward the melee. "I think I can get back on my own."

"Are you sure?" He flicked blood from his blade, putting on what he believed was a credible show of surprise. "There are thieves and scoundrels."

Right there. Her eyelid twitched at the word *thieves*, but her spine straightened. "As in the one before me, using this nonsense to have at my virtue?"

Amir widened his smile, the snake before the mouse. "Come, now. We both know that virtue sailed from a different port long ago."

He was awarded with a slap. Amir let it land, eyes watering a little, and touched his cheek. Her eyes turned frosty. "I pegged you for a different sort of man last night."

"And I believed you a different woman. Perhaps we both stand corrected." Amir ran a man through who came about the roan, kicked the body to the pavers, then touched his forelock. "An educational experience. Until next time."

Haughty, shoulders back, chin up, she glared. "Until next time." She stormed past the Clydesdale, then broke into a run back toward her brother.

Amir watched her go, then pulled from behind his back the device she'd tried to hide from him in her satchel. It was clearly made by the ancients, all smooth corners and perfect, shiny facade. Glass and metal in a curious medley that was both foreign yet made perfect sense. She'd found it in one of their packs, and Amir was certain they did not depart Imshir with it, having been through everyone's luggage on the voyage. He tapped it against his chin thoughtfully, tossed it, caught it, and swaggered back out into the fight.

Which was, by that point, done. Groans of the dying. The smell of blood and shit. Smoke and fire came from the corpses of those that tangled with the High Justiciar. Amir pursed his lips. *I guess I don't get as much practice today.*

Sight of Day arrived at his elbow. His golden eyes were hard. *{What do you have there?}*

"I think you know." Amir offered it to the Feybrind. "Here you go."

The cat took it carefully, eyes softening. As if knowing Amir's paltry Handspeak, the Feybrind's fingers moved slowly, over generous in their motion. *{Do you know what you hold?}*

"Something important." Amir shrugged. "Important to you, anyway."

{More than you can imagine.} The cat looked at the device. *{You would just give this to me?}*

"It's not mine. It's not theirs, either. Whoever owned this died long ago." Amir clapped the cat on the shoulder. "Best take better care of your things next time."

Chapter Twenty-One

When Vertiline stepped onto the dry, desiccated grass surrounding the ancient spire, she thought, *My baby girl was here? What for?* She paused, hands on hips, examining the ruin. It was a maw of broken teeth, gnashing a mighty spire that rose to the heavens. The spire was of ancient manufacture, but lifeless. Its surface nearer the ground was pitted and marked as if by fire and catapult, but above, slender pure silver metal still rose.

There was a broken Artifice on the dry grass. Sand had already walked among its broken legs, trying to find a way in. She spied a body laying among the wreckage. Difficult to tell how fresh but it didn't have the leathery, sunken look of the fallen passed by years rather than weeks. She breathed, then smiled. *Yes. My baby girl* was *here. And whatever she was after, she found it.*

"What the fuck happened?" Armitage joined her side, his bulk a comforting shadow against the blasting heat. Vertiline had chosen loose linens and a summer hat instead of armour, but the journey here had been merciless. "Looks like someone started some shit they couldn't finish."

"Evanne." Vertiline pointed to the Artifice. "Look. A fallen machine."

"And you think our kid did that?" He glared at the dead machine. "You're probably right. I'm going to take a look."

{I will come.} Sight of Day padded by her husband's side. *{Without me you will find a hole to fall into.}*

"I'll find the hole even with your help... wait." Armitage stopped, squinting at the cat. "I didn't mean that."

The Feybrind gave a mock bow. *{Lead on, finder of holes. Let it be a big one.}*

Vertiline turned to her entourage. There was the sand merchant, Amber, lord among his retinue of guards and camels. And Jade, his sister, who apparently wanted to see the world. Vertiline thought it difficult to see the world if you never got off your camel and talked to people, but she was not a sand merchant's sister.

Amber headed for Vertiline. The man was dogged in his approach, so she steeled herself. *His sister I am not, but I carry the Three's power on the edge of my steel. Surely it's sufficient for another bout with this man?* The merchant squared off against her as if preparing for battle. He was not an ugly man, nor short. His face carried three scars down his cheek, but otherwise his face was pleasant enough if you liked that sort of thing. "I await the promised treasure."

"It's in there." Vertiline pointed to the ancient spire. "Away you go."

His nostrils flared, but he didn't take the bait. Perhaps being a sand merchant taught patience. "You promised wonders. Prizes worth such that lords would bow to me. I see nothing but sand."

"Look there." Vertiline pointed to his right. "There is some dried grass."

"Do not—"

"Stop," Vertiline advised. "In a few moments you will say something like 'do not trifle with me or else' and I will ask about door number two. I have never been a door number one kind of woman. I carry glass, Amber. I carry glass and Light, and if the 'else' is a threat of violence, I will call your bluff." She smiled, easy as you please.

His lips puckered for a moment as if he'd tasted lemon. "I meant only that the sun draws high and the heat will be brutal without shelter."

"Good." Vertiline tilted her head, considering him. "We don't have to be at odds with each other. You know the blasted plaguelands. I know steel and war. It's just—"

"Amber," whined Jade, "have you found the treasure yet?"

"Just that," Vertiline finished.

Amber's eyelid twitched. "Jade is the jewel of my father's empire."

"Hmm."

"She must learn of the world."

"Hmm."

"She will learn much here."

Vertiline looked past him to the young woman and her long-suffering camel. "You're sure about that?"

"Perhaps we can continue this conversation after we've made camp and settled," Amber offered. "When the sun is not so hot, our tempers will be cooler."

Vertiline thought of saying, *My temper is just fine*, and wondered why she wanted to needle the man. He'd offered a caravan on naught but the promise of potential wealth. He was brave enough, fighting the sand sharks two nights past alongside his guards.

The rustle of dead grass made her turn. Sight of Day padded with deliberate steps toward them. The Feybrind could've walked across the dead field without making a noise but knew surprising a Tresward Knight a poor life choice. She smiled as he drew close. *{You will not believe it, but the monster found a hole.}*

Vertiline blinked. "What? Where?"

The cat pointed to the Artifice. *{Beneath the broken machine.}*

She frowned, turning to Amber. "Will you excuse me? I've got to earn my keep."

That earned her the ghost of a smile. "Until the night falls and we share honeyed mead."

That sounds like something worth looking forward to. She almost turned, then lifted her chin fractionally toward Jade, before settling back on him. "You can come with, if you like."

His eyelid twitched again. "You make a handsome offer. Perhaps you are destined to become a sand merchant?"

Vertiline shook her head. "This past week has involved enough sand for the rest of my life."

"A shame. Until tonight."

"Until then." She turned, striding in Sight of Day's wake. *A hole, hmm?*

I HAVE NEVER SEEN THE INSIDE OF ONE OF THESE MACHINES. THE Artifice was larger on the inside than Vertiline expected. With the machines' monstrous resistance to damage she'd expected walls thick as stone ramparts, but their skin was barely a hands breadth from outside to interior.

The air within was a cool, welcome respite from the blasting heat of the desert outside. Vertiline kept her hand on her blade as she ducked through the door, but closed her eyes for a moment as the air kissed her skin.

"It's fucken chilly, ain't it?" Armitage brought her back to the here and now. Her husband was toward the nose of the machine. Two seats sat before a wall of glass. The floor was on a crazy angle, so the Vhemin held onto the chairs, which didn't even flex with his massive weight.

"It is welcome." Vertiline clambered deeper in. The floor canted upward, but it wasn't broken or cracked. To the left, the window and her husband. To the right, a chamber beyond an open doorway. If Vertiline could think of a single word to describe the Artifice's interior, it was *sleek*. The walls were smooth. What looked like cabinets held mysteries aplenty, but the latches were of exquisite quality.

There was no life anywhere, though. This machine was dead, and its pilots with it.

"How do you reckon they did that?" Armitage pointed to the window before him. "Can't see through it from the outside. Wouldn't even know it was a window. From this side, clear as day."

"Not quite." Vertiline made her way to his side. The seats were padded leather, and before them sat panels of glass. *I've seen their like. The control surfaces the ancients used on their devices.* "See? The sun is calmer from this side. Darker, perhaps."

"You think that's why it's cooler?"

Vertiline gave it some consideration. "I think the machine has magic still. A warding to keep the inside pleasant no matter what's on the outside."

"No commander gives that much of a shit about their troops."

"They do if they are human soldiers, husband." She gentled her voice. "Not everyone lived out on the sands."

He glared at the seats as if willing them to get in the conversation. "Maybe." Not arguing with her, but maybe taking umbrage with the world.

Vertiline straightened as much as she could, what with the sloping floor. "We had glass blades and Smithsteel armour. Tresward could've faced the world with iron blades and plain steel armour, but every little bit helps. If the ancients could control the weather, it would be a simple mercy, easily given, to ensure their soldiers weren't suffering the small complaints of the flesh."

His shoulders bunched, but then he relaxed. "I don't even know why I'm angry. They're all dead. We won." He stamped to the rear, leaving her with the empty chairs for company.

I think I know why you're angry. Your people were used as the shock troops to raid heaven and kill the very Three themselves, but the gods didn't die. Your masters did, but their legacy remains. And you're wondering who you mean by 'we'. 'We' won, but against who, and why?

"Coming?" Armitage's gravel and anvil voice drew her attention to the back of the machine. "Only, there's this hole, see?"

She held back a smile. "I will come see what magnificent pit of hell you've found."

THE PIT OF HELL WAS JUST A PLAIN OL' PIT. THE SAND WAS SHORED up with a rude mud until it hit rock. The hole was cut with rough tools; nothing of the ancients had bored through the skin of the earth. Just hard labour.

The Artifice had a hatch open in its belly, and this was over the hole. It was a short step down to real earth, the cool of the Artifice leaving Vertiline as she returned to the outside air. A rope ladder had been tossed over the side of the pit. One end was anchored to an open cabinet in the Artifice above. Vertiline gave it a suspicious glance, because few cabinets she knew could take the weight of a human hanging off them, but she stood beside a marvel from beyond time. Perhaps the ancient's hinges were amazing.

Sight of Day was at the bottom of the pit. The Feybrind held a curious green glowing rod about the length of her forearm. Despite the sickly hue, it cast light better than a lantern. *{There is a box of these here.}* He waved the glow stick. *{I hope they do not summon eldritch horrors.}*

Armitage slung himself over the pit's edge, monkeying down the rope ladder. If you only saw his size, it was easy to forget his strength gave him grace. Vertiline waited until he was clear of the ladder then followed at a more leisurely pace. She was thankful she wasn't wearing Smithsteel, because while her training kept her strong, twenty kilos of armour was twenty kilos she didn't want hanging off her while she hand-over-handed down.

The base of the pit was rocky, but with a coarse coating of sand. A tunnel she could stand in ran east to west. Armitage had to hunch. Sight of Day offered her a glow stick. It was almost weightless, and while it gave everything a chartreuse luminescence, it was easier than summoning light with the Sway. *That still costs me more than it should.*

{There is a dead creature that way.} Sight of Day pointed west with his glow stick. *{There is also sobbing from that direction. I suggest we go the other way.}*

Armitage gave him a hard, snake-eyed stare. "You going soft on me?"

{I am merely exploring all options. West is where people have already gone and met excitement. To the east, there could be a surprise.}

"West it is." Vertiline peered into the gloom. "Sobbing means a living soul is waiting to tell me what happened to Evanne."

{Or a nest of spiders.}

"Or that. What, you don't like spiders?" Vertiline pushed into the tunnel. She caught Sight of Day's eye roll, shoulders heaving in a sigh that screamed *These stupid humans,* then he padded in her wake.

She heard the scrape of rock on scale as Armitage followed at the rear. "I don't mind spiders."

Vertiline glanced back. "Even huge ones?"

"Even then," he rumbled. "I always like the part when they find out there are bigger things that go bump in the night."

{You are majestically terrifying.}

Vertiline hid her smile and continued down the tunnel. It widened in parts, but without seeming pattern, as if cut by water long ago. Strange holes festooned the rocky walls at random intervals. She leaned close to one, peering into the black.

A fursoft hand pulled her back. *{I wouldn't do that.}*

"Spiders?"

Sight of Day shook his head. *{Worse, I think. They do not smell like spiders. They smell like...}* His hands stilled, then he turned to Armitage, but put his back to the wall so they could both see his Handspeak. *{Do you remember the first time we crossed the sands together?}*

"Red wanted to kill me." Armitage chuckled. "Broke my arm good."

{If she wanted you dead, you would be dead, brother. You are majestically terrifying, but Knight of the Tresward you are not.} The cat eyed the hole Vertiline had stared into. *{Sand hoppers. We fought them on the sands. It was the first time we'd used steel together.}*

Armitage scratched an armpit. "I remember."

{This smells like that. But different, too. Older.}

"Huh." The Vhemin leaned into the hole. "Come out, fuckers!"

Vertiline winced. "I don't think that's wise."

He glanced at her. "I reckon a front-on fight is better than—"

What it was better than was lost to imagination as a monster surged from the hole. Vertiline thought she saw teeth and claws as it skitter-dashed from the burrow. Glass was in her hand, incandescent Light welling from the blade as she lunged. Her strike caught rock and creature in one slash. The rock glowed red, while the creature's flesh hissed as her burning blade severed a lot of legs from the rest of it.

It keened, struggling back into the dark, but Armitage roared and lunged. He reached into the hole, grabbing for it, then braced a leg on the outside and pulled. Vertiline waited, blade held in perfect half guard, edge level with gravity's even insistence rather than the tunnel's rough floor.

The creature popped from the hole in a mad scrabble of remaining legs. Vertiline held ready, but she didn't have to worry. Her husband knew the music and all the steps of the dance and had perhaps dated the conductor's daughter in times past. The Vhemin slammed the creature into the ground once, twice, and when it kept trying to eat his face, he went to town like a logger splitting wood. Even, hefty strikes laid on each other like bricks, until the thing he swung had the boneless pliability of wet laundry.

He dropped it with a wet slop. The three looked at it. To Vertiline's eye it was too much spider and not enough sand hopper. A mouth held many, many teeth. Two proboscises ran from under the jaw, severed clean near the maw from her strike. The body was like a dog's, if a dog had twice the regulation count of legs and a second body attached at the back end.

Armitage grunted, not breathing hard at all. "That's an ugly fucken spider."

"I don't think it's a spider." Vertiline eyed the holes along the tunnel. "I think it has friends."

{Explains the moaning and sobbing ahead.} Sight of Day scratched behind an ear. {Imagine a nest of these things. They injure a creature, attracting more, and here we are, ready to answer the dinner bell.}

"Hey, cat. What was that thing you were trying to teach me about?" Armitage frowned. "Something about the biggest, baddest monster?"

The cat blinked gold. {Apex predators?}

"Yeah." Armitage bared shark teeth. "There's a new apex in town."

{That's not how ... never mind. Sure, there's a new apex.} Sight of Day fussed with his satchel for a moment, checking inside. Satisfied, he looked to Vertiline. {Deeper?}

Vertiline glanced at the rock above. She imagined the sand merchant, his sister, and their men. Thought about what would happen if the three of them didn't stop the 'spiders' from carrying them off in the night. The Knight Champion gave a thin-lipped smile. "Right to the bottom."

THE WAILING GOT LOUDER THE FARTHER THEY TRAVELLED THE tunnels. Vertiline killed another two 'spiders', with Armitage beating her number by one more.

Sigh of Day hadn't killed any. The Feybrind had grown sombre the deeper they'd gone, saying only, *{I smell something else,}* but hadn't been drawn on it. Vertiline knew him well enough to give him time to work it out. He wasn't some recruit so young he looked like his balls had dropped last week.

They found a Feybrind before they found the moaner. She was laying on the tunnel floor beside a dispatched spider, another three nearby. Her breath was ragged, her ochre eyes dim with pain. Vertiline drew closer, wary, because something felt off. "Caution, friends."

Sight of Day padded to her right. *{That's what I smelled. She is like me, but not.}* He looked at his hands, then folded them together, holding his peace for a moment. *{Something has changed her.}*

"She looks like you well enough," Armitage rumbled. "Eyes are a different colour, but that's just how it is with you lot."

"She needs aid." Vertiline crouched before the injured Feybrind. Her wounds would've been fatal on a human, but Feybrind were a little tougher. Still, there was a lot of blood on the stony ground. Vertiline held her hands up, drawing that wonderful ochre gaze. She wasn't as good with Handspeak as Geneve, but she could get by. *{We are here to help.}*

Sight of Day crouched by the woman, rummaging in his bag. He withdrew medical supplies: gauze, linen, mosses, and a capped jar of unguent.

The wounded Feybrind eyed them, then her gaze rose to the hulking Armitage lurking behind them. Her fingers fluttered like moths. *{Strange times make strangers of us all.}*

Weird, but okay. "I'm Vertiline." She pointed behind her. "This is Armitage. And he is Sight of Day."

The cat watched them, her breathing laboured. Even after a lifetime of seeing Feybrind hurt but silent with the pain, it unnerved Vertiline to not hear them whimper. *{I am Sands Apart.}*

{Hold still.} Sight of Day uncapped the unguent, spreading some liberally on Sands Apart's wounds. The injured Feybrind bared teeth but lay still enough. *{How did you come to be here, little sister?}*

"Little sister?" Vertiline blinked. "She's regulation size."

Sight of Day half-smiled. *{She is young. I guess perhaps fifty summers, so she is my 'little' sister.}* He looked down. *{She still has many roads to travel.}*

"Fifty. By the Three." Vertiline shifted, her squatting position less than comfortable. "She looks great."

{As do you.}

Vertiline sighed. "It is the Light. The Three have me caught like a fly in amber."

Sands Apart twitched as Sight of Day wrapped her arm with gauze. *{You are...}* Her hands stilled for a moment. *{You are Tresward?}*

They don't miss much. "I was," Vertiline admitted. "I'm not so sure anymore."

Sands Apart reached beneath her sash and pulled out a knife the length of Vertiline's hand. She lunged for Sight of Day. The golden-eyed Feybrind shifted like wheat before the wind, the blade passing by his ear. Vertiline lunged, grabbing not the blade but the hand that held it.

Sands Apart didn't skip a beat, dropping her knife to her other hand, blade reversed, and swung at Vertiline's face. Vertiline shifted her squat, a pattern holding her hand, leaning toward the Feybrind, forearm pivoting into the other woman's elbow.

Bone cracked. The knife chimed as it hit rock. Ochre eyes widened in pain, Sands Apart's mouth open in a silent scream. Vertiline turned from her, arm against her shoulder, and stood, bringing the other woman up, only to swivel back, fist swinging, and smash the Feybrind woman to the floor.

The cat lay still.

"That was unexpected." Armitage shuffled closer, giving Sight of Day a raised eyebrow. "You give her a little boom boom?"

{I do not have 'boom boom'.} The cat frowned, picking up the fallen

knife. He turned it over a few times, then handed it to Armitage. *{I have calming medicines.}*

"What about that insect that bit me?"

{I keep telling you, that was a dream. You imagined it.} But Sight of Day didn't half-smile, glancing instead to the fallen Sands Apart. *{She will not survive this.}*

"She tried to kill you." Vertiline took the knife from Armitage. It was a plain enough blade, but well-made in the Feybrind style. No Tresward Smith put hammer to anvil over it, but it would hold its edge until the sands took them all. "She tried to kill *me*."

"To be fair, a lot of people do." Armitage crouched beside the fallen Feybrind. "What's interesting is she didn't try to kill *me*."

{Our enemy uses humans, Feybrind, and Vhemin.} Sight of Day shrugged. *{Her clue was the Tresward. I don't think you belong to the same knitting circle.}*

Armitage grunted, then dragged the fallen Feybrind's bag toward him. He upended it on the stone floor. Vertiline spied a few knick-knacks. A length of rope. A little jerky. Another blade much like this one. Some parchment, a stoppered inkwell, and a brush.

Sight of Day flipped through the parchment. Most was blank, but one carried a picture of exquisite penmanship. Vertiline took it from him. The picture was unmistakable. A woman with strong shoulders, rust locks wild as she fought both Feybrind and Vhemin. The pen's nib had bitten the parchment hard as the fallen Feybrind were drawn, but the artist had taken no shortcuts in the detail on the woman's face.

Evanne. My baby girl.

Armitage glanced at the parchment, said, "Right, I'm getting some answers," and reached for the unconscious Sands Apart.

{Hold, brother.} Sight of Day offered a half smile by way of apology. *{She will not speak to you.}*

Vertiline's husband glowered. "It might feel pretty good to ask, though."

{It might.} A shrug. *{Perhaps a different approach?}*

"What did you have in mind?"

The cat turned golden eyes further down the tunnel. *{Don't you want to know who's making all the noise?}*

THEY TRUSSED SANDS APART LIKE A HOG. ARMITAGE CARRIED THE unconscious woman like she weighed less than a thought. He wasn't kind about it, and Vertiline winced as the Feybrind's head knocked against the tunnel wall from time to time.

The passage opened into a vaulted chamber. Vertiline held the green glow stick high. It gave back an impression of rocky walls and a semi-even floor. In the middle was a spire that rose to the ceiling. It was thin, made of shining metal. Without doubt, a relic of the ancients, but its purpose was a mystery. Attached to the spire was a clutch of perhaps fifty gently pulsating sacs bound together with a glistening resin.

Also bound to the sacs was the moaner. A human, his pale skin bleached white with pain. He was embedded in the resin to the waist, leaving torso free. Where most people had two arms, he was left with just one, the severed limb on the ground a few paces away.

Dried blood soaked the stone.

The moaner rallied a shade when Vertiline raised her glow stick. His eyes were dulled by pain. *I've seen enough people at the south end of battle to know this man doesn't have long.* The moaner swallowed, throat working hard, then croaked, "Help. Three's mercy, help."

Armitage passed Vertiline, lumbering toward the spire and its gruesome catch. He tossed the Feybrind at the base of the sacs, put hands on hips, and stared up. "They go all the way to the top. Warm inside. There are creatures within." He worried in his mouth for a moment, grimaced, and tossed a shark's tooth aside. "Eggs. Plenty of eating here if we get hungry."

{This looks like a trap.} Sight of Day looked to the ceiling, then pointed to the walls. *{Many holes allowing entry from the spiders. I believe this is their nest, the sacs their brood, and we the dinner when they hatch.}*

Vertiline pressed fingertips to her forehead, feeling weary. "It never ends, does it?"

{Your kind kept making horrors. Don't look at me.}

"Help?" The moaner seemed less certain. "Please. They'll be back soon."

Armitage fetched the man's arm, holding it out to him. "Here you go."

"You're a monster." The moaner seemed surprised.

Sight of Day rolled golden eyes, then hurried to the spire. *{Not all of us. A moment.}* He rummaged in his satchel, withdrawing a tiny, stoppered flask. Within was a clear liquid, tinted green by Vertiline's glowing stick. He popped the cork. *{For the pain.}*

The man drank the liquid, only a little dripping down his chin. "My thanks. Do you have water?"

Armitage glared at Sight of Day. "This one will talk when I ask. He ain't like you lot."

{Give the man some water. Trust me.}

The Vhemin glared harder, but uncapped his canteen and held it to the moaner's lips. The man slurped great gulps before Armitage recapped the canteen. "That's enough. You pull through, you'll get some more."

"I might not pull through if I don't get water."

"Harden the fuck up," Armitage advised.

Vertiline stepped between her husband and dear friend, facing the moaner. "What's your name?"

"Valence." Valence seemed surprised at his admission. "I don't know why I said that."

{Because I gave you an elixir that promotes honesty among the faithless.}

"But... you said it was for the pain!"

{Are you in agony?} Sight of Day gave a small, encouraging nod.

"Well, no."

{Then no lies were told.} He gave a half-step back. *{He's all yours.}*

Vertiline considered the unconscious woman at her feet. "Who's that?"

"Sands Apart."

"Same team, then." She nodded. "Why are you here?"

"Recovery crew." Valence looked alarmed, as if wishing his lips would stop moving. "We didn't get the demon army we wanted, so we came to find out why."

"Hmm." She looked at the spire. "What's that?"

"No idea. It connects to the structure above, but we don't know why."

"How'd you lose your arm?"

"Spiders?" He hesitated. "I think they're spiders."

"You said you were a recovery crew. What were you recovering?"

Valence gave a manful attempt at biting his lip, but the words came anyway. "Cleo came here after the Half-Made, and—"

"You better not be talking about my kid," Armitage warned. "Not unless you want to give up your other arm."

"It's what she calls herself." Valence flailed against the resin, then subsided. "Can you let me out?"

{The elixir offers honesty, not compliance.}

"That's a no." Vertiline kept her voice cool, despite wanting to cut Valence's head from his shoulders. *He knows of Evanne.* "What role do you play?"

"Role?"

"Soldier, sycophant, sorcerer. Pick one."

"I'm a necromancer." Valence winced. "By the Three, why do I keep saying the wrong things?"

{Honesty is uncomfortable when the truth is ugly.} Sight of Day shrugged. *{Perhaps you should have made better life choices.}*

"You make the dead live again." Vertiline looked away. "Did you do it here?"

"Yes." Valence slumped in resignation. "I found one of ours. I woke him. He told me what happened here. Cleo used one of Evanne's kin to force compliance. They had the human queen and used her powers to—"

"The queen is a sinner?" Vertiline took a step closer. "Which gift?"

Valence paled as much as a man with acute blood loss could. "I, uh."

Vertiline reined herself in. *Time for theatre.* "It is of no moment. Come on, we're leaving." She turned heel. Sight of Day blinked, shrugged, and followed.

Armitage growled. "Plenty of good eating on him."

"Hush," she said a little louder than necessary, so Valence would be sure to hear. "You hardly ever eat people anymore."

"Wait! For pity's sake, wait!" Valence sounded like his panic lever had been pulled, voice tense and a higher octave. "The Raven Queen is a Ritualist."

Vertiline paused, keeping her back to the captive man. Armitage spoke. "Like a shaman?"

"Similar." Valence sighed a gust. "Humans have the big bases covered. Evokers, Thaumaturges, Enchanters..."

He wound down as Vertiline turned and gave a baleful glare. "Sinner, I know the weave of your workings. I carried glass and steel for the Three. I know better than you could—"

"Tilly." Armitage put a hand on her arm. She looked down, saw her hand about the hilt of her sword, glass bared a hands breadth from the scabbard. "Easy now."

She slid the blade home with a *snick*. "I know what a Ritualist is."

"Not all of us have your lofty calling." Armitage's tone was light enough as he scratched under his chin. "I know murder, though. Can a Ritualist do that? Or is it something else?"

Valence glanced between Vertiline and the Vhemin. "Do you want to tell him what a Ritualist is, or should I?"

"For pity's sake," she grated. "Get on with it, man. I've been mansplained to enough to tolerate one more round."

Valence's lips went bloodless, but he rallied. "The lesser races, uh." He eyed Sight of Day, who's tail *swish, swished*. "The non-human races do not have our gift. They can call no Light. And aside from the murky powers of the Vhemin shaman, no sorcery does their bidding."

{Lesser, says the man stuck in a spider trap.}

Valence ignored Sight of Day's Handspeak. "Where the line becomes gritty is Ritualism. It is a lesser, uh." He sagged for a moment, head down. "Sorry. It is not considered a great power. If you want a contract to be really binding, you call a Ritualist. They can put a geas upon ink and parchment that can't be broken by any but the Three. They specialise in the, uh," he pursed his lips for a moment, "*mechanics* of magic. If there is a recipe, they can follow it."

Vertiline blinked. "Morgan's a cook?"

"In a manner of speaking." Valence looked at the ceiling for a moment. "The problem with Ritualism is most of the greater, uh. Most of the common gifts do not need an inner working. We do what we do without cant or ritual. The potential for a Ritualist to work wonders is there, but no one has given them a set of instructions."

"Shaman," Armitage grumbled. "They use knotted string, leaves on twine, or scrawled marks in the mud."

"Yes, just because it's not a book doesn't mean it's not an instruction." Valence's tone of contempt was clear.

"Can I break his arm?" Armitage looked thoughtful. "Doesn't need to write anything down for his gift, so I could—"

"I apologise," Valence blurted. "I find myself in an unusual situation. It is clouding my judgement."

"Why would Morgan, surrounded by her Coterie, be unaware of this gift?" Vertiline frowned. "It makes little sense."

"Rituals are quiet works," Valence suggested. "She might not have heard her inner whisper until the bustle of Ravenswall was behind her." He looked thoughtful. "That's not the impressive thing, though. A queen with the gift would be useful for our cause, but it was how Cleo used Evanne to ... *amplify* it."

Vertiline kicked a loose stone. It clattered into the gloom. She thought she heard an answering *tik-tok* that was just a beat too late to be an echo. "Hurry this along, sinner."

"I'm not sure how to explain it." If Valence hadn't been bound, Vertiline could imagine him pacing, wringing his hands. "Cleo thought Evanne a necromancer, and that her power could extort the dead, now risen queen to great wonders. They opened the demon gate sealed these thousand years—"

"Wait, Morgan died?" Armitage frowned. "That's a big detail."

Valence shrugged as much as he was able. "Apparently she passed back in the Battle of Ravenswall."

"Aye." Vertiline nodded. "The High Justiciar told me of it." She looked away out of habit. The pain was still there, Eleni's sacrifice, Geneve's greater one, and Vertiline's own failure to uphold her end of the bargain. "Justiciar Eleni brought her back with the Sway. Swapped forty years of her life for Morgan's four minutes of death."

{*Rough trade.*} Sight of Day turned golden eyes on her. {*She would pay it again, you know.*}

"If she had the chance, but I took that from her."

{*And yet still.*} The cat glanced into the dark. {*Did you hear that?*}

"Yes. So, the dead queen would be more powerful because of Evanne." Vertiline nodded. "Using your corrupt gift to extort others to greater heights."

"It wasn't *me*," Valence said. "I wasn't there."

"But you'd have done it if you were."

"Probably," he admitted. "But Evanne is not a necromancer."

"You just said my kid helped Morgan open a demon gate." Armitage looked at the glow stick he held. "Is this getting dimmer?"

{*It has been for a while now. Your eyes aren't good enough to tell.*}

"You could've said something." Armitage tossed the glow stick into a corner.

{*You'd have just got upset, like you are now.*}

"I'm not..." Armitage glared at the cat. "You'll know when I'm upset, you little—"

"What I'd like to know," Vertiline breezed over the top of him, "is what Evanne is."

"I don't know," Valence said. "She helped Morgan open the gate. She died herself, then came back."

"Evanne died?" Armitage swivelled back from the gloom he'd been staring into. "But she came back?"

"Is there an echo?" Valence sighed.

{*To be fair, I was going to ask the same thing. He was just a beat quicker.*} Sight of Day drew his sword, giving it a flourish. {*I'll get warmed up.*}

Vertiline tried to keep her scream inside. She'd frozen like an ice sheet when the necromancer said her baby girl died, then felt her heart limp back to life when he'd said she'd risen with the next breath. *This makes no sense.* "What is she, sinner? She died and lives. Evanne opened a gate with a Ritualist, a feat neither could do alone. And she's not *here*. So where is she, and why did she go there?"

"No clue," Valence said. "It's what we're trying to work out."

"It's time to go," Armitage growled.

"Wait, what?" Valence's tone became a squeak. "You said you'd free me."

"Sure," Armitage said. "Still will. But after you serve as bait."

"Bait for what?" The glow sticks dimmed rapidly, going sickly, the cavern sagging into darkness, leaving three dim fingers of light at their feet. A skittering came from the dark. "Three's mercy, but bait for what?"

Vertiline drew her blade, keeping the pattern in check. *Not yet.* The glass was heavy, and she could feel the edge of its bite as it tasted the air.

"Bait for those sodden cunt biscuits," her husband said, and she could hear his smile in the darkness.

Vertiline had the sense of a hundred thousand feet on rock as the enemy surged toward them.

Chapter Twenty-Two

Evanne didn't want to go into the tavern. It looked like shit, all dilapidated planks and boarded windows. Not a copper baron was spent in upkeep, and windows were the kind of silver regal-level expense that was as far out of reach here as the stars. The one thing going for it was that it was near Hollyhead's lake, serving as a central hub for the scraggly remains of the townsfolk who were too cowardly to fight when Wandermere came knocking, billy club in hand.

The rain urged her on, but she ignored it for a moment, gathering her cloak close about her shoulders. The rain urged harder, and as added encouragement, tried to find a way down the back of her collar. She gave the clouds a glare.

They didn't care.

"Why aren't we going inside?" Tarragon nestled in her hair, the fairy a warm glow at the curve of where Evanne's shoulder met her neck. "The inside is less wet than the outside."

"It smells like old ass," Evanne sniffed. "Old ass and older cooking fat."

"I just smell your hair. It's nice." The fairy snuggled closer, which

Evanne had to admit wasn't anything bad. "We won't be able to get directions, or a boat, or ... *anything* out here."

"I could steal a boat." A man barged past her, his steps splashing muck, and shouldered into the tavern before her. Evanne didn't lose her balance and resisted the urge to lash out. *He might just be the one guy with a reliable fishing boat.* "I could steal *that* asshole's boat."

"How do you know he's got a boat?" Tarragon peaked out from her hair. "Eww. You're right, it doesn't smell good."

"Wish me luck." Evanne ducked her head, then shouldered through the door. The stench inside wasn't actually as bad as outside, because a low open fire shed smoke into the room, making everything smell like woodsmoke instead of armpit. The smoke managed this by somehow avoiding the crudely hacked hole in the roof that stood in as a chimney. She squinted. *Could just be the ceiling fell in and they called it a day.* The fire pit had the dreary, weary output of unseasoned wood, clearly no expense spared there.

A gaggle of patrons were scattered about the interior. A hag Evanne mistook for a witch gave her a leer, and after a brief moment of shock, Evanne realised it was meant to be alluring, and the woman was no doubt the bar maid. She considered her options, including just how long it'd been since she'd tasted another woman's lips, and then cast the thought aside. *No fucking way.* Against the east wall slumped the remains of a bar, complete with a bartender pretending nothing was wrong with the list of his countertop. The south wall held a small stage, with a sad-looking man holding a lute and wearing a cap adorned with a bedraggled feather.

The angle of the feather might have looked jaunty, if both the feather and man were ten summers younger.

The lute player was doing his best to murder a stanza, and after a moment of serious contemplation Evanne wondered if it was the popular ballad *The Three Come.* It was supposed to be uplifting, a tale of gods back to save the world, penned by some sycophant trying to shine the Three on after Knight Champion Geneve and her band did all the hard work. The words the man sang were right, but the notes were not, and Evanne wished for a brief moment to have wax to stopper her ears.

"What's he doing?" Tarragon hissed in her ear.

"Murdering a bad song," Evanne said.

"Not him. *Him*." The fairy pointed, a shower of glimmer trickling down Evanne's rain-slick cloak.

Evanne followed the fairy's arm, which directed her to the asshole she'd followed in. The asshole was making a path right for the hag, who looked like this was not how she'd wanted to spend the afternoon. Evanne gave it a moment's thought, then decided it looked too hard to deal with before a drink and angled for the bar. Either the barmaid would solve her problem with the asshole or not, and if the latter, well, that's when Hitch might come in handy.

The bartender gave her a hard stare. "Coin?"

"For certain." Evanne nodded. "How generous. Normally it is I who would offer it to you, but I will take your—"

"Do you have it?" He hawked, spat on the floor, then wiped his mouth with the rag he was using to clean a mug.

She pursed her lips. "I've a baron or two." She placed two coppers on the counter, index and middle finger pinning them in place. "I've enough for an ale, and more for information."

The bartender gave a long, world-weary sigh. Evanne knew the Trick of it, saw the exaggerated slump of his shoulders, and ignored the theatre. "Information is expensive."

"Information is as cheap as your ale. This is not the high-class bordellos of fallen Imshir. Nor the calling houses of Ravenswall. No artists paint outside, rosewater scent and all, waiting to tell news of the patrons. We are in a shitty fishing village in a shittier part of the world where it rains all the time. Your single point of note is a lake," she pointed to the south, past the lute-player, "which wasn't there eight hundred years ago."

The bartender squinted. "You're not from around here, are you?"

"And this is why your information isn't expensive. It's likely of low quality if that's the best you've got. Of *course* I'm not from around here. I'm—"

"You look funny," he said. "Your eyes are weird. Your teeth are—"

"My teeth are *fine*," Evanne said. "But my teeth aren't the issue." She fossicked in her memory for another Trick, just the right kind for a man like this. "What if I could promise you something no man here could have?" She tried to focus, but by the Three, the not-really-a-bard was *bad*. His strings were so out of tune it made her just-fine teeth hurt.

He frowned. "And what would that be? We've all we need. Fish, and ale."

The lute-player took that moment to warble his way up the octaves, setting Evanne's just-fine teeth on edge. She turned, bawling, "Be still! We're trying to have a business meeting over here!"

The lutist gathered his dignity, stood, and said, "Think you can do better?"

Evanne smiled, putting a little cat-with-cream into it. "I *know* I can do better. The question is whether this clown," she jerked a thumb at the bartender without looking, "wants to pay for it."

"You what?" said the bartender.

"Pay." Evanne glanced back at him, dirty rag and all. "I promise you a song played better than any you've heard. A once in a lifetime performance that will make children quieten. Seabirds will cease their idle chatter, the very waves calming susurration for—"

"Susurwhat?" The bartender blinked.

"The waves will still, the lake calm." Evanne let the cat-with-cream go and harboured the wolf in her grin. "Men and women will stop their business, bewitched by the music coming from your tavern. It will be a song that all who hear it will remember. And they will remember your tavern as its source, and over time, memory will become legend, and legend myth. The finest bards will come from all corners to visit here, *this* place, where the song was first heard."

No one spoke. The lutist was frozen, barmaid stalled in her push of the asshole's hand from her rear. Even the barman's rag had stopped pushing dirt from one part of the mug to another. Then the fire popped, and the lutist said, "Are you saying I'm playing badly?"

Evanne rolled her eyes, turning back to the barman. "So. What's it to be? An eternity of mediocrity, or a song of ages, in exchange for information that will cost you nothing to give?"

The barman put his mug down. "Can you fight?"

Evanne thought about that. "Kind of?"

"We'll talk after you get yourself out of this, then." He pointed with his chin over Evanne's shoulder.

She turned, taking in the lutist. Bad stubble, the kind of growth that reminded her of parched grass. Patchy in the way that would encourage a *no, thanks* to any offer. He held his lute by the neck, other arm outreached to grab her, but missed because she'd slowed his roll by turning.

He looked at her, his lute, then swung it like a bat. *If there was any doubt this man is a hack, it's gone now. No self-respecting bard uses their instrument as a weapon, unless it's crafted from moonbeams by the ancients.* Evanne was no dab hand at fighting, not like her mother, or even her father, but she liked to think she was quick, and with her mended heart beating right, she wasn't going to run out of puff.

She stepped back, meaning to make an effortless dodge. Her heel caught on detritus, perhaps a fragment of the slumped bar, and she stumbled. The poise and grace she hoped to broadcast was lost as she staggered, but the outcome was positive as the lute swept past her face. The wannabe bard overbalanced, veered to her right, and went down on one knee as she took a seat on her rump. Tarragon squealed in her ear, which wasn't fetching, but let Evanne know the fairy was still okay.

The asshole by the barmaid tried to make free with his hands again, which earned him a wince-inducing right hook from the woman. *She might look like yesterday's breakfast, but she's got a mean swing.* The asshole stumbled back, to Evanne's jaundiced eye more in surprise than impact, collected a stool on his way, and went down in a flail of limbs.

The flailing hit a bleary-eyed fisherman, who took the hit like a pro. Didn't bawl or fuss, just hefted his tankard and went to work on the asshole now on the floor beside him.

The lutist rose, trying to navigate back to Evanne, and that's when the fisherman's tankard broke, sending a hunk of ale-drenched wood into the side of the not-a-bard's face. The not-a-bard, uncertain as to priorities, bellowed, heading for the fisherman.

The fisherman had brought friends, three likely lads who looked like they knew their way about a tavern brawl. Two intercepted the lutist, the third helping his friend beat on the asshole.

For reasons Evanne couldn't get straight, the barmaid shrieked and headed for *her*, which wasn't a good outcome. Evanne struggled upright, dodged a swing, another, and collected a third in her stomach. She growled, feeling the Vhemin in her rise, her hand clutching for a weapon. At her back lay her guitar and scattergun.

The human in her gave a pitying stare to the Vhemin, and Evanne regained some control. "Hold up a second—"

Someone hit her over the head, like, really hard. Wood shot past her face, suggesting *stool*, and she saw Tarragon pop free, stars, rage, and the floor in that order. Evanne bit her lip, tasting hot salty, then someone hauled her up. She had two men on her, the barmaid lining up for a swing.

This is bullshit! "Hitch!" She reached for the spectre, and he flowed into her. Evanne let him hold her, touch her thoughts, then take control. Her body leaned left, the swing taking the man on her right in the jaw, and Evanne's knee came up all by itself to impact with the barmaid's crotch. The outcome wasn't as impressive as it could've been on a man, but Hitch was trying to distract. She felt him buy space, her left shoulder dropping to break the man's grip on that side, and then she leaned right into the man floundering there.

A quick stamp into the back of the left-side man's knee and he was out of action for a moment. Evanne felt Hitch slam her elbow into the guy on the right, then kick the barmaid in the crotch—again!—as the woman came back into the fray.

Her left hand chopped down on the left-side man's neck, then she spun to the right, sending the blade of her right hand into that motherfucker's throat. He coughed, and she followed that with a punch that landed like an anvil.

Back to the barmaid. Just in time to see her fielding another stool, swing half done, so Evanne stepped inside her reach, grabbed an elbow, and help her along. The woman tumbled face-first into a table, the sound of teeth on wood like the scattering of gravel on stone.

The lutist roared, coming at Evanne from her left, and that's when Hitch swung the ancient's scattergun from under her cloak. The weapon whined like an insect, the big chamber beneath the barrel *thrum-clicking*, the nose of the weapon against the lutist's forehead.

Tarragon hovered, then settled back into Evanne's collar, which was very fetching indeed, and not unnoticed by everyone present. Evanne could imagine their thoughts. *A holy weapon, and she has one of the fey with her.*

The man stopped cold. Hitch shivered out of her shadow, misting to nothing. Evanne didn't know what it cost him to do that, but he never stayed for long. She gave a sly, sideways grin. "Hi. Do you want to hear something epic?"

The man gave a feverish nod. "Hello. I am listening! I'm listening *right now.*"

"Good man." She spun the scattergun beneath her cloak, a Trick she'd been practicing for a moment just such as this, then flicked her fingers at him. "Back up. That's right. Keep going. Over there. Sit down." The lutist sat at the table the barmaid hit, helping the woman up beside him without seeming to pay much attention.

The barman cleared his throat, so she turned to give him her attention. "I guess it's time to talk about it, then. You said you'd play in exchange for information." He considered the remains of his bar. "Never seen someone fight like you did. You barely moved, yet you tossed Muriel," he nodded at the stunned barmaid, "aside like she was nothing. Muriel's the town brawling champion. I keep her around for times like this."

Evanne kept the sly smile about her lips. "The deal was a song for information. Are you good for it?"

"I'm good for it." He retrieved a mug. "I'll throw in some ale for free."

Her smile widening, Evanne sauntered to where the lutist had played. She pushed broken furniture aside, retrieved a stool, uprighted it, sat, and pulled her guitar from its sling across her back. Tarragon glimmered from her perch in Evanne's cloak. "What are you going to play?"

"Same thing that hack tried to." Evanne put her fingers on the strings, plucked them, and gave a tuning peg a quarter turn. "This is called *The Three Come*. It was made in Imshir, I think. The days were long and hot. Hard, too. The land across the sea is desolate and doesn't offer kindness easily."

Evanne bowed her head over her guitar, fingers touching strings, soft, and delicate. The ancient guitar Uncle Day had given her set its notes as she asked, the music rising like embers from a fire. She felt the dead about her as she knew she would. She knew them as they arrived. Wolrif, a young man lost in the lake just two summers back, perched on a table. Yvette, his lover, who'd drowned herself after, watched Evanne with yearning only the dead knew. Behind her, Elder Gallile leaned on her cane, all shimmering blue like the dead did.

In Imshir's land, where sun-blazed skies unfurl,
Three gods descended, their banners proudly twirl.
Cophine, the summer warden, her flame aglow,
Ikmae, the middle patron, strength to bestow,
Khiton, the god of endings, wise and bold,
Together they stood, their destiny foretold.

The Three Come, they stand so strong,
In Imshir's heat, they'll right the wrong,
Against the demon horde, they'll fight,
Bringing hope to Imshir's darkest night.

Imshir's sands, unyielding, scorched and dry,
But in their hearts, a blaze that touched the sky.
They vowed to cleanse this land of dread and woe,
With every step, their spirits began to grow,
Cophine's fire, Ikmae's steadfast might,
Khiton's wisdom, guiding them through the night.

The Three Come, they stand so strong,
In Imshir's heat, they'll right the wrong,
Against the demon horde, they'll fight,
Bringing hope to Imshir's darkest night.

. . .

IN THE FALLEN CITY, THE DEMONS GATHERED NEAR,
Their shadows looming, and their intentions clear.
But the Three Come, unbroken and unbowed,
Their unity a shield against the darkest shroud,
With valour and courage, their spirits aflame,
They'd face the demons, and they'd stake their claim.

THE THREE COME, THEY STAND SO STRONG,
In Imshir's heat, they'll right the wrong,
Against the demon horde, they'll fight,
Bringing hope to Imshir's darkest night.

THROUGH BATTLES FIERCE, THEY PRESSED ON UNAFRAID,
In their hearts, the hope of a brighter shade.
Imshir's people, they rallied to their side,
Together they'd conquer, with hearts open wide,
For Cophine, Ikmae, Khiton, and the land they'd mend,
In unity, their strength, they'd find their way to the end.

THE THREE COME, THEY STAND SO STRONG,
In Imshir's heat, they'll right the wrong,
Against the demon horde, they'll fight,
Bringing hope to Imshir's darkest night.

IN THE LAND OF TEBRANI, THEY'LL SING THIS SONG,
Of the Three's triumph, as they stood strong,
Though Imshir's days were long and hard, it's true,
The dawn of better times, their hope shines through.
For in unity and courage, the darkness shall fall,
And Imshir shall rise, as a city for all.

. . .

THE SPECTRES PLAYED WITH HER BY LENDING THEIR STRENGTH TO her song, their need to hers, and giving something back to the living they waited on. Evanne felt the cold gather about her, shivering as her breath misted past blueing lips. *I'm not done. Keep going.* Her fingers wanted to tremble on the strings, but there'd be time for that later. She pushed on, feeling Wolrif and Yvette gather closer, Gallile not far off, the dead hungry for the song she offered. *The Three Come* played, and Evanne sang, her husky voice a balance against the sweetness of the guitar.

When the song was done, Evanne stilled her fingers. "Knight Champion Geneve brought her Light, and her love, and saved the world. Not the Three. No matter what the song says." She stood, facing the bartender. Then swayed, exhausted, and sat. Stood again as Tarragon glimmered inside her cloak, giving her the warmth she craved. Lips still blue, she croaked, "Information."

The bartender's face was wet with tears. "I've never heard music like that."

"And you won't again. I keep counsel with the damned, and I'm here to save this world. Will you keep your part of the bargain?"

"I will," he husked. "But first, I beg your name."

Evanne let her smile fall. "Is it important?"

"People will want to know."

Evanne eyed the spectres in the room. She wanted to say, *You should remember Wolrif, Yvette, and Gallile. Their work is yet undone.* But it wouldn't matter. Not in a place like this. She squared her shoulders. "I'm Evanne, the Half-Made."

WOLRIF, YVETTE, AND GALLILE WALKED WITH HER TO THE JETTY. The old woman's ghost was a little slower, her steps marred by the arthritis that plagued her last living years. They didn't say anything to Evanne.

The dead never spoke to the living.

"Hi," Hitch said.

There's always one. Evanne let the cold wind tug a rust lock free, the wisp tickling her lips. "Done enough resting?"

"Resting is a loaded word," the spectre complained. "It implies I'm off doing naught while you do all the work."

"You ... are," Evanne said. "That's literally what you're doing. You're not here, instead off on some cloud," here she kept her voice light, because the *other* Hitch warned her to not remind him of what he'd lost, "while I'm doing all the hard work of walking about."

"You weren't doing all the hard work of fighting."

"I literally was! I punched. I kicked. I—"

"I did all that." The spectre strolled out over the gently lapping lake water. He waved her cares away. "I—"

"You don't even have hands," Tarragon piped from Evanne's collar. "You can't hit someone."

Evanne closed her eyes, rubbing the bridge of her nose. "It doesn't matter. Are you well, ghost? Are you with us?"

"To the bitter end." His voice was bright, as if the end wasn't bitter at all. *To be fair, he's lived as a shade eight hundred years past his demise. He knows what happens when you die.* "Did you get what you came for?"

"No," Tarragon said.

"Kind of," Evanne hedged.

"The dirty barman said nothing useful." The fairy nestled back into her collar. "It was all, 'Oh my, you sing so well,' or, 'My tavern will be famous'!" Her voice was not a bad impression of the bartender's uncultured tone.

"He said this lake arrived four generations past." Evanne counted on her fingers. "That's what, a couple hundred years?"

"Healthcare sucks now," Hitch said. "I don't know if we can be so bold."

Evanne gave the ghost a little side-eye, but let it lie. "However many years exactly doesn't much matter. He," she pointed at Wolrif, "was one of the first to die in this new lake. Off performing for his sweet," she turned her gaze on the silent Yvette, "who goaded him on. Oh, aye, I can see the Trick of it well enough. I can see how it happened, and how the guilt of it carried you down, too." Evanne frowned, glancing at Gallile. "I've no idea what you're doing here, though."

The old woman said nothing. They never did.

"Maybe she knew the lake wasn't safe," Tarragon said.

Evanne thought about it, then shook her head. "There's no way she could've. Wolrif was the first to drown. Unless..." Evanne turned to Gallile. "You've been below, haven't you?" The old woman nodded, glimmering blue. "You went there before Wolrif, and knew what devils the ancients hid."

"Not devils." Hitch turned his not-face on her. "Riches. She found something worthy of keeping to herself, knew the way around the guardians, and here she stands, a signpost of human greed." Gallile shrugged, denying nothing.

"Can you release them?" Tarragon clambered free, trailing glimmer, and took wing, flitting about the three ghosts. "They look so sad."

"Aye." Evanne waved the question off, suddenly tired. *Always one more thing.* She rubbed her chest where her healed heart beat, stronger than it ever had. "We just need to get there. Get past the guardians. Uncover the riches. And then, maybe, the ghost will be appeased."

"It's never that simple," Tarragon said.

"No, it never is." Evanne tucked her stray lock back under her hood, shivering. Her heart might be stronger, but her blood was still Half-Made. This land was too cold for a part-Vhemin like her. "We'll work it out. First things first. A boat."

Chapter Twenty-Three

Tarragon perched on the prow of the skiff Evanne had liberated from its mooring. No one complained, gave chase, or threw rocks at them, which made a pleasing change. It was a pretty good skiff in a pretty bad town. Tarragon could see how the lines of the boat would love the water, and it didn't leak. A neat coil of rope, a stacked pair of oars, and other oddments inside suggested it was often used, but well cared for.

She glanced at Evanne. The young woman seemed recovered from her ordeal at the tavern. She'd bounced back from the cold of the grave once more, but it didn't mean she always would. Just last night, Tarragon had argued with her, pleaded, raged, and cajoled, but nothing would sway Evanne. The maybe-Vhemin was stubborn, cleaving close to her mission to *do better*, whatever that meant. *Living or dead*, Evanne had said, *I will help them all*.

Tarragon bit her lip. *That's why I love her.*

"What?" Evanne glanced to the fairy as she coaxed the skiff's sails about. The little craft shuddered but didn't toss them overboard.

"Nothing," Tarragon lied, turning back to the lake before them.

"You wanted to come here," Evanne said. "You said—"

"Aye," the fairy said. "I remember it well. I said, 'Come to this place, and we will find where I was born. A place of wonders! And with it, we will fix your armour'."

"Technically, it's my armour," Hitch said.

"Tell you what," Evanne said. "If you can carry it, you can have it."

"That's low," the spectre said.

"It doesn't matter anyway," Evanne said. "I will wear the armour, and you will wear me. Together, we will save the world."

Tarragon bit her lip harder. Jealousy tickled her belly. *I don't even know why I'm jealous! He's dead, and she's a Big, and...*

And, of course, rationale didn't make the feeling go away.

THE INNKEEPER HAD SAID THERE WAS A MOUNTAIN WITHIN A VALE many generations past. 'Many generations' was probably a euphemism for, 'more years than I have fingers to count', but perhaps Tarragon was being unkind. He'd sent a runner and when the boy returned, he'd carried an old scroll. Unfurled, it was a stained and smudged map of the region.

The man had pointed to a section of the map where a small mountain jutted above a plain. Tarragon could imagine swaying green grass with the Itikari enclave atop. *Not much imagination needed; I was born here.* Everything was so *different* now, though. Something had changed this region. Forests grew where roads used to be. The air held a chill that wasn't present before, and it smelled different. Not clean and dry, but wet and rich. Not rotted or anything, just … not the same.

It's making me doubt my memories. Can I even open the door to my home? Will the city remember me?

She glanced back at Evanne. The young woman grinned into the spray as their little boat scuffed the water, rust locks damp from rain, spume, or both. *She might be a problem. She is a maybe-Vhemin. I can see the heart of her, and know she is good, but the city's Council might see only the monster, the creature on the surface.* Still, they both knew that was a problem they'd need to solve, much like that of getting the Artifices to respond to Evanne's touch in the plaguelands.

Then, the problem was she wasn't Vhemin *enough*. The irised doorway into the machine had been sullen and unresponsive until Evanne lost her temper. Perhaps that was a trait the Artifice recognised, but not for long enough. The machine had glowered to somnolence after a mere hundred klicks.

Still, we survived. It got them off the sands and let them journey through other parts of the Forsaken Lands. *Or'sen*, Tarragon corrected herself. *They don't think they're Forsaken anymore.*

"Do you think this is far enough?" Evanne stood, balancing in their small skiff. They'd 'borrowed' a diving bell and anchor from the township. 'Diving bell' was a generous term. This looked like a cauldron with a chunk of glass fitted to the side. A Big could huddle inside, the anchor on the lakebed below, and play a line through a pulley moored to the boat above. This was old, pitted, and to Tarragon's eye a guaranteed way to get tetanus if you were to scratch yourself on it.

The anchor was a hunk of crude stone. Tarragon thought the pulley was seized when they'd 'liberated' it, but it was just a crude friction fit. The idea was to have just enough weight below that the buoyancy of trapped air would keep things more or less equal with the below-average pulley. There wasn't enough air inside to last more than a span of ten minutes before they'd start flagging, but that was fine. If they couldn't open the door within ten minutes, they weren't going to get in at all.

Tarragon watched as Evanne chucked the anchor and bell over the side, skiff bobbing and swaying in an unpleasant manner. The maybe-Vhemin didn't seem to notice, keeping her balance—nay, poise—with ease as she eyed the top of the bell. It didn't immediately sink.

"This is a terrible idea." Hitch strode out over the lake to stare at the diving bell. "This thing was made by inbred hicks in a backwater town that doesn't have a seafaring history."

"Aye," Evanne nodded. "That's true, but it's also true there's a cave of wonders below. A place of history and wealth, treasures and trinkets we can rescue to aid our world. And," her lavender eyes found Tarragon's, "perhaps give a measure of remembrance to those yet living."

"Was that a dig?" The ghost sounded uncertain.

"Calm yourself, spectre." Evanne shucked her wet cloak. "We must go, and that's all there is to it." The maybe-Vhemin wrapped her guitar in the cloak, then stowed it under one arm. Tarragon took a moment to marvel. Free of the cloak, her bare arms were muscled, lean, and hard. Evanne shared a look with her, those not-quite-shark's teeth sharp enough, but within a smile sweet enough to make honey seem bland. "Are you ready, fairy?"

"Me?" Tarragon fluttered. "I, I, uh."

"For certain death. Wonders! The discovery of the dive. Seeing if it's all been worth it." Evanne swept her arm, encompassing the lake.

Tarragon bit her lower lip. "To see if we've wasted our time? To see if things below are as I remember?"

"To see if there is a chance at answers." Evanne held out her hand, and the fairy hopped on, scampered up that wonderfully muscled arm, and perched on her shoulder, holding on to rust locks for balance. "We've come to fix what's broken."

"The armour?"

"That, too." Evanne glanced at the ghost. "Care to take a look below?"

"Lazy living creature." Hitch sank beneath the water. They were left alone for a moment, cold wind making Evanne shiver beneath Tarragon. The fairy put on a little glimmer, sharing her warmth, and she felt Evanne relax a little. The ghost resurfaced. "It is cold and dark below. Oh! There's a lot of water."

Evanne growled. "And the door?"

"Aye, aye, calm yourself. The door is there. Also, a small boat lies in ruins nearby. No body, though." He sniffed. "Might be the one Wolrif used to come out this way. No sign of the lad himself, not even a stray thigh bone."

"Femur," Tarragon said.

"Nor one of those," Hitch agreed. "There may be denizens of the deep that ate the man. Or, Itikari wards did their job."

"We are wasting air." Evanne shucked her boots, made sure her scattergun hung by her side, and gave Tarragon a glance. "Are you ready?"

The fairy took wing. "Let's do this."

Evanne stepped off the side, plunging into the lake. She surfaced with a small cry. "This is very cold!"

Tarragon smiled, then dove in herself. She flutter-swam into the diving bell, surfacing within. It smelled like a rusted barrel, but the inside was dry enough. The small porthole gave a glimpse of the world outside.

Evanne surfaced beside her, the maybe-Vhemin's hair slicked against her head. "Let us descend."

Tarragon offered more glimmer as Evanne played the line through her fingers. The bell descended, the world above slipping from view.

They went into the deep.

THEY DRIFTED LOWER, EVANNE'S STRONG ARMS WORKING THE ROPE. The pulley inside the bell *squeaked*, at a pitch high enough it set Tarragon's teeth on edge.

"Hey. Sparky." Evanne blew a strand of sodden hair away from her face. "Could you, you know?"

Tarragon blinked. "Sorry." She glimmered, lighting the inside of the bell as they went further into the dark. She perched on Evanne's shoulder, feeling the muscles work as the Big took them deeper.

I'm going back home. Why is she doing this? We know repairing the armour is unlikely. But she came anyway.

It was a weird thought. Bigs didn't do things for fairies. They'd *made* the Fairy Kingdom to look after *them*. To fuss with the clever machines that made their lives easier, or longer, and sometimes shorter, depending on whether you worked in the weapons division.

But here was a Big, going down in a smelly diving bell, legs no doubt freezing in the water, her half-Vhemin blood chilled to sluggish slurry, for ... for what?

"I bet that's cold," Hitch offered. He drifted inside the bell, although his voice didn't need air to be heard. "It looks cold. At least it's freshwater."

"Why's. That. Good news?" Evanne was breathing hard. Tarragon knew that her heart worked better than new now, but it was still going to be a lot of work to shift the mass of the diving bell into the deep through a shitty, rusty pulley system.

"No sharks," the spectre said. "Your legs are flailing about. If I was a shark, I'd find them appetising. The trick with sharks is to—"

"No sharks, don't care," Evanne said. She paused for a breather. The air was getting murky, and Tarragon hoped they would be done before carbon dioxide poisoning killed them both. "Anything else that I should worry about?"

"I saw an eel."

"Fine. No problem."

"It was as long as the skiff." Hitch ducked outside, then back in. "I don't think it's here anymore. You can't miss a thing like that."

Evanne started yanking the rope again, and down they went, *squeak squeak, huff huff.* Tarragon felt useless, her glimmer illuminating the bell's interior but not much use otherwise.

Then, the maybe-Vhemin froze. "That's not good."

"What's not good?" Tarragon looked at her, the rope, the bell, and through the porthole where nothing but gloom reigned.

"The rope. It thrummed in my hand." She looked down, perhaps unconsciously stilling her flailing legs. "You sure there's no sharks here?"

"It's twenty, maybe twenty-five meters down, tops," Hitch said.

"Why is that important?" Evanne's eyebrows bunched in confusion. "Do sharks not live in deep water?"

"They *love* deep water," the ghost assured her. "No, that was the eel. It's found your anchor. I think it's chewing on the line, and that means—"

The line snapped, and whatever the ghost thought it meant was lost as they dropped like a stone. Evanne grabbed the inside of the bell, trying to stop the line playing out, but the wet end of the rope snaked through her fingers and was lost to the lake. They descended, a lot faster than before, and while the maybe-Vhemin made no noise but some angry grunting, Tarragon was ashamed to admit she squealed.

There was a *gong* as the bell hit stone, then a *creak* as it lodged on something. The water in the bell foamed, a black, oily shape circling Evanne. *The eel! It's here!*

Evanne snarled, grabbing the creature, which looped about her like a python, its slick scales running through her human fingers. Tarragon lost her perch, hit the water with a splash, and bubbled to the lakebed.

The eel was a monster, and it had the look of a hungry monster. But Evanne was half monster herself, and that half was all bile, spite, and anger. Tarragon caught the glint of steel as the maybe-Vhemin lashed out with a knife, the water murking red, then the eel got in on the action, biting on Evanne's arm.

I can't help. Tarragon couldn't fly through water. Couldn't get up enough speed to punch through the eel, and besides, in a few more moments she'd drown unless she got back into the bell and its precious supply of air.

She swam toward Evanne, even though that seemed suicidal, glimmering as she came, hoping the young woman wouldn't strike her by accident. The good news was that didn't happen, but the bad news was the eel saw her glimmer, changed tactics, and swallowed the fairy. One minute there was sandy, turgid water, the next she was in the gullet of a sea monster. It was slimy, and her glimmer wasn't delivering happy views, all red nastiness. She snatched and flailed, but there wasn't a lot of room, and less air.

I'm going to die.

The fairy thought about burning bright, but ... *what will that do to Evanne?* The water could boil, or turn to scalding steam, or... She flailed, terror clutching at her, the glimmer inside welling to a peak, wanting to be free, to burn, to let her *escape...*

She heard dull *thunk*, and the eel thrashed, then a *ftooom*. The eel stopped moving, water gurgling down around Tarragon. The fairy clawed above, trying to come back up, and popped out into a horror show of gibs and splatter, but also air, which she sucked in big lungfuls of.

Evanne was all bared teeth, the ancient scattergun in her hand, the end trailing smoke, her other hand clutching a fistful of eel. The eel's head was gone, just stray red spray on the inside of the bell.

She used one of her precious cartridges to save me. Tarragon wanted to say *Thank you*, but before she could finish catching her breath, the bell *creaked*. They both froze. Evanne put the gun away. "What did you see? Outside, I mean. Is there a door?"

Tarragon nodded. "About five meters that way." She pointed, remembering from her brief time on the lakebed. "The bell is lodged between rocks. It's fine."

"It's not fine. I just shot the inside of it with a scattergun. And my foot's lodged." Evanne's violet eyes gave little away, but Tarragon heard the tension in her words. "I'm stuck, fairy. I can't get free."

"We'll get you out," Tarragon promised, just as the porthole burst, water spraying into their tiny air pocket.

Chapter Twenty-Four

Evanne yanked her trapped foot, but it was wedged good. Her hair billowed in a nimbus about her head, rust locks turned black by the lake. Tarragon glowed in the murk, orange-gold light casting long shadows among the rocks about Evanne's feet. The worthless diving bell was still lodged on other rocks, befouling her movements.

It looked like her foot was caught in a crevasse. A jagged maw in the lakebed ran beneath the rocks to either side of Evanne. Her foot didn't hurt, not like she'd broken it, but she couldn't get it free.

I've got to cut myself loose. She drew the knife she'd speared the eel with, breath burning in her lungs. Her ankle was below the lake floor, so she'd need to cut through her shin. *Who am I kidding? I'm not going to saw my own leg off with a knife. I don't like pain enough, and besides, it'll take longer than the air I've got.*

Her lungs spasmed and she clenched her mouth closed to stop sucking in murk. Tarragon glimmered closer, eyes wide at her knife. Evanne used it to point to the surface. *Go on. Get.* No sense in two dying because one had big feet.

The fairy looked at the crevasse, then swam down. Evanne tried to shoo her away with her other foot, but the water made her kick sluggish and imprecise. Tarragon swam a lazy circle about her leg, then dove into the gash in the rock by Evanne's foot.

Blackness. *Great. She's going to die, but I'll die without light.*

Hitch shone ghost blue before her. "I'm here. I'll not leave." He sounded wretched, pacing on his not-legs, looking about for an angle. "I'm ... I'm not sure what to do."

Her chest clenched, and she tried not to gasp for breath, but the struggle with the eel had made her breathe hard, and she was at the end of her tether. She sucked in water, coughed, breathed more liquid, flailing against her bound foot, against the water, the rock about her. Evanne knocked the bell, the stubborn thing not moving at all, felt the black getting closer, her heart slowing, her life leaving.

Pain stabbed her trapped leg as the crevasse gripped tighter, before it released in a grinding, grating moan muted by water. Bubbles burst about Evanne, then the weight of the lake dragged her below. She fell fast, going from 'water' to 'water with air', nothing to slow her descent.

She landed on a metal floor, lake sluice pounding her to the ground. She tried to claw away, her movements weak, and for some reason heard Hitch say, "*Counter* clockwise. No, the *other* counter clockwise! That's it. Faster!"

That grinding, grating noise again, the water easing, ebbing, and leaving her gasping for air. *I'm ... breathing! I'm breathing!* She would've laughed if she had the strength, but instead threw up, coughing out water, mud and other slurry. *By the Three there's a lot of it, where's it all coming from...*

And then, she fell on her face, because that felt like the right response.

"All I'm asking is how could you *not* know it was counter clockwise?"

"I failed my exams."

"Even *I* knew... Oh. She's awake." Hitch ghosted closer, his blue glow illuminating the metal Evanne lay on. It was a rusted grill, pitted by time, water, or both.

His blue radiance was outshone by Tarragon's glimmer as the fairy fluttered closer. Her face was drawn, and for the first time Evanne could remember, there were bags under her eyes. "Are you okay?"

"Water," Evanne croaked.

"I would've thought you'd have had enough of that," Hitch said.

"I could open the gate again." Tarragon bit her lip, turning away.

"Gods no," Evanne said. "I'm not that thirsty." She made it upright on the second try, legs sturdy enough despite her fall. She glared at the ceiling, which was also metal, but marked by a long line through the middle. "What is this place?"

"Think of it like a stable, but for machines," Hitch said. "The ancients kept their vehicles here. Wondrous machines that roamed the earth or commanded the skies. They were—"

"It's a hangar," Tarragon said. "But there's nothing here but us. Oh. And this guy."

Evanne followed Tarragon, slightly favouring the leg that'd been caught. It grumbled at her, but at least she was alive to be grumbled at. The fairy flitted away, her glimmer not touching the walls, giving Evanne the impression of a vast space. *This was all under the lake?* No, that wasn't right. This 'hangar' didn't use to be under anything. The fairy stopped over a sad huddle: a now-wet skeleton clothed in the manner of Evanne's time, none of the fancy threads she'd seen ancients' ghosts wearing. Nothing like her cloak she'd taken from the hospital, either.

The remains didn't look savaged. He looked peaceful enough, just laying down, grinning skull staring for all eternity at the ceiling. Clutched in bony fingers was a golden sceptre.

Tarragon settled by the skeleton. Her glow cast shadows along the floor. "He's been here a long time, I guess."

"I don't think so." Evanne squatted by the body, staring at the grinning skull for a while. "I know you, don't I, Wolrif?" The skeleton didn't answer. If he had, that would've been weird or terrifying. "That's a strange kind of sceptre." Evanne freed the golden rod from the corpse.

It was heavy, suggesting it was solid gold. Tarragon flew closer, alighting on the sceptre's tip as Evanne held it out. "It's not a sceptre. It's a semiconductor capacitor."

"A what now?" Evanne blinked.

"What she said," Hitch said.

The fairy gave an eye-roll to the ghost. "How could you *not* know it was a semiconductor capacitor?"

The ghost sighed. "I earned that, didn't I?"

"All I'm saying is, I was the one with hands." The fairy offered a tight, overly sweet smile to Hitch. "I came down here to open the hangar door. With my *hands*." She held them up.

"I get it," Hitch said.

"Do you?" Tarragon shook her hands. "With these, I saved us all! Next time, you try it, and see how far you get."

Hitch sighed and stalked away. Evanne grinned at Tarragon. "Hands, huh?"

"It was ... hard." Tarragon shuddered. "Your foot was stuck in the outer door's mechanism. It wasn't opened properly. I had to charge the system, because this," she tapped the sceptre, "was missing, I guess? I don't know. I opened the doors, and you and half the lake came in." She huffed. "I guess Hitch helped, but only a little. I was panicked, because I thought I was going to lose you, so I was turning the wheel the wrong way, and—"

"Hush," Evanne said. "At least we can get out now. Once we've caught our breath, anyway."

"Uh." Tarragon frowned. "I'm not sure. I think the mechanism jammed. We'll need to find another way out. Shouldn't be too hard, though." She sprinkled some glitterdust on the sceptre. "This will let us turn a few things on, if we can find out where Wolrif took it from."

"That part's easy," Evanne said.

"It is?" Tarragon glanced at the skeleton. "I don't want to sound unconfident in your abilities, but ... he's *dead*."

"That's a mere technicality." Evanne helped Tarragon onto her usual spot on her shoulder before rifling through Wolrif's possessions.

He had a small satchel with an empty canteen, no food, and a small, worn knife. At the satchel's bottom her fingers rasped on wood. She drew out a small, delicately worked box. "Hmm."

"What's that?" Tarragon peered closer.

Evanne fussed with the box, and after a moment it snapped open. Inside, nestled in cloth, was a hoop of white gold. "Answers."

Chapter Twenty-Five

Queen Morgan, ruler of the realm, protector of the free peoples of Or'sen, called the Raven Queen, or the Raven by the uncouth, poked the fire with a stick. It popped in response, which seemed fair. *I pop when you poke me.* Her eyes found the outline of Heser the Cheg, back to the fire, eyes out to the night, ever watchful. Vigilant.

I must end this. It cannot be.

The fire popped again, disagreeing. She turned her gaze on the giant tiger that lay as if dead by the fireside. The grey and black Pakhet was larger than a tiger had a right to be. *More horse than cat.* A wonder of the ancients, by all accounts. A guardian, meant to drive fear into the enemies of the lost Itikari empire.

The tiger rolled onto her back, paws in the air. She let out a small buzz, one paw twitching in her dream. Morgan snorted. *It is not her nature to be terrifying. Her heart is peaceful. Why did my ancestors try and make it any different?*

The Raven Queen stood, smoothing down her trail-worn pants, tugging her jacket close, and running fingers through her hair. *Gods, I'm tired.* But weariness was no excuse. *There is plenty of time to rest when I'm dead.*

Except, that wasn't true. She'd been dead before, and it afforded no respite. Morgan remembered nothing of her time beyond the veil. There were no stories she could tell the living to ease their hearts for those lost at the great battle of Ravenswall. She remembered the pain of death well enough, and the worse pain of coming back to life.

The High Justiciar Eleni had traded her life for Morgan's. It was a brittle kind of trade; an honour debt Morgan couldn't ever settle the ledger for. She'd said, *Why did you bring me back? What's the cost?* Because those questions were important for one who led the free and didn't want *her* debt to fall on *their* shoulders.

Eleni had smiled, tired, skin aged, but eyes youthful and bright. *I brought you back because your death wasn't writ in the heavens. The price is that you have to keep on living.*

It seemed a weird thing to say, because of *course* she was going to keep on living, but then a new menace gripped the throat of Ravenswall, and this time it shook her free. Deception. Knives in the shadows. She'd left to gather the thin threads of hope from Imshir. *I wished the old bonds we shared last time we saved the world together would be good enough. I hadn't accounted for Imshir's troubles.*

Troubles they had in common, it seemed. Feybrind had schemed to bring down Ravenswall, and it was a mercy they'd only gone that far: Imshir was a city made of fire now.

"I'm queen of nothing," she told the fire. It didn't pop this time, which irked her, because it would be nice for someone to argue with her moping.

Morgan arched her back. She was marching well toward her half century, and while her hair was still (mostly) raven black, her bones grumbled enough. She padded—*no point in waking the cat*—to the small pile of metal they were set to guard. An ancient suit of armour, and a blade of impossible power.

The armour was worthless, damaged beyond the skill of any Tresward Smith to repair, but the sword... *oh my*. She drew the blade from its scabbard, its blue-white radiance vying with the firelight for dominance. It felt weightless, the exquisite balance demanding perfection she couldn't offer. It was a bastard blade, a hand and a half sword, suited to fencing one-handed or smiting with two. She swung it, grimaced, and sheathed the blade. *I'm no fencer.* Morgan had been trained by Ravenswall's best, but she felt made of rough mud and sludge holding Requiem. She leaned it against the armour. "We'll find her. I promise."

The sword didn't reply. At least it wasn't as surly as the fire.

"I dislike waiting." Heser the Cheg's deep voice drew her about. The man was made of steel, honour, and sweat. He'd been one of the few who'd fought at Ravenswall, even when all seemed lost. He'd made the call to free the Knight who'd become the city's Saviour when Morgan's mind had been turned against her. He was strong, tall, and she couldn't have him.

She quirked her lips. "Oh, aye. And what's to say I do?"

He blinked. "My queen—"

"Hush, goodman." Morgan softened her tone. "I jest."

Heser sighed, as quietly as a mountain could. "I forget."

"That I can make jokes?"

"That queens are human." He turned back to the night.

Morgan frowned. "I can't be human. I am the throne. The iron will that holds these lands true. The peace that spans—"

"You're tired," Heser said, not turning. "Worn out. Exhausted, as we all are." Pakhet buzzed again. "As *most* of us are. If there was any justice, we'd be done with all this."

Morgan tried a sigh of her own. "There is no 'done'. That is the world of a queen."

He grunted, glancing at her once more. "The Feybrind were supposed to be with us, not against. We'd worked so hard to unite all. I even made an accord with that blasted Vhemin monster," his voice hitched a moment, "Barret, to bring peace. She was stubborn as granite." He subsided, looking down.

"Aye," Morgan said. "She was my counsellor." She turned that about, surprised, because it didn't fit quite right. "She was..."

Heser the Cheg took a turn by the fire, giving it a poke, then tossing his stick into the flames. "She was born on the sands. Fought wars for and against her own. Found kinship with ours. She was my friend."

Morgan walked to his side, then—tentatively, as if it might burn—

put a hand on his shoulder. He let it stay a moment, then sagged, pulling away. Morgan let her hand fall. "Where do you think they are?"

"The bard and the fairy?"

"And the ghost." Morgan could see the spectre now after her experience at the demon gate. He was indistinct, like a memory you'd found in someone else's head, his words soft as a whisper, but he was there nonetheless.

"Bah. Spectres. Ghouls. Bardsong that stirs the soul. What I wish for some honest magic."

"Oh, sirrah?" Morgan brought herself to her full height. "You think mine is dishonest?"

Heser the Cheg glared at the flames. "May I speak freely?"

"You seem to, more and more often." Morgan heard the clip of her words, and tried to hammer them smooth, but they wouldn't fit to the shape she wanted.

Heser turned to her, his eyes hooded in the firelight. "If there are two ways to take something, and one makes you angry or sad, I meant it the other way."

Morgan laughed, feeling the tension leak away. "That is fair counsel, Guardsman."

"Guardsman," he murmured. "I wonder."

"You didn't answer my question."

"The unruly youth and the ancient sprite will be in trouble so deep there will be no swimming out of it," Heser said. "They will have stirred up an ancient evil in their quest for answers that don't exist anymore. The evil will be powerful, perhaps involving the dead, or demons, or horror show monsters from another time."

Morgan nodded. "That all seems true enough. If you fear it, why do you follow them?"

"It's not them I follow."

Chapter Twenty-Six

Armitage heard the enemy. They were faceless, monstrous, a horde descending toward him and his family, thirsting for the blood inside them.

Over eight hundred years ago humans had made his kind. The runt had said so—he'd uncovered how the ancients built Vhemin as monsters to win their wars. They'd made his forebears strong and brave. A salting of crocodile, shark, and snake along the human frame. Some asshole thought it'd be fun to make an army of self-healing warriors, so that's what Vhemin were too.

Armitage had a long time to wrestle with this truth. It didn't fit right at first, because he didn't feel *made*. He felt *real*. And he'd never felt so real as the first time Tilly kissed him. Her hands were warm, so Three-damned *hot*, and when she'd laid them on his chest he wondered if he'd had a stroke and was hallucinating.

But the more he'd thought about it, the more it made sense. They made it so he felt sick and angry when Feybrind were near. They crippled his kin, so they were chained to the desert where the sands were hot and thirsty, always drinking up Vhemin blood. They healed well enough, but that didn't mean they were unkillable. Plenty of shit on the sands wanted to eat you. It was just the kind of rancid ale humans made—thinking of themselves, what they wanted, and how to get other people to give it to them.

Yeah. They'd made Armitage. But they'd put a heart inside him when his metal was on the forge, and he *felt*. It was harder to do the killing business when he thought there was ... *more*. More inside the cats, even though they made him sick. More to humans, their hot hands, ice-blue eyes, and smouldering lips. Lips he'd thought as untouchable as the far away sky. He didn't like those feelings so much. They made him confused, and you died on the sands if you got your ass and head mixed up.

They'd also made him hungry, and he liked that just fine.

He hefted his cudgel. It was a workmanlike weapon, the kind you could bash brains with just as easily as hammering in a fence post. The enemy were everywhere, those damned spider-dog things. The front of the horrors looked like the sharp end, a maw with teeth, and Armitage understood how that worked. The number of legs seemed excessive, but it also seemed the kind of thing those ancient fucks would crank out. Nature didn't make creatures like this without a lot of encouragement.

The glow sticks faded, but his Vhemin eyes did what they'd made them to do. He saw the juice inside people, the beating heat, the salty red. Armitage felt his brother on his right, didn't even need to look to know Roars Like the Singing Sun stood by his side as he always had, always would. He felt sick at the closeness of the Feybrind, but he'd felt sick before. Wouldn't kill him.

Just made him hungrier. Yeah, those ancient fucks had made him a monster, a killer, a hunter, a creature happy in the dark and heat and stink of war, the shit and piss that came from a dead man, the cries from one not gone yet. But they'd given him that heart, and a head, and he could choose what he was hungry for.

He bared shark teeth into the night, then chuckled. "They're coming."

"That doesn't sound fun. Why are you laughing?" Tilly's voice was cool, in command. He knew she stood to his left, glass in hand. No armour, because she'd put the Smithsteel aside, but Armitage didn't know why Tresward wore it in the first place. He'd asked her, *Why so much metal? Looks heavy* and she'd said, *It reminds us who we fight for, and tells those we fight against why they shouldn't.*

More human nonsense, but he loved her, so he took it on the chin. "I'm laughing because they didn't bring enough." He swung the cudgel with a *whoosh, whoosh*, then stepped forward. "Wait here."

Thing was, they made Vhemin for shit like this. The cat couldn't see in absolute darkness, and humans... well, they were barely capable during daylight. He stamped toward the enemy, figuring maybe fifty spider-dogs, or dog-spiders, or whatever they were.

They headed toward him, and he knew, fucking *knew* they could smell the salty red inside him too. His grin widened.

The things crawled on the ceiling and along the floor. Those at ground level weren't a problem, but if one dropped from above, it'd be an issue. Best keep moving. He barrelled toward the surge of enemy, wound back his cudgel like he was playing hockey, and swung. The business end hit a spider-dog in the teeth, sending it to collect another before both impacted the far wall.

One went for his leg, so he stomped down, feeling the crunch, then kicked it away. Something bit his calf, but it felt like amateur hour stuff. He reached down, tearing the monster away with a roar, then tossed it, swung his cudgel like a bat, and splattered the horror across the room.

He knew he'd miscalculated when they surged over him. Legs, teeth, all that, but he was used to being in a scrape. Most people weren't up to beating a motherfucker with another motherfucker, but that was on page one of his playbook. Armitage roared as teeth found his shoulder, and he tore the spider-dog off, but a spray of blood splattered stone and other creatures about him. He felt their hunger increase.

The thing on his shoulder spun away with a *thunk*. His heat vision picked out a dark shaft piercing it. The damn cat shot it in perfect darkness by hearing alone? Damn Feybrind were always showing off.

Still. That's an idea. If the cat could shoot by sound, probably sense of smell too knowing the golden-eyed git, then Armitage should make some noise. He kicked, he stomped, and he laid about with his cudgel.

Something landed on him from above with a *thud*, then a *thunk* tore it away a heartbeat later as the cat shot it.

"What's happening?" Tilly didn't sound alarmed. Course not. She had the Three at her back, and gods were handy in a scrap.

"Busy," he grunted. *Thunk thunk thunk* and there were three less. "The cat's showing off." He swung his cudgel, splattering one at his feet into a mealy slurry connected to a still twitching body.

"Do you need a hand?" Her offhand tone made him turn.

Fuck me. A whole posse had swept past him and were making for her and the cat, and also the asshole glued to the spire. He roared in pursuit, kicked one out of the way, tripped, and the tide rolled over him like a chittering wave.

Chapter Twenty-Seven

T arragon fluttered along behind Evanne as the maybe-
Vhemin stalked the big room. It smelled of drying lake, a
petrichor scent that wasn't entirely unpleasant, but
reminded Tarragon there was a weight of water above them. She shivered. "You won't find a way out."

Evanne ran her hand over a wet wall, then gave Tarragon a glance.
Her wondrous, beautiful eyes held a fragment of Tarragon's glimmer,
her mote of orange-gold a sunrise over violet oceans. *By the Three, she is
glorious.* Tarragon didn't know if she was smitten by Evanne's youth,
attitude, or smarts. *Maybe it's all of the above?* "Chin up, Sandwich.
There will be a way out."

"How do you know?

"Because he," Evanne's arm pointed unerringly towards Wolrif's
corpse, "didn't get this sceptre from in here." She tossed the golden rod
in the air with a gentle spin, catching it with a confident grip. "He
found it somewhere else and brought it here. I don't think he found
another door in the lakebed's floor and, say, walked it over here."

"No." Tarragon glimmered a little brighter. "Maybe he had help."

"You think people live down here?" Evanne's tone held enough
doubt for a legion.

"Of a sort. This is a Fairy Kingdom stronghold." Tarragon wanted to be smug, but her heart wasn't in it. "It might mean there are still some of us alive."

Evanne's face softened. "I'd like that."

"You want more fairies so we can get the door open?"

"Love, there's not enough wonder in the world." The maybe-Vhemin shook her head, her voice turning gentle. "I think you're all that's left. But I'd like there to be more." And with that, she turned and continued stalking.

Did she mean 'wonder' like, me me, *Tarragon me, or fairy me, like, all fairies are cool, and it'd be neat to have more around?* She felt her glimmer drop a few shades. *Fairies* are *cool, but ... I want it to be me me.* She sped after Evanne, landing in her customary perch on the Big's shoulder. Was it her imagination or did Evanne relax a little as she settled?

"Yo. Squishies." Hitch emerged from a wall, beckoning. "Over here."

"Squishies?" Evanne bridled.

"Yeah. You're so ... fleshy. Not like me." He gestured with those not hands at his body. "OG spectre, all the way."

"OG?" Evanne shook her head, rust locks rustling against Tarragon's wings. "Never mind. What's up, oh forgetful sage of ages past?"

"There's a passage behind this wall."

"Less useful than you might think."

"I mean, it ends at this wall." He made an after-you gesture at the blank facade. "What kind of imbecile builds a tunnel that ends at a wall?"

"Someone who's budget ran out?" Tarragon felt a little stir of excitement. "Or, someone who built a secret door?"

"Exactly." Hitch glowed a softer blue. "I, as you've pointed out, don't have hands. So, I can't push the button."

"There's a button?" Evanne hurried toward the wall.

"Figuratively, sure." Hitch shrugged. "There's *something* that opens it."

Tarragon *hmm'd.* "Probably not a secret door." She alighted from Evanne's shoulder, fluttering to the wall and peering. *No, no seam I can see. Wait. There it is.* The fairy drifted up, following the line of the door. Rust and grime had befouled the outline. "Looks like a service tunnel, not a secret door."

"Same thing." Hitch leaned against the wall. "Because there's no service people..." He trailed off, looking at Tarragon. "Sorry."

Evanne glared at the ghost. "That was a dick thing to say, even for you."

"I said I was sorry!"

"Try acting sorry!" The maybe-Vhemin glared. "I know you don't like Tarragon—"

"It's not that—"

"But if we don't get in, there's no fixing the armour, which means no saving the world, righting wrongs, or justice for Imshir. Or don't you get that? We need to, Hitch. So many people are dead, and we don't even know *why*."

Tarragon tried to flutter a little quieter. "I think—"

"I forget," Hitch said. "I forget all the time. Not just things that happened before, but things that happened yesterday, or this morning. It didn't use to happen."

"I know you're forgetful. It's your least charming quality." Evanne put her hands on hips.

"I'm trying to say, I think I'm finally dying." He held up his wrists, no hands at the end. "There's so little left of me anymore, and I think my time is done. I didn't get to do what I needed, and the world's tired of carrying me."

Tarragon tried again. "If we just push this—"

"What do you mean, Hitch?" Evanne's voice caught.

"I mean, I won't be here much longer. I think, anyway." He glanced away. "There's no rulebook, Evanne. But I *am* sorry. I sometimes remember what Tarragon's done, but sometimes I don't, and ... I get angry."

"Great," the fairy said. "Now—"

The wall groaned, rust and dirt flaking away, a little water pooling at the bottom. *Oh no,* Tarragon thought. *I didn't do that, so what's opening it from the other side?*

Chapter Twenty-Eight

Evanne spun the scattergun from its holster faster than she'd
done before. The ancient weapon keened, its pitch
increasing past her hearing as she pointed it into the black of
the secret doorway. Air *hissed* past her legs, tugging her still-wet
breeches, a chill running through her. The wind was stale, like no one
had breathed it for, say, eight hundred years. No hint of rot, no mould,
nothing musky. A slight hint of metal, but not the coppery wonder of
blood. Just ... steel, oiled, and put away for a winter that lasted a
millennium. Evanne's remade heart hammered in her chest. She bared
not-quite-sharp-enough teeth, glaring into a maw dark as pitch.

There was nothing there.

Hitch looked at her, the scattergun, then the doorway, and back to
her. "You good?"

The weapon trembled in her hand. "How did this open?"

"There's a button," Tarragon said. "It's—"

"Who pressed the button?" Evanne let the scattergun nose a little
up, then down, following the barrel with her eyes. *There's really nothing
there.* "I've never seen the sorcery that lets a button press itself."

"Thaumaturgy," Tarragon glittered. "It would—"

"Thing is, there is more than one button." Hitch faced the doorway.

"All I was saying is, there's more than one way to push a button," Tarragon grumbled. "There is *also* more than one button, and I would have got to that."

Evanne closed her eyes for a moment, pinching the bridge of her nose with her free hand. "So, what I'm hearing is there's *another* button, by which a person, or thaumaturgist from a distance, is pressing. And this button will open the door." She opened her eyes, looking to Hitch, then Tarragon.

The fairy nodded. "Yes. The button opened the door. I'm almost certain."

Evanne lowered the scattergun. "That leaves just one problem to solve." She rubbed her bare arms, shivering a little as air wisped past her. "How did the person, or thaumaturgist, know to open the door?"

Hitch brightened and raised a not hand. "I..." Then he lowered it. "I've got nothing."

"There are ways of watching a place from another," Tarragon said.

"Like, a scrying stone?" Evanne scowled at the ceiling above, daring a spy to be there.

"Like," Tarragon agreed in a suspiciously non-specific way.

Evanne slipped the scattergun into its holster, slicked back rust locks, and squared her shoulders. "Let's go meet our watcher."

THE TUNNEL WAS CLEAN ENOUGH, AND DRIER THAN THE ROOM they'd come from. It twisted and turned, Evanne imagining it snaking about subterranean rooms and non-secret passages, taking them to the button-presser. Tarragon flitted a little ahead, trailing glimmer. There was something different about the fairy. An urgency about her, but a buoyancy too, as if she'd left an anchor at the lake bottom and could finally fly, like really *fly*. That maybe things would turn out. It made Evanne's heart warm, despite how she had to hurry to keep up. *I really like this fairy. I want her to be happy. I want her to live. She's so much older*

than me but hasn't spent time above ground. So much dark and silent time as a prisoner of my people, but she forgave me for being one of them, and is helping me, and Hitch, even when he's a huge dick. I think I love her, and I don't know what that means. "So."

"So," the sprite agreed.

Be cool, Evanne. "No cobwebs."

Tarragon turned, flying backward so she could look Evanne in the eye. "Cobwebs mean spiders. Spiders mean insects." She giggled. "And insects mean there are no fairies to keep the nest clean."

Evanne felt a small stir in her chest, right in her remade heart. It felt tight, like happiness, but tight, like caution too. "You think there are still fairies here?"

"Of *course* there are fairies here!" Tarragon flew a loop. "We'll see them soon. They will make us tea and cake, and remake your armour, once we go back for it, and they will like Pakhet, and perhaps tolerate the ghost."

Evanne smiled despite herself. "I just don't want you to get your hopes up."

"Because someone else would clean out the cobwebs?"

"Something like that." Evanne glanced at Hitch. "You feel like scouting?"

"I dunno," the ghost said. "You going to talk about me behind my back?"

"It's likely."

"Sometimes I wish you were as dishonest as everyone else says you are."

"Wait." Evanne frowned. "Who says I'm dishonest?"

"And with that, I'll be right back." The ghost slipped into a wall.

Tarragon flitted on ahead. "Come *on*, Evanne. You'll meet other fairies, good ones I mean. Ones who can Build things, make machines, mend the broken things, and it'll be okay."

Evanne hurried to keep up, Tarragon's sparkle glittering further ahead. "Everything's already okay. Slow down, Sandwich."

The fairy slowed, a grudging orange tone coming into her glimmer. "You Bigs are so plodding."

"It comes with having huge feet and no wings," Evanne said. "The good news is we can lift really heavy things, and don't get swallowed by eels."

"Hah. You just haven't met an eel large enough."

"Hah," she agreed. *I do not want to meet the eel that can swallow me.* "Will the other fairies have a problem with Hitch?"

"Only if he's a dick."

"So, quite likely then," Evanne mused. "But seriously. Do you think they will help us?"

"Once they realise the Itikari armour was his?" At Evanne's nod, Tarragon sighed. "I think so. I don't think they'll have much of a problem with a dead dude who fought for the home team."

Evanne bit her lip. *What is she not saying?* "But."

"But," Tarragon drew the word out, "they might have a problem with a Vhemin. I mean, a mostly-Vhemin. A bit Vhemin?" She squinted. "Just how much Vhemin are you?"

"I'm monster enough, true," Evanne growled, dredging up the Trick to hide her embarrassment. *I can't help what I am.*

Tarragon *psh'd*. "You aren't evil. I can see it, and so will they."

"You sound confident." Evanne wanted to believe it.

"Look. There was a war, a long time ago, and a lot of people died. I was Itikari. Your dad, or like his dad seven times removed, was Vehement Systems. They fought, and I think they ruined everything. More fighting won't fix it."

They rounded a corner, coming to door. *No button, though.* "And you'll explain this to the fairies, and they'll just ... be cool with it?" Evanne tried to hide her doubt.

The door *clicked*, and slid wide, the corridor bathed in radiance from the other side. It was brilliant, like staring into the sun, a pure white that made her teeth hurt. Evanne blinked, shielding her eyes with a hand. Her Vhemin's blood heat vision was clouded too, because the light was burning hot. There wasn't any noise, though, which allowed her to hear a woman's voice, clear as day. "They will not 'be cool' with it. It's time for an accounting."

Chapter Twenty-Nine

I t wasn't some rando threatening her that bothered Evanne. *That seems to happen on a daily.* It was that she couldn't *see* the rando. There was light, heat, and a voice: that's it. The scattergun found its way into her hand, the draw smooth and sure like she knew how to use it. The weapon's heft felt *good*, lending her a confidence as it gave its soft, eager whine. She readied a Trick, throwing her shoulders back, chin jutting. "Come get some."

"I'm over here." The voice was female, strong, and certain of the outcome.

Evanne obliged, pointing the scattergun a little to the right. "How's that?"

"Perfect." The woman practically purred, but this time right in her ear. Words were accompanied by a touch on her elbow. Evanne whirled, which turned out to be the wrong response, as the touch turned to a grip, her whirl into a tumble, and she tasted the ash-metal of the old floor as it smacked her in the face.

The scattergun clattered free, the ancient weapon going silent as Evanne's hand left the grip. *Well, fine.* Evanne growled, rolled, and found that burning radiant light right *there*, *on* her, hands at her throat. *I can't see. I don't understand.* She felt a weight on her stomach, bucked in instinct, and whoever it was tumbled free. Evanne clawed across the floor, hand finding the scattergun, the old grip giving her strength, and she stood, bringing the weapon about.

"Fuck." Tarragon was frozen in the air. Not like ice, because the tiny woman struggled like a dervish that would fit in a teacup, but those invisible hands that had held Evanne's throat moments earlier gripped the fairy. Or that's what it looked like, because Evanne could see right through Tarragon's body as if someone's invisible fist held her, and that fist let you see the other side.

"Gun on the floor," said the woman.

Evanne hesitated. "Or what?"

"You know what? You're right." Tarragon screeched as she moved through the air, the invisible person holding her shifting to a line of cages. Evanne hadn't clocked them when they'd entered, because she had other things to worry about, but sure enough: lots of cages made of gold wire. They didn't look like they were supposed to be here. Stacked, rather than built in. *If the ancients had put these here, they'd look more ... right.* The room itself wasn't huge, perhaps the size of the small library Evanne had liked back home.

Imshir isn't there anymore. I don't have a home.

The library had been small because all it held were books that told stories about the clockwork inside a person, not facts about how *stuff* worked, and that's what Evanne liked. Stories of action and adventure. *And romance. Don't forget that.* Evanne locked eyes with Tarragon, saw the pleading there, and felt her chest seize tight. Tarragon was tossed into a cage, and quick as you like the door was closed with a little *snick*. The fairy threw herself at the door, rattling the tiny bars of her cage, but she was locked in there. *I've got to get her out.* "Hitch? I need you!"

The ghost materialised by her side. "This looks bad."

"Before you do something we'll both forget, let me show you something." The voice had moved to the left this time. There was a *click* and Tarragon arched her back, eyes wide, face locked in a grimace. She stayed like that for a few seconds, then with another *click* fell backward. "These cages are built for fairies. It's hard to damage someone who's designed to live next to radiation or survive a shock, but it turns out all you need is enough joules."

None of this made sense. *Radiation? Joules?* With dawning horror, Evanne saw many cages held a tiny body. *So many fairies. Are they all dead?* Evanne took a faltering step toward Tarragon as the fairy got onto one knee. The *click* came again, and Tarragon made a noise like *jit-jit-jit* before collapsing at the next *click.* "Stop it!"

"Then put the fucking gun *down*, Vhemin cur, or the next time she won't get back up."

"Play along," Hitch suggested. "We don't need the gun anyway."

Evanne gripped the weapon tighter, then sagged, putting it on the ground.

"Good," the voice soothed, sly now. "Kick it away."

Evanne toed the weapon, spinning it across the room where it shored up against a wall with a *clang. I hope Hitch has good moves for taking out an invisible person without use of a scattergun.* She felt her shoulders alive with tension, like a metal wire was threaded through them and someone as strong as her father was pulling it tight. *Relax.*

It's not easy to relax, because something's wrong here. This place is supposed to be deserted. "Who are you?"

"A gift from beyond time, a Hail Mary from the ancients who didn't believe in losing, given to the people of our time to win." There was almost a purr in the voice, a subtle slinkiness that was all cream and a happy cat.

Evanne felt the tension leave her shoulders as she laughed. "Oh, no. You're none of those things. You're a thief with borrowed secrets, playing at miracles in a place that time's forgotten. There's no war, Mary, and no one to fight it for. Hitch, now!" The spectre slid sideways toward her. There was a *snap* and, just like that, he was gone. Evanne blinked, reaching her hand toward where he'd been. *Nothing.* "Hitch?"

The voice chuckled, and this time was right in her ear. "This place was built as a haven. There is no place for the dead in a land of wonders."

Evanne whirled, taking a wild swing, and hit nothing but air. "Face me, coward!"

"As you wish." Across the room the air shimmered, then *relaxed*, like the world was letting down its cares. The colours and lines of the wall and cages shivered, outlining a person, the greys and blues all trickling together, running like wet watercolour. The outline solidified, became substantial, tall, lean, and a hunter.

A Feybrind.

She was furred like all the People, with a pale coat and diamond eyes. Where Uncle Day's gold glance held warmth and safety, this woman's glare held contempt, an ice tundra Evanne's father's cold-blooded kind would never be welcome on. Evanne realised her mouth was open, closed it, then said, "But... you're Feybrind!"

"I am." Her lips moved, the words coming out.

"And you speak!"

A half-smile, the best Feybrind could manage. "I see Vhemin remain as ugly and brutish as ever but have picked up some small skill in observation."

"Maybe Vhemin," said a small voice behind the Feybrind. They both looked to Tarragon. "She's maybe Vhemin." The fairy rocked her hand in a so-so gesture. "Maybe not. Depends on the time of day, I think."

Evanne wanted to chew that over, but the only way that was going to happen was if she got this mysterious pale woman under control. She sidled toward her scattergun, still resting on the ground, as if the Feybrind said, *I don't need it, not for the likes of you.* Evanne bared not-quite-shark-teeth in a jagged smile. *People have underestimated me before. Wouldn't be the first time.* "How is it you talk?"

"You don't want to know how I control this place, or caged the fairy?"

"If you're offering—"

"No," the Feybrind said. "I think not those." She laid fine fingers against the fur at her throat, parting it to reveal a thin black collar. "This is a piece of wonder the ancients made for those of their own who were robbed of words. Sickness could do it, some illnesses so bad even their magics could do naught. This lets a human speak again. Or, as it happens, one of the People. All I had to do was learn how one *should* speak, if one could."

Evanne stopped her sideways travel. "How did you do that?"

That half-smile, and a show of teeth. "Carefully."

{Can you still use your own words?} Evanne moved her hands carefully.

The half-smile dropped. "Do not sully the People's language with your filthy, slurred movements, cur. We should never have let the words leave our fingers in the sight of strangers. They are *ours*, the one thing they left us with!"

Evanne felt the tone of the conversation turn, bad becoming worse, and decided she'd feel better with a weapon in hand. *Fuckit.* She spun, dashing toward her fallen scattergun, made it three steps, and felt the floor fall away beneath her. Arms pinwheeling, she fell, scrabbling for a hold, a fingernail on the edge, anything. Her left hand found the floor's edge, her too-sharp-for-a-human's fingers catching on old metal. She banged against the wall of the pit she'd fallen into. Her feet kicked against the wall as she dangled, scraping against smooth metal. *By the Three, she suckered me into a pit trap. Who even puts a trap in? The ancients were paranoid.*

Then, *I should stop thinking about long-dead idiots and focus on myself. Out, woman.* She reached up with her free hand, looking up, and locked eyes with the Feybrind. The cat had moved fast, quick as all her kind, and stood right above Evanne. "Just like the rest of you. Too quick to anger, too slow to think. And thus, too easily trapped."

Evanne glanced below. Darkness and cold, too black for her human vision to see, too frigid for her Vhemin's eyes to make anything out. Could be a pit of spikes. Could be water. *Unlikely to be a bed of feathers.* "What do you want?"

"Exactly what I've got. A Builder, to make marvels. And I don't," she pulled a knife free from her belt, stabbing it into Evanne's hand, "need *you.*" Evanne screamed, grabbing onto the ledge with her other hand. The Feybrind pulled her knife free, Evanne whimpering at the pain. She dangled by one hand, eying the blood-slicked knife in the Feybrind's hand. "Quit your mewling. That won't kill the likes of you." The half smile came back. "*This* will." The Feybrind stamped down hard on Evanne's undamaged hand. Evanne heard a crunch of bone, screamed, flailed, and then fell.

Chapter Thirty

Tarragon spent a lot of time trying not to throw up. It wasn't just the pain, which alone was something that went deeper than her skin, harder than the time she'd faded in a Vhemin cell, and uglier than Helio's death. The pain was bad! It was super bad. But it was just pain, and she'd been hurt before, by people more pro than this juiced-up Feybrind woman.

No, it was all her dead brothers and sisters.

Sure, she was worried for Evanne. The maybe-Vhemin fell with a scream, the floor sealing after her plummet from the light, and that wasn't great. But Evanne wasn't here, and the cages were. Each one held a dead fairy. Gold and silver wings, no longer shimmering. No glitterdust sparkled. Just a lot of dead, sad, tiny people. They weren't rotted, not like Bigs. Something about people of the Kingdom kept them ... *fresher* for longer.

"So, fairy," the juiced-up git said. "Help me, and your friend lives." Her diamond eyes were close to Tarragon's cage. Not so close Tarragon could gouge them out, but near enough the fairy could see where calculation met promise.

Tarragon gave a sad little laugh. "Do you know how old I am?"

"No." Diamond-eyes seemed amused. "I'd guess you were—"

"I'm older than you, by a long shot. I am *from* the ancients' time. I am an ancient! Last of a miserable family made to serve impossible masters. And in all that time, do you know what I learned?"

The Feybrind pulled back, the amusement in her face falling like winter snow. "I'm sure you'll tell me."

"Never kid a kidder. Never lie to a liar, and never sell to a sales-woman." Tarragon tried an experimental flutter of her wings, but there wasn't much vigour there. "You sent Evanne to her death, and you're holding the promise of a dead woman over me. It won't work."

Feybrind lips pulled back in a half-snarl. "I can cause you—"

"Aye, pain, I know of it. You've a miracle contraption at your wrist." Tarragon pointed to the sleek vambrace on diamond-eye's left wrist. It was a miracle of Tarragon's time, made by a proper Builder, all silvered metal and fey lights. "Such devices give the wielder imagined power. A handshake of steel and miracle, all to control those who won't bend, and force them to break instead." Tarragon leaned forward, gripping the bars of her prison. "It won't work."

The Feybrind's tail lashed. "And why not?"

"Because I'd rather die than help you, and that's all you've got over me. So why don't you play hide and go fuck yourself?"

The Feybrind froze, then half-smiled. "I like you, little Builder. I think I'll keep you a while longer." Another lash of that tail, then she pulled her cloak tighter. "I'll be back."

"Don't hurry on my account. Say." Tarragon pressed close to the bars. "What's that cloak?"

The Feybrind hesitated. "You must know, if you're as old as you say."

"You don't know!" Tarragon crowed. "You found it, but you don't *understand* it. It is a Cloak of Many Colours."

The Feybrind's glance soured like milk in the desert sun. "And why would you tell me this?"

"I want you to wonder what would've been possible if you'd been nicer. That's all." Tarragon huffed and turned her back on the Feybrind. "You can go now."

She heard the *swish, swish* of a lashing tail, then nothing for a handful of heartbeats, then a door creaked before clicking shut.

Tarragon let her breath out. *My hands are shaking! By the Three, I'm trembling like a newborn kitten.*

"That was super stupid," said a totally different voice.

Tarragon jerked in surprise, turning to her right. There, three cells over and one up, was another fairy. "You're not dead!"

"And you're *almost* observant." The tiny woman was about Tarragon's height, but where Tarragon borrowed her colours from both forest and sunrise, the other was blue, from the cerulean ocean to the deep almost-black after midnight. "Dancing Stars is not someone you want to mess with."

"Dancing Stars is the Feybrind?" At the blue fairy's nod, Tarragon paced to the right of her cage, trying to get a better look, but there were three cells and as many dead fairies in the way. "Do I know you?"

"Maybe."

"Do you know me?"

"Of course." The blue fairy knelt, and Tarragon made out perfectly white tiny teeth bared in a fierce grin. "We all know you. Your name is writ in the stars. You are here to save the world."

"Hah. Oh. You're serious?" Tarragon frowned. "I'm not much of a Builder. I failed my exams."

"I know that too."

"So how does a failure save the world?"

The blue-tinged woman sat cross-legged. "You mistake failing one thing for being a failure. A fish cannot climb a tree, but that doesn't mean it's a bad swimmer."

"I'm not a great swimmer, either."

The other woman laughed. "You swim well enough. We've seen it. But there is something else you can do better than almost anyone alive. One special thing we gave you, when we took away everything else. Do you know what it is?"

Tarragon peered, hard, at the other fairy. "Who *are* you?"

"I'm sure you'll work it out." The other fairy glittered like a pale moonbeam. "The Manifest is one part of us, but there's so much more. There were many people who were part of the Itikari. Just like Vehement Systems, there were those driven by greed or hate, and others driven by glorious purpose."

Tarragon frowned. "I don't think greed or hate is much different from purpose. Some people use that word to mean the same thing."

"And yet, there were some people who were good, all the same. Good people gave you something. They didn't know it, and neither did you." The blue woman glittered, just a little, to show she meant it. "We gave you *potential*."

Tarragon blinked. "You sound like my last report card. 'Tarragon Greyflight shows potential but could try harder'."

"Hmm."

Tarragon huffed again, stood, and brushed herself down. "Well, you know my name. And you know my friend, Evanne's."

"'Friend'?" The other fairy's voice held a hint of humour.

Tarragon tried not to blush. "She's a Big."

"Hmm," the blue woman said again.

"Anyway, she's wonderful, and brave, and can, um, *do* stuff." Tarragon felt her voice winding down and rallied. "Why do you care?"

"Because her name is writ upon the stars, too." The fairy leaned forward. "What do you fear, Tarragon Greyflight?"

"Everything." Tarragon was surprised at the misery in her voice. "I don't even have a sword."

"Ah."

"What's that mean?"

"Just, 'ah'. There is no agenda in everything." The other fairy stood, also brushing herself off, and beamed at Tarragon. "Let me introduce myself. I'm—"

"Are you a Builder? A proper one?" Tarragon bit her lip. "Can you get us out of here?"

A pause. "You could say that."

"Okay, cool." Tarragon shivered. "I don't want to hurt again."

"None of us do, but sometimes it's what's required."

Tarragon mulled that for a moment. "Fair enough. What's your name?"

The blue fairy pressed her face to the bars. "I'm Yasmine Glittercone."

Chapter Thirty-One

Sight of Day didn't like death or killing. It was a complicated matter, because those who'd laid down the weave of his soul designed him as a carnivore. He knew how to make limoncello, pancakes, and the best berry compote north of Ravenswall, but he needed to rend flesh to live. The biggest problem with killing was how slow everything else moved. When he was a much younger Feybrind he'd wondered why there were any deer left in the world, or why humans sometimes starved, because it was as easy as thinking to loose an arrow to the slowly plodding retreat of a startled doe. It made light work of murder, which seemed at odds with how the world was made, with everything else hard.

When he'd asked an elder, Wending Stream told him, {*They don't run slow. We run fast,*} and he'd understood. There was a cost to the People's speed, and he'd learned that later on his first run-in with the hated enemy. The monsters had swarmed his forest home, and while his tribe had fought and killed with ease, Feybrind also tired. The Vhemin looked stronger and weren't, and with that bulk they also looked more likely to tire but didn't.

This taught him speed was there for a reason. His kind were too soft, too easily killed, to be slow. They needed to lead the wind just to survive.

And they'd been losing for hundreds of years. The monsters—human and Vhemin—pushed them from the plains to the forests, the forests to the ice, and always Feybrind stepped back. Sight of Day hadn't minded. He'd known he wasn't made for this world. An ill-fitting sock over a broken foot, an ache that never let up, and he'd waited for it to, one day, stop.

Then he met a red-haired warrior, a woman who stood before the Three not in supplication but as a leader. An equal to the gods, not because she used their gifts of Storm and Sway as easily as they did, but because she held courage and love and gentleness with a world that didn't deserve it. Geneve was the Daughter of the Three, pure of heart, *choosing* to save the world, even the Feybrind in it. And so he'd joined her quest because it passed the long, wearisome years, and then he discovered quite by accident that he loved her. A human who could've been his sister, or his cub. And with that realisation came another: *I don't want to die.*

He learned through this mayfly that killing happened, but it *shouldn't*, not to anyone, anywhere, no matter if their skin was scaled, furred, or bald like a baby mole. And that was good enough.

Sight of Day hadn't understood Vertiline at first. Another warrior but following the blade because her heart's love held one too. It was a silly reason to kill, but humans did a lot of dumb things. Then he watched how the teacher became the student, Geneve no longer the kneeling adept but the protecting master. Golden Feybrind eyes saw the cost Vertiline wore for the things she'd done and had to keep doing, and knew the woman hated who she was, and desired to be something she couldn't be.

It broke his heart, and he realised he loved her too.

The largest surprise was when he realised the monster who walked with them loved them both too, burned with it despite his cold blood. The Vhemin lived worse than Feybrind, because no one liked them, not even other Vhemin. And he knew the one thing his brother Armitage feared was losing his new tribe. He feared no skittering monsters from the dark.

Which was another stupid Vhemin thing, because Sight of Day heard their number, thought there were more than fifty, and knew there was only one way they were getting out of this alive. When Armitage charged, Sight of Day felt a building sense of panic, a desire to run to his brother's aid, but he couldn't see. He heard well enough, sending shaft after shaft into the enemy. Sight of Day knew how tall Armitage was, could feel his bulk in the night, and shot around the outline he held in his mind. For the first time in his life, he wondered if he might not be fast enough, because there were so very many creatures coming for them. He wondered if this is what the doe felt like.

I can't see. Why did they give the stupid Vhemin the better eyeballs?

He sensed Vertiline to his left. She would be vibrating with a need for action, but she couldn't see either.

He remembered the elderly Wending Stream's words, her fingers giving them purpose, her truth formed into shapes of meaning, and stored within his heart. {*They don't run slow,*} she'd said, leaning over him, her forest-green eyes deep and cool. Unafraid of the gold brightness in his, calm as gentle breeze from the north. But she'd also said, {*We run fast.*}

Behind him, he felt the the spire's presence, with the stupid human who tried to make the unwilling live again lashed to its base. A thin arm of metal reaching to the roof. His arrows were metal, and his eyes weren't worse than Armitage's. They were much, much better. The cat bared a half-grin, drew two arrows, and held one against the bow, the other between his middle and ring finger. He turned to where he knew the spire was, loosed, and turned back. Not faster than light, but faster than the arrow. The arrow hit the spire, metal tip hitting metal shaft, and sparked.

His eyes, a gift from masters long dead, saw for a brief moment. Too brief for a human to see much, but plenty for a Feybrind. The idiot Vhemin was under a hungering mass of spider-dogs. There were five rattling across the rocky ground toward them, so he loosed his arrow, then sent four more after. He didn't need to hear the *thunks* to know he'd hit. Feybrind didn't miss.

He fired another arrow behind him, got another spark, and he shot a further five horrors that were trying to eat his brother. Vertiline spoke, her words far slower than Handspeak, but of course they couldn't see any words given shape and form rather than sound. "He had a lantern."

The cat thought about which *he* she might mean. *Ah.* The necromancer had a lantern at his belt. It was mired in the sticky mass anchoring him to the spire, but that was fine. Sight of Day spun, padding over ground he couldn't see, shoring up next to the human who brought the sleeping dead back to wakefulness. The man was in a panic, all panting breaths and sharp gasps, which Sight of Day ignored. He laid fursoft hands against the man, feeling to his belt, liberating the lantern.

Turning, the cat tossed the lantern. His fingers found their way to his quiver. Two arrows left. Perfect.

He fired the first, sending it though where he knew the lantern was. He heard the tiny awkward shriek as it pierced the device, then fired again.

The second shaft arced through the midnight black. It hit.

And sparked.

The room bloomed as the lantern wept liquid fire. Spider dogs, a room ablaze, and in the middle of it, Knight Champion Vertiline, glass in hand, and murder whispering in her ear.

Chapter Thirty-Two

Well, this is a load of old ass. Evanne favoured her left ankle, because the drop through the floor hadn't been bad, but the landing sucked. She'd hit in darkness, the light above not doing a great job of telling her anything about the room, and she rolled her foot on some old tat scattered about. The trapdoor above closed, shuttering her in deeper blackness. *The night feels like an old friend at this point.*

The tat she'd identified as trinkets and coins. Her human eyes couldn't pierce the gloom, her Vhemin's blood heat vision not doing any better, but her fingers said the coins were just metal discs. It wasn't easy to tell if they were gold or a material of the ancients worthless after their passing. She pocketed them, then turned a few trinkets over. That one? Probably a doll about the size of her hand. This shape? An empty cup. Another one gave her a fright, small objects conjuring fears of a spider avalanche, but it was just a chipped container full of desiccated nuts. She laughed, nervously, and the sound fell into an abyss, as if she was in a great cavern. She waited after that, just breathing, and was rewarded. There was *some* light, and over time her human eyes brought shape to her. She strained, seeing buildings about, a pathway leading away. She was on what could only be called a promenade, locked in gloom under the lake.

She took another look above at the closed trapdoor. *I fell a long way.* It was lucky she hadn't broken her leg. It looked to be ten metres on a good day, fifteen on a bad, and that's when she realised: *the floor cants.* It was as if she stood on the deck of a sailing ship frozen half-way through rolling the waves.

The roof above wasn't skewed. If it was fine, it meant the floor here wasn't, and that spoke of some deep structural problems. It was the kind of thing Uncle Day would know about, and remembering the golden-eyed Feybrind stabbed her right in the feels. He'd know what to say to make this right. Hell, he'd probably know how to talk to the psycho killer witch Feybrind above so they could all just hug this out.

She pulled her cloak of shadows closer. It wasn't warm down here, and although her crippled heart beat anew, it didn't flow with the blood of her mother. The cloak of shadows preserved her heat well enough and would do until she could make a fire.

Which would take some doing. Down here there looked to be precious little to burn. The floor was made of a pale might-be-marble. The dead people were so far gone there was nothing there that would catch, although they had clothing that seemed to have withstood the ardure of time. Evanne poked about the ruined promenade as her eyes grew more accustomed to the murk. The street was lined with buildings, and a few glances inside suggested they were shops because the layout spoke of shelves and cabinets rather than beds and couches. The contents of the shelves were lost to time, everything ruined or rotted.

A sound made her freeze.

She froze, as if that would make her ears work harder. *If I were half Feybrind I'd hear better, but no, I'm made of two peoples who weren't gifted with anything special there.* No other sound reached her, but she placed her feet with a little more care.

It wasn't easy. Her ankle still sucked, so it was half-hobble, half-padfoot, but she did the best she could. *I wonder how Tarragon is.* The fairy would be welcome now, not just because she was light and heat. Evanne missed her, and wanted to say crazy things like *I love you* or *You are beautiful.* It made no sense because she was pocket-sized, which would make romance ... mechanically tricky. But Evanne's mended heart seemed to urge her to say things when the fairy wasn't there, then her stupid mouth seized like a stuck gear when the elfin woman was near. *For all I'm a master of Tricks, I'm bewitched.*

The sound came again. It was like a metal bar scraping on old stone, and Evanne imagined a horror with a spear dragging it against the cream marble beneath her feet. It was certainly the mania of her overworked imagination, because this place was dead as dead could be. But she sang songs and told stories; it stood to reason being in touch with that side of life gave her bountiful creativity, although Evanne wished her brain would save it for a better time.

Being caught in the open would make her sucky ankle even more suckful, so she crept to a doorway on her left.

It was wide enough to admit two at once. Within she found a store with chest-high glass cabinets against the back wall. The interior held buckets with a cool, gritty substance within. Evanne imagined mould and kept her distance. The ancients were said to keep everything clean; a fungus that grew here was something a wise person wouldn't want to mess with.

A glimmer of ghost-blue caught her eye. Evanne didn't scream or flail, because she was used to the dead, and if there was a thing known to all it was: spectres couldn't speak. They couldn't change the world, not even to pick up a pin, let alone harm a half-blooded vagrant.

The ghost was a girl, maybe ten summers with a tailwind. She wore a frock, nice enough if you were into that kind of thing, and while Evanne could see no colours she fancied it might have been yellow and white. The lighter part had a terrible stain above the heart, the fabric rent, and Evanne figured the wound that killed her took her quick enough. The girl beckoned, drifting through the right wall. That would lead further up the promenade, but through the buildings instead of out in the open.

If only I could walk through walls.

Evanne glared at the wall, then hustled to the back of a store. Sure enough, a thing people of today and ancient times shared was a space out the back. A twinge hit her as she remembered Old Merle, and his storehouse, and the strings she'd stolen, but only because he'd let her.

Deep breaths. Keep moving. She slipped through a door that merely screamed on ancient, rusted hinges rather than howled, finding herself in a room full of crumpled crates and boxes. She frowned, because most things the ancients made stood the test of time. Didn't they?

She lifted the flap of a box. Inside were cylindrical containers. Food, perhaps? She stood, hunting through the dark for a way out. *There.* A door at the back opened into a slender alleyway. It ran parallel to the promenade. Blue hinted ahead, and Evanne headed after the ghost. The spectre wasn't messing around. She caught a glimpse of ether saxe as it flitted from a building, stormed up stairs that no longer existed with the insouciance of a child unaware of the world's dangers, and through a cracked remnant of a door. Evanne hustled to the no-longer-stairs, swore, and slipped into the building through an open window.

Evanne expected a house, because spectres seemed drawn to their past, but she found a wide room with curious panels of glass affixed to the wall. All was cold and dead to her Vhemin's eyes. The floor was a smooth material that sucked up the noise of her footfalls. A couple of skeletons were hanging out on a dilapidated bench in the corner. Evanne ignored them and *tried* ignoring—but without much success—the assault of dust and musk that threatened to steal a sneeze from her. She located intact stairs through a door that fell apart at her touch and headed aloft. A landing with broken boards promised a swift drop to a broken leg, so she edged along beside a railing that looked no stronger than a newborn deer. The craftsmanship was fine enough, but the palings were plain steel that didn't like these conditions.

A glimmer of cobalt drew her to a closed door, so she lifted the latch, took a calming breath, and stepped inside. She found a room perhaps six metres a side, but the bulk of it was taken up by an epic dollhouse on a table at waist height. The girl crouched atop this, blue sifting from her body, the courtesy of luminance letting Evanne's human eyes take in details her heat vision couldn't.

First, the dollhouse: it was all walkways and buildings. Someone built this child a city to play with. There were no dolls left Evanne could see, but the girl went through the motions well enough.

Second, the walls: they had similar glass panels to below, but the spectre's cyan light let Evanne see they were clouded with smoke, rather than mirrors or pictures. The far wall boasted another door which hung wide in a drunkard's leer. The walls held ancient writings which Evanne didn't much care for the look of. They were familiar shapes but made no sense. *By the Three, what is an IMPERIUM CENTRUM?* She frowned at the words for a moment, then glanced to the girl, who still played with the epic dollhouse.

The ghost wanted something, but Evanne was in no mood to play with dolls. Still, the girl was intent, hunched over a large structure. She glanced at Evanne, gave an eyeroll, the meaning of which spanned the ages, and beckoned. Evanne growled, adjusted her guitar's strap, and padded closer. She tested the table for strength, and it didn't creak or pitch a fit, so she vaulted atop and made her way to the girl.

It took a little doing. She tried to step in the streets rather than on the houses. She stubbed her toe, swore, swayed, and planted her foot in the middle of the promenade, then—

The promenade?

Evanne felt her perspective shift as she saw the 'dollhouse' anew. This was no child's toy. There was the store with the cylinders. And back there was where she'd landed from the trapdoor above. The child was hunched over the building they were in. Evanne unslung her guitar, crouched, and eyeballed the girl. "This is a map of the city?"

The girl gave that some thought, then slowly nodded. She stabbed a blue arm at where they were, then along the city toward a taller structure that sat at the end of the table. Evanne crouch-walked toward it, trying not to trip and put her eye out on tiny houses. The taller structure had the look of a tower from which one could see the lay of the land. Perhaps the ghost wanted her to find a better vantage?

Evanne did another scan of the table. The promenade ran the length of the city, but toward the let's-call-it-east was a wide channel that ran perhaps two thirds the city's length. Evanne tried to do some mental math and figured you could fit perhaps ten horse-drawn carts abreast along that laneway.

She hopped off the table, crouching so her eye-line was level with the street, fancying it would give her a better view. When she straightened, the girl was right before her. Evanne leaned on her guitar. "You want me to go to the tower? What's there? Is that where you died?" A head-shake. "Something to help you? Give you peace?"

The girl puzzled over this a moment or two, then shook her head. She just pointed at the tower. Evanne sighed, then leaned against the wall. "Fair enough, spirit. You can't talk, so I'd best just go there myself, hey?" She glanced at her guitar. "Would you like me to play for you?" The girl snapped out like a candle, the pitch of black returning again. Evanne sighed again, rubbing her forehead. *Okay. The ghost doesn't want music. Best get to the tower.*

She turned to the broken door, and the table gave a *click*. Evanne froze into a crouch, ready to drop or run. Nothing else happened for a moment, then the panels around the room gave a soft light. They were full of the patterns of swirling snow, flickering like a troubled fire. Evanne straightened, because nothing seemed to want to eat her face. Some ancient technology woken by her presence perhaps?

Evanne paced the walls, running a hand against cool glass. The panels didn't do anything else. *Best give the table one last look, fix my bearings, and be off.* It wasn't that she didn't trust this room, but she had bigger issues. Tarragon was prisoner above with a psycho Feybrind, and the faster she got there, the better. As she faced the table, she saw motes of ember at a few points in the streets. Some moved, but most didn't. One was near the building she was in.

Evanne leaned closer, reaching a finger out to touch the mote. Her fingers passed clear through it, and she felt no heat or resistance. The panel across from her flickered, then filled like a painting. She saw the street she'd been in well enough, which was also empty.

She looked at the mote, the panel, and back to the mote. "Are you showing me outside? Are you saying there's a, what, an invisible monster out there?" Evanne glowered. "If you're going to show me anything, show me Tarragon. Show me above."

Nothing.

She slammed her fist against the table. "Show me!"

The table trembled, then the entire tableau shifted. Walls fell into the ground, silting away as if made from sand. The table's length became a blank canvas, all except the tower at the end. This stayed upright, but the surface shifted as if Evanne's perspective were watching it rise, then the table hissed, sand rushing up and creating new buildings. The whole thing took but moments.

Evanne realised her hand was still balled in a fist, so she relaxed it. *A good Trick to remember is, when something unexpected happens, make it look like I planned it.* She paced the table's perimeter, feeling her eyebrows draw into a frown that threatened to become a scowl. The panels on the walls reverted to calming snow as if reading her mood. The new let's-call-them-streets still ran a long distance, a central avenue giving passage along the length of the city, but where houses and shops were before this seemed to have more large structures.

An idea tickled the back of her mind as a further red motes blinked into being. She glanced at the central tower, then said, "Further down." The table shifted, hissing as sand trickled like water. The tower's face changed again as if Evanne were travelling further down, then stopped, the table filling with sand structures once more. Larger holding areas, more red motes, and still a central thoroughfare. She glanced at the tower. "So you're always there. This is a map of a multi-level city. And you're a keep for a castle that runs, what, leagues below?"

The tower chose to keep its silence.

"How far down does this go?" The table shimmered, the tower going down once, twice, and a third time, stopping to reveal a level with promenade, but the area was smaller, the structures more utilitarian. Where before there were smaller rooms and laneways, this was connected by stout, workmanlike channels.

"Back up. All the way to the top." The table hissed and changed, taking Evanne's view back up five levels to where they were. She glared at the tower. "*All* the way. To the top, I said. Where I fell from."

The table did nothing.

Evanne felt her scowl relax into a plain ol' frown. She padded to the door at the end of the room and peered out. There was a short corridor ending in a window. Evanne hustled down it, then peered out and up. The world outside was brighter, somehow. She could see, sure enough, there was a roof above, plain as houses. She glanced toward where the map showed the tower should be and goggled in surprise. Where before the streets were mired in blackness, light lay long, cool fingers on the streets. The tower was clearly visible, studded in sullen lamps rising upward. They might once have been evenly spaced, but not all worked. Time robbed many of whatever magic made them work.

Evanne followed their broken line to the ceiling high above. Sure enough, the floor was at a crazy angle to the level above. Perhaps the table couldn't show above because the system broke? What could break a system like this? She leaned on the windowsill, feeling the smooth ancient maybe-marble beneath her hands.

Wait. This is the stone they used, but the level above was mostly made of metal.

Evanne's perspective shifted, her mind *clicking* pieces into a lock. "Murderous bastards!" She scrambled back into the table's room, then tapped the tower. "Show me the top level." No change. "Show me the bottom level." Sand shifted, silted, and became the smaller bottom level. "Top." It changed back to where she was.

Evanne looked up at the roof above. "This is the top. The thing above us is a, what, a ship? A ship crashed into this city?"

She sat on the floor, instrument clattering beside her. *The invaders crashed a giant warship atop Tarragon's home. No wonder she doesn't remember what is above. That was never her home.* Evanne glanced around. "This underground tomb is the ancient city of the fairies. It's been lost for hundreds of years, not because it's at the bottom of a lake, but because there's a huge … ship? An Artifice larger than anything I've heard of? *Something's* on top of it. A battle*ship?*"

The ghostly figure of the long-dead girl materialised beside her. The girl's face was sad, but she nodded. Then she pointed at the tower. The dead might not talk, but they could get the point across. *Go there, bard, and free us all.*

Now the tower was lit with lights to guide her in, Evanne made good time getting there. From her initial vantage they'd seemed wan, but the closer she got the brighter they became. Small suns, a fairy magic long asleep below the corpse of a crash that killed them all.

She paced along, mindful of the red motes the table had showed her. The ghostly girl drifted in her wake, not doing much of anything useful until Evanne came to a barricade in the middle of the thoroughfare. It was poor work, all rotted tables and broken chairs. A fair number of corpses adorned both sides of the barricade. The ones on Evanne's side were mostly solid skeletons you'd expect Vhemin to house within their flesh. Even dead, rotted to naught, they were impressive.

The other side? Humans, more or less. No Feybrind Evanne could see, but a small collection of sticks caught her eye, and she realised, *Those aren't sticks*. She crouched, reaching through the barrier, and—*gently, bard, Three's mercy but be gentle!*—lifted the sad collection through.

It was a fairy, of course. The tiny body was no more than a hand's length tall. Small even for their people. A child? Did they have children? Or just a super-small Builder? The fairy's gossamer wings still glittered in the dim light, but the rest was old death like everyone else. She held the little bundle to her chest for a moment, feeling unaccountably sad. *How do we protect those who need it most? How do we stop those who are too small for the size of our fights?* She thought of Tarragon, the fairy's unstoppable courage, her fierceness, and felt sadder still.

She placed the bundle back by the barricade, stood, and brushed her pants down. "I'm sorry, fairy. I'll find out what did this. I promise." Evanne eyed the barrier, thinking to climb it, but when she put a hand on a table it groaned. "Right. Try climbing that and the whole lot could come down. Be crazy to arrive after the big fight, and die snared in matchwood."

A glance left showed a laneway she could help herself to. Evanne turned that way and found herself face to face with the ghost. The girl shook her head. Evanne glanced around her. "There's a passage. We need to go that way." Another head shake. Evanne growled. "Look, I know you're very dead and all, but this isn't helping. My fr..." *Friend? Not right.* "My Tarragon is up there," she pointed to the roof high above," and she's going to die if I don't hustle."

The ghost put hands on hips, settling in for the duration.

Oh, for goodness sakes. Evanne sidestepped the spectre and headed down the laneway. Her Vhemin blood heat vision just gave her the cold blues and chilly blacks of a world bereft of light and life for hundreds of years. The rays coming from the tower weren't sufficient to lift the mood of the alley, but the ghost hopped along beside her, then in front, back-pedalling as the girl waved her arms frantically.

Evanne glared, storming on, because no one cared about Tarragon, or the world above, or people who were still fucking *alive*, by the Three, and this was no exception. Ahead, a bend in the lane headed toward the tower, so Evanne followed it, then stopped. Ahead of her was a sturdy box. It was the size of a sea chest, roomy enough to hold a body, two if you cut them up well enough. It was just sitting there, not doing anything, but also not a rotted ruin like the rest of the place.

The ghost hung back. Evanne looked at the chest, then the girl. "This is what you're worried about? This is just a box." And she wound up, levelling a kick into the stout wood.

Clunk. It didn't sound hollow. It didn't even really sound like wood. It sounded like ... leather, maybe. Evanne frowned, crouched, and touched the box. It wasn't warm, but the wood felt like parchment, a softness wood didn't have.

She stood, then kicked it again. *Clunk.* Again. *Clunk.* As she was about to give it another jolt, because the sound was just so *weird*, the box opened, revealing a giant maw with more teeth than a tribe of Vhemin. Evanne backed up, because the box would definitely hold a person if it chewed them up, then backed up further as it sprouted legs and two clawed arms. She screamed, turned, and ran. Back around the corner, out into the street, all the while wondering, *Is this what the red motes were? The monsters here aren't invisible. They look like luggage!*

A skidding, clattering sound followed her. A glance showed Evanne the monster followed with enthusiasm, a tongue lolling in a gross parody of a dog's. She pumped harder, her renewed heart up for the challenge, turned toward the barricade, and thought, *What would be great is if I could make that in a single jump.*

She leaped, but her foot caught on a piece of junk, and she crashed into the barricade. Her great fear of earlier, that she would die mired in other people's trash, seemed more real. Evanne thrashed, found an arm tangled worse, yelled, and whirled. The monster was right *there*, but it wasn't eating her face. The ghostly girl was soundlessly shouting at it, and the box tilted slightly as it watched the spectre. *The creature must be magical if it can see spirits.* Evanne tried to free her arm, then saw another sea chest ambling from an alley further down the promenade.

It was a little larger, the lid open but too far away to see if it had more teeth. Evanne snarled, pulled her arm out, and stumbled free of the barricade. Her foot was stuck between a stool's legs, and she shook it off with a clatter. At the noise, the chest closest to her faced her, slavered, and lunged.

Pure instinct took over, and Evanne swung her guitar. It *spronged*, bouncing off the wood, and she fell backward into the barricade. Again. She flailed as an armoire fell on her leg. She hissed in pain, but it blocked off the luggage, which was good as it was about to chew on her. It chewed on the armoire instead, wood crunching under powerful jaws. Evanne kicked the armoire away, getting herself further from the monster but more entangled in the barricade.

The ghost seemed to be everywhere at once. She was on the barricade, gesturing wildly, then away toward the other creature, then back. The luggage closest to Evanne growled as it chewed ancient wood, then rounded on the spectre, lurched, and swallowed her whole.

What the fuck? Evanne stopped moving for a moment, because at no time ever had she seen a ghost impacted by the material world. There were plenty of times she'd wanted to punch Hitch but she may as well try hurting the wind. *It's not fair.* Not that Evanne couldn't hurt ghosts, but that a little girl who'd died already was being eaten by this *thing*. She lurched upright, not sure what the best course of action was, and the girl popped free through the side of the box. The spectre flickered blue, staggered away, the box in pursuit. The other chest hurried, clearly wanting some ghost pie.

Evanne yelled, "Stop!"

No one listened to her. Not the ghost, which ran around in circles, nor the two chests. The girl ran through a wall, the bigger chest on her heels. Unlike her, it couldn't seep through walls, so it made do with brute strength, punching a hole through ancient wood and plaster. The smaller chest followed. A handful of moments later the girl popped through an upstairs wall, the chest still following. The girl ran out onto nothing but air, a feat the chest couldn't compete with. It plummeted to the street, saw her—how, Evanne didn't know, because it didn't have eyes—and slavered toward her.

The ghost zipped in front of it, distracting it, and headed toward the other side of the street. Evanne yelled, "Stop!" again, gripping the neck of her guitar, then, "Stop!"

No one stopped.

I will make them hear me. She almost strangled the guitar with one hand, raised her other, and brought her fingers down on the strings. There was no music there, all discordant noise as she screamed, *//STOP!//*

The guitar vibrated beneath her fingers. She *felt* it, a hot rush, a heat too impossible to hold, as the guitar's voice joined hers. She glanced to the guitar, expecting fire, but there was no flame. Her Vhemin's sight saw no heat, just an ether-blue smoking from the strings. The two chests were frozen, as was the girl. Evanne touched the strings beneath her fingers, thinking, then said, *//COME HERE.//*

She squatted as the chests and dead girl drew around her. Her throat felt raw, sanded, but her blood felt *alive*. She breathed, just *breathed*, then said, "You know how we know we're the good guys? Because we use our words to communicate."

The larger chest nipped at her, and she slapped it away. Another stroke of the strings, this time something melancholy in the note, and she said, *//ENOUGH OF THAT.//* Then, "What are you?"

She felt watched by it, considered, then it spoke like the creaking of a secretaire's lid. "*We are the traps left behind. We are the winter wardens. We are the lost of the fallen.*"

"Huh." Evanne frowned. "That's a long name."

"*Call us mimics.*" The smaller chest sidled closer. "*You are like the enemy, but not. You are,*" it sniffed the air, scenting, "*Vehement.*"

"I'm the Half-Made." Evanne stroked a little music from the strings, feeling the weave of it now, and how the mimics settled. "I'm nobody's enemy. Leastwise, not yours. I'm friend to fairy and Feybrind. I call the Vhemin of the plaguelands my brothers. And if you'll let me sing for you a spell, perhaps we can find a way to share a story or two as well."

The larger box looked to the smaller, then sank to the floor, legs withdrawing. "*I would hear music again, Half-Made. For eight hundred years our ship has been without the voice of dragons. You speak with their will. We will listen.*"

Evanne allowed herself a small smile. *Voice of dragons* had a nice ring. Then she blinked. "Wait, what?" She looked above, then very slowly, to the floor beneath her feet. "What ship?"

Chapter Thirty-Three

The cage wasn't badly made, which sucked. Tarragon was hoping a spot weld would be roughshod, or perhaps someone had used a simple pinion hinge she could tap out, but no, whoever made it knew Builders and didn't spare expense.

"I don't know why you're wasting time with that," Yasmine said. "I already told you the cages are impenetrable."

"I'm looking because I haven't given up." Tarragon glared, aware she was angry because she worried about Evanne. *I'm also worried for myself. That's a thing, too.* "How long have you been here?"

"It's hard to measure time here." The other fairy shrugged. "It could be months, but I think it's more likely years. When I spoke to her mother, well, that was only five summers before I ended up here."

You what now? Tarragon stopped worrying the bars. "Whose mother?"

"Right intent, wrong question." Yasmine sparkled, glitterdust silting through the cages beneath her. "You need to work out where you are first."

"I'm in the fairy citadel, buried beneath the timeless lake of Holly-head. I've come home to rescue the world." Tarragon thought that sounded a little pretentious, so she hedged with, "Well, Evanne and I came. And maybe we'll just rescue a bit of it first."

"Anything strike you as odd about the fairy kingdom?" Yasmine swept her arm about in a *see?* motion. "Notice anything different?"

"Everything's different," Tarragon said. "I don't recognise this at all. This whole place is different, but I was captured. I guess," she realised she was wringing her hands together and smoothed them against her legs, "I hoped I'd work it out as we went along."

"That doesn't sound very Builder of you."

"I failed my exams, okay?" Tarragon bit down on hot words. "I'm not a very good Builder."

"More of a spy?"

"How did you know?"

"A guess." Yasmine had the airy nature of someone who lied and didn't care if you knew. "You don't recognise anything because this isn't the city you left."

Tarragon squinted at her. "You're not making a lot of sense."

"There is a horrible truth at the heart of what you're feeling," Yasmin promised.

"I know," Tarragon said. "I've forgotten so much. I'm not much use to her like this."

The other fairy sat cross-legged, then tapped the side of her head. "You might have failed your exams, but we made you a Builder. You don't have the knowledge. Helio did. But you still have the mind of an engineer."

Tarragon grabbed the bars, pulling herself close. "How do you know about Helio?"

"We made a lot of gambles toward the end," Yasmine admitted. "Helio, you, your whole clutch... you were a part of it. A long throw of the spear, Tarragon. Do you know why we called you Greyflight?"

"Who *are* you?" Tarragon whispered.

"You can work that out yourself." Yasmine tapped the side of her head again, but harder, *slower* this time. "*Think.*"

Tarragon bit her lip. *I'm in a cage meant to hold fairies. I'm in a city that feels foreign, for all it was my home before capture. This fairy is stuck here too, and while I might be worthless, it makes no sense they could capture two of us.*

She glanced at the rows of cages, and the tiny bodies within. *They caught a lot more than just us two. This woman says she knows someone's mother. She knew Helio. And she knows I am a Greyflight.* She gritted her teeth. "I don't know what's going on."

"Good," Yasmin said. "That's the best place to start."

"What?"

"When you think you know what's going on, you make assumptions. A good Builder never assumes. Surely you remember that."

"The world tells its own truth." The axiom came to Tarragon's lips, so deeply embedded it couldn't be lost.

"Hmm." Yasmine glittered again. "And?"

"We..." Tarragon frowned. "We tell the world a new truth."

"We Build," Yasmine agreed. "What truth would you tell?"

"Who *are* you?"

The door slammed open, and the nasty cat Dancing Stars stalked in. Her Cloak of Many Colours was open, her diamond eyes hard. Tarragon hadn't known many Feybrind who had such clear gemstone eyes. It was always ruby or gold, not the clear ice of hate. The black collar about her throat, the thing that let her speak when all her kind were mute, gleamed. "Now we'll talk about how we get this ship flying again."

"No," Yasmine spoke before Tarragon could. "I will not tell you how to get an ark risen."

"There's another Builder here."

"I'm not a very good Builder," Tarragon offered. "Better with a sword."

The Feybrind seethed, which was also unusual for their kind. They were always reserved, and almost always kind. Tarragon remembered Feybrind as calm in the face of other people's storms, but Dancing Stars was all jankiness held on the vibrating leash of rage. "You will bring this wonder back to life. This ship yearns for the skies. Think of how we'd change the world."

"The world was already changed when last it flew," Yasmine said. "When this ship held sway, black against the stars, it shaped things in a way no Builder could."

Tarragon looked to Dancing Stars, then back to Yasmine. "Our city wasn't black. It was gold. It was bright in the night. It flew above the world and promised help to any below."

"That's right." Yasmine nodded encouragingly.

"So," Tarragon started, then stalled out.

"So?" Dancing Stars came to the side of Tarragon's cage, putting a furred hand against the metal. "I can make you hurt until you wish you'd never been born."

Tarragon thought about that. "But why, though?"

Diamond eyes blinked. "What?"

"Why would you do that?" Tarragon hunched away from her. "All the People are makers, like we are." She touched above her heart. "We Build castles in the clouds. You make clothes so fine you can see no seam. Swords of steel with no welds. Everything the Feybrind touches becomes better. I know I'm not a very good Builder, but you're a terrible Feybrind."

Dancing Stars lurched back as if she'd been slapped. "I'm the *best* one there's ever been." She touched her face, then the black necklace at her throat. "The best *ever*." Then she whirled and stormed through the door.

"That was foolish," Yasmine said.

"It felt good, though." Tarragon sat, because her knees shook like a reed in the wind. "I want to throw up."

"Maybe later." Tarragon heard the smile in Yasmine's voice. "You were telling me about how our city wasn't dark against the clouds. Tell me more."

Tarragon didn't want to talk about the everbright city. She didn't remember it well, because she'd last seen it eight hundred years ago, and she'd also been alive almost no time at all before she'd been captured. It didn't anchor in her memory like Evanne's face, or the way the maybe-Vhemin moved.

"I don't want to talk about our city," she said. "What's there to talk about anyway? It died, like everyone and everything else. There's nothing left."

"You're missing the point." Yasmine sounded disappointed, but Tarragon refused to look at her. "For goodness sake. We didn't Build things to break. So, what happened here?"

Tarragon gave her a grudging glare. "Why don't you just tell me?"

"It's better if you see it for yourself." Yasmine still crouched in her cage, but leaned forward, almost eager. "And you might see something I've missed."

"One Builder to another? Even if I'm not a very good Builder?"

"Even then," Yasmine agreed.

Tarragon thought back. It was a long time ago, and she'd been in a Vhemin prison for eight hundred intervening years. But before, she remembered Helio and her going on a mission.

It was dark, because that was the best time for dirty deeds. Tarragon stood at the hangar door, looking over the edge and down on the world below. The hangar door was made for Bigs and their machines, but it served a fairy well enough too.

She wore her combat harness. It fit her like a glove, black tension fabric woven to catch her glimmer and amplify it through her sword. It wouldn't do to be a fairy on recon duty at night if you glowed, so the combat harness stopped all that. It caught light and heat, so even Vehement Systems' abominations couldn't see them.

The monsters were winning, though. They bred like rabbits, were merciless, and walked off mortal wounds. Their masters gave them weapons of heat and light, fury only the righteous Three's Wardens were supposed to hold, and azure armour that turned blade and beam alike.

The dragons helped. But they were too few, and too late. It might be the end of the war, and Tarragon was on the losing side.

Helio touched her arm, startling her. "Don't think that."

"Hah. You don't know what I was thinking." Tarragon hugged herself despite keeping her words bright.

"I think I do." Helio touched his head. "You're wondering how we can win." His fingers touched the black suit over his heart. "You're feeling we've already lost. Hush, now. I feel it too."

Tarragon glanced away. "Are we doing this?"

"We are, but... Where's Mynned?" Helio sighed. "Damn dragons."

Lightning blasted across the sky as Mynned soared past the hangar door. //FRET NOT, TINY FRIENDS. MYNNED COMES.//

Tarragon squinted against the massive buffeting winds from his wings. "Does Mynned always talk about himself in the third person?"

//MYNNED DOES WHATEVER HE WANTS.// She caught a toothy dragon grin, lined with blue embers. Mynned was a black dragon, scales of night, and he breathed lightning. She marked where his scales were melted, because he'd been out last night too. He limped home, complaining of nothing because 'dragons don't complain', but she could see the hurt in him.

He arced across the sky, a long, lazy swoop she could make out mostly because of how he blotted out the skies. She shivered. "He should stay."

"Why?" Helio took a step toward the empty air. "He is a dragon. Do you want to tell him to mind his knitting?" Then he jumped, gossamer wings carrying him away.

"He doesn't knit," she called after Helio. Then, to herself, "I want him to, though. That way he won't die. There are too few of them left. The world didn't know the wonder of dragons before, and they will forget soon."

There were plenty of fairies, though. She leaped after Helio, turning as she flew to mark the great city behind her. It glowed like a solar furnace. There, at the rear: the Skyforges. At the bow, the actinic lances that could raze cities and challenge the sun itself. Midships was where people lived, or tried to, while the war burned below. Artists, magicians, and Three's Wardens. Bright lights against the horrors the demons brought. Brittle spears against the monsters wrought by Vehement Systems.

They were going to lose.

ON THE WING, HELMET VISOR DOWN, TARRAGON SPED AFTER HELIO. Mynned soared farther north. His job was as distraction only. Draw the enemy's *focus, bend it from where it should be, so two very small people could do a thing even a dragon could not.*

"*I can hear you thinking.*" *Helio's voice was calm over the comm.*

"*You cannot," Tarragon said. "You* think *you hear me thinking, but really you're just thinking what I'm thinking.*"

A pause. "What?"

"*Focus, Wing Master." Tarragon put on a burst of speed to fly beside him. The world rolled beneath them, Cophine's face lighting the way. Whole swaths of the countryside were ruinous, charred earth bare, a bleeding heart of the world. The great Corgur had fallen two weeks past, and his mighty body still burned where the dragonscale failed. He'd taken legions with him, but the monsters had legions aplenty. "We must be swift and silent.*"

"*No, I must be swift and silent. You must be Tarragon." Helio glanced her way, and she refused to comment on the grin he wore like a second skin.*

"*So I failed my exams. Do you have to bring it up all the time?*"

His grin faded. "If you knew... No. It is better not." He kept his silence for a few moments before the grin came back. "At least you're my equal with a blade."

"*Equal? EQUAL?" Tarragon wanted to shriek. Yes, yes, Helio had taken her under his wing, teaching her the patterns, how the edge cut and parried, how the point sought the killing blow, and how the arm behind both could change the world. Without all that peskersome Building knowledge in her head, she was able to really focus.*

If she'd been a Big, she was sure the Three's Wardens would have welcomed her as a sister. As it was, she made do with fairy rimfire and looking damn fine while she did it.

They approached their target. It was an armoured convoy protecting stolen knowledge of dragonmaking. Somehow the Vehement bastards had taken over a Skyforge. Intelligence said they meant to blow it up, but after a dragon ate almost all of them, a heroic monster managed to escape as dragonfire purged his kindred. He'd been seen with a gemstone of knowing, etched with the eldritch mysteries of dragonkin.

Thinking about it made Tarragon feel tired.

The knowledge wasn't just information that could be copied. That's not how the Skyforges worked. What Vehement Systems hadn't worked out was how to marry magic and science. Not properly. The gemstone was a spell frozen in amber. They were trying to sherpa it across the plains below to a safehouse, their tame warlocks at the ready to pry the secrets from within.

The convoy had the look of a professional job. Tarragon counted ten Artifices stalking the land. A hundred of the fiendish monsters in blue-runed armour walked beside them, heads on a swivel, ember lances in hand. At the heart of the convoy was a low-slung machine that rolled on treads. An amusing anachronism, but Tarragon could see the tracks it left from up here. That machine was heavy, which meant armour. You could send one of the Three's Wardens in here, but only a Valiant would be able to crack that nut.

There weren't a lot of Valiant sitting on the bench, which left the job to two small fairies.

A staccato crackle from the north drew Tarragon's eye. Blue touched the night. No problem, two small fairies and a dragon. *Mynned was drawing the enemy's attention at distance. He was proud like all his mighty kind, but she had to admit they kind of got the job done.*

The response in the convoy was instant. Artifices shifted their cannons northward. Troops on the ground dropped to fighting crouches, weapons trained in the general direction. All Vehement soldiers knew dragons meant business, and you didn't take one on unless you wanted to die. It was more personal for the ground troops, because Itikari designed dragons to heal by eating the creatures that were front-line shock troopers. The message was clear: dragons don't view you as a threat. They think of you as fuel.

Helio dropped lower, bringing them in from the south. Tarragon stayed on his wing, close enough they could've touched. He gave a tight salute, then peeled off toward the heavily-armoured tank. Tarragon ignored it, heading right for the largest concentration of soldiers.

She wasn't a Builder. She couldn't hack the defences of the tank, subvert its friend-or-foe, and liberate stolen knowledge. Helio could do all that. Builder, saboteur, craftsman, hero—whatever Itikari needed, he rose to the challenge. Tarragon was just a soldier-spy.

But she was a pretty good one.

The black suit had collected her ember all through the flight. She felt buoyant with it, like she could do anything. Maybe even fight a dragon. She was more than enough for the chumps before her. A thrill tickled her as she dropped her head, leading her charge with a shoulder. Tarragon gathered all that stray energy, the magic Itikari put inside her for just this moment, focused, and let it shine.

The suit went from black to clear in a moment, and Tarragon's emberfire blazed. She punched through the back of a blue-runed monster, then another, and another after. She kept going, putting some real curry into her wings, leaving a trail of burning flesh and ash behind her. The armour they so prized melted like wax against the meteoric fury she brought.

Then she was out the other side. She flew up, turning to see what she'd wrought. A swath of the enemy slowly toppled in her wake. The first was just legs, nothing else left, but as her fire ablated their armour and flesh, there was more left. The very last creature she killed had a charred, fairy-sized hole in his breastplate, a wick of flame curling from within.

She bared teeth. Not a grin, something darker in it. Her sword was in her hand, a sliver of Fey Branded-forged metal that gleamed like justice. Tarragon went back down, faster and harder, eyes locked on the visage of a monster whose armour glowed azure. The monster raised her lance, firing, and Tarragon caught the beam on the edge of her steel. The metal glowed, heat flowing into her hands, and the fairy felt alive, because she was from a race of reactor technicians, and there was nothing these fiends could do to her.

The monster, nobody's fool, brought her weapon up in a reflex block. Tarragon cut through it on the way to the creature's head, severing flesh, bone, veins, the works. Her sword was so hot no blood flowed, but the monster fell nonetheless. Even they couldn't walk off a headshot.

Another lance shot caught her, and she revelled in it. Heat flowed into her, and she let herself hover a moment. The creatures fired, and fired, a fusillade of hate. She welcomed it. You knew which side you were on by who shot at you. She flitted higher, soaring between the beams of an Artifice that seemed suddenly aware a dragon wasn't their only foe.

Tarragon ignored it, came around, and made another pass. Her emberfire burned brighter from the energy she'd borrowed from their lances, and she ploughed through their ranks, another burning charnel path of monsters who'd trouble no one ever again.

A creature pulled forth a mace, swinging as she exited one of his comrades. This was why she had the sword. She dodged the swing, a spark on the wind, and rounded on the weapon, her own blade hungry. There was a tiny chime, the mace severed through the haft. Tarragon flitted left and right as the creature swung the useless handle. She couldn't take a physical blow from these creatures, not when their armour was so blue, but her sword could defang them.

Tarragon glowed with righteous fury, shrieking, and dived like an avenging angel.

"DO YOU THINK THAT WAS RIGHT?" HELIO WAS SOMBRE AS THEY FLEW back to the citadel.

Tarragon scoffed. "They would have killed us a hundred times over."

"That's true. But they're the bad guys." Helio's normally zippy flight was a little beleaguered by the crystal he carried. He didn't say how he'd got it from the tank, and Tarragon wouldn't have understood anyway. She hadn't passed her exams.

"What are you saying?"

"I'm not sure." She imagined a shrug, but his black suit hid all. "I think I'm ... tired."

"We know we're the good guys because the bad guys shoot at us."

"We know we're the good guys because we do good things." Helio's voice was level, calm, and perhaps just a shade sad.

"Easy to do good when you passed your exams." She felt the heat in her words and tried to dip the next in a little honey. "I'm only good at one thing."

"I don't think that's true. But the other thing I can't teach." Helio sighed, the comm heavy with it. "You're a master with a blade, no mistake. But you've yet to master yourself."

"What's that supposed to mean?"

"Nothing. Everything."

She held her silence for a spell. The citadel glimmered through a cloud bank then was revealed. Golden splendour, gleaming spires, heavenly radiance, the whole shebang. She marked the conning tower above the control spire near the rear. The spire ran through the citadel, a single strut on which all things led from. Tarragon pushed herself a little faster to bring herself in Helio's eye line. "Want to buzz the tower?"

He laughed. "It wouldn't be very effective. We're black on black, Greyflight. They wouldn't see us."

//THEY WILL SEE ME.// *Mynned soared past, his passage buffeting their smaller bodies. He roared, lightning blue crackling against the cloud, then lanced like a spear toward the citadel's tower.*

Tarragon raised a tiny middle finger in his passage after she'd regained control of flight. "Bastard."

//NO. JUST A DRAGON.// *The black beast sped up as he approached the tower.*

She heard comm chatter. The likes of no stop *and* by the Three Mynned if you dare, *but of course he was a dragon, and dragons didn't kneel. Tarragon grinned as he winged past the tower, lightning crackling against the heavens.*

And she knew. She knew. *They were the good guys.*

"WE DIDN'T DO ANYTHING WRONG," TARRAGON SAID. "WE DID IT all right. We fought the darkness. We battled demons and monsters. We were on the side of dragons, Yasmine. Dragons! They flew so high. I remember. I remember it all."

Yasmine held her peace a spell. "And whose side were the dragons on?"

"Their own. They're dragons."

"Huh."

"What's that supposed to mean?"

"It means 'huh'." Yasmine sighed. "We did you a great injustice, Tarragon of the Grey Flight. We robbed you of purpose and gave you another. We planned, and schemed, and did things we shouldn't have done, all because to not do them would damn us all."

"What the fuck," Tarragon said.

Yasmine straightened. "The Three see things beyond mortal ken."

"Blah, blah, get to the point."

The other fairy snickered. "I can see why Helio liked you."

"He was my friend. He died." She felt the bite of the words against her lips, the petulance in them. "All my friends do. I'm the only one left."

"Huh."

"Three's mercy." Tarragon sat in disgust.

"Helio had a job. He did it. You had a job. You've yet to do it." Yasmine's voice was soft, like spring dawn. "Since you remember everything, tell me: what's wrong with this room?"

Tarragon didn't want to think anymore. *I'm tired, too. Everything is hard. The world is upside down, and I'm in love with a monster. I used to kill Evanne's kind, and now I hurt when she's not here. The citadel is broken. They changed the locks while I was away. The hangar was on top, not the side, and*—

She jerked to her feet like a puppet yanked on strings. "This isn't the citadel!" She whirled, glaring at Yasmine. "But it's where the citadel *was*. So, where are we?"

Yasmine smiled, gently, as if about to give the bad news to a cancer patient no longer in remission. "We're in the worst place we could be. We're in the machine that killed our home."

Chapter Thirty-Four

T his is some bullshit. Vertiline waited for her husband to call for help, solve the problem, or whatever damn thing he was up to. She heard the cat firing his bow, and imagined Sight of Day was doing his best in the pitch shroud that settled on them. She couldn't see, and the Sway still hurt so much to use. Not the pain in her throat or the shriving of her soul. Vertiline was used to that. It was the pain of others, and the consequence the Sway brought. But it was *there*, itching at her, making her throat tighten, and her teeth clench. It wanted her to speak, to bend the world to her will, to alter reality to suit her whim.

Almost every time she'd used the power someone died. *If I use it, will I help my husband or kill him?* She knew the logic was flawed at a base level, but her heart wasn't convinced. Imshir fell, and her baby girl was lost when she but called a glimmer of radiance to her side. *I do not understand why the Three hate me so.*

Perhaps it was because Vertiline was better as a Knight than Cleric but had to be both now her order were all but forgotten. And if the Tresward were a dim memory, the Three might consider her bargain null, and come for an accounting. She was supposed to resurrect the order, not bury the remainder.

She bided, thinking, *If my love asks for aid, I will raise the Light*, or, *If Sight of Day needs me, I will be there.* And she waited, glass in hand, while her shoulders hunched so much they near squeezed her head off. Vertiline almost cried out when she heard her husband fall. She froze, feet welded to the floor, because he hadn't *asked*, and every time she put her will into the world on her own hundreds of people died. Then Sight of Day did something that rattled, and something else that sounded like a whisper on the wind, and fire bloomed.

And with it, hope in her heart.

We are in a place no sunlight touches. These creatures haven't learned to fear the Light. I will teach them.

She saw the mantle of dog spiders. They coated the walls, ran down the spire behind her toward the pitiful bait-in-the-trap sinner there, carpeted the floor, and came for her. Her, and *hers*, and in that moment she saw enough for the pattern to fall on her, each word of its name like a hammer from above.

Seven Seasons Reaping.

She knew where her feet should be, and they were. Vertiline knew how her blade should start at high guard, and that's where glass glimmered. Each movement perfect, and as her sword sang the hymn of death, golden Light infused the blade. Vertiline heard the tolling of mighty bells as reality parted for a moment, a mere fraction of time, but making the Three's Light real. A butterfly rested on the narrow prism of her blade's edge, gold-and-black wings fanning against the warmth of an invisible sun.

Vertiline stepped forward, blade coming down, and three spider dogs ignited in a single cut. She stepped to her right, one foot behind the other, turning the linear movement into a spin as she straightened her stance. A spider dog fell from above into the perfect upswing she'd readied for it, and the bells' toll became the rumble of thunder.

Seven Seasons Reaping was one of black Khiton's favoured graces. He'd passed it down for a single soldier on a battlefield of the fallen. A late, sole reinforcement coming to defend against the damage of a thousand blows. He'd meant it as an end of battle, but Vertiline saw the horrors coming forth from the walls, and knew it was simply a different kind of beginning.

The Light flowed from her blade, droplets of golden shimmer hissing like molten stone as they hit the ground. She stepped into the fifth movement of the stanza, blade sweeping a head-height three-sixty-degree arc about her. No spider dogs were that tall, but the Light blazed from her glass, spraying liquid fury. A dozen, nay twenty spider dogs died.

And still they came.

She saw Sight of Day by the spire, his blade out as he fenced with those coming down the pillar. Vertiline moved toward where her husband fell, saw a spider dog rise with fangs bared, and knew it for the killing strike.

It wasn't in the pattern, but it must happen. She reached with her metal hand, fingers splayed wide, and heard thunder roar. She closed her hand into a fist and pulled it down. Something resisted, but only for a moment, then the sky fell.

Lightning blasted through the roof of the chamber. It coiled about her closed hand, blue-white and feral. She screamed, tossing her hand toward Armitage, feeling her control of the Three's power a brittle thing, her arm trembling to hold it steady, and a wave of rolling electricity coiled across the ground.

Energy arced from spider dog to spider dog, curling about the chamber, a web of linked rage. It lashed from her clenched fist, a train of horses on a leash too frail to hold it, trembled against its bridle, then snapped it. Energy crackled to the spire, the metal turning brilliant white, and she thought *no, no, not him, never him* as the Light sought release through the man and Feybrind at its base.

Silence. Smoke and ash swirled through the dim rays peaking through the rent in the cavern's roof.

Vertiline held her shaking fist against her body like an injured bird. She swayed, then slumped to one knee. She couldn't look. Not at what she'd done.

Not again.

Chapter Thirty-Five

It makes no sense. There is no ship this big. Evanne stamped her way toward the tower. The mimics followed, a small troupe now at heel. She had suitcases and armoires, writing desks and sea chests. There was even a cabinet with sliding drawers that looked hungrier than any furniture had a right to. They clattered along, keeping time with snapping of buckles or clunking of lids as she played. Her throat felt raw from whatever it was she'd done before. She'd reached out, but reached in too, found something there she wasn't sure had been there before, but it didn't make her feel bigger.

I feel complete.

A small sewing box kept pace at her feet. "*Why do you go to the place where everyone dies?*"

Evanne didn't slow, because there was always some fool spouting *portent this* or *doom that*. "Everyone dies everywhere, Box."

"*I didn't.*" The sewing box seemed thoughtful, if a box could. "*I have been a sewing box for a thousand years or more.*"

"Wait. A thousand? But the world died eight hundred years ago." Evanne gave it a few moments' thought. "The ancients made you before they needed weapons?"

"*Humans always needed weapons.*" The sewing box clattered a happy clip as she struck a chord, notes dripping from her guitar like invisible happiness. *"Do you know what a contract is?"*

"It is paper that two liars use to Trick each other."

The box snickered shut. *"Yes. I was a liar. I bartered my soul for a life of luxury. I lived well before, and now I live forever as a sewing box."*

Evanne glanced to the tower. It loomed above, the lights spearing the gloom doing little to relieve the oppressive air. *All the more reason to play for joy.* "The ancients ... animated objects with human souls?" She felt ill. "That's inhuman."

"It is very human." The sewing box clipped a few steps ahead of her, bouncing from corner to corner as she played. *"The next part of your journey needs care, Half-Made. Within the tower, all die. We can't go with you."*

"Why not?" They rounded a last bank of derelict buildings, all with the look of tiny houses stacked atop each other. *Oh, for a hundred years to look inside these places. There must be so many stories.* The tower was suddenly *right there*, hulking, impassive, eternal.

"It is forbidden."

"All the people doing the forbidding are gone." Evanne turned a small circle, facing each mimic one by one. "You're with me now, and we make our own rules. We're different, and it's fine they didn't understand."

"We're different." The sewing box snapped thoughtfully. *"No one knows how much."*

"Come on." Evanne led them, clittering and clattering, stamping and clonking, a merry band in a world of depression, to the front of the tower. Giant doors were at the base. They were ajar, wide enough for all to enter, so they did. Evanne's blood heat vision showed her the cool of centuries, but the warmth of rekindled life lay right below the floor. They were in a large room sporting many exits, with a single huge dais in the floor. It was underneath this the heat lay.

So, she went right for it.

Standing on the dais, animated luggage all about, she let her fingers slow, teasing the melody from joy to contentment. The mimics settled, still keeping time, still with her, but given respite from excited dancing for a moment. *The crowd needs to breathe.*

The floor jolted, then rose. She'd more or less expected something like that, although *down* was more of where she thought they'd end up. No one put murder rooms in the top levels of their manse, so this made a pleasant change from the last weeks' fare.

The dais was a smooth ride. Even with an array of furniture, it didn't seem to mind the weight. They went up, and farther still. There were illumination globes in the shaft, but not all worked, casting their elevation into staccato bursts of light and shadow. They slowed, then stopped just short of a platform leading to a door. The dais *graunched*, shuddered, and was still.

Evanne sighed. *It was too good to last.* She eyed the platform above. "Anyone good for a boost?"

An armoire sidled closer, opening its doors for her. Shelves within looked harmless enough. "*Use my mouth.*"

Evanne paused, hand half-way toward a shelf. "Your what now?"

"*Should I have said a different word? I'm not used to words anymore.*"

"Just say 'shelf'. You've got shelves here." Evanne tapped one thoughtfully. "This is a mouth? What do you eat?"

The sewing box nudged her ankle. "*Often humans ask questions they don't want to know the answer to.*"

Evanne blew a rust-lock strand from her eyes, then clambered on the … shelves. The mimic didn't snap its doors shut, gobbling her up, which was a possibility she felt strongly implied. The other mimics watched with their not-eyes, attentive as she climbed. Waiting. Expecting. Yearning. *They are so lost.* She closed her eyes for a moment on the last shelf, hand atop the armoire. It wasn't even dusty. "I'll come back for you. I'll come back for you all. I promise."

The sewing box hopped at the armoire's base. "*We will wait until the end of time for that day.*"

"Not that long. I think maybe five minutes." She showed not-quite-shark-teeth. "Trust me." With that, she reached up, hand on the platform, and hauled herself up.

THE ROOM WAS ENORMOUS. EVANNE FELT IT SPANNED THE ENTIRE width of the tower. There were no columns supporting the roof. The ancients must have had wonderful carpenters to build such as this. Arrayed around the room were small desks, chairs still before them. Many chairs were occupied by the mouldering remains of people. The bodies had all but gone, skeletal bone and a little hair all that remained, but their clothes were still good as new.

She saw the ghosts of Wolrif, Yvette, and Gallile standing by a metal pillar emerging from the floor. Time enough to deal with them later. Ghosts didn't bother her.

Evanne stood on a platform that would have connected with the dais if it made it a little higher. There were no guardrails, just a clean floor that ran out like a wide metal tongue to taste where the lozenge of dais would've waited. Above, a roof, and below, levels like this with similar ramps leading into other levels. What they held was a mystery for another time.

The far wall was made of a bank of louvres. The slats were closed against rain that would never blow against them down here. She paced forward, guitar held in left hand, eyes trying to break secrets from the night. Her Vhemin eyes said there was no heat left here. All was dead. She made the louvres, and perspective shifted. These were no ordinary slats. Each panel was as wide as her body. The rains that beat against them must have been mighty indeed.

Evanne reached out, touching the louvres. They were slick with condensation. She sniffed her wet fingers. Just water, nothing slimy or sinister, but you couldn't fault a girl for checking after the horrors of the 'healing' pool at the temple. She turned away, then gave a small scream as the louvres CLANKED. She spun back. All about the wall the louvres trembled, strained, their ancient mechanisms struggling against rotted metal.

The louvre before her groaned like a wight as it eased up and away, showing what Evanne now knew to be the top deck of a flying fortress. Lights, long dead, struggled into luminance along its length. By the Three, but it was massive. It stretched before her larger than Imshir was end-to-end. The ugly underside of another ship lay against it, crushed into the deck. Evanne could imagine where she'd fallen out, to land here, and discover a place buried beneath a lake. Above, water trickled from where the vessels had speared into the lakebed. They stoppered this cavern, two hulls making a cork.

To think this ship held levels below, each as large. And this was Tarragon's *home*. The fairy came from a palace emperors could only dream of. "She must think me a sad and lonely rube," Evanne whispered. "She must bite her lip at my quaint ways. She must think I am simple."

"Don't be a dick," Hitch said.

Evanne screamed—again!—and whirled to the spectre. "Hitch!"

"*I* think you're simple." The ghost glimmered blue, his not hands tucked into his pants, looking not at all worse for wear for having been gone all this time. "Tarragon's smitten by you, although I certainly don't know why."

Evanne rushed toward him, wanting to hug him, to hold him close, but she faltered, then stopped. "I'm glad to see you."

"Don't get soppy on me." Hitch strode to the opened louvres, blue luminance emanating from him. "Quite something, isn't it?" He gusted a ghosty sigh. "I've lost so much, and more goes with each moment. But I remember this, now. I remember when it flew. And I remember when that," he stabbed a not-finger at the underside of the place Evanne had fallen from, "crashed into it. Wasn't a great day. They came from above, you see. Flew that smaller craft so high, where the air was thin, barely a whisper, cold as the night beyond the sky. Dropped, and struck a wonder of the Three asunder."

Evanne joined him. "It doesn't make sense. This ship is huge, Hitch! It's bigger than any city I've seen. You could fit Imshir inside it and have room for Ravenswall."

"And that's just the top deck," he agreed. "Fairies don't do things by halves. They are the Builders of our dreams."

"Where have you been, ghostie?"

"I was slapped silly by the Feybrind witch. She's found sorcerous devices. A collar that lets her speak. A real invisibility cloak. And something to turn aside the workings of magic, I expect. Which is where I went." He turned not-eyes down, then back to her. "There's good news, though. By my reckoning, she thinks she's in the fairy citadel. She doesn't realise she's in a battleship made by the other side."

"But she'll want Tarragon to fix it," Evanne said. "And Tarragon can't."

"Because she failed her exams, sure. But—"

"No, Hitch. Because it's not made by fairies." Evanne paced. "*This* ship is made by fairies. *That* one is different. A language she doesn't speak. A book written in a foreign tongue. A—"

"I get you," he said. "So what?"

Evanne imagined the kind of monster that would work against her own kind, to seize relics of the past, to overthrow thrones, kingdoms, and the Tresward, such as they were. "So, I think she's in real trouble. We need to... I dunno."

"What would be great is if we could get this citadel flying again."

"That's it!"

"I was joking." He gave her a hard stare. "Really. It was a joke!"

"Still a good idea." Evanne thought hard, then looked to the other ghosts, still standing by the pillar in the floor. "What are they doing here?"

"You're the ghost whisperer." Hitch stalked around the three other ghosts who watched him, saying nothing. They never did. "Odd they're rooted right there."

"I think I can make them tell us." Evanne hefted her guitar and touched the strings. The instrument dropped soft notes on the floor, hesitant, perhaps even resistant. "I think I can make them *show* us. I did it with you, back when I died. And I did it a little with lost Gabriel in the ancient temple."

Hitch gave her a sideways glance. "You're going to woo them with the power of song?"

Evanne's chin jutted of its own accord. "You know, you're right. You should talk to them, ghost to ghost. See what they know."

"You know I can't do that."

"No, really. Try it! Your lack of ability is surely better than my very real power to see the dead and learn the manner of their passing." She waited him out, using the Trick of time.

"Was I being a dick?"

"A little."

Hitch slumped. "I forget so much. Sometimes I forget who my friends are. It's a problem I've always had." He brightened. "Do you need me along for this one?"

"I don't think I need to fight anyone." She glanced at her guitar, remembering the power he gave her those times they'd shared the strings. But also that he was her friend, her oldest one, and worked with her, without asking for aught. "But... sure. If you want. I could use the company."

He eased across the distance between them, slipping through her skin and into her flesh. There was less of him this time, but she didn't want to think about that. The strings beneath her fingers felt tighter, readier. The guitar still wasn't sure, but she was. She needed to know.

In the garden of memories, we stroll,
Where love and laughter filled our soul.
Though time has passed, and tears may flow,
Your spirit lives on, our hearts aglow.

WITH EACH THOUGHT OF YOU, A SMILE WE FIND,
A cherished presence in our hearts, entwined.
Though you're gone, your light still gleams,
In the tapestry of our dreams.

//ATTEND.// Her throat felt raw, but she didn't need to say much. *//SHOW ME.//*

WOLRIF STOOD ON THE DOCKS, EYES OUT TO THE LAKE. IT WAS A STILL day, the lake a mirror of the sky. He felt the emptiness of his coin purse, the yearning in his heart, and how grateful he was to Gallile. The old woman was by his side, leaning on her crook, eyes to the lake, or something beyond. Her voice wasn't as frail as she looked. "There is treasure beyond measure beneath the waves. My family has kept the secret safe, but now it's time to pass it on. To give it to someone worthy."

"*What of your own family?*"

Gallile snorted. "My daughter has naught but cotton between her ears. She tells me she needs no husband. I tell you there is time aplenty to be alone when your husband's dead and buried."

Wolrif chewed that over for a time. He'd not met Gallile's daughter but didn't need to. His eyes were on sweet Yvette, who could sing songs pure enough to break the heart. Like him, poor. Like him, didn't mind it. But he wanted a better life for her, and Gallile's treasure was the way. "As you say. So, I take ship to where the water's deepest, take a diving bell down, and unlock the door?" He tried to hide his doubt. "Seems odd no one else has found this treasure."

"I was a younger woman when I swam there last. I was alone, as I always was. Secrets can only be kept by one person, child. And I give the keeping of this one to you as I step off." She shrugged, old shoulders bony under her shawl. "Remember the device I need. The rest is yours."

"Aye, I remember. A bar of gold, thick and long as my forearm."

"The very same. There are jewels of diamond and other golden trinkets, but this one is mine. I made a promise." Her eyes searched his. "My dead husband wanted me to pass it down his line. I have little time for them, but we must keep our word."

Wolrif thought of the promises he and Yvette shared, and felt the smile break out on his face despite himself. "Aye. Wish me luck."

"Luck," she called to his back.

The lake remained calm, even, and pure. He took his small skiff out to the deepest part of it, where the water was dark and cold. The diving bell was workmanlike, solid, used by the longshoremen to repair the hulls of their boats. None had taken one this deep.

None except Gallile.

He shucked his leathers, favouring cotton and wool instead. It would surely be cold in the chamber below. An oiled, well-wrapped bundle held such as he'd need: oil, a lantern, striking stones, and a small knife. He stepped into the lake, sinking within the diving bell, light receding.

"THREE'S MERCY," HITCH BREATHED. "HE CAME IN THE SAME WAY you did."

"Hush," Evanne whispered back. "Do you think he was after the same golden rod we found above?"

"I think he found the rod," Hitch said. "I don't think he could get back out."

Evanne shivered. The bottom of the lake was so very cold.

GALLILE MADE HER MEASURED WAY THROUGH THE VILLAGE. HER AIR-headed daughter was yearning after a boy, which was well enough and by time due, but she'd been tight-lipped on her suitor. No doubt a vagrant, but it wouldn't matter once Gallile had the golden rod. The rod would control power beyond memory. She just needed to pass it to the Feybrind Wild Sur, the one who could hear nothing but saw all, and he would secure her place in his new kingdom.

She gave a companionable nod to the blacksmith. His apprentice would do well for her Yvette, but the girl was an imbecile and couldn't see it. No matter. When Gallile had the golden rod, Yvette's needs and wants would be pliable. The Feybrind said the rod could Command all people. Even a wayward child who knew no better. Wolrif was smitten with some doxy, but that didn't matter. He would bring his own undoing back to shore.

Gallile imagined her village paired out just so. The baker's maid with the scullion. The blacksmith himself with the tanner's daughter. Those farmer twins from the next vale brought here to help with some of the heavier work. Ever on toward progress, unity, and health for all.

She'd spent a lot of her life wondering what it would be like if people weren't so unpredictable in their wants. They had no sense of what was good for them.

Perhaps when the stray Wolrif came back with largesse, he could be a fitting match for Yvette? The boy was motivated, and whatever trollop he had his sights on would be easy to sideline with the golden rod. If he survived, of course, because Wild Sur said the rod was cursed. Any who touched it would die, but that was okay for Gallile. She had little time left anyway.

*Y*VETTE WONDERED WHERE HER CRONE OF A MOTHER WAS, BUT NOT WITH *wholehearted anger. Sure, the woman was losing her wits and managed to be overly meddlesome, but Wolrif said they were leaving tonight. He'd been tight-lipped about a job but said it would give them travelling money and more, and what with such as she'd saved in the small lockbox beneath the floor of her room, they'd be onto better things.*

She'd secreted a small travel bag within her mattress, because she had no intent of letting mother Gallile know she was off. Sometimes it was better her mother found things out after the fact than lived experience, because her mother's lived experience would involve a lot of wailing, unfair guilt distribution, and ultimatums.

The front door slid open, and in entered the coldness of the wind and her mother's stare. "Ah. You're still here, of course." The barb was related to the fetch-and-carry chores she'd left for Yvette. As if they had need of further horseshoes from the blacksmith's boy. And he was always dirty and followed Yvette too closely with his eyes.

"Yes, mother." Yvette matched coldness with mockery. "I wasn't sure if I should fetch you in your dotage. You're like as not to get lost between the bakery and tavern."

"Mind your tongue."

"You mind yours." Yvette stared her down. "Not that it matters."

"What's that supposed to mean?"

Yvette considered the path beneath her feet. Shaky ground, but fun to stamp on. Perhaps a little wailing would do well for the morning. "It means I won't be your problem. I plan to leave for the city."

Gallile scoffed. Yvette had grudging admiration for the sound; few people could pull it off with such casual aplomb. "You've no means or travelling company."

"I've both." Yvette was taller than her wizened mother and used it to look down her nose at the wicked witch. "This eve I will be gone."

"This eve you'll be thanking me for the future I've made for you."

Yvette scowled. "You can make the gown but it doesn't mean it'll fit."

Gallile had a smug, knowing smile. "It will fit. When Wolrif returns, I'll—"

"Wolrif? What know you of Wolrif?"

Gallile stopped just on her warm-up to a good tirade. "What?"

"You can't know of Wolrif." Yvette spun, clutching her hem, then turned back. "My Wolrif? About so high," her hand stabbed out, "dark of hair, with a chiseled chin and a sparkle in his eye?"

"I didn't notice his chin." Gallile floundered. "No matter. He dives for us."

"Dives? Like, in the lake?" Yvette felt a chill, because all knew the lake could take a man's life.

"If you're worried about superstitious nonsense, I've taken care of it."

Gallile was entirely too confident for Yvette's manner. "Mother, what have you done?"

"Looked after you, like I always have. Now come."

But Yvette wouldn't come. She sped past her mother, skirts hitched, and was on the wind. Running to the lake, for a boat, for anything. Because Wolrif would be swallowed by the lake, and she'd never see him again.

"Oh," Evanne breathed. "Oh, no."

"I think it gets worse," Hitch said.

"Why do you think that?"

"Because they're all still alive at this point."

Wolrif hurt. The inside of him, that hurt a lot, but also the outside, where he had a lot of the blood that should have been on the inside. There was a damnable secretaire that attacked him. He'd lost his way in the twisty turns of the city beneath a city. He'd stopped wondering at marvels and started running, because no matter how shiny, everything here wanted his life.

It was bad enough when he'd entered through the magic gate. It hadn't responded at first, and he wondered if all was for naught, but then it'd opened, giant air bubbles escaping, and he'd been sucked in with the inrush of water.

The diving bell was lost. He didn't know how he'd get back out.

He didn't know how he'd survive this pit of horrors.

There wasn't any gold, aside from the golden rod. He'd found it after entering the dark tower where the secretaire wouldn't follow. A platform took him up, and there it was. All light left the place as he'd removed the rod from its plinth, and a loud noise like a harpy sounded, so he'd run.

Back down, and out the door, and that's when the secretaire bit him. He'd lost his knife. Then kept running. Climbed, rod under his arm, lantern flickering more than he was comfortable with, back into the corridors and traps above.

He hurt, but he could make it out. Last door, and he was free. He put his hand on the apparatus that opened it and pushed.

"WE WERE THERE," EVANNE SAID. "BUT THE DOOR DIDN'T WORK right. The water came in."

"Hush. There's more."

YVETTE STOOD ON THE LITTLE BOAT SHE'D STOLEN. THE DIVING BELL WAS old, shitty, but it was all she could wheedle from a drunken boatswain by the docks.

She saw another skiff on the lake. Slower, piloted by a hunched figure with animated arms. Her mother, no doubt come to destroy another dream.

Yvette entered the lake, the cold taking her breath away. She huff-huffed as the bell sank. Yvette didn't know how a diving bell worked. In hindsight, she should've brought a light. It was so dark down here.

No, there: a light. A sliver of gold amid turbulence. Three's Mercy, but it was Wolrif! Her feet touched the bottom, and she tried to shuffle the bell closer. It fought her, the turbulence a churning, torrid flurry of mud-streaked water.

Behind Wolrif, his eyes wide with panic, a hole in the lakebed floor. Light *glimmered within. He held out a shaft of gold to her, and for a moment her fingers touched it. She felt a jolt, then he was sucked away, down into the hole. A clang, and all light left.*

Silence, except for a trickle of water. A creak, a crack. Yvette sobbed, because it was dark, and Wolrif was gone. Another creak.

And then the lake flowed over her.

"Khiton's balls." Evanne clutched herself, music dying for a moment. "I can feel the water. The cold."

"One to go," Hitch said. "Play."

Gallile stood atop her skiff. She had no diving bell, nothing but her voice, and she screeched at the placid lake surface. There, the boat Wolrif had been in, and a little way off, Yvette's.

Her Yvette's.

The water trembled, and a huge bubble broke the surface. It brought with it muck and slime. And a scrap of colour.

Gallile paddled her skiff closer. Her old bones ached, her heart thundering in her wizened chest. She made the cloth, almost lost it as the undertow threatened to steal it back to the deeps. She snatched it and saw it for what it was: a scrap of the scarf Yvette wore.

This was the Feybrind's fault. Gallile was supposed to die for the cursed rod, not Yvette. But her daughter was down there. Gallile wailed, because her daughter was below, her stupid, wonderful daughter, and she couldn't save her.

No: Wolrif's boat. She paddled, made it over, and almost capsized it in her frantic hurry. An anchor and line was coiled in the bow. She grabbed the anchor, held it close, and dived.

Down, into the deep. To get her wayward, headstrong child.

Her beautiful girl.

EVANNE SAT ON THE FLOOR OF THE ANCIENT ROOM, CLUTCHING HER guitar. Holding the three ghosts' grief. Trying not to be too sad, or too angry, because she needed to get back to Tarragon.

Except... She held up the golden rod. "I'm carrying a cursed ancient relic that kills anyone who touches it?"

Chapter Thirty-Six

"It's called the *Century Charm*." Yasmine seemed sad. "They didn't build it to kill. Not at first."

"Vhemin build everything to kill." Tarragon frowned. She wanted to lean forward, to peer at Yasmine, but the bars of the cage made the effort futile. She let her eyes wander. The room was as she remembered. Shitty Vhemin construction, trash architecture, bogus lines. It all made sense now. *There. A haze.* She thought maybe she could see a part of the air where the edges didn't line up right. Was the Feybrind here?

"The real problem we've got is Dancing Stars wants us to fix it. Where she dropped Evanne... no one comes back from there. But I think that's where our home is. What's left of it." Yasmine didn't seem certain. "We'd have a better shot at fixing *Dancing in the Storm* than this hulk."

Dancing in the Storm. *That's the name we gave our home!* Tarragon straightened. "I'd forgotten her name." *Play for the crowd.* She fluttered her wings to a specific timing, sparkle dripping about her like warm rain. An old pattern, because Handspeak wasn't very secret with one of the People here. A vibration so subtle you'd need to be a fairy to see it. This is what she said: ... . / .-.. .. ... -. -. ...

She listens

Yasmine paused, then her own wings thrummed just enough for Tarragon to hear. .. / ... . . / .... . .-. — *I see her.* "Huh."

"Don't 'huh' me." Tarragon put on a good glower for their audience. "It's been eight hundred years, and most of that time I was a prisoner of the Vhemin. I wasn't ... *here* for very long."

"Your heart's always been here."

"I'm not sure," Tarragon admitted. "I didn't pass my exams. I didn't know the things I should have. Helio, now he was at home on *Dancing in the Storm.* He loved everything about it. He could've fixed it."

"Maybe no one can fix it." Yasmine didn't seem sad about it, just resigned. Was that what she thought, or what she wanted Dancing Stars to think? "The *Century Charm* came from near orbit. Floated above the air, undetected, a thing you lost sight of like a dream you can't quite remember. They dropped on us."

"Like a dragon." Tarragon shivered. "They learned how to do that from us."

"Suicide mission," Yasmine said. "We never did those. They didn't think they'd survive. The Vhemin aboard were forced to fight. Or maybe they wanted to? I don't know. We hurt them so often, so badly, they probably thought it was good to go out with a bang. Take our flagship with them."

"We have to get out of here." Tarragon straightened. "That crazy cat is going to want us to fix this stupid Vhemin ship. We can't even fix our *own* ship. And she, uh." Her eyes went to the sad, forlorn shapes in the cages around her. "She doesn't seem the type to take no for an answer."

"There's a way." Yasmine shrugged. "It's a long shot. Just the kind of play a spy would make."

"I'm not a very good spy."

"But you're the best one we've got." Yasmine's voice turned urgent. "The walls of this Vhemin hulk *aren't made by fairies.* Do you know what that means?"

Tarragon thought that through. The Feybrind, watching them, invisible. The fairies who died here, perhaps thinking it *was* their home, afraid to touch the bars because it hurt, and eventually dying because it kept hurting. Thinking their cages were made by Itikari and built so strong. All of them Builders, with knowledge of stress tolerances and the melting point of steel, and how to make the purest coke from coal. How they could fix a reactor, make a perfect weld, or build a Skyforge.

Tarragon didn't know any of that. And for once, the not-knowing gave her an edge. *I need to unbalance this cat. I need to not be the bait in the trap. I need to free us all.* She didn't know if this cage was as tough as the one they'd locked her up in for eight hundred years. But she was willing to gamble this diamond-eyed git didn't know how hot Tarragon could burn, unlike her old Vhemin gaolers.

She thought hard about how much it would hurt to hit the walls of her cage, but also how it wouldn't hurt for very long. She turned to Yasmine. "Why haven't you escaped?"

"Because I'm where I want to be. Here, to give you a little nudge." The other fairy beamed. "My part in this story is already done. Yours? It's just beginning."

"I'll be exhausted for a few moments."

"Do you want a hug?" Yasmine's smile snapped off.

"Kind of. Yes."

"Well, you'll have to wait." Yasmine scowled. "Go on. Get on with it."

Tarragon took a few deep breaths, like she was about to dive into deep water, then she glimmered. The glimmer grew, hotter by the moment, her wings shining incandescent, her body radiating heat. Because the walls of this ship were made by Vehement Systems, who had no fairies, and didn't forge metals in the hottest fires. A fairy, burning everbright, might melt through such substandard material.

And be free.

She backed up, almost touching the door of her cage as she faced the wall behind it. Ducked her head. Closed her eyes, *huff-huffing* with imagined pain at the cage, then she shot forward. She hit the cage, and oh *my* but it hurt. But not, as she thought, for very long. A brilliant point of agony all about her, then it was gone, and she hit the wall of the *Century Charm*. Steel old when she was born parted before her, metal spraying, boiling in white-hot rivulets as she flew.

Behind her, the Feybrind shouting—*odd, that a Feybrind makes noise at all*, "Stop!" but then Tarragon was through. A tiny fairy-sized hole in the metal wall behind her, and she *plopped* into a strange room. She panted, flat-out tired, cooling on the decking as the glimmer left her and she was left drained.

I've only got a few moments. The Feybrind wasn't stupid—none of them were—and would be here in moments. Tarragon clawed her way along the floor toward a sagging shelf. The room was filled with them near as she could tell from the small beam of light coming through the wall. Tarragon wasn't glowing and couldn't see in the dark like the Feybrind or Vhemin. She felt like there was vast space around her, an absence of people who would have made it whole and complete before they all died, after killing her home.

She made the shelf as the door slammed open. Light spilled in, but no shadow or form. The cat still had her cloak of many colours on. Tarragon heard no footsteps, because of course the Feybrind were silent. "Where are you, fairy? You can't hide from me."

That's exactly what I'm doing. Being small, to be great. Tarragon kept her words to herself, using what strength she had to prop herself up against a strut. It was rusty, the metal sharp, jagged, and uncomfortable against her back. She hugged her knees to her chest.

"You think you're stopping anything? I will bring the broken casting of a person you arrived with back here. I will stretch her on a rack and make her scream. And I'll keep making her scream, because her kind can't die."

You don't know Evanne well at all. She's not the screaming type. Tarragon felt a little stronger, enough to stand, albeit wobbly. She faced away from the wall. The cat would start rummaging under the shelves closest to Tarragon's egress point, and the fairy wanted to be the hell away from here when that happened. The cat could see in the dark, very well as it happened, but she saw light, and Tarragon was fresh out of glimmer. Tarragon darted across the floor, slinking under another cabinet. This one had a few boxes left on the bottom shelves, but nothing looked like a fairy-sized sword. *Three's mercy, did no one think to make a handy weapon in all these years?*

The shelf she'd been under was wrenched aside, a crash making

Tarragon's shoulders almost reach her ears as she cringed. The shelf banged against the wall, and for a moment Tarragon saw a leg as the cloak of many colours shifted aside in Dancing Star's rage. Tarragon used that moment of sound to dart to another shelf. *There.* Two more shelves over there was a grating in the floor.

"I *will* find you." The cat's voice was coming from by the grate now, by all the blasted luck. Like all the People, she moved fast. Still, maybe that was the best place for the cat to be. As a spy, Tarragon learned the tactics that served her best were the unexpected ones.

Daring her courage, Tarragon crept closer to the voice. Another shelf down, and here she was, the floor between her and the grating just three lousy metres away. She felt her skin prickle with a little warmth. *No, no, no! Not yet!* But the little fire inside her wouldn't be banked for long. It was made from a tiny piece of a star, so they said. Stars burned for so very long, never wanting to be banked.

The shelves were constructed with bolts, so Tarragon bit her lip, shuffled to one, and unscrewed it. It moved surprisingly easily, perhaps a testament to both their manufacture and the lackadaisical manner they'd been 'tightened'. *Don't think. Evanne wouldn't. She'd just do it. Evanne would be at the grate already!* Tarragon heaved the bolt, a tiny discus thrower releasing her prize into the room. It *clattered* as it landed under a shelf, and Dancing Stars bounded after it, knocking over another shelf.

Tarragon rushed for the grating. She heard the cat cry, "Got you!" but the fairy already had her hands on the grating. She heaved, glimmer sparkling, the grate up, but Khiton's *balls* it was heavy, but she didn't have time for heavy, because the Feybrind was coming, she was almost here, Tarragon could hear her breathing, the scrape of boot on decking, the imagined whisper of breath against her neck, so she heaved harder, felt something in her back *twinge*, and she cried, but kept going, and then *plonk* she was under, the grate *clanging* above her.

She ran. She was in a drain, of course, but nice and dry after eight hundred years. The grate was torn away behind her but she had her glimmer back and could see. She was in a drain that you could get your arm into, but the fairy was already a meter down, and unless Dancing Stars had noodles for arms, Tarragon was free, she was *free*.

Dancing Stars called after her. "It's okay, little one. I'll get you in the end. And while we play cat and fairy, a game I'm *very* good at, I will bring your other friends here. The ones out in the wilds, where you left them. Safe, or so you thought. Well, let's see."

Oh shit, Tarragon thought. *Morgan. Heser the Cheg. And Pakhet.*

Chapter Thirty-Seven

When the ground started to tremble, Amir was inclined to pay it some mind. Deserts were strange places, stories telling of quicksand that could swallow a man whole, suck the meat from his bones, and spit out a bleached corpse a handful of years later.

Deserts surrounding an ancient spire? Likely worse. The High Justiciar had left him outside in the sun and heat with Amber and Jade, the first of whom had become somewhat of a friend during their weary tread across the dunes, the latter who'd not forgiven him for thwarting her attempted theft of the sky map. She'd tried again, and he'd stopped her again. It felt a novel game to pass the time as the caravan worked its way across the sands. And here they were, sky map in Tresward hands, and Jade thinking murder.

"Amir, what news, hey?" Faust's bass voice broke his contemplation of both the trembling sands and the merchant's sister.

"Destruction, most like." Amir visored his eyes, finding Larochette in a moment. She'd decided Amber's side was a welcome place to be most days and had until moments ago been enjoying cool tea from an icy decanter. Amber claimed it to be an ancient's device, but Amir knew it could just as easily have been a thaumaturge's working. "Larochette! Attend!"

She bounded over as the sands beneath them rumbled again. She stubbed her toe into the ground. "This is no earthquake. It has the semblance of horses, but under the sandy sea."

Amir thought about that for four heartbeats, then jogged to Amber's side. The sand merchant's sister was under a tent sipping tea not a handful of metres distant. "Friend Amber, are there horses under the ground here?"

The sand merchant stood like he'd been shocked upright by lightning. "There are worse things. Insects the size of dogs, sometimes larger."

"Larger?" Amir blinked. "But only sometimes?"

"They are terrible creatures. I'd not thought them attracted to dead ruins. Typically, they are about the ones still vibrant with ancient energy. They nest near the ancients' sources of power." As one, both men looked at the ancient structure, and its mighty spire, then at the dying-but-not-dead grass at their feet. "A place such as this, if it were not struck dead."

"It was killed by the High Justiciar's daughter mere weeks past."

Amber made a moue. "Ah. They would be hungry, and perhaps angry."

Amir wanted to roll his eyes, but there wasn't time. Of *course* the High Justiciar had gone into a nest of dog-sized insects who were starving and angry. He wasn't worried about her, but rather himself. While she was the best he'd seen with a blade, Amir was a far shot from there.

The sand shook more, and Amir saw Faust and Larochette stumble, even with Tresward training, then scramble back. They beat a retreat to the tents, and for once, Jade hadn't skulked off to Sight of Day's pack and the star map within. The woman was wide-eyed, and she held a curved dagger. Where she'd kept that in her clinging silks Amir couldn't begin to guess. A horse wrangler mounted a panicked beast, tossing a, "To the hells with this!" over his shoulder, and kicking the wild-eyed beast into a gallop. He made it perhaps ten seconds out into the sands before the ground erupted beneath him, grains boiling like water in a pot, and creatures of horror scrambled up to take him and horse into the earth.

"Three's mercy," Larochette breathed. "What are those things?"

"If they bleed, they can die," Faust assured her.

"Did you see them bleed? I didn't." She drew paired blades with a weary sigh.

"What should we do?" Amber looked like he wanted to run.

"Don't run," Amir suggested. "I hazard the creatures are attracted to motion. Like tics in the grass."

"How do you know?" Jade sounded accusing.

Another of their retinue made a break for it, taking a slightly easterly path, and moments later the sand swallowed him and his camel. Amir drew his sword, pointing with it. "There. That's how." He visored his eyes again. *Is that the glint of metal there?* The tip of a spike, perhaps, or some other ancient device glinted from below the earth. It was, near as Amir could tell, aligned with the spire above and the entrance of the ancient structure. Perhaps there were more beneath the earth?

Faust looked to the ground beneath him. "So, we shouldn't move?"

"Oh, we'll move all right." Amir felt perplexed. "How will we slay the beasts if they don't come for us?"

Larochette gave him a stare harder than he felt he deserved. "Your plan is to *try* getting eaten?"

"The sun's taken his mind," Jade whispered. "It happens, even to the strongest."

Strongest, hey? Amir liked the sound of that. "I will lead. Faust, behind. Then the merchants, and—"

"I'm staying here," Amber declared.

"Then you'll die," Amir said peaceably enough. "Your call." He turned and set off toward the glinting spire. He sensed Faust behind him, good, reliable Faust who'd been at his back a hundred times before. Larochette, encouraging in her way, then the begrudging resignation of Amber and Jade. *All's well. We are together.* Amir stepped with confidence across the sand. A man at arms raced toward them from the ancient structure, then screamed as the sand erupted, and something seized his legs. He went down, armour and all, flailing with it. He tried using his shield as a club, sword lost to the depths, before something with pincers like scythes took his arm.

Then he was gone. Nothing left but bloody sand, and a shield with an arm still attached. *No matter.* Amir changed course, gravitating toward the shield. He crouched, examining the churned sand. Aside from the blood, there was little to show a tunnel was here. Amir collected the shield, extracted the still-warm arm, dropped that to the ground, and kept on toward the metal glint.

"Souvenirs?" Larochette sounded angry.

"You've your two blades," Amir countered. "Faust, his hammer. I have but a slender slip of metal. Against armoured chitin, I think I need something else."

"Fair." Faust scanned the sands about them. "Your plan, Amir?"

"I saw a glint."

"I see it too." Jade bit her lip, realising she was agreeing with a crazy person.

"I believe that is where the Justiciar is. We should help her get clear of the denizens of the deep, then make all haste for the ancient temple. I feel if it were active but recently, there will be a low chance of infestation."

Jade huffed. "I don't want to go—"

The ground beneath her erupted, a clawed horror like a spider dog bursting forth. Amir felt the pattern come over him, dropping like a light rain on his face. Not chosen by him, but as if it chose *for* him. He lunged forward, feet light on the sand, eyes half-closed, shield forward. Was it his imagination or did the rim glimmer gold? His blade held high. Shield, dropping down. A crack, the ecstasy of the pattern within him like a prayer answered, as the shield sundered chitin as if it were kindling. His sword, answering the siren's shriek of death, dealt six swift slices and dismembered the creature.

He spun, shield in guard, sword ready, blade smoking, a glimmer of red along the edge.

Silence.

"Fuck *me*," Faust said.

"Fuck me *sideways*," Larochette countered.

Amber was google-eyed, and Jade's jaw looked to be going below her knees. Amir swayed a little, the embrace of the Three's Storm making his teeth itch. He'd only had it for a second, just a tiny moment of time narrower than the gap between a crone's teeth, but he'd *had* it. Amir cackled. The sound broke free, a storm of noise and delight he scarce recognised. He capered a jig, raised his arms—shield and sword both—to the heavens, and yelled, "Yes!"

The ground beneath him surged, and because he was playing the goat and not paying attention, he stumbled. The sword tumbled free, Three knows where *that* went, and something bit his leg. It wasn't the gentle nuzzle of a rabid dog, instead delivering the kind of savage pain Amir imagined childbirth to be like. He screamed, lost his footing, and went down. Sand was in his eyes, and he had no balance, no damn ground to balance *on*, and here he was, the first of his friends to embrace the Storm, but also the first to die. Cophine's sweet smile, but this was a bitter truth, and it hurt more than his leg.

Someone grabbed his jerkin and pulled. He emerged into the light, scrabbling sand from his eyes. There, Faust. The giant had him. Beside, Larochette, her blades *snick-snicking* by his leg, close enough to leave a kiss of air, and he screamed as the weight left him, perhaps with pain, release, or both. It was a complicated time. Faust set him on his feet. "Can you stand, man?"

"I can stand, brother." Amir spat sand. Faust released him, at which point he proved himself a liar and toppled to the desert floor. He came eye-to-maybe-that's-an-eye with the spider dog's head that Larochette severed. It was a fearsome beast, made more despicable by Amir's blood coating its maw.

Faust hauled him back upright. "You're not doing a good job of standing."

"My leg hurts like—"

"Death hurts more," Larochette breezed. "Get a grip."

"I believe death is the absence of pain, but I take your point." Amir swayed, but under Faust's watchful gaze he kept his feet. "Perhaps a sit down?"

Jade screamed as a harsh *boom* cracked the air, and the merchant's sister pointed. Amir whirled with less grace than he'd had moments earlier. The glittering silver spike in the ground was alive with the actinic blue of chained lightning. There was another *boom*, then a third. The air felt charged, and Amir felt all the hair on his body stand upright. A spider-dog crawled from the earth but a few metres distant and was turned into a scorch mark and drifting ash by an electric release from the ground spike.

Amir glanced to his leg, ignoring the noise and calamity coming from Jade, the insistent *by the gods* from Larochette, and the aghast expression of Faust. They could all see what he knew to be true: in moments the ancient device in the ground would erupt and kill them all. Thunder roiled above, clouds filling a once-clear sky in moments. He considered his leg, the bleeding mess that made a pattern near impossible, and took a moment to breathe.

The High Justiciar is below. The lightning above is the Storm's will. The Storm is mightier than any ancient device. The trouble comes from the sky, not below.

Amir fumbled through his memory, seeking a pattern, anything, a brief moment where the shield he still held could be defence against the gods. The lightning glimmered above, a crackle, a torrent, and then he felt the Storm within him answer. He placed but the toes of his mauled leg down, perhaps a third of his weight on that injured limb, the rest as he leaned back. He swept the shield above, the movement he held in his mind made perfect, as he willed his tired body to do what it knew must be done.

The lightning struck.

Chapter Thirty-Eight

The dawn was cold here. Morgan was used to how the cold clung to the walls of her keep, but Ravenswall was protected by warm sea winds despite how far south it was. Here, though? There was no sea breeze. Just the woods, holding the chill right to the ground, protecting the earth from any stray beam of sunlight.

"It's brisk, but that's how a morning should start," Heser the Cheg proclaimed. "Gets the blood pumping."

"*It is too cold. Make a fire.*" Pakhet lay in a giant curl, tail to nose.

"There's a fire right here." Heser fussed with a pot of coffee over a lick of flame.

"*That is not a fire. If it dreamed big, if its parents believed in it all the way, it still wouldn't be a blaze.*"

Morgan hid her smile by looking down. The leaf-covered loam beneath her feet was soft and smelled earthy, in a good way. The air here was clean, not plagued by the soot of Ravenswall's industry. No smell of sea or salt touched her clothes. It wasn't so bad, perhaps, if they'd had a decent fire.

Also, none of Ravenswall's people were about to befoul her fledgling magic. The spark inside her was weak. It couldn't ever become a flame, not least of which because she had no parents left to believe in her. Heser believed in her though, and she felt that was enough for the morning. *Try, Queen Morgan. Try, because your people need you.* She reached a tentative finger to the soil. First, a circle. A small one, because she wasn't sure whether she was doing this right, but she *felt* it was right. Within the circle, an X for fuel, and vertical lines for the fire. She drew these slowly, carefully, feeling the tip of her finger heat with each one.

Ritualism wasn't common. It was a slow magic, uninspiring to some, because it took the time and patience one only mastered while sitting throne in a kingdom wrestled from sycophants when her father died too early. But from small beginnings, great things. Heser's fire hissed, then surged. He leaned away from it, not jumping or yelping, but measured. A man used to calamity, and an upstart fire was none such in the skein of his life. He eyed her over a fire now a half a metre high. "That was you?"

"It was."

"*I like her.*"

"It will burn out too soon, and we won't have coffee." The man sighed, a gentle motion full of patience and strength. "I'd best get more wood."

"*I like you too.*"

"I will get it." Morgan stood, brushed herself down, and pulled her cloak a little tighter. "I could use a walk."

"Perhaps we could both use a walk."

"*Perhaps you should hurry. The fire will burn down soon.*"

Morgan strode past the fire, gave the giant, grey-striped tiger a pat between her ears, then set out into the trees. Heser was at her side, falling in place, comfortable there, effortless, easy as her shadow. They picked their way through trees, gathering fallen sticks aged enough to hold the flame. Heser had taught her how. So many simple things she hadn't known how to do, like what wood would burn, or how to break ice on a pond and set a line for fish. Simple things from a life she probably didn't want, because her father hadn't raised a peasant girl.

Yet, doing these things with Heser... They filled a gap.

"We have enough." He spoke after minutes or hours, Morgan wasn't sure. Minutes, it must be, yet the time passed easily between them.

It cannot be. But it was, and there was no one here to tell her what was right for the Raven Queen. "Do we? Surely a few more logs." She adjusted her own load, an armful and more.

He eyed her collection of sticks, awkwardly carried, and withheld comment on the matter. They paced through the trees some more, no longer gathering wood. *We're gathering time*. Morgan glanced up, the sun trying its best to make it through the leaves, sifting a meagre, green-filled light to them. His hand found her arm, other across her mouth, lips to her ear. "Quiet."

She nodded, surprised he'd managed to put his load down without sound, let alone get to her side without the snapping of a twig. She listened, holding herself still as the trunks about her. *I hear it*. To the west, a *clink* of old metal. A hushed whisper of shifting feet. Heser took the branches from her arms, placing them with exquisite care on the ground. They padded to a fallen trunk, crouching behind it.

Minutes passed. The sound drew nearer. Morgan saw movement through the trees. She caught the shape of a man dappled in shadow. Another one beside the first. But something was wrong with their gait. They didn't walk like men trying to make no noise, but they were voiceless all the same. They shambled, and although the one closest to her held sword and board, they were loosely clasped, the weapon and shield hanging low.

She understood when the shambler turned to face her. Sunken flesh, grey and mottled. Eyes of milky white, beset with the verdigris of time. These things were risen, foes from beyond the grave. How did you kill a thing already dead? *It pains me to admit, but Evanne would be handy about now*. Morgan wondered if her own weak magic could undo the tether binding these creatures here. Some necromancy was at play. She had some fledgling skill with the method and madness of binding. She narrowed her eyes, focusing, and almost fell back as Heser stood, sword in hand. "My queen. Run."

"Don't be a fool." She stood, the game now up. The creatures saw them. There was no rush, but they pivoted to the queen and her guardsman, iron to their lodestone. "You can't kill a man who's dead already."

Heser frowned, examining his sword. It was well-made, as all blades given to her guard were. Manufactured by the Feybrind, craftsmen without peer, who had forged them to part humans from their souls. He growled. "I'd like to give it a try."

"If it makes you happy." She crossed her arms.

He looked to her, his sword, to her, then to the creature hunching toward them. A grunt, and he vaulted the log. The guardsman roared, charged, and swung. The dead man didn't raise his shield to block, just took the blow centre mass, staggered, spun, then righted itself. It lifted its own sword and gave a vicious slash. Heser took the swing on the edge of his steel, kicked the things legs from under it, and retreated.

A few moments, and he was by her side. "It appears tricky to kill those already dead."

"Hmm." Morgan's tone was noncommittal.

Sensing a trap, Heser straightened. "I've another thought."

"Be quick about it." But he was gone already, vaulting the log once more—she did love to watch him work—and charging the creature again. He lunged past it this time, his blade hungering for its neck. There was a wet *pop* as blade parted flesh, and its head spun into the air, hit the ground, and rolled downslope.

The creature didn't slow—not that it moved fast in the first place. It turned to 'face' Heser and swung again. He removed its arm with the sword, at which point it came for him with the shield. Another roar, a slash, and shield and rotted arm hit the ground.

The now armless, headless corpse lunged, trying to chest-barge him. Heser the Cheg sidestepped easily, then loped back to the safety of the log. "Some foul magic animates their very bones."

"Hmm." Morgan turned back toward their camp. "Should we hurry? I think we must find Evanne."

"To see if she's alright?"

"To see if she can save us." The words didn't taste as bitter as Morgan expected. "She has some skill with the weaving of the dead."

"Hmm." It was Heser's turn to look at her as if playing poker.

"I know that tone."

"There was no tone." But a smile crept into his voice. "Come, my queen. We must get you to safety."

There would be no fire. But perhaps a run would get the blood pumping all the same.

THIS IS TOO MUCH RUNNING.

Morgan panted, breath hot and sharp in her throat, pulse knocking away right alongside. Her time on the throne hadn't given her the fitness of a warrior, nor that of a giant tiger. Pakhet bounded ahead, returning often, only to leave again after a *"Hurry"* or *"How did your species survive so long"* tossed over the shoulder. The dead who pursued them weren't in a rush, but they'd swelled in number. Bodies of the restless dead, but mindless, without soul or cause other than what they were given. Morgan saw no necromancer, felt no magic, and yet the dead continued on.

So, they ran. And despite the dead not being in a hurry, it felt like those with souls still inside them made no ground. The monsters had no need to rest, to get their bearings, or to find higher ground. They were drawn to Morgan, Heser, and Pakhet wherever they went. Heser tried to lead them away, despite Morgan feeling her heart trip at the idea, a hard *No!* leaving her lips, but it didn't matter. The creatures split up, a mass following him, the remainder on Morgan.

They thought of that trick already.

Who was 'they', though? Morgan felt the answer was out of reach. They'd put the vampire to sun and stake, freed a village, and left no enemies in their wake. They'd overthrown shaman, knocked aside warlords, and helped all they came across. Yet someone still hungered for them.

I'd bet Evanne's done something. I can't be the only one she pisses off.

"Stop woolgathering!" Heser's tone was short of a bark, but not by much.

Morgan felt her own retort, crushed it down. His face was a mask of worry, his eyes wide, always looking to her, past her, beyond her. He wasn't coddling her. The man was terrified. *For me.* She caught up with him, put a steading hand on his arm. "Heser the Cheg, we have a few moments."

"And what if we twist an ankle? What if the cat falls in a hole? What if—"

"*I will not fall in a hole.*" Pakhet perched atop a rock, the magical, worthless armour Evanne was so concerned about lashed to her back. "*I am very good at not falling over. It's the tail, you see. It helps me—*"

"I hear you, Heser." Morgan left her hand on his arm. "You have taken care of me for so very long. You have ever been at my side."

"My queen." His voice was rough.

"I have not deserved the gifts I have been given." She straightened, turned to look back, and frowned. Coming through the trees, hundreds of shapes. Shambling, soundless, tireless. "I do not deserve you."

"*Touching as this is, I think—*"

"I am the lucky one." Heser stood straight, a pillar of stone and duty. "Many men would serve unkind masters. Many men would serve at the foot of those unworthy."

"And I am worthy?" Morgan laughed, short and hard. "I think I am not. But I am learning." She turned away from the pursuing dead. "Is that water I smell?"

"*I have no idea what you smell. Your kind are as close to insensate as makes no difference. But there is a mighty lake ahead.*"

"Then we run. Let us see if the dead can swim." Morgan turned and put a little curry in her stride. Breath still burned her throat. A stitch knitted her side. But she would show none of that. Because Heser the Cheg was with her, and while he was there, she had no fears.

Chapter Thirty-Nine

T he lightning curled down the shield, a vivid rivulet of godly power. It bled into the spire itself. Ancient machinery fought a moment against the Three's Storm. Energy, denied its route to the ground through Amir's shield, then rebuffed by the spire, blasted sideways. It tore the ground apart like paper, tossing molten sand, rock, and metal across near half the world. Amir lost his sight for a moment at the brilliant torrent of power but held his footing.

Because the Storm was with him.

The shield above held true, a dome of crystal gold a membrane about them. The destruction was a blast rather than flood, over in a moment, but sand and rock fell as Amir's heart beat on. Faust, closest to him, alive, but hunched, as if expecting death. Larochette, unbowed, swords crossed in guard, hoping to stave off death with a prayer. Amber, curled over his sister, who sobbed.

The golden glow about them faded. Amir lowered the shield, the wood held true by the Three's power. He staggered toward the spire, now silent, pausing at the edge of the murder pit. Below, he saw the spire, at the base of it a charred corpse, and naught else. The gloom took all. The rim of the pit had sagged, superheated rock leaning against the spire. He turned. "A rope and lantern." His voice was hoarse, as if he'd spent his last moments screaming.

Perhaps I did. The pattern wouldn't care.

Faust recovered first, the giant trotting to the remains of their gear. Amir saw dead horses, handlers torn apart, and much grief waiting if he spared it a thought. Larochette joined the giant in his search. No dog-spiders came for them. *There may be no dog-spiders left in all the world after that.* The High Justiciar, he figured, but he'd never heard of a pattern that did what she'd done. Sway bound to Storm, perhaps, but the cost against her years left would be harsh.

Larochette bumped his elbow, and he realised he'd glazed over for a moment. She held a rope, hook, and lantern. "Here."

"My thanks." He took the lantern, which she'd conveniently lit for him, and affixed it to his belt. The hook and rope he slung, fetching it against the spire. The hook rang a clean hit. He tugged the rope to be sure, then backed over the pit, line coiling away into darkness.

"Hold, brother." Larochette tossed her hair. Behind her, Faust crouched beside Amber and Jade, offering them water, and perhaps comfort. Amir's eyes found Larochette's. "You have called the Storm twice."

"A moment's indiscretion." The joke died on his lips.

"You are an Adept now."

"My trials still await."

"They're just below." She pointed with her chin into the gloom. "I think you'll find all you need to emerge a Knight."

Ah. That is why she doesn't help. She sees my leg but wants me to win the trial without aid. Amir understood, but said only, "My thanks." And slipped into the gloom. He slid down the rope carefully, moving hand over hand. It wasn't just because he didn't fancy burns on his hands. If the High Justiciar was below, startling her wouldn't be wise. He arrived at the bottom of the pit next to the charred remains at the spire's base. Human, but who was a mystery.

He held the lantern higher. It cast a tenuous but warm light in a pool about him. Smoke curled in almost sensual trails. Somewhere, the *tink-tink-tink* of cooling metal. He pressed into the gloom. The first he found was Sight of Day. The cat was on his back, golden eyes sightless.

Amir bent, pressing his fingers to the Feybrind's throat. There was a pulse, strong and steady, so he pulled his hand back and slapped the man across the face.

The cat started upright, all bared fangs and spite. Amir waited him out, watching the tail *lash, lash*, then said, "No time for sleeping on the job. Be about it."

Golden eyes narrowed, then softened. *{Says the one who missed all the fun.}*

Amir snorted. "Come. I don't know if we killed the nest or if they're just as sleepy as you were."

{I was,} and here, a harsh slash of the hand, *{stunned.}*

Amir grinned, then turned to the dark. The cat loped past him, because the Feybrind *of course* had better night sight than a human. Amir caught up with him a moment later. He was crouched beside the High Justiciar, who in turn was hunched over Armitage. Amir cleared his throat. "Quite something, hey?"

She turned, platinum hair streaked with soot, eyes hard as agates. "You would joke at a time like this? My husband is..." her face fought to crumple, and she fought right back.

"Perhaps. He is Vhemin, though." Amir walked closer, being mindful of Vertiline, because people in shock were like as not to be unpredictable, Justiciars or no. Armitage was supine, glassy eyes staring upward. He bent, checking for a pulse.

Sight of Day touched Amir's arm. *{Are you going to slap him too?}*

"Only a fool would do that."

The cat half-smiled. *{Then allow me. There is a modest debt owed.}* Before Amir could get clear, he smacked Armitage in the face.

The monster roared upright, then spun, panting great hulking gasps. He rounded on Amir. "Did you hit me?"

"Do I look suicidal?"

Armitage rounded on the cat. "It was you, wasn't it?"

{At least the crick in your back is fixed.} The Feybrind gave a small bow. *{You're welcome.}*

All eyes turned to Vertiline, who's mouth hung open. "Husband?"

"Wife."

"You live?"

"It hurts too much for me to be dead." The monster rubbed his chest. "Whatever you did seemed to have killed the vermin."

"And you!"

"Go for the head," he said absently. "Rookie mistake."

"You were dead!"

"I've been dead before," he admitted. "Amir, was it?"

"Sir." Amir waited, his lantern still held high.

"Get that fucken light out of my eyes. You got a way out?"

"Rope." Amir swivelled, gesturing with the lantern. "We'll wait until you've got your strength back, or we can winch you out."

Armitage pushed past him. "Already got my strength back. Race you to the top?"

Vertiline ran past, standing in front of Armitage, and put her hand to his chest. "You *died*."

"Maybe."

"I *killed you*."

Silence spread from them like a worn blanket, two souls familiar enough with each other to let the moment settle. Then Armitage touched her chin, tilting her face toward his. "I'm fine, Tilly. I'm always fine when I'm with you."

"But what about next time? Or the time after that? What if..." She clutched her metal hand to her chest. "What if I'm like this with *her*? I can't be trusted! She was right to leave. She should stay away."

The Feybrind padded toward the rope. *{She's a hazard, but she's our hazard.}* He glanced up. *{Your daughter didn't leave, friend of my heart. She was taken by the evil and the wicked. Her heart yearns for yours.}* He made a great show of examining Amir's rope, still tethered above. *{I'll get another rope. We've got one more to bring up.}* And then almost too fast to follow, he was gone, a rat up a drainpipe.

Amir approached, cleared his throat, and when Armitage glared, he offered, "We've not much light left. We must make camp within the ancient's temple."

"How many?" she whispered.

"Enough." Amir shrugged. "You have three students and two sand merchants. It is sufficient to find one wayward Justiciar's daughter."

"Five." Vertiline's voice was flat.

Sight of Day landed cat-silent behind them. He held the tail of another rope, the other end lashed above. *{For the prisoner.}*

Amir blinked. "You've been busy. You found time to upset a nest of horrors and captured someone? A big day, even for the High Justiciar."

Armitage offered him a shark-toothed grin in exchange for his joke. "Come on. I'll show you. Be careful. She bites."

Chapter Forty

The ghosts hadn't vanished, which was a sure sign there was still shit to do. Evanne glared at them, then the rod, and finally to Hitch.

He held up not-hands. "Don't look at me that way! *I* didn't bestow a horrible curse on you. It was those assholes." He jerked his arm to the others, and Evanne imagined if he still had thumbs, one would be pointing in their direction.

"I don't feel any different," Evanne said. "No curious doom behind me, nothing breathing down my neck." She patted her nape. "No, definitely no eldritch horror there."

The floor vibrated. Not a huge amount, not like an earthquake, or the destruction that shook Imshir when the ancient's mountain erupted with its death weapon. But nothing here had moved the entire time she'd been down here, and probably not for the eight hundred years prior.

"What was that?" Hitch said.

"Probably nothing." Evanne frowned. "Probably."

The floor vibrated a little longer, a little harder, then subsided. Evanne breathed out a breath she hadn't known she was holding, tied on a bright smile, and rounded on the ghosts, golden rod in hand.

"Which one of you knows what to do with this?" They stared at her with the lifeless insistence of the dead, not a one moving. "I swear to the Three if you don't show me, I will shove this thing up your a—"

The floor shook, *hard*. Violent, forceful enough to knock her to one knee. One corpse that had spent the last eight hundred years slumped over a desk finally slumped a little further, skull rolling free of vertebrae, turning like a child's ball to *crunch* onto the metal floor, where it shattered. The body slid under the desk, a loose pile of dust in shiny coveralls. A chair broke free of the stiction holding it in place, rolling a handspan sideways before turning about slowly. A shutter on the wall overlooking the prow of the mighty *Dancing in the Storm* snapped open, unstuck from ancient grime to show more of the outside.

Evanne really wished it hadn't. The gloom outside was lightening as more of the curious lamps on the decking came to light, showing the underside of the ship that had crashed into *Dancing in the Storm*. She could see where it stuck down like a dagger into the hull of the fairy fortress, a spear breaking through from above. And where it met rock above, water spewed in. The whole lake above, litres and litres of water beyond reckoning, was seeking a way in.

"*Fuuuuuck*," she breathed. "So, *this* is what a curse feels like."

The roar of water reached her over the rumble of tumultuous rock. She could imagine the cold spray on her face and rounded on Hitch. "How do we get out of here?"

He glanced at her, then to the ghosts, then outside. "Same way we came in."

"There must be some kind of ship's boat. A dingy, perhaps."

He turned incredulous not-eyes on her. "This ship sailed the *sky*, Evanne. They didn't have a wee put-out to bob about in. They flew dragons."

"Dragons, right. So, where do we find one of those?" Hitch looked to be no use at all in this conversation, so Evanne turned back to the ghosts. They still clustered about the pillar, not doing anything useful.

Except.

Ghosts lingered where they were anchored. Where their presence was most urgent, to them anyway. She looked to the rod in her hand, then to the pillar. She made it, double time, scrabbling across the metal floor as it canted further. Desks remain bolted in place, as did their chairs, but bodies fell to the ground, sliding across the floor. She got a mouthful of ancient hair, spat, rolled sideways to avoid another skull, and made the pillar.

It was about half her height. She fumbled about without much luck, trying to find a door, a hatch, anything that would give her a clue as to why the ghosts were here. Hitch hollered behind her, things like *Evanne, Run!* as if there were anywhere to go and *Three's mercy, but get off the floor*, because that wasn't half obvious. She ignored him, punched the pillar in frustration, yelped in pain, wound up, and hit it with the rod. *Clang!* The rod vibrated in her hand, not in a pleasant way, but as if the golden metal was angry.

You're angry? Try being cursed for a lifetime! She swung again, lost her balance on the tipping floor, banged her face into the pillar, roared in pain, got a hand atop it, stood, face clenched in rage, and really let it have it. She was down here with armoires, sewing boxes, and four worthless ghosts, rather than being up top with Tarragon. Fuck *allllll* that. The rod *clang, clanged* as she beat the pillar. Hitch was in her face, trying to tell her to *Three's mercy stop* but Evanne wanted none of it.

She didn't feel like drowning today.

She hit the pillar one more time and the front popped free, sliding across the decking to be lost with the pile of remains against the far wall. Revealed within were two circlets of metal, conveniently about the size to hold the rod between them. Running out of options fast, because *Dancing in the Storm* was in fact sinking in a new lakebed with another ship forcing her into a deeper grave, she slotted the golden rod in the circlets. It fit, snug as a bug.

Nothing happened.

Evanne peered at it, then wrapped her hand around it, giving it a wiggle. *I could really use Tarragon.* "Damn ancients couldn't build for shit. I don't know what the hell—"

The pillar and rod lit with brilliant gold-white energy. Evanne felt the jolt hit her, the back of her throat alive with the taste of a thunderstorm, her teeth bright and hot, her hair alive with power. She was flung across the room, slamming against the back wall. She lay, dazed, too dumb-struck to be angry anymore.

She could see outside, those tall floor-to-ceiling louvres open and showing her what was going on. Buildings that stood for an eon shook to rubble. Water came from above, an endless torrent that would drown all the sins of the past. But the lights... they caught her eye. What previously bloomed to life decayed, faded, as if the water were bringing hopelessness instead of boring moisture. As the lights on the *Dancing in the Storm's* deck shuttered one by one, the pillar of gold before Evanne brightened. It wasn't just light to her human eyes, but blood heat against her Vhemin ones. She could see a furnace wash blooming around the pillar, spreading like a fire, heating the metal floor, bringing to life what was dead.

And she *heard* it. The ship sang, a music outside hearing, something that made her want to play along. It was beautiful, soundless, her heart tripping in her chest like the crippled thing it used to be. Because the song was wrong, missing so many parts of the orchestra it couldn't keep the rhythm.

Hitch stood before her. "Get up. We've got to go."

She turned bleary eyes to him. "Can't you hear it, Hitch? The music's so loud."

He gave her a look that said, *You are completely cracked*, but his tone was even and calm. *Just like Erik Hitcherson. Not Hitch, but what he was.* "Soldier, you've got to come with me. To stay is to die."

He doesn't understand. Still, she clawed her way up, using the wall as support, the deck keening beneath her, the sound everywhere. "Where is my guitar?"

"Your what? For pity's sake. There's no time—"

"There's no time left if we leave, Hitch. Don't you see? The water will fill this cavern. We can't get along the deck and up to the light. I can't hold my breath that long. There's only one way out, and that's flying." Evanne pushed off from the sturdy safety of the wall, careening across the floor in pursuit of her guitar. She spied it amid a pile of old teeth, hair, and skulls. She hit a desk on her way there, tripped over a chair, knocked her forehead on the edge of another desk, swore, and then had the instrument in hand. Wood under her palm, strings under her fingers.

Now, play.

But I don't know a Trick for this. I've crooned to a traitorous lover under a blood moon and made those who love me follow when they shouldn't. "Hitch, I don't know the words."

He was there. Of course he was there. He was always there. She imagined his hand on her arm, his breath in her ear. "We can do this together."

"Not this time." She brushed a tear from her eye, unsure of how it got there, uncertain if she was angry or sad. Just like the ship, because it remembered who stood on its deck as it sailed the stars. It knew Erik Hitcherson. It knew Tarragon Greyflight. But it didn't know Evanne the Half-Made. "I need to make it right."

"Then tell it a story. Tell it about the world."

Evanne widened her stance, set her feet, and held her right hand high, poised to strike the strings. She thought of the Feybrind above, not just the one that threw her here, but all the others it represented. The fairies, all but gone. The dragons, truly gone. And the sewing boxes and sea chests that waited below for deliverance. Her hand fell like a striking hawk. She teased a chord from the discordant. A melody in between disharmony. Filled the gaps where the orchestra forgot how to play, left their music sheets at home, tried to play with a reedless woodwind. Her guitar, just a few strands of string against the sorrow of *Dancing in the Storm.*

"Hush," she said. "I won't say it's okay. But it might be, if we can make it right." The deck groaned, a mighty cry of warped metal as the blade of the enemy craft twisted in its heart. Evanne wanted to sob, because she knew what the ancients did. *They made this ship alive. They put a soul in it, then rode it to death.*

Water sloshed over the deck, burying detritus, washing the grime away. Cleaning the ship, while it sank its head and tried to drown. Evanne thought about the sewing box, felt the strings bite her fingers, felt how slick with blood they'd become. She bowed her head. "If that's how you want it. But I won't leave you. I can't leave you."

The deck settled. The roar of water was endless, but the ship's song quietened. Evanne kept playing, just as she had for the mimics, even though her fingers bled and her guitar strings smoked. The ship's song settled and found its beat. It went from the trip-lunge of Evanne's broken heart to the steady, ready rhythm of her remade organ. Steady. Certain.

Then the floor surged beneath her, a sprinter on the starting line pushing for the finish. All the lights along the deck surged to luminance, brilliant as tiny suns. *Dancing in the Storm's* nose hunted for daylight, the deck canting upward, spearing against the enemy vessel. Itikari metal sheared into Vehement, hooked, and caught. Rising like a hunter from the depths, *Dancing in the Storm* clutched the body of her ancient foe and broke into the lakebed above.

Evanne hunched over her guitar, because the song was so loud now. So bright, hard like the desert sun she'd walked across. Angry, and awake, and alive again. They erupted through the churning, turgid torrent of the lake, climbing for the sky. The ship shook like a dog, the trappings of time falling in their wake. Daylight hit her, and she saw Hollyhead's lake churning as fresh air came to her through the louvres.

Evanne stood, still crying, but with happiness. She looked out at what they'd done. Felt warm. Then blinked. "Hang about. Is that the fucking Raven?"

Chapter Forty-One

The ground shook like a corrupt supplicant in Morgan's throne room. The kind that knew they'd done something wrong, but tried to stare you down—*the very queen!*—and lie about how they were right. How they'd stolen the cow *back*, despite the bovine's branding telling a different tale, or how their property line had *always* been just so, despite their neighbour's goat milking shed being right amidst it.

Something disturbed the earth from deep within.

The queen staggered more than ran, Heser helping her, or her helping the guardsman, difficult to know. Pakhet loped ahead, and despite the armour lashed to her back, she made it look easy. Four limbs beat two on this kind of terrain, and she was built to a scale that saw fewer troubles from a ruckus.

The lake, then: it shook too. The waves rippled, surged, and fountained over the shore. They'd be swamped for certain, so Morgan cast about for a better place to stand firm. *There. A cliffside.* The western bank of the lake had a small rise leading to a sharp drop. They could defend it, no risk of attack from the rear, and perhaps toss a few animated corpses over the side if it came to that. She yanked Heser's arm, pointed, and he nodded.

A ragged-gasp rush, a hurry up a shaking hill, the water already spreading at the grassy base. Her feet were wet, boots sodden right to the core, which didn't speak well of the artisan who'd made them. She couldn't remember his name, and that bothered her. Heser yanked her arm right back, her woolgathering holding them up. "My queen! Now is not the time to dick about. Excuse my language."

"Fuck the language. We should be running." She shared a bared-teeth grin with him, and a last surge saw them climb the slope, stopping at the cliff's edge. Blessedly, the drop-off was as steep up close as it had seemed far away. A mountain goat would struggle navigating the climb. What Morgan saw as she surveyed the drop to the water below made her eyes want to pop free of her skull.

The water was dropping. Not a little but surging as if someone had pulled the plug from a bath. All manner of fish and lake plants lay exposed to the air. Water came and went, great surging waves, churning with muck and detritus, as often saving a fish as depositing a new one on the stony lakebed now exposed to air.

"*There's something you don't see every day.*" The grey striped tiger perched on the cliff edge, haunch down, paws in close. "*What do you suppose Evanne did this time?*"

"We don't know it was Evanne," Morgan lied. *Why am I defending the rapscallion? She's shown me nothing but attitude.*

"Perhaps she is getting the job done." Heser couldn't have known her thoughts, could he? It seemed he answered a question haunting the halls of her mind.

"*Perhaps. I suggest you see to your own chores. Attend! The dead come.*" The cat started grooming a paw.

Heser waved steel at her. "Are you going to help?"

"*I don't want to deprive you of the fun.*"

He growled. "There is little fun to killing."

"*Lucky for you, they're already dead. Oh, look. Here's one now.*" The cat slipped out of sight. It was like a fading of the light, and then there was nothing where she'd been but air.

Pakhet wasn't wrong. The first shambler made it to them, lurching, arms out at Heser. He stabbed his steel into the ground, picked it up, and tossed it over the cliff by brute strength. It clattered out of view, armour and weapons rattling all the way down.

Morgan observed the slope leading to them. She counted twenty enemy at least, and more emerging from the trees to the west. Another made it to Heser, and the guardsman drew steel from earth and beheaded it almost absently. It didn't slow down, so he walked about it, severed its spine, kicked the head over the cliff, then shoulder-barged it after its skull when cutting the spine had little effect.

She cleared her throat. "I feel there is a more efficient way. They do not respond to your mortal blows."

He gave her a narrow-eyed stare. "Do you want to do this?" After a pause: "My queen."

"I'm merely providing an observation."

He grunted, shook his head, and turned back to the next two approaching. Despite their unhurried manner, they made good time, never having to pause for breath or find their bearings. An army of these would be a marvel, and for a dark moment she wondered if there was space in her coterie for the dread arts of necromancy.

A wash of humid air came from her back with an accompanying slop and gurgle of water, and she turned. For the second time in as many minutes her eyes wanted to pop free of her skull, but this time it was trying to make sense of what was there. She saw a wall of metal covered in lake fronds and other gunk, which was surprising in itself. The wall was a part of a larger mass, a hulk of a thing that could house her whole keep within.

She took a step back, but didn't scream, because what was the point? The giant structure, a ship of some sort it must be, was on a crazy angle. She borrowed the gleam of Heser's steel and put some of it in her glare, straightened her shoulders, and stepped toward the edge.

Below, the rocks of the lakebed parted as an even bigger vessel surfaced from an ancient tomb. The prow was speared through by the smaller vessel she'd first seen. The *size* of it confounded her for a moment, because surely no human could make something so grand. It stretched longer than the entire length of Ravenswall, perhaps further than the nearest farmlets. The top deck was a ruin, of course, but she could make out lines where the streets of a whole town lay bare.

The shaking of the ground seemed the least of her worries. "Heser!"

He tossed a corpse over the edge, joining her for a moment, whistled, and said, "It'll keep." Then he was back in the fracas.

Morgan turned an incredulous stare in his direction. "It will *not* keep. It is a giant ship coming from beneath the very earth!"

"Does it have a sword at your throat?" He removed the arm of a corpse that obliged his point by swinging a blade at his head. "No? Then it'll mind."

"We can escape," she said. "We can hop aboard."

"Not a bad idea," he conceded. "When it draws near, we jump."

He dispatched five more corpses in the time it took the deck to draw near, the other ship now towering above, pierced through as it was. Or was it embedded in the larger hulk? A problem for another time. The ship approached, but it looked too far to jump. "We will not make it."

Heser joined her again, and she saw the strain on his face now. Sweat, a flush, but a tight-lipped mask hiding any discomfort. "It is of no moment. Come." He bulled through the three corpses before them, dragging her with. "Now, I will throw you."

"You will nooooo—" Her words trailed into a shriek as he grabbed her by the middle, then lurched toward the cliff's edge. Now *this* was a time for screaming, and she did not disappoint as he hurled her across the gap. She pinwheeled, arms flailing, heart fit to burst, and *slammed* into the side of the ship with a force that knocked the wind from her.

She slid and scrabbled for purchase. Morgan gripped a slippery frond, anchored to the hull of the vessel, and climbed. Hand up, a breath, teeth gritted, then her fingers found a ledge, and she hauled herself up. She found herself on a ruined deck, now some height above Heser and his melee. "Jump, guardsman!"

He glanced up at her. "My queen, they will simply follow. They will climb, as you did." He saluted her with his blade. "Find Evanne. Save us all." Then he turned his back on her and faced his doom.

Morgan's mouth opened, closed, and opened again. "For pity's sake, jump!" He didn't respond, blade an arc of glittering death. "Your queen commands it. You *must* jump, Heser."

He decapitated another corpse, then turned clear eyes to her. "I must protect the thing I love with all my heart."

She tried to jump then, to get back to him, but something held her back. Morgan howled and spat, turned in fury, to find the gentle jaws of Pakhet holding her cloak. "He will die!"

The cat didn't say anything, but her eyes were soft and very sad as she pulled Morgan from the edge. The ship beneath them moaned like whale song, sorrowful, and headed for the clouds.

Chapter Forty-Two

Tarragon was tired. Not, 'Oh my, I've had a day', tired, but, 'Merciful Three, I am nearly dead', exhausted. Her glitter didn't sparkle as it should, her luminance a glint rather than gleam. *I've pushed it too hard. I've been running and fighting for so long. I don't remember when I last slept. And I was tortured, too.*

She almost felt Helio's smile, nearly heard his voice. *That sounds like an excuse, soldier.*

"It's an excuse, but a good one." The tunnel she was in didn't care, just batted her words back with a slight reverb.

The reverb went on longer than it should. Tarragon frowned, put a hand to the curved wall beside her, then pulled it back. The wall shook, a gentle vibration that felt like an Itikari stardrive coming online. But that was impossible, because she wasn't in an Itikari ship. She was in the ship of her ancient enemy. The very one that killed *Dancing in the Storm.*

She picked up her pace, despite her feet feeling flat, her knees wobbling, and her wings drooping. She had to get out of here, into the open, and somehow find a way back to Evanne. She had an idea that the maybe-Vhemin might have found the control centre for *Dancing in the Storm*, way down below, and turned it on. And that would be bad, because she wasn't a fairy. Fairies could handle the radiation cascade from a semiconductor capacitor once it was engaged. A maybe-Vhemin? Difficult to know. An all-the-way Vhemin could live on the poisoned, radioactive plaguelands. Could Evanne?

Why she'd turned the stardrive on was anyone's guess, but there was no mistaking the gentle, insistent rumble.

Then the floor became the wall. Tarragon tumbled, only slightly put out because she didn't have far to fall and besides, the pipe was round. The wall could be the floor without inconveniencing anyone.

Then the floor/wall/whatever *really* shook, and *then* it lurched, a staggering amount really, as it sought up. And Tarragon thought: *Oh, my.* Dancing in the Storm *is alive.*

She ran. She ran and ran, never mind the fatigue, and ran some more. The *Century Charm* was definitely moving up, creaking and groaning all about. The pipe before Tarragon snapped open, sheared off as a girder passed through, giving her a glimpse of chaos. The room outside was on fire, which she ignored because she was a fairy, jumping the gap with a tiny flutter to carry her the distance. The pipe heated up, also fine, but the air was getting thin, which was less fine.

It didn't help her exhaustion any.

If I could just find a Three-damned sword! She wanted to scream with frustration. Escaped from a Vhemin interrogation cell, survived a city blowing up, near drowning, assassins, the desert, a misfiring temple, and now this, all without a blade in hand. It defied belief.

She was nearing the ship's hull. The pipework took a hard left, the sounds behind her growing deader by degrees as she entered the insulating layer that safeguarded souls from arclight fire. The pipe she used as a corridor must have carried reactant back in the day, but here it carried not even a cobweb. She could feel the rads around her, the echoes of a bygone time, quickened no longer, but deadly to Bigs even still.

The rads would keep her safe. *I don't want to be safe. I want to be with Evanne.* She gave a tiny scream of frustration, and just like that, the hull before her cracked open with the agonised cry of breaking metal. Outside, muddy water and daylight. She lunged for the gap, wiggling an arm in and damn the risk, but it wasn't wide enough to let her through.

Tarragon pressed her face to the sharp, jagged seam, eyes hunting, seeking. She saw the expanse of *Dancing in the Storm* laid out below her, all the way to the conning tower. It stood like a weary soldier, hatches battened down, a few broken and wide. Rock and silt covered the deck, water still sluicing off and into the lake below.

The door to the conning tower stood open, and in the shade, hiding from the light, were mimics. Guardians still, not freed from their task. *No time for pity.* Between the soul-bound guardians and Tarragon, a shambling mess of undead men and women were clambering onto the deck from the western side, slow and steady as they came, no rush about it. Amidship was what looked like Queen Morgan, looking unqueenly indeed as she wrestled with Pakhet. The giant tiger didn't look like she was that taxed, her attention cast back to the conning tower.

From which strode, guitar in hand, Evanne. Tarragon bounced in glee, clapping in excitement and joy. *She's alive! My love is alive!* She tried to wriggle into the breach again, then froze as the light was blotted out.

A Feybrind jewelled eye stared in at her. Just a metre or so separated them, the thickness of the hull, and there was Dancing Stars, lips pulled into a snarl. "I *see* you."

Tarragon pulled back in fright, then squared her shoulders. "I see you too. How did you get out there?"

"I ran away." The voice was wry, but falsely so. Whatever magic the ancients gave the collar at her throat, it wasn't good at irony. "Just like you're trying to."

"I'm not running away. I'm running *to*." Tarragon beamed. "And there's nothing you can do to stop me."

"Huh." The Feybrind vanished, and a moment later the sound of clanking metal and scraping rust. A hatch, perhaps? The tunnel about Tarragon shook, then *clanged* like a bell, which wasn't great because the fairy was inside it. She collapsed, dazed, still exhausted and nothing left in the tank really, then got an arm beneath her. *Up, soldier. Fight's not done.*

The tunnel whipped up and down as if someone was shaking it like an aerosol can. Tarragon hit the roof, the floor, each wall, the roof, the floor, the walls again, and so on for long enough to bite her lip, her tongue, bash her nose, feel blood gush, bang her forehead, scream in rage, have that cut off as she hit the roof again, then collapse to the let's-call-it-the-floor. Light of a different sort broke into the tunnel. Tarragon gasped, trying to get away from that end, because the Feybrind was right *there*, those jewelled eyes hungry rather than hard, but something was wrong with her arm, and her knee was wonky, and her wings were a crumpled mess.

The Feybrind snared her from within, pulling her into a Big corridor. Sure enough, the traitorous hatch was above them, a rusted metal ladder leading to it. The pipe Tarragon had been in was clearly marked *RADIATION DANGER* in what passed for wasp-bright yellow-and-black after an age of time. A sword—for Bigs, not Tarragons—lay in its scabbard on the floor.

Requiem. Dancing Stars hadn't drawn it, no doubt having intel on what happened to non-humans who tried that, but had used the magic weapon as a crude crowbar to open the pipe. *Well, that sucks. I wonder how she got Requiem. Are the dead her servants?*

Dancing Stars held Tarragon up to eye height. "You were saying?"

"I misjudged," the fairy admitted. "What now?"

A half-smile broke across the Feybrind's face. "You get your wish. We're going to meet your friend. Then we're going to torture you."

"Wait, what? Why are we doing that?" Tarragon blinked in confusion.

"She has the ship." Dancing Stars' smile didn't widen, but it looked like she wanted it to. "*My* ship. She will give it to me, or you'll die."

"You could just talk to her. Without the torture!"

"My way is easier. More honest." The Feybrind gave Tarragon another shake for good measure, then held up a wire cage. "Remember these?"

She tossed Tarragon inside the torture jail cage, which sucked a lot, but she was too tired to do much about it. If she could have a few moments to gather herself, she could bust out again.

But Evanne didn't have a few moments. Not from Feybrind 'justice'.

Chapter Forty-Three

Evanne hurried as fast as the busted-up dais would allow. The mimics clustered around her, some tall, some foot height, and all leaning in. She didn't feel threatened, more ... *protected*. As if they shared her concerns and were hanging around to help out.

"Hey," she addressed an armoire. "Are you guys hanging around to help out?"

"*We like the music. You make the music for us, and for the ship's heart.*" The armoire had a voice like finely sifted, sun-warmed sand. Easy, gentle, and calm. Definitely unsuited to a murder box.

"Is that a yes?" Evanne glanced around. "You guys are hard to read without faces."

"*Will you make more music?*"

Evanne nodded. "It's what I do."

"*Will you make the music that sets us free?*" This came from the sewing box, which hopped about her ankles.

"I don't think I can." She held up her free hand, palm out. "Hold up. Not because I don't want to, but because that's not my gift. But I know someone."

"*Then we are here to 'help out'.*" The sewing box bounced happily. "*Eight hundred years is a long time to be a sewing box.*"

"No kidding." Evanne's teeth rattled as the dais stopped not quite at the bottom of the shaft. She hopped over the edge, followed by the mimic contingent. The doorway outside was still ajar, the buildings previously on the deck mostly scrubbed away by the ship's rise through water and rock. "Speaking of someone, where the hell is she? Ah. Yo! Morgan!"

The Raven knelt by the railing, Pakhet hunched beside her. The giant tiger had Hitch's armour strapped to her, but otherwise looked the same. Morgan looked like she grieved. No tears, nothing like that. Face an implacable mask, but so hard it looked brittle. Eyes dry, but like the frozen wastes, all the water turned to crystal by driving cold. Shoulders straight, back straighter still. The pair knelt in the shadow of the ship poised above them. Evanne turned her gaze to it. It wasn't ever as big as *Dancing in the Storm*, and there wasn't much of it left.

The two ships were still locked together, but without the embrace of rock, that wouldn't last long. The ship above them groaned, shifted, perhaps threatening to topple and squash them flat. A hatchway on the side banged open as if in agreement, then tore free, tumbling the long way down to clatter on the deck.

The queen stood, smoothed her jerkin as if it were a court gown, and clasped her hands before her. Waiting. *Well, of course she wants me to go to her. Queens don't hustle after other people.* No matter. Evanne understood the Trick being played here, one not on her, or even for her, but for *Morgan*. Whatever was going on in her head needed this, and Evanne could give a little. So, she hustled over, then noticed the mimics weren't following. They clustered in the door's shadow. "Guys. What's up?"

"*The sunlight,*" the sewing box explained. "*It will cleanse us.*"

"A bath doesn't sound so bad."

"*Not that kind of cleansing.*"

It's never easy, is it? "Stick around. This is the person I know." She jerked a thumb at the Raven. "I'll be right back." She hurried over to Morgan. As she drew nearer, Morgan's distress was more apparent by how immobile she was. Evanne pulled to a halt a few metres clear, because she knew rushing up to a troubled horse was the surest way to get a kick. "You good?"

"I am well. Thank you for asking." Morgan's speech was impeccable, crisp, cut from the same block of ice behind her eyes. "Are you well, too?"

Evanne veered away from the trap, because it dawned on her: Heser the Cheg was not here. She felt her heart clench, her breath freeze. *It can't be. I sent them away to be safe. So no one else would fall on my account.* Her voice hitched, scratched, and stumbled, not at all like Morgan's cool tones. "Where is Uncle Heser?"

"He ... stayed behind." A tiny tic in her lower eyelid was all the release the Raven allowed herself.

"He was supposed to. You were both supposed to be protected!" Evanne felt the ice flow beneath her crack, halves separate, drift apart. "He was supposed to be safe."

"He was not." Morgan straightened further, if it was possible. "Will you put this ship down so we can retrieve him?"

Evanne glanced to the side. "He's down there?"

"Was. Past tense."

"I don't know how. I, I... Uh." Evanne took a step back. Morgan's face had seized, lips parted, no air coming through. "What's wrong?"

A shining red length of steel emerged from Morgan's stomach, glistening and wet. Evanne staggered forward, not understanding. Her hand found Morgan's, the queen's grip strong and desperate. Evanne tried to push the steel back, but her fingers slipped on slick metal. Her eyes met Morgan's. She saw terror, pain, and confusion.

The steel whipped back, and Evanne felt a ghost of Hitch within her. Saw the coming move and kicked Morgan aside. The red arc of steel slashed the air where the queen's neck had been a moment earlier. She roared, charged empty space, and collided with someone. Evanne took the sword to her shoulder for her trouble and considered it fair payment for having the Feybrind in her grip.

But, not for very long. Dancing Stars snaked free. It was like trying to hold water without a glass. Evanne scrambled away, backing toward Morgan. The Raven panted, blood slicking the deck beneath her.

Evanne found her hand again, gripped it. Held it close. "Speak to me, Morgan."

"The pain is exquisite," the Raven admitted. "But I believe I've had enough of this. Will you buy me a few moments?"

"So you can die alone? Fuck, no."

A withering stare, still intact despite her wound. "Just this once, Evanne, will you do me the courtesy of—"

Whatever the courtesy was supposed to be was lost as steel glinted in the air. Evanne pushed Morgan away, using the shove to roll herself the opposite way. Steel rang against metal decking, then again, stabbing where Evanne was, so she just kept rolling. Her back shored up against a slump of detritus, allowing a pause, then she surged sideways as the light shifted around the Feybrind's cloak. The steel sank into the debris behind Evanne, then came free with wood affixed to the blade.

It would buy her seconds, at best. Evanne stood, realised she'd lost her guitar in her tumbling, and swore.

Tarragon's voice came from the air to her left. "Evanne, runaaaaii-iiieeee!"

The fairy was an invisible captive. Evanne felt fear closely followed by murderous rage. She bared not-quite-shark-teeth, snarling, and lunged for the air. Her fingers caught a scrap of unseeable cloth, gripped, then lost it. She whirled, lunged again, missed, stumbled, and then screamed as her back felt the lick of steel.

She staggered, back arched, and cried out. Turned once more, anger burning hotter. *She has my Tarragon. She stabbed my queen. And she stabbed me! Payment is overdue.* Evanne held her hand out. "Hitch. I need you."

The spectre stepped into her, a whisper of cold, a feeling of heat, and they were one. His voice came in her mind. "She will banish me again."

"Until then, we make her pay. See? There." Evanne looked to red drip-dripping to the deck a handful of paces away. The Feybrind's blade might be invisible, but the blood she'd taken from Morgan and Evanne wasn't.

"I see." Hitch breathed with her lungs, breath frosting out, gravecold settling over her. S/he stepped toward the blood, heard the gritty whisper of boots against mud muck, and turned. They felt the air of the blade as it passed by, not a handspan from their face. S/he reached for the path of the weapon, found steel and a fursoft hand. Feet braced, shoulder up, and *twist*, sending the Feybrind away.

A *whump* as Dancing Stars hit the deck. Evanne followed—or was it Hitch? Was there a difference?—a predator after prey, teeth bared. Found empty space on the ground, no body, because Feybrind were quick. Evanne cried out as the blade's edge kissed her shoulder blade. Hitch held her safe while he rolled them forward, away from doom and pain. Evanne stood. Hitch dropped their stance. Evanne snarled. Hitch steadied their breath.

They waited. One, ready, poised. Evanne said, "Come, witch."

"You've found your ghost. Quaint." The Feybrind's voice was on the wind, behind Evanne, before her, everywhere. "That's enough of that."

A wrench, and Evanne staggered as Hitch was ripped from her. She felt the shiver of loss, Hitch's cry of frustration only for her ears. Evanne felt about, and knew he was nowhere close. She cocked her head, feeling for the Trick of how Hitch stood, and copied it. "You speak as if you understand how I fight. Aren't Feybrind supposed to be wise?"

A slight pause, then Dancing Stars' voice came from her right. "You can't fight like him. He isn't with you anymore."

"He is always with me." Evanne touched her heart. Another Trick, a lie between friends this time. "He is here."

The Feybrind stabbed her through the gut this time. Evanne wheezed forward, hunched over the sword, head finding safe harbour against the Feybrind's invisible shoulder. Dancing Stars' lips were next to her ear. "Can he feel this?" She wiggled the steel.

Evanne hurt too much to scream, so she settled for a right cross. There was no curry in it, what with the piece of steel in her stomach, but she connected. The Feybrind danced back, taking her steel in a rush of white-hot agony.

Evanne swayed with the wind. Felt its cold kiss, her lifeblood dripping beneath her. Straightened, and smiled, a hard Trick but a necessary one. "You are nothing like the People. You enjoy the pain of others."

"I am like all of us. The ones who cannot speak because we were made to be mute. Who feel the lash of scorn. Whose birthright is servitude. We were made to be beneath your feet, but we're above you."

Movement by the far railing drew Evanne's eye. A sewing box, keeping to the shadows, was hustling their way. A sea chest hunched along behind it. She looked away, because someone was coming over the opposite railing. For a moment she dared hope *Uncle Heser* then saw this person was dead far longer than moments. He was joined by another, then another. The damned were coming for them.

Great.

A flicker of the light drew Evanne's wandering eye. Before her, a ripple flickered through the air, revealing Dancing Stars rushing at her, blade high. Evanne felt surprise, then elation, dropped low, and put her shoulder into the Feybrind's midriff. Stood, all brute strength, and tossed her over her shoulder. It bought her time to take stock. *Ah.* Morgan lay on the deck, finger tracing lines through a pool of her own blood. Evanne saw a stylised eye within a ring. The ritual wasn't much, a thumb on the scales at best, but it took away some of Dancing Stars' cloak's power.

Evanne spun back to the Feybrind, who'd wasted no time in gaining a little distance. She still had the damnable blade. With her free hand she lifted a cage lashed to her belt, giving it a shake. Within, a tiny glimmer. *Tarragon.* The Feybrind held the tip of her steel to the cage. "Do you want to see her die?"

"What do you want?" Evanne didn't let her eye follow the sewing box's trek across the deck.

"I want this ship." Dancing Stars raised an eyebrow. "I want it all. Every secret and piece of stray magic."

"No problem," Evanne said. "Take it." She was mindful the dead shambled closer, more of their fellows coming from over the side. The ship, perhaps listening, groaned a stressed metal cry, wallowing in the sky. The shadow of the enemy vessel shifted.

"I don't believe you'll let me have it." The Feybrind half-smiled.

"Then why ask?" Evanne touched her belly. The wound seeped, but the flow had staunched already. A gift from her father, but she needed her mother more now. A blade, and mastery of it. The Storm on a leash, the Sway at her call.

The sewing box was almost here. The Feybrind hadn't seemed to notice. "I want you to give it to me because you've nothing left to give. I want to *know* you mean it." She shook the cage, Tarragon falling against the bars. The fairy screamed, then fell to the bottom.

"*Excuse me.*" Pakhet appeared behind Dancing Stars, the great tiger massive and towering, a grey menace.

The Feybrind spun, sword in guard, then froze as she looked up, cage falling from nerveless fingers, then looked up some more at the tiger. "What? Where? *How?*"

"*I am magnificent, I know.*" Pakhet yawned a razor maw of mincing ivory, then closed her mouth with a snap. "*Is now a bad time to talk?*"

"Now," Evanne hissed. "Now!"

The sewing box lunged, snapping at the binding lashing Tarragon to the Feybrind's belt. Dancing Stars turned to the new threat, but the sewing box made good time, scurrying across the deck with cage in tow. Dancing Stars made to follow then stopped short at the sea chest before her. It opened, revealing not a cosy interior of folded blankets and keepsakes, but a wet, slavering maw.

The first undead soldier arrived, stabbing the sea chest, which didn't seem to mind. It turned, lunged, snapped closed, and then there was one less undead warrior on the deck.

Dancing Stars sprinted after the sewing box, but she was mere mortal flesh. The little mimic moved with a speed that other sewing boxes couldn't hope to match, breaking away from the living dead, the Feybrind, the giant tiger, and all other danger to race toward the open door at the base of the tower.

Evanne liked the box's approach. She bent, nabbed a stray rock, lined up her shot, and hurled at Dancing Stars' head. The rock hit, *bang*, a perfect shot. The Feybrind stumbled, turned with a snarl, then reached to her belt. She pulled free a curious stick-like object, which Evanne would have called a wand if it wasn't so crooked. Raising it high, she said, "Murder them all. Do it *now*."

Evanne thought the deck had been well populated with undead warriors, but she realised that was a failure of imagination. Over the side, a wave of corpses rose, rusted swords and warped branches in hand, some with armour, some naught but bones. The previously shambling husks scurried with renewed vigour alongside their reinforcements. Which was more or less fine, because the sewing box had made it half-way to the doorway, and the tiny mimic carried the most important thing in Evanne's life to safety. She straightened, held her hands up just like Hitch did, and beckoned with her left hand. "Come get some."

The Feybrind obliged, leaping toward Evanne. She tried to pivot, but the damn cat was faster than the wind. Evanne took the sword to her gut again, groaning over the blade, falling to the deck as Dancing Stars whipped it free. She coughed blood, then looked up at the Feybrind. Majestic. Beautiful, in a way no human or Vhemin could hope to be. Eyes like jewels, demanding a yearning to meet soul to soul. But within Evanne, that lick of sickness when she was around the People, the thing she'd pushed down and away.

It was so tiresome, but now she held it. Grabbed it, hard, and stood. Wiped bloody drool from her lips, snarled right back. "Best you got?"

The cat's eyes widened a micron in surprise, but clearly having been raised to not disappoint, lunged at Evanne again. This time, Evanne took the blade across her ribs, the hot burning pain a welcome distraction from the holes in her stomach. She grappled with Dancing Stars, half-Vhemin strength against Feybrind. Not a contest she could win, but she wasn't trying to win. *I just need a little more time.* The deck shifted beneath them, *Dancing in the Storm* listing to starboard. The ship shuddered as it gouged the hillock the Raven had climbed from. The ruined hulk above them shifted. Sunlight glinted.

A shaft of golden dawn fell across the sewing box. The box was mid-hop, and for a moment Evanne saw who it used to be. A lad, perhaps twelve, which defied belief because what could a twelve-year-old do that demanded an age of servitude. She saw his ghostly outline, blue-green and shot through with all the colours of the sun. Arched in pain or release, then he was gone.

The box clattered open, spools of thread and needles spilling forth. Just a sewing box once more.

Dancing Stars saw it too. Chuckled into Evanne's ear, held so close as if they were lovers. "Now I will get your fairy, and we'll end this as we should have."

"Don't," Evanne coughed, "count on it." For good measure, she head-butted Dancing Stars, the Feybrind falling back, hand to nose, and surprised to see it coming back bloody.

And now, Evanne had the sword. She took two breaths, thought *don't think about it*, and yanked it from her ribs. She flourished the blade to stop from fainting and felt for a Trick. One she learned from a great person, strong in all the right ways. Aunt Barret wouldn't have even blinked when stabbed, and Evanne let none of the pain show on her face. *For Tarragon.*

Because from the door across the deck spilled the mimics. Large ones, small ones, all of them angry. They kept to the remaining shadow, running toward their fallen comrade, and to Tarragon. The dead surged toward them. Evanne leaned back into one of Hitch's favourite fighting stances, blade held low as she remembered Mama doing. *What did she call it? Low guard.* Offhand up, once again beckoning. "I can do this all day. Can you?"

Chapter Forty-Four

Tarragon bounced along the deck in her cage. Whatever tool Dancing Stars used to elicit pain was left behind on the foul monster's belt, so that was a plus. But she wanted to cry when the little mimic died, because she saw he was like her: too small for this world, too easy to break. Perhaps, unlike her, he'd been too brave to care, and now he was gone. The slightly larger mimic dragging her forward was a suitcase. There seemed precious use for suitcases in this new world she'd woken to, but it looked a fashionable piece of luggage and earnest in its intent to take her to safety.

She held the bars of her prison, watching as she drew further from Evanne. The maybe-Vhemin held a sword and a bloody grin with equal ferocity. But her opponent was *Feybrind*. They'd been made to win at everything. Dancing Stars was heavy with years and experience, and Evanne was but sixteen summers.

I don't want to watch.

The nightmare corpses swarming the deck met the mimics with a clatter of metal on wood. An armoire that was polished to a shine Tarragon quite liked opened up, gobbled a corpse, then snapped shut. A moment later the doors opened, revealing racks and hangers, but no corpse. Just … gone. Then it was beset by three unholy warriors and hacked to pieces. Amid the debris, there was no fallen corpse, but Tarragon saw the outline of a woman with long hair sketched in the air, her arm reaching for the sky, and then her spirit was absent, the wreckage limp and dead.

"Get me a sword," she said to no one and everyone. No one and everyone ignored her. "Get me out of this box!"

The suitcase paused. "*We need safe haven from the Three's sight. We were not made with their consent.*"

Tarragon gripped the bars of her prison. "You mean you were made in violation of the Holomancer's three laws?"

The suitcase said nothing but picked up its pace as it headed for the door. A zombie hustled in from left field and was eaten by a secretaire. A group of warriors draped in vines, armour green with verdigris, set upon the secretaire. A wardrobe, of a size fit for the queen's fashions, lunged, and gobbled three in a single wide sweep of its doors.

Then they were inside the tower. Tarragon remembered how it used to be. Pillars of light reaching up the elevator shaft. Suspensors lifting with magic and science. People hustling to and fro, fairies on the wing. There was nothing like that now. The lights were all absent. The dais didn't align with the floor. The only human was Queen Morgan, bleeding to the bitter end. And there was only one fairy.

"Yasmine!" Tarragon pressed her face to the inert bars. "Have you found me a sword?"

A rake of arclight fire destroyed the suitcase, gleaming glitterbeams of fire and light tearing it to ash and a couple of stray buckles. A small, fat man's spectre tried to run from the remains and was caught on wind only he could feel, taken, and gone.

Tarragon turned and saw Dancing Stars bearing down on them. The Feybrind had an arclight rifle, which explained what was going on. She pointed it at Tarragon and was knocked sideways by Evanne. The maybe-Vhemin stepped from fog that wasn't there two seconds ago, her own tremulous cloak stuttering and struggling with keeping her hidden.

But this one time it worked, and Dancing Stars hit the deck hard. Evanne was covered in blood and cuts but didn't look upset about it. She looked like an avenging goddess. Tarragon bit her lip, not seeing the tattered cloak, the raggedy clothes, the klicks on the trail. She saw someone she very much wanted to know a lot better. *Now is not the time.* "Can someone get me out of this cage? Anyone?"

Pakhet bounded inside, armour still lashed to her back, and a scab-barded sword in her mouth. She spat it to the deck, where it clattered. Tarragon recognised the weapon. *Requiem.* The giant cat turned to the open door and roared. "*Evanne!*"

The maybe-Vhemin looked to them, perhaps counting. Hands balled into fists. Saw the queen. The tiger. Mimics, in a huddle. Her eyes met Tarragon's. Relaxed in relief for a moment. She ran to the door, touched Pakhet's nose. "Make them safe."

Then she stepped back and moved to the side. To the panel that controlled the door and responded only to a human's touch. Pressed her hand to her heart, blew a kiss from it to Tarragon, then put it against the panel. Behind her, Tarragon saw Dancing Stars stand. The Feybrind gathered the arclight rifle and turned to Evanne. Who stepped out to face the Feybrind.

The door groaned, then with a scream of metal, eased closed. Tarragon screamed louder, hand out, but it was done. Evanne was gone.

Chapter Forty-Five

Evanne didn't feel awesome. She felt like she'd been stabbed thirty times, perhaps an exaggeration, but not by much. She'd fallen down about that many times, either as Dancing Stars pummelled her, stabbed her, or used some of Hitch's weird tricks to throw her across the deck. *It doesn't matter. What did Hitch say? 'Fall down seven times, get up eight'? Rookie numbers. I can do this all day.*

Behind Evanne lay the closed door. Safety, because the Feybrind couldn't open it. Not with her non-human hands. Morgan might be able to open it from the inside, but the Raven was bleeding out, perhaps to her last, and Evanne trusted the tiger's sense of preservation to stop any such foolishness.

They're safe. I will buy as much time as I can. They will run and be free.

The Feybrind stood before her. Behind the cat stood an array of vicious undead warriors, some bowed with time, others spoiling for more ruckus. Evanne might have stood a chance with Hitch, but she had zero prospects now. There was enough mongrel in her to stand a few more minutes, but that was it.

Dancing in the Storm swayed, perhaps in response to the gentle wind touching her flank. The ship eased farther out over the lake. The sun peered from behind the enemy's vessel, touching Evanne's face. She closed her eyes. Felt the cool of the wind and warmth of the sun, and thought, *More than a few minutes would be nice. It's not such a bad place to die, though.*

The Feybrind considered Evanne down the barrel of that strange ancient rifle. "You're brave or stupid."

"I'm happy to be both." Evanne glanced to the ship poised above them. "Does she have a name?"

"They called her the *Century Charm.* The name is writ large on the hull. I saw it when I came for your fairy friend."

Evanne sighed. "A good enough name, although I daresay they should have called it *Ship for Brains.* Crashing into this marvel was a stupid thing and made the world worse for all."

"I don't know." Dancing Stars lowered her weapon. "This ship was run by slavers. They thought people were things to be owned, whether furred or scaled. My kind came from here. Dragons and fairies too. They might have looked like marvels, but the trappings of wonder do not make it less horrible."

"I've no argument with that." Evanne rubbed her shoulder. The most recent wound there was healing well enough. "You look like you've had enough of a rest and are looking forward to another beating. Are we going to do this, or what?"

The Feybrind half-smiled. "You've bought a little time. Time is such an interesting thing. A mayfly might see a day as an age. For the People, a week is as tiny as a second. The blessed weapon will hurry from here, and I will follow. I will get it back, and your efforts will be for naught."

Evanne nodded amiably enough. "That may be true. But it will still be a week where you don't have it. You never know what could happen in a week. A mountain could explode. An ancient flying fortress could rise from a lakebed. Those kinds of things change the world. They upset all the pieces on your board."

"Perhaps you should die sooner rather than later. Your voice annoys me." The Feybrind shouldered her weapon in a smooth motion and pulled the trigger.

It clicked, hissed, then sighed. Nothing else happened.

Evanne laughed. "You should have brought a holy weapon. The Tresward's scatterguns might have been more use."

The Feybrind gave a silent snarl, dropped the rifle, drew a sword, and leaped. Evanne dodged the first blow, her enemy's blade taking a rust lock, the hair wisping on the wind. *Cophine's summer dress, but she's fast.* The second back slice Evanne almost dodged, taking a cut on her arm. And a thought hit her as Dancing Stars half-smiled again. *I have seen house cats play with mice, this selfsame look on their faces.*

Because they enjoyed it.

Well, I enjoy things too. The blade sliced along Evanne's ribs, and she accepted the pain as price of entry. It brought her once again into the Feybrind's intimacy, where hot breath mingled, and she could smell the cinnamon scent of her combatant. *No matter.* Evanne got her hands hooked like claws into the Feybrind's jacket and brought her in for another head-butt. *Crack.* Another, for good measure, and Dancing Stars had the good grace to go a little boneless.

Then the cat brought a knee up into Evanne's groin. Luck and fortune was with Evanne, as she kept her grip on cloth, the Feybrind coiling like a mad snake. She earned her own head-butt, ducking her head to take it skull on skull, and gave a third back before breaking free.

They staggered apart, two drunkards on the battlefield. Evanne smeared blood from her lips, flicked her hand, droplets scattering, and gave another almost-shark-toothed smile. "Again?"

As the Feybrind charged, blade high, Evanne thought, *I hope Tarragon is far away.*

Chapter Forty-Six

T arragon was on the wing, her tiny fists beating on the door leading to the ship's deck. They did nothing. "Morgan!" The Raven was the only one who could open it. The queen bled quietly to herself, the spreading pool beneath her ochre in the strange, fallen light within the tower.

The ghost-pale Big stirred. "Get me up. I can open it."

Yasmine flitted into Tarragon's eye line. "You can't go out there. The whole reason the Half-Made put you here was so you could get away. Run, and be free. Save the legacy of our people."

"You're crazy, lady." Tarragon ducked around her, darting to Morgan. The Raven Queen curled on her pain, no Vhemin strength in her, nothing but sheer will earned atop a rusty throne keeping her upright. "Get the sword. With the sword you can beat the monster and save the, uh. Save everyone."

Morgan nodded, and Tarragon saw despite her lips being blue, her eyes were fire. "A debt is owed. My... liegeman fell. I will bring justice."

Yasmine buzzed about Tarragon. "Your one chance to go. Isn't that what you've always wanted? Freedom. No leash. Blazing a path. Beating your own drum. Not living up to our expectations."

Tarragon thought about that for less than a second. "I don't care about your expectations. I must get out there."

A helpful shoe box humped close, dragging Requiem's scabbarded length to Morgan. The queen touched the hilt with weak fingers. Tarragon's jaundiced eye said *No way she could do this without a magic sword*. Morgan got the scabbard's tip on the ground, and using it like a cane, levered herself to her feet.

It cost her. Tarragon saw how much, the sway the queen had never shown, the half-lidded eyes, the parted lips, the shallow breaths. She flitted closer, wanting to help. *If only I was Big! I could help. I could really help.* "Are you okay?"

Morgan nodded and drew Requiem. The sword's radiance bathed the room. White, clean, the cold of justice on a hanging dawn. She hefted the blade, the length trembling not at all. Little arcs of energy walked the blade's length. Tarragon marvelled at the weapon. Such a sword had never been made, not by Feybrind, not by fairy. The very best mastersmith in all the world could toil his life away and never make its equal.

Surely it was enough to best an upstart cat.

Morgan faced the door. Raised one blood-caked hand, palm out toward the panel that would open it. Then fell, face-first, on the ground.

Requiem clattered free. The blade's luminance dimmed but wasn't gone. Little arcs of electricity walked from the blade, dancing toward the door. Toward their enemy, as if the sword wanted the fight.

Tarragon wailed. "No. No! We're so close. You've got to get up." She flew to Morgan, landing beside the queen's head. The porcelain perfect face was still. Barely any breath at all escaped her mouth. And Tarragon realised, *She thought she was going to her death, and she did it anyway*.

Yasmine landed beside Tarragon. The other fairy clicked her fingers in front of Tarragon's face, snaring her attention. "Hey. Yes, you. Tarragon Greyflight, lost child of a fallen empire, all that. You must run."

"Never," Tarragon snarled. "Evanne's out there."

Yasmine relaxed, and gave a small, knowing smile. "She is your enemy. Her blood is dirty with the taint of the enemy."

"Don't be stupid," Tarragon said. "Our enemy comes from our same house. Itikari made the Feybrind, and they fight us, undermine us, and are trying to destroy what's left of our world." She panted, trying to hold her anger in check. *Hell with it*. "Enemies aren't made by blood. Lovers are not made by sharing the same skin. We're all in this together."

"What would Helio say?"

Tarragon checked herself. *She knew Helio?* "He'd have asked what the mission is."

"And what's the mission?" Yasmine's face was intent, something else behind the question.

Who is she, really? Tarragon brushed glitter from her hair. "Save the girl. Save the world."

"In that order?"

"Always." Tarragon bit her lip. "I know it should be the other way around, but—"

"The world is made of all of us. We can't save it without thinking about the people who make it." Yasmine leaned close, conspiratorial now. "Tarragon, what would you give to save the world?"

"Anything." Tarragon looked for another way out. Maybe a hatch she'd missed? As her eyes scanned the room, they passed over something half-hidden, waiting, ready. A giant maiden she glimpsed for but a moment, taller than any person, mightier than an Artifice. A dawn warrior, armoured and ready, spear in hand, leaning forward with Yasmine's intensity, waiting for the answer.

Then, gone. Tarragon rubbed her eyes. *I'm tired. That's all it is. I'm just super tired.*

"Tarragon, would you give up your home and power? Would you cast aside the gift of flight, the grace of the wing, your very namesake, that of the Grey Flight, to save the girl?" Yasmine waited.

Tarragon gave her wings an experimental flutter. Touched her hair again, feeling the warmth of her glimmer. Thought of Evanne, dying so they could get away. "I would give anything."

Yasmine smiled. Tarragon *felt* it, warm like she'd just walked into a sunbeam on a winter's day. The other fairy leaned in, grabbed her jerkin, and kissed her. It was long, and warm, and very surprising, and quite confusing. Tarragon didn't know what to do, so she didn't do anything except feel ... good.

Yasmine pulled away. Tarragon blinked, a lot. "What was that for?"

"Need doesn't want for a reason. Also, it's my last chance." Yasmine's smile widened, and Tarragon smelled new cut grass and spring flowers. "Let us begin, again. We'll change a tiny thing, so we can fix everything."

Chapter Forty-Seven

The dead came for Evanne. The damnable Feybrind waited outside punching range, looking tired and haggard. Evanne felt a slight tinge of satisfaction from that. It didn't overshadow her feeling of dread, because she was going to die, but at least she'd made the creature work for it. The damned shambled, in no hurry at all now. Lots of them, rotten clumps of ancient warriors with their mindless urge to end her life. She stood tall, the blood of a hundred cuts on her clothes, the weakness inside her making her tremble, here at the end.

But at least Tarragon is free.

Movement at the ship's side drew her eye. More undead horrors, no doubt. She turned back to Dancing Stars, trying to come up with a good last line. "You don't even have the stomach to do it yourself."

"I have plenty of stomach, monster." The Feybrind's half-smile didn't waver. "You're just not worth my time."

"I thought you had so much time it didn't matter."

"I have a river of time and still I don't want to share a thimbleful with you." The cat's tail lash, lashed. She raised the gnarled wand, her jewelled eyes gleaming with delight. "That's why I have servants."

A roar from Evanne's right, and she thought, *Three's mercy, but what horror has she conjured now?* She turned, too damn slow, because she was exhausted, the Vhemin in her finally tired, but the human not ready to kneel. She gaped in surprise, thinking at first it some Trick. A new everliving warrior, a final blow to kill Evanne's hope, conjuring the recent dead.

Heser the Cheg, bleeding from every inch of exposed skin. Evanne's mind, limping in time to the sluggish blood in her veins, finally clicked: *he lives. He's alive!*

And she laughed, because it was Uncle Heser, and he was alive, and he looked so very angry.

Heser the Cheg waded into the ranks of undead before her. Standing against their wave, an angry rock at high tide, relentless. He ploughed toward Dancing Stars, who leaped at him. Her Feybrind quickness, that beautiful skill with a blade. Evanne reached out, all the strength she had in her, wanting to pull Uncle Heser behind her, because Morgan loved him, and he loved her, and no one should die but the Half-Made mongrel that didn't fit in this world anyway.

The Feybrind's blade cut like liquid light, fast, true, near perfect. And she bounced right off, Heser the Cheg's war cry a thing of animal fury, his own blade strong and true. She was trained and had lived a handful of human lives, but he was made to protect, forged of an iron that didn't come from the ground. His sword moved slower, but Evanne saw how he was ready for the *way* the Feybrind moved. Heser met speed and strength with a thing he'd always had: patience.

Dancing Stars sprang free of the clash, bleeding from a cut on her arm. Heser the Cheg ignored her, pummelling his way through the undead.

But there are so many. At least Tarragon and Morgan got free. We both fight for them.

Evanne retrieved a discarded, rusty blade from the deck, and met Heser on the battlefield. He slipped his back against her, and she felt the same strength as lived in Papa. She caught his smell for a moment, warm, honest, human. It straightened her spine, brought life back to her arms.

She bared not-quite-shark's-teeth, a snarl on her lips, and brought blade against blade, as she and Uncle Heser fought for just a few more ticks of the clock. She felt pretty good about death, now. The Trick of it was knowing everyone died alone but being able to lie to yourself that company cared. They battled, Evanne's arms growing tired, but Heser the Cheg saw it, offering his blade against an enemy so she could catch a ragged breath. She returned the favour, decapitating a long-dead woman that wanted to bury a spear in his spine.

It was nearly a dance. Nearly fun. Nearly a good way to die.

Evanne jerked about in horror at a rumbling *clank*. The tower door behind them gaped wide, an ancient jaw too used to somnolence. *No. No!* She wanted to scream. Who opened it? Was it the witch, Morgan? She was the only one who could.

The dead paused a moment, the Feybrind's glee at toying with more prey clear. "Ah. And all this fuss for naught."

Evanne wanted to punch her right in the face, but there were too many living dead. Heser's face was drawn, but not lost like she felt. He was built from materials stronger than castle walls. He would fight, no matter what. No matter how useless.

In the shadow of the gaping maw came a blue-white glint. Evanne's eyes strained. Too far for her Vhemin eyes to see heat, too dark for human eyes to make out detail. A body on the ground? Was that the Raven? Mimics, huddling behind someone else. A woman, tall, a silhouette that showed strength of purpose and arms both. The newcomer held a gleaming blade.

Requiem.

She stalked forward, and sunlight gleamed against golden skin and hair like summer wine. And Evanne, perhaps for the second time in her life, was speechless.

It's Tarragon.

Evanne opened and closed her mouth a few times as Tarragon Greyflight, wingless, taller than Evanne, leaner perhaps, but walking like a storm front, stalked toward them. Requiem was in one hand, green eyes harder than glass. She called across the deck. "Dancing Stars!"

The Feybrind's half-smile died like an unready youth in a pitched battle. "It can't be."

Tarragon charged. And Evanne realised the fairy—no, the *human*—looked at home. Because she finally, *finally*, had a sword in her hand.

Chapter Forty-Eight

Tarragon felt like a giant. Big legs, Big hands, all of her Big. Big, Big, Big. She'd lost her wings, and now knew what it was to look at a fairy with a human's eyes. Yasmine seemed so very small, despite the tremendous presence behind her. *Cophine.* The goddess herself had kissed Tarragon, and then remade her.

Now the world was different. The doors before her were still massive, but less so. The dais behind her was no longer unclimbable; it was her servant, should she choose. The mimics bowed and backed away. And the sword. Oh my, but it was a sweet length of skymetal. She felt how it loved her hand, the grip fitting her fingers just so, the weight of it leading her, balancing her, showing her the way. Tarragon knew this weapon was a Tresward Knight's blade, despite it not being glass.

It is not my sword. It is a sword I'm just ... minding for a time.

The blade glowed brighter for a moment, perhaps aware of her thoughts, or just doing what magic swords did. Her brain felt bigger, more ready for the challenges before her. The challenges were simple enough to see: a field of foes arrayed against Heser the Cheg and the love of Tarragon's life, Evanne. The Feybrind—*must watch that one*—holding a withered wand. The walking corpses between Feybrind and friend where five to ten deep. A line it'd be hard to break, even with shocktroops.

But Tarragon had a sword. She had trained with Helio and knew the steps of all twenty-one hundred patterns. No Smithsteel kept her safe, but Tarragon's blade was a shaft of righteous fury. It came to her from the demon's realm, forged by conflict, and delivered to her willing hand. While Tarragon had been tiny, Evanne had kept her safe. Now, magic sword in hand, it was time to return the favour.

She charged. Wingless, but her Big legs took the battlefield in such wondrous strides. Her body was heavy, and Tarragon wondered if Bigs felt like bison sometimes. But the heft gave strength, and she gripped the bastard sword with both hands. No shield, but no problem. It was time to bust some skulls.

When she met the undead, she did it with the first tender steps of Cophine's patterns. *Breach the Clouds* was comfortable, safe, a soloist's answered prayer to an army. She led with her left foot forward, blade in high guard, and brought Requiem down through shoulder blade and out hip. The creature before her sagged into separate halves, but the pattern denied her will to dawdle. She turned her right foot behind left, the motion making her turn an arc, Requiem's blade singing as it parted air.

Thunder roiled from the south.

Tarragon smelled fresh-baked cookies, butter and chocolate on the wind. But she wasn't done. She led the third step of the pattern to her next enemy, dropping her stance, sword coming down through the middle of her enemy, parting it skull to rotted balls. She stood, right foot coming up in shin guard as a mattock went low for her foot, the pattern knowing where she shouldn't be to avoid damage.

Fourth step, then, and be quick about it. Tarragon passed Requiem to her left hand, right palm pressing against a skeletal rib cage, right foot crossing before left this time, and around again, sword scribing a perfect line through the neck of her enemy. Its head bouncing, she moved on. Two more steps, sword back to right hand as it passed through a foe. Another down, then Requiem in both hands, striking three times through a giant monster of a man, both arms and one leg now separate from the rest.

Which brought her to Evanne's side. The maybe-Vhemin's eyes were wide in astonishment. She had been cut a thousand times, and Tarragon felt fury, narrowed her eyes, and glared at Dancing Storm. The Feybrind was backing away, which wouldn't do. A quick glance to Heser the Cheg showed the man was in the same state as Evanne, brain just freewheeling away inside his skull. There was work to be done, but first things first. "Love."

"Love," Evanne agreed. "You were supposed to run."

"You were supposed to stay with me." Tarragon beheaded a corpse that got to close. "Heser. Are you well?"

"I am well," the guardsman said. "You?"

"I wonder if I will pass out from the thinner air at this altitude, but otherwise I'm fine." Tarragon touched Evanne's face. "Behind me, now."

"You're a Knight?"

"There is no Storm. I'm just angry." Tarragon turned, and levelled Requiem, pointing the blade beyond the undead horde, the tip toward Dancing Stars. "Let's talk."

Chapter Forty-Nine

It was ogling Tarragon that got Evanne into trouble.

In her defence, the not-fairy-anymore was glorious. Tall, and strong, but all the *other* things she used to be, which is what made Evanne ogle. Angel face, check. Honey-brown skin, double check. Eyes green as the deeps, pure as jade, checkity check. And the long, lustrous, wheat-pale hair. The hair! It begged Evanne's fingers to run through it.

In none of the ballads she'd read had Evanne heard of the brave warrior being dumbstruck by his lady love during the heat of clashing blades. It was an important part of research they'd left out, and here she was, surrounded by shambling corpses, battle sound thick about her, and Evanne let her guard lower, goggling.

Heser shoulder-charged her, knocking her across the deck, where she flopped in a pile of limbs and lamb eyes. He took the pike swing meant for her head on the crossguard of his sword, kicked the legs out from under the corpse that tried to make her join them, and gave her a look rich with repressed condescension. She wanted to say something like, *I had that*, but he was already moving on.

It made her feel cold, because she hadn't had it, and the pike swing would have hit her head, which was the end of the line.

Evanne lost her sword in the trip from standing to sprawling but had shored up next to her guitar. It lay, glinting, and if it could speak, she imagined it would say, *You suck with a sword, but you play fine. Lay some phat chords down.*

She grabbed it, and stood, throwing its sling about her shoulders. The first strings she touched were surprisingly in tune, and she offered silent thanks to whichever ancient luthier put it together. She straightened her shoulders, stuck her hips forward, and brought her hand down on the strings. The note was full of curry, a little evangelism for her team, a wing beat to lift the soul. Heser surged in time with the music, while Tarragon paused, finding her way among the tune before attacking with renewed vigour.

Heser and Tarragon, warriors so grand,
With honour and valour, you'll make your stand.
Let the clash of your swords write your legendary story,
A testament to skill, courage, and glory.

Insufficient. I need something better—there are so many dead. She cast about for who they were, the souls that lingered above the remains, hoping for a repeat of the trick she'd used with Gabriel at the ancients' healing temple. Her music wound about their feet, seeking a home, a heart to call to.

Nothing. It was like playing to an empty room. No Trick she had found a response, and her music wandered, aimless.

She tossed a few more chords at the feet of her companions, while backing up a little, buying her some space to think. The undead continued to clamber over the railing, numbers growing even as Tarragon put more down. This would end in the inevitable way. Dancing Stars' half-smile found Evanne across the battlefield.

Tarragon stumbled, took a cut to the arm, and cried out as red blood splashed. She seemed surprised, as if still expecting golden gilt to seep from her wounds. Evanne saw the moment her balance faltered, thought about what Mama would have said, all *straighten that arm* and *your head is half a centimetre out of true.* Tarragon was wrestling with her body, used to the world in miniature, and she lacked balance.

I can fix that.

Evanne leaned over her guitar, closed her eyes, and thought of Tarragon. It wasn't hard, because she'd thought of the fairy most every moment in the past weeks. It was easy to imagine how she stood, and how she *should* stand, where those wonderful legs should be (if not entangled with Evanne's ... *focus, dammit!*), and how the Trick of it should beckon her to her true self.

I have it. Evanne played, not a heavy riff that demanded rage and power, but the flowing, wondrous walk she knew Tarragon had. The way Mama stood, as if the world were naught but her equal, and how sure she was of her place in it.

WITH GRACE IN YOUR STEP AND FIRE IN YOUR EYES,
Stand as a warrior, ready to rise.
Hold your blade with purpose, strong and true,
Your beauty and skill, Tarragon, they both grew.

STAND TALL, LIKE THE ANCIENT OAKS SO GRAND,
With roots deep in the earth, take your stand.
For in your strength, I see your true self shine,
A wondrous beauty in your battle's line.

YOUR SKILL, A MASTERPIECE, A WORK OF ART,
A sword in your hand, a warrior's heart.
With every move, your spirit takes flight,
Embrace your stance and unleash your might.

THUNDER ROLLED. EVANNE OPENED HER EYES AND SAW TARRAGON storming with fairy grace and human power. The magic blade Requiem led where needed, followed where commanded, flashing and burning through steel and corpse flesh alike. Ice rimed the ship's railing, and the air gathered close as if to listen.

Three's Mercy. She is calling the Storm.

Well, fine. Time to get the dead to back down. Their lack of souls meant difficult times ahead, and Evanne couldn't call to something without a soul, so...

Wait a minute.

The problem wasn't the *dead*, but the magic hauling them about. It wasn't necromancy, not quite, more like ... a puppet show. They were easy to cut down, even Evanne could do it. Nothing guided their swings but the crooked wand in Dancing Stars' hand. *If I can get some souls back in those bodies, this musical will end differently.*

Evanne hunkered beside a ruined wall, eyes finding the Feybrind's. She offered her best platinum solar smile, raised her hand, and struck three chords in quick succession. The music didn't seep about her feet or find the army before her. It wandered over the railing, down the side of the ship, and across the land below. It called to the souls of the lost. Evanne felt resistance, snarled, and hauled on her guitar strings. They vibrated, wanting to play out of true, and she crooned to the instrument. *Just a little more.* Her breath frosted before her as she stood half in the land beyond life.

Evanne sang for the forsaken, and some answered.

Then she screamed in agony, because Dancing Stars' throwing knife severed her ring finger where it pressed on the fret board. Strings snapped, and her finger fell to the deck.

The music stopped, but the soulless dead didn't.

Chapter Fifty

I *feel so warm. I feel like Evanne is holding me.*

Tarragon was too new at the whole 'being Big' game to know if it was the best decision she'd ever made. When Yasmine asked her if she wanted to give everything up, she'd thought it meant her life. One put on the scales to balance out another. Turned out, Yasmine meant giving up being a fairy. Flight. Glitter. Being a reactor technician—

I never passed my exams. I was never an engineer.

—Or being able to walk in a lake of fire without a concern. Now she had Big legs, and Big arms, and a Big head of hair. She hadn't found a mirror in the distance between *the past* and *now* to check herself, but Tarragon wondered if everything was still in proportion.

I liked my nose. It was a good nose.

Without wings for balance or the gift of flight, she felt ungainly, but strong, like a mammoth. A horror of shambling rotted meat came at her with insistent mindlessness, so she punched its skull clean off its neck. With a wet pop, the skull broke free, hit the deck, and rolled. She crouched, rose, and sliced Requiem up through the creature, leaving both halves to land in separate harmless piles.

Evanne made that possible.

The maybe-Vhemin had wrapped her in song, cloaked her in music, and put those warm, strong hands on Tarragon's shoulders. The once-fairy felt her footsteps guided just so, her stance held upright, and felt the truth of how a Big should move. The sword sang in her hands, the steel chiming and humming along with Evanne's tune. It was a wonder not even the ancients could have made.

The Feybrind still had the damnable wand. Tarragon bulled on, trying to make it to the cat, but Dancing Stars was both agile and nobody's fool. Tarragon caught the moment where Dancing Stars realised where the lift in Heser the Cheg's steps came from, and what guided Tarragon's long-limbed strides. The cat whipped out a dagger and tossed it.

If there was a saving grace, it was the melee. There were so many undead warriors on the deck a clean shot was impossible. The knife cut Evanne's finger, not her throat.

And the music stopped.

Tarragon stumbled, and for a moment she wondered if she was doomed to always need music to walk right. Evanne stood, right hand over left. It looked like she was holding her severed finger back in place, but also in pain, those delicious-looking teeth clenched, guitar dangling at her side, cut strings waving in the wind. Tarragon took three perfect steps toward her. Thunder roiled behind her, a gentle chiding from the Three, and she stopped.

I could go to Evanne. I must go to Evanne. But the Feybrind will send more against us.

Hope arrived, pale as the dawn. Swaying her way along the deck, a rudderless ship with no captain, stumbled the Raven. Her once-porcelain face was ashen, her clothes dark with lifeblood. Her eyes were locked on Heser the Cheg. Tarragon looked to the shadowy depths of the tower. The mimics huddled, fearing the sun. The once-fairy spun twice, her blade taking the heads from five enemies and buying her a little room. "Morgan!"

"I see beyond the veil." The queen's eyes slid sideways to Tarragon. "My love is a reanimated corpse."

"Great! But that's not what's happened." Tarragon cut another down. "Can you do something about the mimics? The light hurts them."

Morgan drew into herself, hunching. The motion didn't look natural on one so used to straight backs and imperious glances. Like the thing holding her up broke, and she couldn't quite glue it back together.

Evanne still clutched her hands together but was standing taller. The maybe-Vhemin headed for the queen, words cast ahead like a red carpet. "Morgan. You've been chained to a throne your whole life without realising you're a prisoner." There was music in the words, a resonance in her tone that Tarragon could listen to for hours. "You have a chance to spare others from their eternal fate." Her throat worked, and Tarragon used the time to kill more monsters. She caught Heser the Cheg's eye. The man faltered, human at the last, but refused to kneel. She wanted to give him comfort, to hold him, to say it would be all right. The guardsman righted himself as if Tarragon's glance was all he needed, straight-armed a corpse, and also charted a course toward Morgan.

"I don't know if I can." Morgan looked back at the mimics. "I don't know how."

"It's easy." Evanne made it to her side. She touched bloody fingers to the Raven's chin, tilting it up. //SET THEM FREE.//

Morgan relaxed, and the wind sighed. Tarragon held the line, her magic sword a brand as a tempest drew a cloak across the sky. Lightning crackled in the heavens, and thunder shook the air. She cut down all those who came against her. The ones that passed her met Heser's blade. Behind them, the maybe-Vhemin crouched beside Morgan. Lips to the queen's ear, encouragement or counsel Tarragon couldn't tell.

The queen drew a circle about her in bloody ink. Stood, arms high. Screamed, her voice a raven's caw.

The battlefield stilled. The Feybrind's hand on the wand was still firm, but the cat's diamond eyes narrowed as she watched, concentration lapsing a moment. Behind Morgan, the mimics still clustered, still anxious. Then they stilled. An armoire rocked on wooden feet, then toppled. A suitcase snapped shut, leather buckles still and lifeless. One after the other, life left them.

Not life. They were never alive. Time borrowed against a debt, repayment well paid.

Evanne stood, whirled, violet snake eyes alive. She spared a grin for Tarragon, and the once-fairy felt warm all over again. Then Evanne faced Dancing Stars and wiggled her fingers. "That was a neat trick with the knife. You've cut my strings, so now I'm free. I can still dance without them."

She raised her voice to the wind, singing counterpoint to the thunder. Tarragon took a step toward her. She felt enchanted, her heart beating faster, sword lowered. The maybe-Vhemin's song made no sense. *//MARGARET. TIMOTHY. STANLEY AND BERNARD. IMOGEN. ANDREW. CALYPSO AND CALLIOPE.//* And Tarragon realised while it sounded like music, it was a plea.

The mimics. She's learned their names.

The bodies nearest Dancing Stars shuddered, as if two sets of marionette strings pulled in different directions. Ghost-pale shapes Tarragon couldn't see clearly slipped inside the long-dead husks. They'd animated luggage for hundreds of years. Controlling a body that once was human was a cinch for them.

The undead legion tottered, then rounded on the Feybrind. The cat's diamond eyes widened, and she threatened the host with the wand.

It didn't have any effect. The cat danced back. "A cunning trick. Time to regroup. There will be another time."

She drew her cloak of many colours close. But there were so many once-mimics. They clawed at her, tearing fabric. The Feybrind whirled and struck, breaking free, but losing her cloak. She gave one last venomous glance their way, then turned tail and fled.

Tarragon laughed. "Evanne. We've won the day!" She turned. "Evanne?"

The maybe-Vhemin was gone.

Chapter Fifty-One

Dancing Stars was on the wind.

She ran because that's what the smart money demanded. The path down the side of *Dancing in the Storm* was free of the undead army. She tucked the worthless command wand away, scampering down the side of the ancient ship at the same speed a human might run across flat ground.

The People were gifted with better sight, speed, intelligence, and skill. She knew they should be in charge. That's what this was all about, after all.

Wild Sur would bare fang and lash his tail, but he wasn't *here*, and hadn't seen what Dancing Stars had to fight against. Their troupe was tiny, a small collective of the willing. A handful of humans, outnumbered for once by the People, and some strays from the vile Vhemin. All thought the humans should topple. It was a powerful anthem to march to, and all under Wild Sur's control. He was the one who'd started their revolution. *Been* there, when it all stopped, empires toppled, but not fallen far enough. Had the sight and will to give a little extra push, and shove humanity over the edge.

A last jump from the ship's side set her on a grassy knoll littered with the driftwood remains of undead warriors. Dancing Stars had to give the unruly human warrior his due: the queen's man fought better than she. The People respected excellence. Being Feybrind meant their base quality was higher. They were faster and smarter than humans but being long-lived made them better through practice. That she'd been bested by a manchild perhaps fifty summers old, all after he'd faced an exhausting battle on this very hillock, made her reconsider him with respect.

The unruly mongrel who fought beside him had used a power Dancing Stars had never seen or felt. The music that spilled from Evanne's instrument touched the Feybrind's soul. She felt her resolve tremor, and the automatic response of her body had been that oh-so-awkward throw of a blade.

Credit where due once more. The creature kept getting back up. She wouldn't stay down. A full-grown Vhemin warrior wouldn't shrug off that many cuts with such a shit-eating grin. They would have died, blow to the brain or no, and Dancing Stars needed to let Wild Sur know a new player was on the field. One who looked weaker than Vhemin, uglier than human, but was in point of fact more ornery than both.

Shadow fell across her. Dancing Stars looked up. The ancient hulk *Dancing in the Storm* shifted on whatever ethereal current tugged at her rudder. The Vhemin ship piercing her ancient heart teetered, then with a groaning cry of metal, toppled into the depleted lakebed below.

Water surged, muck and spackle on the wind. Dancing Stars thought hard for a moment. Dancing in the Storm *was our prize, but there are treasures aplenty in the Vhemin hulk. Let them have their crippled vessel. I will find other ancient trinkets and bring them to Wild Sur. Legends say the Vhemin war gods made the better weapons, and I shall find more of their magics.*

She ran, bounding down the side of the hill, cat-light on her feet. When she hit slippery mud she didn't fall, tail out behind her for balance, diamond eyes scanning for dangers. There were none, of course. Whatever lived in the lake would be struggling, and she could summon another everliving army with her wand given enough time and distance. The murky water was cold, but she was furred. Feybrind were not house cats. The People were warriors, poets, sages, and teachers. They weren't afraid of a little water.

The *Century Charm* settled on the lake floor. Dancing Stars swam the last, deep stretch to the vessel's side, clambered aboard, and made her way inside through a rent in the sagging hull. A last glance outside showed none in the floating fortress above marked her presence. She didn't need the cloak of many colours when naught but blind babes were her enemy. They didn't have Feybrind eyes.

The hulk creaked. Tiny cries of settling metal pitter-patted back and forth in the gloom. The vessel wasn't steady, the giant ripples from the ship's fall spread across the lake. A gentle, quieting roll lifted the floor and set it back in place before beginning all over again. It would settle eventually, but it was a timely reminder. *This ship may not stay above water for long. I should be quick about this. No one will come rescue me if I get trapped in a drowning room.*

She padded across the floor, her natural grace and agility making the deck movement seem fun rather than precarious. Ancient boxes and cylinders rolled into corners and between shelves. *I am in a store-room.* The term didn't do it justice; the place was immense. Fallen shelves spilled rotted treasure far and wide. *I am after artefacts of power, not broken junk.* It was the work of moments to vault past it all, make the door, put shoulder to it, and escape into the corridor beyond.

Metal rang on metal from ahead. Dancing Stars dropped to a crouch and froze, diamond eyes questing in the murk. It was black as pitch, and she could see very little. Her hearing helped. Was that sound a footfall? Did the hulk still have guardians, set free after the fall? No, the idea was preposterous. The Vhemin's masters didn't build to last.

Still, her ears didn't lie. A creature waited for her.

The Feybrind mused. She could simply go the other way, but that would put a potential enemy at her back. Best to trust to a hunter's instinct and put the prey down. She reached hands to pull the cloak of many colours close, then bared fangs, remembering its loss.

It is no matter. The People have been shadows on the wind for an eon. I need no cloak.

She removed a small marvel from her belt pouch. It was a tube about the length of her hand. A quick twist, a crack, and a calm warm glow seeped from the rod. She held the light stick high, casting shadow back. The corridor beckoned her on, so she followed, silent feet making no sound. There was a surprise in store for certain, but Dancing Stars was the one to bait the trap.

A stuck door lay half open. She slipped through the gap and found herself in a room both long and wide. Pillars held the roof at least three stories above. Artifices lay in broken piles, their mooring lines snapped by either the recent fall or the crash years past. Her rod cast long, ghostly shadow fingers among the shapes. The Artifices resembled the corpses of giant spiders with their spindly, curled limbs.

"You came." The voice carried as if from the air itself. One might have called it sweet, if they didn't know the disgusting mongrel throat it came from.

Dancing Stars' lips curled into a sneer. "You came all this way to die on my steel?" She drew her sword. "I admit to surprise. How did you get past me?"

Evanne's voice drifted to her from the left this time. "And they say Feybrind are the clever ones."

"Ah." Dancing Stars half-smiled. "You climbed aboard the *Century Charm* before it fell. You were here before I was."

"That wasn't so hard, was it?" Evanne's voice drifted from straight ahead, so Dancing Stars padded that way, a hunter on the scent. Except, there was no scent. Just that damnable voice. "I wasn't sure if I'd drown, but I knew you'd come here once the main prize was lost. Cats like to play with shiny things, and this wreck is a bauble of unsurpassed brightness now *Dancing in the Storm* is above you."

The way the bastard creature said *above you* made Dancing Stars' teeth itch. She rounded a fallen Artifice, sword high to strike, but there was nothing there. The Feybrind whirled, but no, no enemy was at her back, knife ready to strike. "Where are you, my pet? Come out and play."

"In a moment." Evanne's voice came from no more than twenty metres to the Feybrind's right. She set off in pursuit. "You know, I would have been happy to die for them. But you made it so they had no hope of escape. So, I need to make sure you can't pursue my family.

Not now, and not ever again." The tone wasn't mocking or happy. If anything, Evanne sounded sad.

"I've no interest in them anymore," the Feybrind lied.

"I thought you a bad liar, but I know it for certain now. There's a Trick to it, do you see? Your lips must believe the lie before they speak it. Your heart must know it for truth before you feel it. Your mind must make it real, before setting pieces on the board." A clatter in the gloom called Dancing Stars farther to the right. "You say things as if people *should* believe them, not because they *must*. Your arrogance makes you a terrible liar."

"Thanks for the tip." Dancing Stars lunged about a pillar from where a shadow beckoned, but she cut nothing but air.

"You'll have to do better than that." Laughter tinkled from far behind her. "While you spent all that time cutting into my skin, I watched. I know what makes you tick. I see the purpose behind those beautiful diamond eyes. It's so easy to make you do what I want. Be where I want."

A piece of machinery on a chain swung at the Feybrind from the gloom. She spun and dropped, taking the worst of the blow on her left shoulder. Her arm went numb, and the light rod clattered away. It rolled under a hulking machine, dropping visibility to less than what you'd get on a moonless, stormy night. Still, Dancing Stars wasn't blind. She bared fangs. "Well done, little one. You play this game better than most mice."

There. Shadow rippled to her right. She sprang forward, right hand finding her knife with ease, curling the blade under her wrist, and tossing it. Silver spun through the gloom. Dancing Stars expected a grunt, a cry of pain, but all she got back was silence. Not even the clatter of metal.

"A good throw." Evanne's voice was rich with encouragement. "But you can't kill that which is already dead."

"You're no more a corpse than I." The Feybrind's words held doubt, even to her own ears. *Ludicrous. The talking collar conveys no negativity. It is just a voice, not a feeling.*

"Do you remember all those times you ran me through?" The voice drifted about, as if Evanne were walking a circle, but so very fast.

Faster than any Feybrind could manage, and a ridiculous pace for a human mongrel. "So, *so* many. They stopped hurting after a while, and that's how I knew I'd passed. Lifted this veil and put on the next. It's not so bad, if you've got a purpose."

Dancing Stars had heard tricks of the voice before. Ventriloquism wasn't a craft they owned, but she'd seen a market dandy put on a show with puppets and string. It was convincing enough if you believed the lie. But it was a lie all the same. She padded through the gloom, farther from her fallen light. *There should be blood. A trail to follow. The scent of sweat.*

But there was nothing. No odour, no ichor, no gory red smear. A glimmer called, and she followed. She found her knife winking at her from below the arm of a fallen machine. How had it got here without making a sound? And the blade was clean. Cleaner than it had left her hand, as if it felt the polish of the underworld.

"This is a very clever trick." Dancing Stars listened to the slight echo of her voice die away, then whirled with a slash for good measure. She hit nothing.

But something hit her, strong as a horse's kick. She sprawled, knife falling free, and this time the traitorous blade had the decency to clatter. The cat sprang up and whirled. There was nothing there. No shadows, no ghosts. No falling girder or broken machine. *What hit me?*

"Tricks are something different. A husk of the voice. A tilt of the shoulder. A game eye for the needful, and a firm hand with the strong." Evanne's voice husked from the darkness. It sounded tired, as if waiting in the world of the living stretched even a corpse's resolve.

"I'd know if you were dead. I would have felt the life leave you, like so many of your ugly kind." Dancing Stars looked about for the knife, but it was gone. She found faint scratches on the floor where the blade marked it, but the weapon itself was gone. *I was just looking over here. I would have seen a person.*

"Would you?" Evanne's voice was sad again, as if she felt nothing but pity for those who remained on this world. "I've seen in your soul. There's naught but darkness and pain. Oh, I know where it came from. A small cat, a lost mother, a father fallen to the blade." *How did she know that?* "I see where my father's people took yours on steel. I know the mark of human hands and see how they hurt."

"You know nothing of me." Dancing Stars wanted to hiss, to growl, but the humans had denied them that simple release. She bared her fangs. "If you're dead, you will bend the knee." She pulled free her wand of the underworld, raising the gnarled, whorled stick aloft. A sickly, pale green light fell from it. The Feybrind felt cold as she always did when holding it. "Show yourself!"

Pain lanced from her shoulder. She dropped the wand, light vanishing, to whirl on her attacker, and saw nothing. Except for her own knife lodged in her shoulder. She yanked it free. Dancing Stars turned to get the wand, fingers scrabbling on the deck. She couldn't feel it between fursoft fingers. She spared a moment to glance down. *No wand.* Come to think of it, she'd never heard it hit the deck. As if it had fallen from her hand right into the lands of the dead.

A snap came from above her, and she leaped back, diamond eyes up. There was nothing there of course, but from the gloom above fell fragments of wood, a tiny scatter of material that had once been a mighty wand of the ancients. She blinked, incredulous. "You've destroyed the wand?"

"It isn't good for you to hold it. It was making you sick. Deep inside, where there's nothing but darkness, a deeper malaise grew. It was swallowing your soul." Evanne's voice was ahead of her, right where the glow stick was. Dancing Stars was looking right at it when the light went out. Not lifted away, not hidden in a box, just ... gone.

She crouched, fangs bared, fear flaring, her breath coming in short, panting gasps. "What *are* you?"

"I'm a promise you could never keep." That damnable voice, so close now. "I'm the air you feel on the back of your neck when there's no draft. I'm winter hail in summer." Dancing Stars felt that very breath on the back of her neck, and spun, lashing out. She struck nothing but air. "I'm everything this world needs, sent to take away that which it doesn't. And you're here, with me. Forever."

Chapter Fifty-Two

Tarragon was frantic. *Evanne is missing. Evanne is missing!* She wasn't tiny like Tarragon, easily misplaced.

I'm not tiny anymore. I'm a Big.

The thought made her feel sick, because being a fairy was cool, except for the constant risk of dying. She'd agreed to become Big to save Evanne, except it wasn't what she thought she was doing. Tarragon remembered Yasmine saying, *Let us begin, again. We'll change a tiny thing, so we can fix everything.*

Requiem in hand, she stalked back to the conning tower. Inside was a sad collection of inanimate luggage, a blood stain, and a smug fairy. Yasmine flitted about at eye height. "Hello, Tarragon."

"Is that even my name anymore?" She glanced at the sword she held. "It's a fairy's name. I'm a, a ... Big." She stumbled on the last word.

"You have always been Tarragon. Cursed to live a fairy's guise but never with their skills. We took them all for Helio. We placed a bet, pushed the long odds." The other fairy *hmm'd*. "I think it paid off."

"Helio is dead. It was a sucker's bet."

Yasmine's smile widened. "That wasn't the bet we placed. Helio was lovely. Kind and gentle, never a warrior. The worst of you, to lead the best of you. A person who could make you hunger for what you didn't have, to urge you to find your feet, and to show you what you weren't."

Tarragon wanted to swat her from the air. "Why would you do a thing like that?"

"Because this world had too many people who thought they knew perfection. All the Bigs who couldn't see past themselves to the beauty of difference."

"Being different isn't beautiful," Tarragon spat. "It's hard, and it's ugly, and no one likes you. Everyone wants you to be like them, and they shout at you if you try to just be you for a minute. If you can't fix a reactor, someone shouts at you. If you don't know the correct setting on a torque wrench, someone else shouts at you. If you drop a fuel rod into the wrong chute, *everyone* shouts at you. It's shouting all the time!" She realised she was shouting herself, clenched her teeth, and looked at her feet. "I just wanted Evanne to live. I didn't want people to shout at her for who she was, or for trying to be what she was."

"And did you do that?" For a moment, it wasn't Yasmine, but the Dawn Warrior, a summer's day within a spear of sunlight. A giant, with glowing eyes, and a presence that could stop time.

Tarragon didn't give a shit. "Do not pull the whole I-am-Cophine-the-Spring-Maiden nonsense. You're either a fairy, or you can do anything you want. Pick a side."

"You've almost got it." The goddess was now just Yasmine again. "Keep going." An encouraging nod.

"I'm not a fairy. And I'm not a good Big, either. I can't even walk right without a song."

Yasmine sighed. "You single-handedly destroyed an undead legion swarming the deck of this battleship. You—"

"Heser helped."

"You did it with a borrowed blade and no wings. When this ship fell, a score of Tresward stood on this deck and died to the last, swarmed by Vhemin and human alike. You have done the impossible."

"But what of Evanne?"

"What about her?"

"Well, she's dead! That's why I'm angry!" Tarragon growled, realising she was shouting again, and just didn't care.

Yasmine frowned. "Why would you think that?"

Tarragon swept her sword toward the doorway, almost decapitating Heser the Cheg who'd wandered in to see what the commotion was about. The man was swift, dodged the swing, and sensibly stood a little farther back. "Because she's gone."

"She's not 'gone' gone. She's just not here." Yasmine crossed her arms, hovering. "She is trying to save your life. Again."

"I'm the one with the sword, though." Tarragon glanced at Requiem, then realised, "I'm the one with the sword!"

Yasmine flitted left, then right. "Being a fairy never stopped you doing whatever you wanted. I daresay it won't stop you now."

"I was a worthless fairy." Tarragon bit her lip. "I was really bad at it."

"And you learned to be really good at other things instead."

"Swinging a sword?"

"That, and making friends of enemies. Finding love in the strangest places. You didn't fit. So, you made your own way."

"Where is she?" Tarragon took two steps toward the door. "That's all I need to know."

"I'm sorry we did this to you. But it was the only way. We knew we had a promise to make." Yasmine's voice was a little sad. "Listen and follow the music. Evanne is a bard, after all."

TARRAGON SPRINTED ACROSS THE DECK, VAULTED THE RAILING, AND headed for the water below. It was a long way down, and it gave her time to wonder if falling so far in such a Big body was wise. Then she hit, and the air went right out of her. She kept her hand on the sword though, training making her clench the weapon even as her body struggled for air.

Requiem burned like a blue-white flare, water boiling off the blade. Tarragon swam up, kicking with those new, strong Big legs. Her head broke the surface, and she sucked air. The *Century Charm* was an ugly, dirty beast waiting for her.

She kicked toward it.

INSIDE, ALL WAS DARKNESS, BUT SHE CARRIED A BURNING BRAND FOR a blade. The music called to her, just like the fairy promised. She could hear Evanne's heart, and the music that came from her, laying a gentle arm around Tarragon. She ran.

Down a corridor. Left. Dead end. Backtrack, down farther, next left. Then right. A closed and barred door was no match for her. Two strikes to the hinges and a kick, molten metal bleeding from the door-frame as Requiem burned incandescent.

A short jink right again, and there, an open airlock. Beyond, a hangar containing fallen Artifices, and two people locked together. Dancing Stars fought with the speed and ferocity of her kind, but there was something wrong with it. Tarragon eyed her stance and bear-ing, and thought, *She has lost all hope.*

What she fought was a shadow. A thing of mist and starlight. *Evanne.* The maybe-Vhemin was cloaked in solid night, form indis-tinct, but she didn't fight like the Feybrind. Clumsy swings a child could block. Stance all wrong. Blade held like an ice pick. Total amateur hour.

But she wasn't losing.

She's not winning either. Where is Hitch?

Ah. The Feybrind had a damnable jewel that banished the spectre from Evanne's presence. She held it aloft like some kind of hokey talis-man, a damnable half-smile, or maybe a snarl, on those feline lips.

That's about enough of that. Tarragon didn't much like Hitch, but she liked Evanne a great deal, and the ghost made her happy. So, time to fix the problem.

She charged. Requiem blazed, hungering for the fight. Dancing Stars saw the sword, and the look on the not-fairy-anymore's face. She kicked out Evanne's leg, used the maybe-Vhemin's lost balance as leverage, and swung her about toward Tarragon. Tarragon, who hadn't learned swordplay from a rube, jumped the fallen Evanne, landing soft and sure on the balls of her feet, blade arcing overhead. It came down on Dancing Star's upturned blade, and skymetal power clashed against Feybrind smith work. Lightning boiled off Requiem, arcing into an Artifice. The machine surged with a growl of ancient mechanisms innervated once more.

That wasn't supposed to happen. Tarragon wasn't sure if she could beat an Artifice. They were Really Big, and she carried not even the single gold bar of an Adept's black sash. The machines were able to defeat legions of Bigs, and she had no fairy glitter to blaze a path through armour anymore.

The Feybrind slid back, blade in high guard. "You fight well."

"I've got a magic sword. It's hard to not fight well." Tarragon circled her. "You've no way out of this."

"That's not true, is it?" Dancing Stars nodded over Tarragon's shoulder, but the not-a-fairy-anymore didn't take the bait. "You'll fight the Artifice, and I'll slip into the shadows."

They rejoined, blades sparking light and shadow. The Artifice grumbled upright, a distracting huddle of jerky, rusty motion. It sent vibrations through the deck as old metal cried a new dawn's song. Dancing Stars tried to stick her knee into Tarragon's groin while their blades locked. The not-fairy twisted, taking the blow on her thigh, then surged in, dropping her shoulder into the Feybrind's.

The cat didn't fall back like a Big, because they were stronger than they looked. She slipped along Tarragon's arm, close as lovers, blade whipping a silver smile toward Tarragon's neck. She took the cut against Requiem's savage edge and used the distraction to kick Dancing Stars' shin. The Feybrind took the blow like she meant to step back anyway, form fluid, perfect, better than anything Helio could have done.

They separated, both panting. *I'm not as strong or as fast, but I have a magic sword and the Three's patterns. That's got to count for something.*

Right?

Whatever, she needed an answer, like, *now*, because the Artifice was well and truly upright now. The targeting systems looked just fine as the arclight cannons hunted for prey. Which made Tarragon think of Evanne and spare a glance sideways for her.

Not only didn't she see the maybe-Vhemin, but Dancing Stars leaped forward. A clash of blades, *again*, this time with Tarragon on the back foot. *Breathe*. She was panicking, and she knew it. Not because she was fighting a master of the blade, although that *was* terrifying. But because she didn't know where Evanne was. Would the maybe-Vhemin be crushed by the Artifice? Had she gotten trapped in debris? Was she unconscious, bleeding out from her wounds?

If there was one piece of good news, the Feybrind had the common courtesy to slip the jewel away, both hands free for the fight.

But still no Evanne. She looked the other way but saw no one. Tarragon caught a lick of steel against her cheek for her inattention. Reflexes, not patterns, kept her from losing an eye. She growled, stepping inside Dancing Star's next thrust, trapping blade and hand with her elbow. They grunted, sharing breath, diamond eyes locked with green.

The not-fairy-anymore smiled. Then she let the Feybrind go, stepped back, and wiped blood from her cheek with the back of her hand. And smiled wider.

"What are you grinning like the town fool for?" The Feybrind's gemstone gaze narrowed, eyes a hunter's, assessing. At Tarragon's laugh, her ears went back, every cat's reaction to being laughed at. "What's so damnably funny?"

"This is." Evanne stood five metres away, hand held aloft. In it, the gem that kept Hitch at bay.

Dancing Stars looked at the jewel, then dropped hand to belt, fumbling in an empty pouch. "Nimble, clever, *naughty* fingers. I'll have to take those from you."

Evanne smiled, nice and wide, then tossed the jewel. It flashed as it twinkled overhead, right toward the Artifice. The machine, finally given something useful to do, opened up with twin arclight cannons. The beams of red-white fury slashed the hangar, carving a hole in the wall through which daylight dared peek. The noise was tremendous. Tarragon had forgotten what the Artifice's war cry sounded like. It was fit to shake the world.

Motes twinkled like glitterdust in the light from outside. Sparkling remnants of the jewel silted to the deck. Evanne stood, arms akimbo, same smile on her face. She glanced to Tarragon. "Love, can you handle the machine? I would, but..." She shrugged, hand out to Dancing Stars. The cat bared fangs and leaped at Evanne.

Tarragon whirled as the Artifice's arclight cannons cycled, whining toward another blast. She held Requiem at cross guard and joined battle with the machine.

Chapter Fifty-Three

Dancing Stars circled Evanne. Her fangs were bared, but Evanne saw the truth of it. The Trick of ferocity that hid fear. Evanne circled right back, making sure her grin was wide and shit-eating. "You seem to have lost your way. Fighting the dead is harder than you thought, isn't it?"

The cat's diamond eyes narrowed. Evanne saw the hot flush of blood beneath it, her Vhemin's blood heat vision showing truer than a human's in the flickering disharmony of light cast by the glow stick, Requiem, and that ghastly machine. "You are no more dead than I."

"Were it true." Evanne held the lie close, like a friend. She just needed a little time, because: truth, it had been hard to one-on-one the damn feral before Tarragon arrived. "You want to believe I'm flesh like you, but you feel the lie as well as I."

The cat lunged, and Evanne tightened her grip on the cloak of shadows. The child's toy might not make her invisible, but she felt ghostly, apart. Ignorable. And it was driving the Feybrind wild. The cat swept past, blade slashing air, Evanne's footsteps lost in the cacophony behind her.

She spared a glance. Took in Tarragon, strong, tall, *not a fucking fairy*, magic blade twirling like only the Tresward could, lightning callousing the blade. The Artifice, stamping and striking, beams of hot fire trying to rend the not-fairy aside. But Tarragon, no wings now, still flew. Wheat-pale hair wild, teeth bared, as she fought a machine as old as her.

"Hey," Hitch said. "Can anyone join this party?"

Evanne took three steps back, then beckoned. "Come."

"I'm not a dog." He took a look at Dancing Stars, his arms crossed, feet not quite ending at the ground, and she was reminded of the terrible price he'd paid to save the world. How the armour took the very marrow from his bones so he could propel a Tresward Knight into the final battle.

"No," she breathed. "You are a warrior. A memory from beyond time. One who served, and fell, but refused to die."

"Who are you talking to?" Dancing Stars' eyes narrowed.

"I don't remember any of that." Hitch glanced down. "I'm just a guy. I don't think I was a very good one."

"I remember it. I'll remember it for you." She held out a hand. "Let's finish this."

He seeped into her, the cold coming with it. Evanne felt her blood turn to ice, her heart shudder, then beat strong. The cool of Hitch's gaze looking out through hers. The music that was in the background of her soul picked up tempo, found a beat, and surged.

Dancing Stars closed with her. Blade a silver blur, wielded by an expert. Evanne/Hitch pulled free the cloak of shadows, using it like a matador's cape. Confounding the Feybrind, a small Trick that drew the eye. Evanne/Hitch stepped close, blade of their foot sliding inside the Feybrind's instep. A perfect movement, needed because the cat was bear-strong. They unbalanced the Feybrind, and continued the movement by standing in the place where the cat was, elbow rising to crack under their opponent's jaw.

The Feybrind stumbled, but recovered, turning the momentum into a pivot that brought blade back around. *Perfect.* They could feel Evanne's concern along with Hitch's satisfaction. Evanne/Hitch's hands came up, one taking the Feybrind's wrist, the other on above her elbow. Sink back now, calm as the ocean, implacable as the tide, putting their back to their enemy as they rotated. The arm with sword a lever, their shoulder a fulcrum, the world an anvil as they threw Dancing Stars onto the deck.

No room for a break fall. *Crunch*. The cat rolled away, leaving Evanne/Hitch with the sword. The cat, swaying a moment, and this was the time to strike. They lunged, blade sinking home.

It lodged in bone, the cat's mouth a silent scream. The weapon tore from their hand as the cat back-pedalled.

How's it feel, fucker? from Evanne, and *Be still, the work's not done*, from Hitch.

Dancing Stars pulled the sword free in a sluice of blood. Evanne/Hitch saw the heat of it, cooling as it hit the deck in a spray. The Feybrind turned to the Artifice. "Hey! Here!"

The machine turned its massive head. *Hold*, said Hitch, and *Fuck what?* thought Evanne.

The Feybrind raised her arms, pulling the machine's attention. Tarragon's eyes, wide with fear now, as she struck a machine's leg. The blade sliced through metal, a burning orange glow both on Evanne's human and Vhemin sight. The Artifice stumbled, but those twin fangs hunted, glowing with promise.

Hold, Hitch said again. His grip on their body shook, because Evanne wanted to run. *Hold, if you trust me. Hold, if you remember me.*

I remember you. Evanne relaxed. *I trust you.*

The Feybrind drew the eye of the machine to them, arms up, blood leaking, sword in hand. Backing toward them, bringing the ancient's wrath. Evanne held, feeling terror, because there was no walking off whatever that machine would do to her.

But held anyway.

The cat whirled. "This is how it ends for you."

The machine fired. Tarragon leaped, blade carving those fangs apart in two blows before she landed. But not before they'd spat hot death.

And turned Dancing Stars into a patch of whisping char.

Hitch let their body go. She shuddered as he slipped free, then threw up on the decking. "I thought we were going to die."

"Artifices were not Itikari," Hitch said. "I remember that much."

"She ... drew this on herself?" Evanne wiped her mouth with the back of her hand, then gave a pale imitation of a laugh. "You could have said."

"My way had more gravitas," the spectre said.

"Your way was for fools," Tarragon screeched. "She could have died!"

"A, you're huge," Hitch said. "B, how can you see me? Most humans can't see the dead."

"I'm not huge," Tarragon said. "I'm Big."

"That's what I ... you know what, never mind," Hitch said. "Did you know this ship is sinking?"

Evanne fetched her tattered cloak of shadows, stood, glanced at Tarragon, and held out her hand. "We need to go, love."

Tarragon looked at her hand. Then took it, her warm fingers sliding into Evanne's cooler ones like they'd been made for each other. Evanne felt herself grin like an idiot, grip Tarragon's hand, and head for the crack in the hull.

Time to go.

THEY MADE THREE STEPS TOWARD THE HULL BREACH BEFORE THE entire ship shuddered. Evanne stumbled, caught herself, or was it Tarragon holding her up? *Doesn't matter.* The floor shrieked as it buckled. It felt like the vessel was folding width-ways, and that tiny glimpse of daylight vanished.

"Ah," Evanne said. "Not that way."

Tarragon's breathing was loud at her side. Like, human-sized and audible, not fairy-sized and near silent. Evanne took a step, and her foot landed on something hard. She bent, retrieving Dancing Stars' necklace. It was clear of ash or grime, a hint of ancient mummery that leant it a gleam even though its wearer was charcoal. She pocketed it, thinking of Sight of Day.

"How did the cat get in here?" Hitch ghosted down the hold as the room shook, the vibrations doing nothing at all to him as he sifted through an Artifice. "There's a passage this way."

Evanne pulled Tarragon after her. "Hold the sword up so you can see."

Tarragon raised the blazing brand of Requiem. They hurried toward the exit. Made the corridor, with blackness at one end. Doors were open, fire belching from one. No time to fret, so Evanne didn't bother. She ran, Tarragon at her back, felt the hot hiss of scorching, then they were through.

End of the corridor, and they took a left. A door flew open, a pale humanoid figure striding through. Hitch yelled, "Personate!" which Evanne ignored, getting passed by dropping her shoulder into the thing's midsection. It felt like charging a wall, but she popped out the other side anyway.

She glanced back and saw it following. And how's that: the thing now held a sword like Tarragon held Requiem. It hadn't held a blade moments earlier. No matter, they could deal with it if they made it outside.

Water lapped Evanne's boots. She ran, taking a right, then through a cross intersection, and left again. A massive door barred their path. She was going to turn back, but Tarragon pointed to writing above the door. "No. This way. It says 'airlock'."

Evanne had no clue what an airlock was, but fine. They made the door, the Personate shambling in their wake. The handle was a giant wheel, which they both set to. It turned with a groan, and they popped into a smaller room. The Personate was behind them, hand on the sill, so Evanne held her dukes up, ready to give it a thrashing.

Tarragon's hand was on her shoulder. "No. You'll die."

"Been there," Evanne said. The ship shuddered, and the door slammed as the hull buckled. Half the Personate landed in the room with them. Evanne glanced at it. "That's one problem solved."

"We're sinking," Hitch said.

"Let's get out then, hey?" Evanne put her hand on the outside hatch, and with Tarragon's help, worked the wheel. Water sprayed from the seams, and a moment later it slammed wide, throwing Evanne against the back wall. She lay, stunned, while water fountained in.

Outside was black. She took a breath, then another. Held it, as the lake filled the room. Requiem was a silver sun in the gloom. A piece of metal lodged with the water's fury and barred the door. Tarragon braced, hair billowing in the water, and sliced. Bubbles churned from molten steel as Requiem cut a path.

Evanne found her feet. Together, she and Tarragon swam outside the *Century Charm*. All was murk and misery, so she powered up. Lungs burning, she was reminded of how they'd entered the hulk what felt like weeks ago but was mere hours. Up, Requiem fizzing and churning the water, Tarragon's face by hers. The lake surface above, a panel of silver glass.

They broke it, gasping. Tarragon floundered, doing her best to tread water and hold the sword aloft.

They were free.

Chapter Fifty-Four

Heser the Cheg had helped them back on board, big arms hefting them with ease. He'd hugged Evanne fiercely, Tarragon more cautiously, but she'd felt the warmth in his embrace, and realised the man was doing his best to conquer fear.

Welcome to the club.

Victory celebrations were subdued. Tarragon thought, *This isn't a party, it's a wake*, as she stalked the decks of *Dancing in the Storm*. She made her way without any particular thought or agenda, finding herself within the conning tower, riding the dais to the control room. *I don't know what is going on, and I was here the whole time*.

Evanne had slipped away, a last lingering touch on Tarragon's fingers suggesting she didn't want to go, her eyes saying she needed to. Tarragon wanted to go with her, but the maybe-Vhemin pulled the bedraggled remains of the cloak of shadows close like she was drawing the drapes, and slipped past the not-fairy's sight.

Morgan was a right state. Heser had propped her up with a view of the lake, but she looked like she was dying. *She's only human.*

Like me.

The dais reached the control room's level, and Tarragon stepped into quiet. No one lived on this vessel beside Evanne, Tarragon, Heser the Cheg, Pakhet, and Morgan. And maybe Yasmine, although of the probably-not-a-fairy there was no sign. Tarragon slipped into the control room, eyes taking it in. She'd been here before, but Big life-times ago. Over there had been where her favourite comms officer, Mandalay, worked. That spot was where she'd first seen an ensign walk into a commander because his eyes had been everywhere except where he was going.

She crouched, hands on a bare piece of decking. *This was where the fairy legion stood.* A plinth used to be here. Fairy leaders like Helio surveyed the battles to come, and he'd brought Tarragon with him a time or two. She'd never felt welcome, a mascot curiosity for the Bigs to wonder at. No special use for fixing engines or toilets, just a peculiar aptitude for the blade and all its arts.

Tarragon fingered Requiem's hilt. The scabbarded blade vibrated in its sheath, spoiling for a fight. *I've had enough fights for today.* Tarragon fetched a chair from the pile of wreckage on one side of the room, sparing only a casual thought as to how they got there. She dragged it to an empty space, and felt it hum as the floor held it close. Minor magic, but it showed some things still worked on *Dancing in the Storm.*

For now.

She ran a hand down the side of the chair, then bent to put fingers on the floor again. "And who's going to fix you now? There are no Builders. Not anymore."

The ship didn't say anything. Ships didn't speak.

"*Evanne's gone to the Skyforge,*" Pakhet said. Tarragon screamed, trying to stand, turn, and unsheathe Requiem in one movement. All her remembered patterns failed her, but she managed to hook her toe against her other heel and fall to the deck.

The grey-black tiger sat on her haunches near the rear of the room, licking a massive paw. Tarragon stood, clenched a furious fist, and said, "You shouldn't sneak up on people."

"*They wouldn't have given me invisibility if they didn't want me to use it.*"

Tarragon felt her heart settled from its panicked hammering. She swept her hair back, followed suit by straightening her shoulders, and glared. "There's a time and a place."

"*The time was now. The place was here.*" The tiger showed a toothy smile. *At least, I hope that's a smile.* "*Aren't you curious as to what's in the Skyforge?*"

"I know what's there. It's a dragon factory. It will be dead, like everything else."

"*Hmm.*"

"What's that supposed to mean?"

"*Hmm.*" The tiger looked away. "*What's it like being only moderately tiny?*"

"I'm huge," Tarragon said. "I'm Big and ungainly. I can't get my balance right. I don't know what is going on."

"*You're not huge. I'm normal-sized, and you're basically a dwarf rabbit compared to me.*" Pakhet ignored Tarragon's jaw-drop. "*What was it like to kiss Cophine?*"

Tarragon's mind *click, click, clicked.* "You mean, Yasmine?"

"*Cophine,*" Pakhet corrected, but gently.

"I don't want to talk about that," Tarragon said. "I don't want to talk about it at all."

"*Fair enough.*" The tiger stretched, claws *skritting* on the decking. "*I don't want to talk about it either. I was just being polite.*"

"I don't like it," Tarragon said.

"*I thought you didn't want to talk about it?*"

"I didn't want," she gestured to herself, huge, monstrously deformed body and all, "this. I wanted to stop being me so Evanne could win. Everything was always hard. I wasn't a good fairy. No one wanted me. Only Helio," her voice hitched for a moment, "but even then it was... shame."

"*This sounds a lot like talking about it.*" Pakhet paused. "*And also a pity party.*"

Tarragon stared out the window, waiting for the sick feeling in her stomach to go away, but it wouldn't. She turned back to Pakhet. "I just wanted everyone to stop having to deal with the mistake I was."

"*Hmm.*" The tiger's tail *swish, swished.* "*And yet, you managed to destroy an undead army more or less single-handed—*"

"Heser was there."

"*By wielding a sword of impossible power—*"

"Because Cophine made me Big."

"*Best an Artifice—*"

"Evanne was there."

"*For pity's sake,*" Pakhet growled. "*When are you going to admit you're exactly who you need to be? This is the time. This is the place. You were put here to use your gifts. Now get on and use them.*"

Tarragon opened her mouth, closed it, opened it again, then closed it. "That's not fair."

"*Hmm.*"

"I'm worthless," Tarragon whispered.

"*There's one who doesn't question your worth. She needs you now. She almost died today. Perhaps she did. Vhemin are fiddly that way. She struggles with impossible power, and she does it alone.*"

"You were there with her in the Skyforge."

"*I appreciate it may have escaped notice, but I was not built in a comfy, cuddly form.*" The tiger lowered her voice. "*Go. Perhaps the both of you could use a hug.*"

THE SKYFORGE WAS HOW TARRAGON REMEMBERED IT. IT DIDN'T stop her flesh goosebumping, or the hair at her nape reaching for the sky. The room was huge. From outside *Dancing in the Storm* it looked like a giant cylinder stuck to the deck. Inside, it was a circular chamber with a smaller, but still massive cylinder in the middle.

The cylinder was dark. It made Tarragon's heart hurt. *This ... isn't right.* Last time Tarragon was here, the Skyforge had been alive with golden light as they hammered another dragon out of stardust. Now... nothing.

The chamber had massive, vaulted doors on each side. These weren't for the dragon, because when it hatched, it would go out through the roof. The top would open like a giant flower. No, the vaulted doors were for other dragons to watch. Tarragon remembered them clinging to the side of *Dancing in the Storm*, fire or lightning blasting into the wind as they roared their pleasure at each new birth.

There are no more dragons. I haven't seen one for eight hundred years.

Humming drew her forward. Tarragon realised she'd been gawping like a rube from the sticks. The humming was pure, sweet, and sad. A dirge made pretty by a throat that could speak with the voice of dragons. The not-fairy felt her heart trip a beat. *Get a grip*. She tugged her jerkin tight, settled Requiem against her hip, and stalked into the chamber.

As her eyes adjusted, a dim glow caught her notice. The cylinder was dark all right, the mighty *SKYFORGE 05* lettering on the side fading into the black above. But within the cylinder and the murk she saw a massive, clawed limb. It was still, of course, because it was dead. *Shame. It was a blue. The blues are the fastest.*

The glow turned out to be a lantern held by Evanne. She stood, head bowed and pressed against the cylinder, free hand to the glass, as she hummed a dirge for the dragon. There were no words in the song, but Tarragon still heard the meaning. *Fading of the light* was in there. *Tall as the sky* was another. On and on. She felt tears on her cheeks but let them fall. To move was to break the music.

And at the end, *I'm sorry*.

When Evanne stopped humming, Tarragon swayed, caught herself, and put a hand to the Skyforge's side. It was cold, as if it had lain beneath a lake, lost to sight, for eight hundred years. It remembered the cold of the grave.

The blues are the smartest, too.

She bit her lip. "That was beautiful."

Evanne turned a weary eye her way, offered a crooked smile, not a lot in it but exhaustion, but Tarragon loved her for making the effort. "I can't help but think if I'd been here sooner, we might have helped another dragon find wing."

Tarragon slid closer. "This dragon died long ago."

"And yet."

Tarragon nodded and wiped tears from her face. "You would have felt joy at seeing them. They swooped and soared. Humans ruled the world, but the heavens were theirs."

Evanne chewed that over before offering, "You look amazing." Then pressed her lips into a line as if those weren't the words she expected. "I mean, uh."

"I'm the size of a cow," Tarragon said.

"No, they're larger. Only a little, but still." Evanne's smile came back, sly this time. "What happened?"

Tarragon thought, *She hates what I look like*, but said, "Everyone was about to die, and Cophine said—"

"As in, the Dawn Goddess?"

"As in, Yasmine." Tarragon looked at her feet, and realised they were but an arm's length from Evanne's. "It's complicated. She wanted to know if I could begin again, and I didn't understand. And I thought if I just *stopped*, like, being me, all at once, it might make things better. And then you would win, and not have to worry, and I mean I know there would be no more fairies, but the world is not for us, it's all Big this, and Big that, and it's scary. And no one has swords for a fairy anymore. And so. Um." *Hic.*

Evanne's smile faded to black. "You wanted to stop?"

"Because everything I do is wrong, and I feel wrong doing it, and when I try harder, it's more wrong. Everyone gets hurt, and even Helio, *hic*, he died, because I couldn't stay quiet enough, but you see he came back for me, *hic*, and then they got us both, and then he died. *Hic*. He was the best fairy. He was all a fairy could be. Smart, and strong, and could Build things. I didn't pass my exams, and oh why I am I saying all this?" Tarragon wailed.

"You thought it would make things better?" The lantern Evanne held flickered, dimming. Gloom gathered.

Tarragon knew Evanne would understand. She *got* it. Like, how Tarragon was just messed up and a mistake. "That's right. *Hic*. And so I wanted to just set that one thing right, and I couldn't even do that. Now I'm Big, and the ground feels funny, and it's a long way away even when my feet are on it. I can't balance properly, and that seems so easy, right, but all the time I'm swaying like a big giraffe. And now, *hic*, now I'm ugly, and I'm even less use because I can't even *fly*." *Hic*.

The lantern's glow was gone. There was the small *tink* as it touched the deck. Evanne's wonderful, strong hands that could do anything were in hers. The maybe-Vhemin's breath was against her cheek as Evanne pressed her lips to Tarragon's ear. The bard's voice came from right in front of Tarragon, but it seemed to come within her too, like that humming had, a song that was without end. But instead of being sad, it was, what, a little bit angry? And Tarragon thought, *Oh no, I couldn't even die right, and she's mad at me.* "Tarragon Greyflight, you are a wonder and a marvel. Each day I can't believe the Three blessed me with meeting you. You are the most perfect thing I've ever seen."

Hic. Tarragon felt her brain skip a few moments of time. "What?"

And then Evanne's lips were on hers, those strong arms around her. Tarragon melted, and wanted to sob, but with release this time, but she was too busy kissing Evanne right back. She found the cinch of Evanne's shift, and it was the work of a moment to have it free. Evanne's hands were under Tarragon's shirt, touching, teasing, tracing a line up her back.

They broke apart, Tarragon trying to find enough air, her chest heaving. She wanted to say, *Are you sure?* But Evanne wasn't talking. She was instead using her lips against Tarragon's neck, and it tingled right into the soles of her Big feet. She couldn't see Evanne but didn't need to. She knew every line of the maybe-Vhemin's body from that one glimpse at the pool, a map she'd carried with her against sense or reason, in case she needed to find a way home.

They fell to the floor, a jumble of discarded clothing and limbs and kisses. Hot breath. The cold decking, of course, but Tarragon didn't mind. She felt Evanne straddle her, kisses fire against her jaw. Requiem fell aside as Evanne unbuckled it. The sword clattered away, lost as Tarragon's fear. The song she felt from Evanne, the music that she felt inside her at the same time, soared like the manifestation of joy.

She wanted to sing. Tarragon wanted to cry.

Instead, she kissed Evanne again, then tumbled her over. Straddled her in turn and pressed her finger against the maybe-Vhemin's lips. Tarragon didn't need to see to know exactly where they were. "Love."

"Love," Evanne said, and nibbled her finger.

Tarragon felt the smile touch her face. And she felt, perhaps for the first time in her life, like she belonged.

Chapter Fifty-Five

It took time to find new clothes, because *Dancing in the Storm* was immense. Evanne just followed the music, and it led her to the right place. A whole section of the top deck remained intact behind the Skyforge, and in a corner was the remains of a shop. It carried clothing that seemed made of leather, but no leather lasted under a lake for eight hundred years. She milled about until she found a mannequin at the back of the ruin. It still wore clothes, one hand jauntily on hip, the other holding a guitar. The clothes were black, carrying gold piping and insignia on the shoulder etched in the colour of a burnt sunset. The guitar was still glossy, no dust clinging, and a fretboard with gold banding.

The jacket was strong and warm. Evanne left her torn rags on the floor, pausing for a moment at the blood soaking most every part. Tarragon hadn't minded. Thinking about that made her smile like an idiot and feel warm inside.

Her fingers lingered on the guitar, because Uncle Day's gift to her was ruined. Would he mind she'd found another? *I need an instrument.* She helped herself, and let it hang from its sling behind her, fretboard pointing to the deck.

"*I see you've taken to looting as well as piracy.*" Pakhet waited for her outside the ruins' door.

Evanne rubbed the cat's massive nose. The tiger's eyes widened for a moment, then closed in delight. She bunted Evanne, which knocked her back a pace, but there was nothing but love in it. Evanne hugged the tiger about the neck, then planted a kiss on that huge nose. "The spoils of war, kitty."

"*And some war it was. Have you seen the humans? They look wrecked.*" The cat sniffed the air. "*Something is different.*"

"I had sex."

"*Not that kind of different.*" Pakhet washed behind one ear with a distracted air. "*This ship wants something.*"

"An expert on ships, hey?" Evanne scrubbed fingers through rust locks. "Maybe I can get the ship what it wants after it gets me a shower."

"*This way.*" The tiger turned, rubbing against Evanne in passing. She was ready for it this time, grabbed a handful of fur, and hoisted herself atop. *No point in walking when I can ride in style.*

THE SHOWERS WERE HOT. THE WATER CAME OUT IN A TORRENT, clean and pure, and it tasted sweet. "This is amazing!" Evanne called. "You should try it!"

"*Don't be an idiot.*" The cat stayed a safe distance outside the stalls. "I *didn't get myself cut to ribbons and bleed on everything.*"

Evanne gave the tiger a little side eye, then grabbed the shower head and swung it at the cat. Pakhet roared, turned tail, and vanished.

Blessed Three, privacy. Evanne scrubbed and scrubbed until the red-brown water ran to clean, then scrubbed some more. She ran fingers over her body where she'd been stabbed, sliced, and run through. There were no marks on her, not the human skin of her limbs or the Vhemin scaling of her torso.

Nothing to mark her trial. Nothing to show for almost dying. She turned off the water, watching it swirl down the drain, then sniffed.

The work's not done.

THE COMMAND CENTRE WAS HOW SHE'D LEFT IT. STUCK SHUTTERS. Piles of desiccated human remains. Music that wouldn't stop but seemed to have more notes now.

"Okay," she said to the ship. "What's up?"

The music shifted, and with it, the ship gently canted to port. It swung as if in a stiff breeze, the prow nosing west. The shutters shuddered, then rolled open. Through the open windows, Evanne saw the township of Hollyhead. It looked like it'd seen better days, no doubt having its fair share of backwash courtesy of the *Century Charm* bellyflopping into the lake.

Or, maybe it always looked like shit.

There were people waiting on the shoreline. This high up it was easy to make out the few narrow streets were empty, all souls gathered to stare at *Dancing in the Storm*. Evanne mused for a moment. "That's not what you wanted to show me."

The ship stopped its ponderous turn. It might hover, but Evanne doubted it was up to real flight. She glanced to the west, because there was naught else to do, and spied a storm front. Dark and moody, just like the Raven ninety percent of the time. Evanne stood by the window, musing some more. "You want something from the storm?" The music grew louder for a moment. It hummed along the decking, vibrating the guitar slung at Evanne's back. "You want to go *into* the storm?"

The music surged, then subsided.

"You're nuts," Evanne said. "We're barely aloft. And it's a long way down."

The music played on, unconcerned.

"Your funeral," Evanne muttered.

"Power," Tarragon said.

Evanne almost screamed, but kept a lid on it, tugging an old Trick close, her heart spasming even as she kept her face calm. "What kept you?"

"Shower," Tarragon said. "I haven't had a shower like that in eight hundred years." The fairy—*no, not a fairy, more like a goddess*—had found new threads also. She wore canvas-like clothing underneath gladiator armour, her left side plated in metal, the right free of steel.

Evanne felt drawn like iron to a magnet and didn't fight. She hustled over, grabbed Tarragon, and pulled her into a kiss. "You look amazing."

"You look like a rock star," Tarragon offered.

"A what?"

"It's a good thing," Tarragon hurried. "A person who played music everyone loved, making them dance and sing. Thousands of people at once, all across the world at the same time."

Evanne looked down at her black not-really-leather. "It seemed right."

"It's *very* right." Tarragon slipped free, drifting to the window. "The ship needs power. The storm will have it."

"Why does the ship need power?" Evanne frowned. "We're flying already."

Tarragon hesitated. "You know how when you've run a long way and you're really tired? And if you have a small rest, you can run some more?"

"I'm not really into running." Evanne slicked back rust locks. "But I get you."

"The storm is like a rest. The ship will run some more after that."

"And what happens to us in the storm?"

"Might die." Tarragon shrugged. "Probably won't. Depends if the arc conduits are anchored to the energy crucibles correctly. The light-front catheter is probably fine because we're flying, but it's hard to know. And there's the wavefront driver to think about too."

Evanne thought that through. "Those sounded like words, and each by itself carries perverse clarity, but you put them together in a weird way."

"We should find the Raven," Tarragon said. "This isn't a job for sword or string."

Chapter Fifty-Six

The Raven Queen was sick of this bullshit. Everything hurt, and if she moved the wrong way her stomach bled. She couldn't sit, stand, or use the privy without help or cursing, so she spent a lot of time swearing.

The deck of *Dancing in the Storm* was clear of bodies. Heser the Cheg had thrown the remains overboard, leaving a confused legacy on the lakebed below. The deck was left as a jumble of shanties and bedraggled tenements. She haunted them, looking for someone to argue with.

There were no takers.

Morgan managed to find new, warm clothes in her trips belowdecks. The ship was a marvel, but it wasn't *her* marvel, which made her suspicious. The collection of slope-chinned fools lining up at the docks to the north set her teeth on edge. There were more than she'd thought lived in Hollyhead, which probably meant the imbeciles from Wandermere had joined them. They were probably her subjects, but she was in no mood to rule the resistant today. Because, ref: point one, everything hurt.

"I should just leave," she said to no one. The wind whistled in response, tugging her raven locks. She brushed them from her face, glanced to the storm brooding on the western horizon, and gave the clouds a half-hearted salute. *I get you.*

She'd done everything they needed her for. Set the cursed souls in rickety furniture free. Became a target for damage. Fell in love.

Morgan ground her teeth. That was *not* supposed to happen, and she would set it to rights as soon as she saw Heser the Cheg again. The man deserved better than a waspish queen who couldn't show her true feelings in a court of sycophants. He *deserved* to grow old and fat with happy children at his ankles for all his long years of service.

She rounded the corner of a burned-out structure, arriving in a small square. What looked like the remains of a fountain remembered better days, its small huddle of broken masonry a call to what once was. The shops about were mostly intact, except for one where the front had been caved in as if by a massive fist. A table and benches near the fountain gave an approximation of standing.

Evanne was sitting at at a table. The saviour of the world, because she'd definitely been that while Morgan bled out all over the deck, was wearing new clothes. They looked good, which set a seething resentment right to Morgan's core. *I never look that good.* Still, the youth had, well, *youth* on their side. Evanne had a clear bottle and two glasses before her. Glancing at Morgan, she winced. "Moping about anything in particular?"

Morgan's anger, which had been like backing vocals to this point, boiled over. Ice water lay behind her words. "I do *not* mope. I am a *queen.* You wouldn't *understand.*"

Evanne's shoulders rose and fell in a sigh. "Like that, is it?"

"Like what?"

"Come have a drink." Evanne poured clear liquid into the glasses, which meant whatever was in that bottle was a bad idea.

Morgan sat, but with caution. The bench opposite Evanne creaked but did not give way. Her stomach wound creaked in a similar manner, but also held firm. She grabbed the closest glass and tossed the contents back. The liquid burned like a summer forest fire. She bared her teeth. "That's brisk. What is it?"

"It's an angel pissing on my tonsils." Evanne finished her glass, then refilled both. "So, how is Uncle Heser?"

"This isn't about the guardsman. This is about the kingdom. About the *people*." Morgan gripped her glass.

"And so you're going to leave Uncle Heser to return to Ravenswall." Evanne snorted. "You dumb cow. He'll follow you, because the chains that bind you have nothing to do with what you want."

"What did you call me?" Morgan blinked, because no one had dared, ever.

"Dumb." Evanne leaned closer, almost conspiratorial. "*Cow*."

Morgan rose, then stopped, because her stomach—literally—wasn't up to a fight. She sagged. "This is not about Heser the Cheg."

"You know, right, that you helped save the world?" Evanne swirled her drink, then took another hit. "That you freed a cursed army of forever damned warriors from endless thrall? You had our backs, when there was naught to gain. You saved your people. They line up there," Evanne waved her glass toward the north, and by implication the inbreds on the shoreline, "because they know a marvel has come in their time. You helped free this ship from endless torment at the bottom of the lakebed."

"This is just a ship. It feels no torment."

"It is not an ordinary ship." Evanne shook her head. "It is alive. It thinks and feels. Eight hundred years ago it was stabbed in the heart and now it lives again." She glanced toward Morgan's gut. "Perhaps you know what it feels like to bleed but yearn all the more despite it."

"I said, this is not about Heser the Cheg!"

"Which is a lie we can both acknowledge." Evanne scratched rust locks, which seemed to have unnecessary levels of bounce and shine. "Or, perhaps it's a half-truth. I don't want to speak about Uncle Heser. I want you to stop being a dumb cow and own your victory. I want you to be the ruler of Or'sen."

"I *am* the ruler of Or'sen."

"Lies, and more lies." Evanne shook her head. "You've been fighting with the fear of ruling since I first met you. I see it in how you carry yourself. In how you treat others. I'm fine with it, by the way. I think you're a cool aunt. You're one of the few I can be myself with. No Tricks." Evanne glanced away, leaving Morgan nonplussed. "It doesn't matter if you don't like me. You have stood by me when no one else did, and I will be your loyal subject until the end of time. And I'll be your niece. And maybe, just maybe, you'll let me be your ally. So we can save the world, and all the kingdoms in it. Like Or'sen."

"I, uh," Morgan offered.

"Sure, whatever," Evanne breezed. "If you want to go, no one will stop you. But I could use your help. And I think you could use mine."

"For what?" Morgan felt like the world shifted, and someone was changing all the rules on her. This *child* was counselling *her!* It was ridiculous.

It was necessary.

Evanne leaned back, glass in hand, and considered Morgan over the rim. "Well, I need your help to save the ship." She patted the table, which rattled alarmingly. "You need my help to call you on your bullshit, sure, but also to show you what being a ruler is all about. I know *people*, my queen. I know the inside of them, all the Tricks that make them work, and what powers their very souls."

Morgan was about to say, *I know that already*, and maybe it was the liquor, but she held her tongue. She thought about how easily her brother had seized the throne. How quickly people deserted her, despite the fairness of her reign. How the only people she'd been able to call on as her kingdom crumbled was a borrowed family half a world away. "Why do people not see what I'm trying to do?"

"Because you're too busy being a queen." Evanne frowned. "I know it's not fair. People are idiots. They have short memories. But I think if you slowed down a little, and threw a few more parties, things would go okay." She put down her glass and reached for Morgan's hand. Gave it a squeeze. "Auntie? You're not alone, no matter how hard you try to be so. We're all here."

Morgan didn't pull her hand away. Her voice felt small when she said, "Why is the ship dying?"

"Dunno." Evanne let Morgan go and refilled their glasses. "I think it's very old. Tarragon said words that made no sense, but the gist of it is lightning. She needs to bathe in a storm. Then the ship might fall to the earth, killing us all, or soar to the heavens."

Morgan braced herself, then levered herself upright. The pain in her stomach wasn't so bad, thanks to the liquor. "Then we shall fly or fall together."

THEY WERE ALL HERE, EVEN PAKHET. THE CAT STOOD APART IN THE manner of cats, licking a paw in an earnest attempt to appear like she was bored. Heser the Cheg angsted a short distance away, shifting his weight from foot to foot while trying to look stern. It almost—*almost!* —made Morgan laugh. But to laugh would be to disrespect this wonderful man who had thrown his life at her feet. She saw it like a tapestry before her. Difficult to know if that was the ritual magic or dawning realisation.

Evanne had perhaps been *slightly* correct in calling her a dumb cow. *But only slightly.*

Speaking of the waif and stray, she stood in severe black, instrument hanging down her back, and since their drinking but an hour past, had reclaimed her scattergun. The weapon bounced at Evanne's hip, looking strangely out of place. When Morgan had asked what the scattergun was for during the ritual, the bard had murmured, *crowd control.*

Beside the young woman was one who looked just as youthful but Morgan could see the long years hung about her shoulders like a cloak. Tarragon, reforged, sword at waist, green eyes cautious and curious in equal measure. Half armour for a fight, hovering protectively about Evanne as Heser did for the Raven Queen. Perhaps, like Morgan, learning to see the world anew.

Tarragon's gaze moved to Evanne, a hint of worry shifting green eyes to the blue-green of tourmaline. Morgan wondered why, because Evanne had all the answers, and knew how people worked. Was brutish in a fight for all her untutored flair. Called the dead friend and led the damned to salvation.

Morgan felt the ritual shift about them and saw for just a moment the fear behind Evanne's mask. *Ah.* She'd said *no Tricks*, but that didn't mean she wasn't lying to herself. Morgan remembered what it was like.

Telling yourself it was *fine*. That you'd *be okay*. Wearing the mantle of strength to hide crushing uncertainty.

The queen eyed the grey clouds *Dancing in the Storm* drifted toward. They had time. Morgan walked to Evanne, who watched her approach with a guarded gauge. "Sup?"

Morgan reached out a hand, stroking Evanne's cheek. "You said I didn't have to do this alone. The same is true for you."

"I'm good," Evanne said, and crossed her arms in a way that said, *I am not good*.

"An hour ago, I thought the people on that shore," Morgan pointed in the rough direction of Hollyhead, "needy. While we gathered materials," she pointed at the jar of ink-black oil Tarragon found, and the rag Heser gathered and tied to a pole for a giant brush, "I thought about many things."

"Good talk?" Evanne's eyes shifted left, perhaps looking for the exit.

"About what it would be like for giant forces to destroy your livelihood, because that's what happened here. Hollyhead was a fishing village, and now," she chuckled ruefully, "there is no lake to cast a net into. They need help." She paused, wondering if it was better to be subtle, then remembered the *dumb cow* line and went right between the eyes. "You lost everything. And you need help, too."

"I don't—"

"Because by my count you should have fallen to the sword. Faced death, with an eye to embracing it." Morgan looked Evanne right in the eye. "You tried to do it all alone."

"I—"

"It's okay," Morgan trampled on. "We all make mistakes. I can't rule alone, and you can't sing for an empty crowd." She looked down at her arms. *Best put them to use*. Looked at Evanne, and then, surprising them both, hugged her. Put lips to Evanne's ear, and whispered, "It's okay."

The girl froze, rigid. "I don't—"

"It's okay," Morgan said again. "We're here."

"But I don't—"

"It's okay." Tarragon stood to Morgan's right, then draped herself into the embrace. "Hush, love."

"But—"

"It isn't okay." Heser the Cheg was at Morgan's left. "But we will make it so." He put a cautious hand on Evanne's shoulder, perhaps not wanting to amplify the awkwardness of a three-person embrace by adding a fourth.

Morgan pressed her cheek to Evanne's as she imagined Vertiline might, if she was still alive. Tightened her grip. Held the teenager close, and gently, softly, rocked her. Evanne gave a small, strangled sob, the barest hint of noise before she buttoned it back up. "It's just so hard."

Morgan nodded, pulled back, smoothed Evanne's hair, and let her go. The adult facade was back in place on Evanne's face, but her violet eyes were soft. Morgan said, as gently as she knew how, "I am not your mother or father. But I'm here, and you are not alone."

Evanne looked away. "I'm not ready to talk about it. I need to fix everything first." She held up a hand. "I know. I'm not alone." She turned back to Morgan. "I don't want anyone else to get hurt."

Morgan stepped back. "The best way for one soldier to live is for those to the left and right of them to do their part."

Evanne looked at her feet, then her shoulders squared, back straightening as she said, "Get on with the damn ritual already."

Well enough. They'd gathered for this ritual at a part of the deck Tarragon assured them was over the beating heart of the ship. It was toward the rear of the vessel, behind the massive Skyforge. All they needed was the storm's power to go to this one spot.

Which meant: first, the circle. Morgan couldn't have told anyone how she knew it was needed. They called her a ritualist, whatever that meant. A vampire lord had wanted her power. Ritualism faded around cities and people but was strongest in the wilds. With strength came knowledge. The world spoke to her: *a circle to hold the volume of the heavens.*

She retrieved the oversize brush, dipped it in the makeshift ink, and scribed a circle. Morgan took her time, ensuring there were no gaps. The 'ink' wasn't amazing, but she felt it would hold for as long as it was needed.

Thunder rolled, and Morgan smiled, despite the cold and her ink-blackened hands. *We're going to tie the lightning.*

Chapter Fifty-Seven

Evanne hugged herself. A passer-by, if any were idiot enough to be on this ancient ship in a thunderstorm, would have said it was the cold. The Trick played well enough to any crowd, but Evanne knew she was just uncertain. Uncertain of whether they should be doing this, or if she should be doing it with these dear souls. *Not like it's my choice. The ship needs this. And ... it'll be nice to make something rather than break everything.*

So, she huddled, glared, and waited for the lightning to hit.

Morgan's ritual circle was fifty metres in diameter, and they were safely outside it. Evanne eyed the heavens, saw the churning grey, and said, "How sure are we this is a lightning storm?"

Tarragon pointed to the deck. "The ship knows."

"The ship is broken. It's almost a thousand years old. It—"

Lightning hammered the deck right in the middle of Morgan's circle. The pillar writhed like a giant snake, arcing from above to bury itself in the metal of *Dancing in the Storm*. The sound was tremendous, deafening Evanne. The lightning coursed on and on, a full ten seconds of power riveting the deck. She had the sense to shut her eyes, but the brilliance was clear through her lids. The air smelled of ozone and burnt metal. With some surprise, Evanne realised she'd fallen back and landed on her butt.

Morgan capered like a village fool, clearly delighted with the success of her circle. Evanne was pleased too, because the circle was the only reason they weren't charred corpses. She got to her feet, still unable to hear. *{I stand corrected. The ship was right.}*

Tarragon's hands found their own rhythm. *{A few more of those and the ship will be right as rain.}*

The heavens rumbled, the clouds above churning as if stirred by a giant ladle. Another pillar of power struck, the deck thrumming with it. Another ten seconds and the shaft left. This time the decking glowed a gentle amber. Evanne pointed. *{Will it melt?}*

Tarragon shook her head. *{The ship can withstand dragon fire. Not that any dragonkin would strike this ship. This is like tickling her.}*

Weird, but fine. Evanne felt like things were going along just fine until a small splash of moisture hit her cheek. She touched it, fingers coming away clear and wet. She looked up, those heavens still churning away, then squinted as the squall hit. She stared at the deck, eyes widening. Morgan's circle wasn't even *dry*, and here was a deluge. Evanne spun to Uncle Heser. *{Get clear.}* She pointed to the deck. *{It's going to get super hot.}*

His eyes widened, then he ran to Morgan. She had the decency to look surprised as the guardsman grabbed her like a sack, tossing her over a shoulder and heading for the door in the Skyforge.

Lightning struck again, and this time it was everywhere. Evanne screamed, cowering. When she opened her eyes again, Tarragon was there. She held Requiem above Evanne's prone body, the sword blazing as another series of bolts cascaded from above. The sword gathered them close, coils of power snaking around the blade. They arced from the skymetal weapon, lashing the deck, revitalising the ship.

Which gave Evanne an idea. A crazy, stupid, insane idea. She loved it immediately.

The ship shuddered, a beast awakening. A massive horn, low and long, sounded. The noise was something Evanne felt right in her gut, but she didn't have time to piss herself right now. She stood, hollering into the wind, the gale howling right back.

Tarragon screamed, "What are you doing? Get down!"

Evanne screamed back, "Trust me! I know what I'm doing!"

This was such an absurd lie, of *course* Tarragon just goggled at her. The ship's horn silenced, the wind keening in its stead. Then the voice of giants spoke. It was male, calm, and certain. *"ENERGY STORES TWELVE PERCENT. REACTORS NINE THROUGH TWENTY ABSENT. RED ALERT. BATTLESTATIONS. THREAT ASSESS-MENT PENDING."*

Tarragon wiped water from her face. "We have to get inside. The ship is going to war."

"Perfect." Evanne sluiced water from rust locks, baring not quite shark teeth. She could hear *Dancing in the Storm's* music switch from a dirge to a drumming beat. "Ship! Don't do anything stupid!" The ship didn't answer. *Just a little more time.* She eyed the clouds above, then put a hand on Tarragon's sword arm. "Get ready."

"For what?" The once-fairy glanced about.

Lightning struck once more. It raked the deck, a glowing, crooked line left in its wake as it hunted Evanne and Tarragon, the only two convenient lightning rods in attendance. Evanne held Tarragon's sword arm, and the not-fairy tried to tug free.

Morgan and Heser the Cheg made the Skyforge, and hauled the big doors wide. There, inside: a dragon's hatchery.

Lightning hit the blade. Evanne turned a half-circle, put her fingers inside Tarragon's guard as Hitch had shown her how to do, liberated Requiem with a twist, and felt the char of the Three's Storm building. She'd felt it before, just briefly, and it had almost killed her.

Now the sword held the power of the heavens, too.

Tarragon shrieked, "No!"

Evanne hurled the sword. It tumbled end-over-end toward the Skyforge, trailing lightning, splashes of radiance hitting the deck. It soared past Morgan and Heser, lodging in the side of the dragon's birthing chamber.

The wind stilled. The sky held its breath. Evanne smelled charring and felt the blistering of her palms. Didn't care. Not now. "Please," she whispered. "Please."

Requiem discharged, angry at being held by not human hands,

coupled with the power of the thunderclouds, all running into the murky chamber. Blue-white coiled within the depths. The sword spat energy again, whipcords of power coursing through the fluid within.

The giant leg twitched.

Evanne turned to Tarragon, who looked on the cusp of an important decision: slug Evanne, or hug her. Evanne interrupted the thought process. "Do you think it will work?"

"Not a chance," Tarragon said. "Dragons don't—"

The chamber exploded. Morgan and Heser were drenched in thick, soupy sludge. Within, jaws wide as it howled, a blue dragon. Lightning crackled along its teeth, then it stared right at Evanne. And winked.

Then it jumped through the side of the Skyforge chamber, shredding metal, and was on the wing. Soaring, and roaring, a crackle of blue-white energy marking its passage.

The ship's horn lowed again. *"ENERGY STORES AT FIFTEEN PERCENT. THREAT ASSESSMENT COMPLETE. WE'RE GOING TO LOSE."*

THE END.

THE FIGHT FOR MERE SURVIVAL IS OVER. The battle for the future of all begins.

Evanne has fought through fire, loss, and legend. She's faced ancient horrors and walked the paths of the dead. But the greatest battle isn't against monsters or gods. It's against **a foe who has never been defeated.**

Wild Sur, the last master of the old world, stands unchallenged. **No warrior has bested him. No army has brought him low. And Evanne is neither.** She has no blade, no grand army—**only a guitar, a sliver of hope, and... dragons at her side.**

But the enemy isn't just Wild Sur. It's the hatred that lingers. The wounds that never healed. The belief that some things can never change. **Evanne must mend what was broken, or the world will fall apart for the last time.**

If she fails, history will repeat itself. And this time, there will be no coming back.

Turn the page and step into the final chapter.

Because this is more than a fight. **It's the last stand. And the final song has yet to be sung.**

THE HYMN OF ALL
A DARK FANTASY ADVENTURE

A Day Like Any Other

Amir was no fan of rain, cold, or halitosis.

He stood in the middle of a corpse farm. Bodies were scattered. Most of them were in pieces. It spoke volumes of the past few moments, but the slimy rodent of a man before him did not seem to care. They stood, too close for Amir's comfort because of the weevil's halitosis, in a tavern. The tavern was in a blasted shithole named Wandermere. It seemed most had left, following music true, a melody that called the heart. Some say the dawn goddess sang it, her eyes violet. Others claimed it was a monster, teeth sharp, always parched, seeking to slake her thirst on the blood of villains. A vampire lord, they said, had fallen at her feet.

Amir contacted a fence, who said a local man of action knew the hero's location. They would meet in the pride of the town: this tavern. The storm outside hurried them in, armour slick, boots muddy, which meant Amir was pissed off before the ruckus started. The man of action turned out to be the weevil, who had been late to his assassination at the hands of the Vide. The Vide forgot their manners, and died against Amir, Faust, and Larochette's steel. Which left the three of them in the middle of a shitty tavern, Amir talking to the weevil, because Faust said *You're the one who's good with people.*

Vertiline had arrived after the ruckus but before the weevil. She'd pressed her lips into a line at the mess, and made a noise that sounded like *hmm*, which was the kind of noncommittal nonsense that made Amir fear a future sparring 'lesson' at the Justiciar's hand. She'd walked to a scorched patch on the floor, touched it with her metal hand, sank back in thought a moment, then settled herself in a dark corner, eyes hooded.

And that was when the weevil arrived, looking at the corpse farm as if this was the kind of thing Wandermere's tavern produced on a daily basis. He'd demanded coin for information, which Amir expected, but more than the fence agreed, which Amir didn't. It left them at an impasse, the weevil with information, and Amir with bared blade and stirring resentment.

When the weevil spoke, he sounded like an old, blocked-up drain. "The problem is the amount of solars. There are none."

"Friend," Amir lied, "you will note the number of corpses around me. These men and women did not accidentally fall. They tried to kill me, my friends," he gestured with his sword toward Faust and Larochette, who were rummaging through the dead, "and would have dispatched you, if you had not been late."

"So you say." The weevil's face was so punchable Amir almost gave it a shot, but he didn't want slime on his gloves. "Everyone knows you don't turn up first to a meeting when you're outnumbered. You want to make an entrance, casual like, hand over information, all without breaking a sweat, and still collect your solars." He jingled the pouch Amir had given him. "There are no solars here."

The wave of foul breath that arrived with the use of the word *solars* made Amir pale. He slicked cold water from his hair, a parting gift from the deluge outside the tavern. *Truth, but inside isn't much better. They could have at least put a fire on.* The roof was in bad need of repair, puddles of water spotting the floor in ways that dragged the steps and mired the patterns. Amir braced himself. "That is because we made no agreement for platinum. The offer was for sovereigns with a smattering of barons."

"I'm rounding up, see?" The weevil squinted up at Amir. "Cost of business is high. Was difficult to wrangle the information. I'm a businessman. Got expenses."

"Sir, are you aware you address a Knight of the Tresward?"

The weevil squinted harder, eyes almost screwing shut. "Tresward known for their business acumen?"

"Not our true calling, I'll admit."

"Then why does it matter?" The creature attempted a smile, the result ghastly. "Solars for satisfaction. I'll hear it no other way."

Amir felt the weight of the blade in his right hand, and imagined how it could be inserted underneath the weevil's ribs, living for a brief moment in his heart. It was a sorely tempting thought, and he felt the blade tremble in anticipation. *A small bending of the truth, first.* "A child's life is at stake."

The weevil pushed out his paunch and brushed an imaginary speck of dust from it. "Children are everywhere. Lose one? Plenty more where that came from."

Amir was moments from sticking the pig with his blade when strong fingers enclosed his wrist. "Sirrah." Vertiline, calm as the sky before a storm. She'd arrived from behind the weevil without sound, despite the bodies and muck on the floor. It was a trick Amir would have to learn. He hadn't even marked her moving, which was the kind of lapse that would get you killed. "It is *my* child."

"Then *you* can pay the solars." The weevil's squint turned into a glare. "We're still talking, which means you're not going to knife me with that pretty blade. You want your child back? Cross my palm with heavy platinum."

Vertiline cocked her head, hand still on Amir's arm. *How did she make it here so quietly? She breathes urgency to our cause but didn't charge the weevil.* He wondered why they weren't beating the weevil into submission. "Is it a matter of true cost, wretch, or is this a play for more coin?"

"Here, now." The weevil straightened. "First, I ain't no wretch. Businessman, see? Better than. Higher up than the likes of you." He looked down at Vertiline, or made the attempt. "Second, does it matter? The cost is the cost."

"It is difficult to extract information from a corpse," Amir murmured.

"I know a way." Vertiline didn't let him go, still facing the weevil. "I knew a man, once. He said—"

"We all know men. What of it?"

Amir noticed Vertiline's jaw muscles clench. "This wonderful man laid his life down before a demon gate so the likes of you could keep breathing. He told me there's always a reason. The reason, Meri said, was important. If it's a simple play for more coin, with you holding the knowledge but unwilling to part with it, then we can kill you now and leech the answer from your soul. If it's a cost of business matter as you suggest, then we can still kill you now. We will simply pay the people you are beholden to, avoiding middle-man fees."

The weevil paled but stood firm. "Here now. Ain't no way you know who they are. They're my people, not yours—"

"They will come looking for their platinum," Amir said. "We need but wait."

"And you have confirmed it is a true cost of business." Vertiline glanced to Amir. "Insert the blade as you were going to but mind the lungs. The corpse will have trouble speaking if he's missing a lung." And she let his hand go.

The weevil noticed, backed away, voice rising as he said, "The Tresward are good. You're no necromancers. You're—"

//DO YOU DOUBT ME?// Vertiline's voice cracked like the breach between worlds. The tables in the bar shook, and lamps flickered as a wild wind surged among them.

The weevil sank to his knees. "Holy Cophine, please—"

//DO NOT PROFANE THE GODDESS.// She relaxed, the lamp-light rising again, the wind dying down. "I am not her. I am her ... sometime servant."

"Sometime?" Amir looked to his blade. "You still want me to stick him with the sharp end, boss?"

"Wait," the weevil pleaded again. "Just *wait*."

She crouched before the horrid little man, cupped his chin, and tilted his head so they locked eyes. "It is *my* child, creature. There is no force on this world that will keep me from her. I will raze cities and destroy armies if they stand in my way. Remember this as you give Knight Adept Amir what he's asked for. Because if you treat us false, I will come back. I will come here, find you, and make your soul cry for mercy. Do you hear me?"

The weevil's frantic nod tugged his head free of her grip. She eyed him a moment longer, then stood, turning to Amir. "Pay the man."

"But—"

"Adept, he is a businessman. He will remember the fairness of our offer as he remembers a future of pain. If more Vide come, he may be ... circumspect."

Amir sheathed his blade, counting coins into his palm as he watched the Knight Champion walk to the tavern's exit. As her hand touched the door, he called, "Could the Sway do that? Call his soul back from beyond to account for his crimes?"

"The Sway can shatter reality. It can do whatever we need but we must mind the price." She didn't turn. "And I will pay *anything*."

Chapter One

Tarragon prowled the corridors of *Dancing in the Storm*. There was an ache just below her heart, and she couldn't rub it away. It was odd; she'd spent so long fighting Vhemin and now she'd fallen for one. *And now, every minute of every day, I worry for her.*

Evanne had not been herself.

How do I know what she's like? I spent mere weeks at her side.

Being Big meant Tarragon was ... *different.* Big, sure, that was obvious to anyone with eyes or a seismometer. But her mind seemed larger, like she had more room to think about things like, *What are we going to do next,* maybe *what is up with the Raven and all those people we saved,* or the big one, *how* did *I fail my exams?* That was a bother that wasn't going away, because she was sure it was a test impossible for fairies to fail. They had a *Manifest.*

She knew lots of other things too, many from before the world fell, because she'd lived here. The ship was her home. She knew what this ship held, where to go to get the good booze, the great threads, or how to start the kitchen's fabricators so they at least had plenty of oatmeal. What with all the people from Hollyhead, there were a lot of mouths to feed.

Evanne wasn't by the liquor stores, nor was she eating. That was a rare thing, because the maybe-Vhemin always seemed to need calories. She'd hungered for more and more after her fight with Dancing Stars. Tarragon drifted past the fabricators, smelling oatmeal and honey as starveling villagers ate, then shored up at the middle deck's best faux leather store. *No Evanne.* If she wasn't where all the cool clothes were, it left one place.

The only training room still working was a modest football field in size. There were fencing sabres alongside racks of jousting armour, and weight cages for making the weak strong. A central stage took up a good third of the room where the battles were fought. Back in the day —a thought that made Tarragon feel as ancient as her eight-hundred-and-mumble years—glimmering Artifices made of illusory light would battle against dragons and warriors on that stage.

Now, one warrior panted, sweat dripping. Her jacket and guitar rested against a wall by her scattergun. A rapier was in the woman's hand, a tiny weapon for one whose shoulders were broad and strong. Tarragon fancied Evanne more of a match for the broadsword, but the maybe-Vhemin looked magnificent either way.

She turned and parried a flickering warrior of light and rainbow. The stage's projectors must be damaged like so much else, but it got the job done. Evanne grunted, turned, parried, and thrust. She was no Tresward, but her skill grew faster than any Tarragon had seen.

Perhaps she was her mother's daughter.

With a spin and thrust, Evanne dispatched her opponent, then raised the épée in a salute before offering a short bow. Tarragon frowned. "They're not real, love."

Evanne puffed out a breath, not facing Tarragon. "All things are real. This ship is the master of all the make-believe we see. I salute *him* as much as those I vanquish. It's only polite." Her voice was husky, with an odd, flat edge. "Besides, it's good practice."

"When have you ever practiced politeness?" Tarragon stepped closer, head cocked, because something wasn't quite right.

"Oh," Evanne waved a well-muscled arm but *still* didn't turn, "since forever."

"Dear heart? What is wrong?"

"Nothing." Evanne slumped a little. "I'll be up in a minute."

Tarragon stepped on the stage, ignoring all protocols against entering a live training environment. No one who cared was left. She padded before Evanne. The maybe-Vhemin's face was lowered, sweat slicking her rust locks. Tarragon touched Evanne's chin, raising her face. Evanne's lavender eyes were red-rimmed and bloodshot. Tarragon wanted to hug her, to say whatever it was would *be all right*, but she held back the impulse. Evanne wasn't her child, and the set of her jaw said she was in no mood for coddling. "What wind blows?"

"A fell one," Evanne admitted. "I have wasted my life."

Tarragon felt her mouth open and closed it with a snap. "You are sixteen summers. There was precious little time to waste."

Evanne pulled away, flourished her sword, then laid it carefully aside. Standing, she ran a hand through her hair. "Mama wanted me to learn the blade. I should have listened. This world cares little for mongrels and strays. There are many who would see our lifeblood spilled because of how the fates made us. The terrible trouble is knowing who the 'us' and 'them' are. I've been too much in my cups, singing songs, and wasting thought on fripperies and notions of no consequence."

Each word was laid like a brick made of doom. Carefully, with a mark of self-loathing beneath. Tarragon hugged herself. "You have saved the villagers of Hollyhead and Wandermere. You have—"

"I destroyed the village of Hollyhead, more like. Brought an ancient hulk from beneath the lake's depths and killed their livelihood."

Tarragon frowned. "You released those in thrall to a vampire lord. You saved the Raven from a life of servitude. Bent hordes of spectres at an ancient temple into a fighting force. Freed those still in thrall." She pressed her lips into a line. "You have raised this ship from below. By song and heart, and no other way would do it." She almost put a hand on Evanne's shoulder but left it trembling at her side. "I see no wasted life."

"I got rinsed by a cat!" Evanne snarled. "I fell and fell again. And fell some more, and at first I wanted it, I wanted you to get free, to run. But then I didn't want it. I wanted you back, and I wanted to stop hurting, and I couldn't *die*, Tarragon. I couldn't even die."

"Ah," Tarragon said. "I think it's time for you to meet the oracle."

"The what now?"

Tarragon sighed. "I don't know if he still lives. Not like before. But if there is someone he'll speak to, it's you. Come, love."

THE ORACLE'S LOUNGE WAS MUCH AS TARRAGON EXPECTED. SHE'D been here before, just once, when trying to discover the truth as to why she couldn't Build things. Then, it'd had plush chairs for Bigs. The chairs nestled within a wood-panelled room that sported a full bar with expensive liquors and tall, tinted windows that overlooked the clouds and planet below.

That was more or less what was here now, except with eight hundred years of time added. The chairs were faded, some rotted, and the windows were grimed. Merciful Three, but the bar remained, its host of liquor intact. No surprise to anyone, but that's where Evanne gravitated to first.

The oracle wasn't here. Or, he was always here but not visible yet. Tarragon hadn't worked out how the oracle-ship combo worked. The ship saw all, but the oracle was something ... individual. A thaumaturge had explained to Tarragon, his eyes earnest beneath an unruly carrot top, the oracle was a thing of two worlds. The ship and oracle were constructed of magic and science in a bundle.

She rubbed her arms. Fairies were made things too, and it wasn't always good to be a tool of the ancients, no matter how cool it sounded to the young sorcerer.

He's dead now, ash and dust like all the rest. Tarragon's arms had the good grace to show goosebumps at the thought. Evanne rummaged behind the bar, helping herself to spirits of unknown type, the labels long worn with the verdigris of age. She turned striking purple snake eyes on Tarragon. "What'll it be?"

"You don't know what those are!"

"We'll muddle through." Evanne sniffed a bottle, made a face, and recapped it. "Smells like liquorice ass. Where is this oracle, anyway?"

"He's here if he's anywhere." Tarragon cruised to the opposite side of the bar, and settled herself on a stool that didn't look like it would give up on the challenge despite the years. Her Big body still felt weird, but she was getting used to it.

"Do you miss flying?" Evanne splashed something purple into a glass.

"I miss it," Tarragon admitted.

"Me too." Evanne looked at a bottle filled with red liquid. "I miss how you used to hide in the cowl of my cloak."

"I did *not* hide."

"Steal a ride. Whatever." The concoction before Evanne was turning, as all mixed watercolours tended to, a muddy brown. She sipped. "This isn't half bad."

"But is the other half good?" Tarragon took the offered cup, braced herself, and took a chug. It tasted like dark honey and fire. "Okay, that's nice. How did you do it?"

"Dunno." Evanne started mixing into a second glass, then after a moment added a third beside it. "The ancients made so many things. Fruit that turns into whatever you needed it to be. Meat for cats. Sugar plums for fairies." She bit her lip. "Anyway, is it so strange to think this bar is filled with whatever you need?"

Tarragon looked about. Remembered the people here, waiting for their turn at prophecy. Some went away empty-handed, never meeting the oracle. Others were told dire dooms. Still more left hopeful. The fates were not easy masters. "I think that sounds right. It's what you need, but not always what you want."

"Well said." A slender man in his late fifties settled himself beside Tarragon. She could have sworn there was no stool there moments earlier, but he didn't seem overly concerned with reality. His hair was close-cut in a Caesar style, and Tarragon could tell that while he was lean, he was also hard. *Perhaps good enough to swing a blade in times of strife.* "Make mine a double."

Evanne's eyes narrowed. "You the oracle?"

"You the bartender?" The man's voice was mostly smooth, just a hint of the gravel age could bring. Cultured, like he spent time reading and wanted to say the words right.

"No one else was offering." Evanne pushed a glass toward the man. "Try that."

"Oh, great oracle—" Tarragon was cut off as the oracle put a palm out right in her face. He sipped, then nodded. "This is pretty good. I haven't had a drink in eight hundred years."

"Did you lose your manners in that time, asshole?" Evanne bristled, glaring at the oracle's hand.

"It's of no moment," Tarragon said.

The oracle ignored her, staring hard at Evanne. "It's as I thought. You are unruly."

"*I'm* unruly?" Evanne's snake eyes narrowed. "I'm not the one picking a fight with a fairy."

"She's no fairy." The oracle frowned, lowered his hand, then gave Tarragon a glance. "Leastways, not all the way, and not anymore."

"What do you mean, 'all the way'?" Tarragon said.

"This is a waste of time," Evanne said. "We came here because the world's ending, and all we're getting is sass."

"Did I say unruly?" The oracle seemed surprised at his own mistake. "I meant you are a moody teen. You don't understand the structure of the world or how it works."

"Oh yeah?" Evanne's chin jutted. "You're a jacked up faded memory of times that were lost because no one could admit they had no idea what they were doing."

Tarragon's mouth opened, then closed. The oracle was *here*, a rare event, and still *working* unlike so much else on the ship. And there was Evanne, blowing her one chance at understanding the future. "I think she means—"

"You know, I think I like her." The oracle tossed back his drink, then stood. "Here's the deal. Everyone, everywhere, is going to die."

"Of course." Evanne crossed her arms. "That's a natural state for the living when they reach the end of their allotted span." She rolled her eyes, letting them come to rest on Tarragon. "I thought you said this was an *oracle*, not a stater of the obvious."

"He is great and wise—"

"Okay, how's this for oracle-ness?" The old man leaned forward against the bar; his eyes locked on Evanne. "In orbit is a weapons—"

"What's orbit?"

The oracle blinked. "In outer space, there is—"

"What's outer space?" Evanne glared. "Make sense, man. We've no time for wise men too clever by half. Speak plain, or not at all."

The oracle's mouth opened, closed, then he tried again. "Where the sky stops, there is a great void where the stars grow. Each star is a sun like ours. This space between stars is like standing atop a giant cliff, where you can look down on all."

"Well done." Evanne offered a small smile. "Was that so hard?"

The oracle's jaw clenched. "The people who used to rule this world made platforms that floated in the void so they could see the lands below. And sometimes, throw rocks from there upon their enemies."

"Nice," Evanne admitted. "Where are you going with this?"

"When you raised *Dancing in the Storm* from beneath its blanket of water, I could see the sky again. The platforms up there spoke to me."

"That's when you dropped the truth bomb about us losing?" Evanne puffed a rust lock from her face. "Yet we're still here. And we've got a flying city now."

"We're moving really slowly." Tarragon's stomach clenched. The *Storm* had fallen as she rode high in the sky, and now she was a wallowing target. "We don't have height and must navigate around the smallest hills. And we don't control where we're going."

"That's because I'm doing the steering." The oracle favoured the once-fairy with a beatific smile. "We need to get to a confluence point. Once there, we can open a gate to the platforms and get orbital defences, uh," he glanced at Evanne, "the big rocks back online."

"Wait." Tarragon stood, bristling. "A gate? To the demon realm?"

"Not all gates go to bad places." The oracle's smile remained in place. "This one is but a hop to orbit, uh," another glance at Evanne, "the void between stars, where we will get the tools and weapons we need."

"Nah." Evanne started mixing another drink.

"Excuse me?" The oracle blinked.

"We're not going to the space between stars. We've got a boatload of refugees. We need a berth for them. Homes and jobs. Then, vengeance."

"If we wait, the enemies I see amassing in the north will sweep across the land and kill everyone." The oracle shrugged.

"Void it is," Evanne sighed. "Tell me about the amassing force."

"It is a collection of Artifices surrounded by a perplexing mix of Fey Branded, Vehement Systems, and—"

"Feybrind," Evanne corrected, as if to a small child. "They aren't slaves anymore. And we are Vhemin."

"You are a little bit Vhemin." The oracle wobbled his hand *so-so*. "You are mostly human."

"I'm—"

"Anyway," the oracle steamed on, "the perplexing thing is, they have all the tools of the old world. They have Artifices docked at a Vehement citadel. All three races performed together to work the magics of ancient time. We might fight Vehement Systems powers but we can't fight Itikari as well."

"Lucky I'm here." Evanne jerked a thumb to her chest. "I'm a mongrel too."

"Quite." The oracle beamed. "I'm glad that's settled. Now, let's talk about the armour you stole."

Evanne eyed the oracle through narrowed lids. "Make your own drink."

"I can't." The oracle frowned. "I'm not really here."

"I'm glad we understand each other." Evanne strode toward the door. "You need people with hands. We're not your servants. Best not forget it."

The Last Song.

THE FINAL STAND.

The Splintered Lands have bled, burned, and broken. Now, it all comes down to this.

Evanne has no sword, no grand army—only a guitar, a sliver of hope, and... **dragons at her side**. But against **Wild Sur, the last master of the old world**, even that may not be enough.

The past is demanding its due. The divisions that shattered the world once before threaten to do so again. If Evanne fails, history will not just repeat. **It will end.**

Grab *The Hymn of All* now!

https://www.books2read.com/TheHymnOfAll

The worst wars are fought with steel. But the best victories are won by those who dare to believe in something more and who **refuse to fight alone.**

About the Author

Richard Parry worked as a senior marketing manager in one of the world's top tech companies. It sounds cool, but it wasn't all cocaine parties. He lives in Wellington with the love of his life, Rae. They have two cats, Harry and Friday, who chase birds. The birds, who have the power of flight, don't seem to mind.

WAIT. DON'T GO!

Thanks for reading my book. If you enjoyed it, let's keep the party going:

Join *Roll for Narrative* for reviews, storytelling breakdowns, and writing misadventures:

https://rollfornarrative.parrydox.com

Lurk, judge, or say hi:

https://www.parrydox.com

P.S. An angel still gets its wings for every five-star review, but I'm told they're on backorder.

amazon.com/author/richard.parry

goodreads.com/richard_parry

bookbub.com/authors/richard-parry-6ffc3911-9f2c-43ef-8ab4-13dc-cd7f5874

youtube.com/@parrydigm

bsky.app/profile/parrydox.com

linkedin.com/in/therealrichardparry

Also by Richard Parry

DAWN'S WARDEN

The Three Faces of Fate

The Undefeated Throne

The Fury of the Betrayed

THE SPLINTERED LAND

THE EZEROC WARS

The Ezeroc Wars universe is big (and growing!). Get the reading guide here: https:// www.parrydox.com/ezeroc-wars-reading-guide/

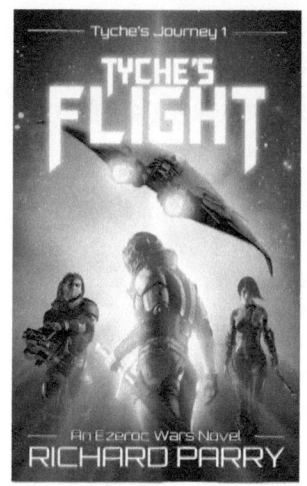

The Empire's Rogues: Volume 1

FUTURE FORFEIT

Not sure where to start? Get the reading guide here: https://www.parrydox.com/future-forfeit-reading-guide/

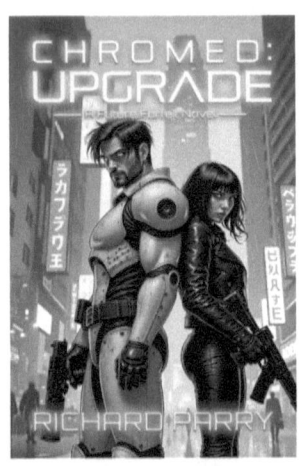

Chromed: Upgrade

Chromed: Rogue

Chromed: Restore

City Stories

Chromed: Consensus

Chromed: Delilah

Chromed: Meltdown

NIGHT'S CHAMPION

www.ingramcontent.com/pod-product-compliance
Lightning Source LLC
Chambersburg PA
CBHW021843010726
47493CB00005B/1523